THE RAGING ONE
THE SUNDERED LANDS SAGA BOOK I
LEXY WOLFE

DESERT DRAGON PUBLISHING

THE RAGING ONE

Copyright © 2026 by Lexy Wolfe

All rights reserved.

Book Cover by Lexy Wolfe

Second edition 2026

Published by Desert Dragon Publishing

ISBN: 978-0-9840003-8-8 (Softcover)

ISBN: 979-8-9886376-0-8 (Hardcover)

ISBN: 978-0-9840003-9-5 (Ebook)

PREVIOUSLY PUBLISHED

THE SUNDERED LANDS SAGA

The Knowing One (Boook 2)
The Timeless One (Book 3)
The Fallen One (Book 4)
The Unforeseen One (Book 5)
The Shattered One (Book 6)

GUARDIANS OF EMERALIS

Divinity Impaired (Doom and the Warrior) (Book 1)

EMERALIS SYNTH CHRONICLES

Ravenhawk (Book 1)
Bishop To Queen (Book 2)
Of Two Minds (Book 3)

COMING TITLES

GUARDIANS OF EMERALIS

Chance Encounter (Book 2)
Dragon's Rest (Book 3)

CHAPTER ONE

A GUST OF WIND swept through the thick trees, shaking the clinging drops of rain free from the new leaves of the upper canopy to fall on the three riders far below. Dead leaves soaked from the spring rains muffled the sounds of the horses' hooves as they picked their way along the narrow road. A forlorn howl nearby brought the mounts up short. The nervous horses pawed the ground, forcing their riders to take a moment to soothe the animals.

At least...two riders offered a soothing presence. "Stupid beast!" the middle rider seethed, jerking the horse's head around. The sharp movement caused the rider's hood to fall back, revealing the finely shaped face of a young, blonde woman hardened by a scowl twisting her delicate features. "It's bad enough we must be out here; must you misbehave?"

"Relax, Journeyman Amelana." The lead rider lowered his hood, leveling a cold, disapproving look at the woman as the wind ruffled hair black as midnight. "You're going to attract lupines by making your beast thrash like that. Is that what you seek?"

The woman's gaze shot upwards, her pale blue eyes wide with surprise. She shook her head with tiny, furtive motions, loosening the reins, which allowed her mount to calm. "Of course not, Ash." She averted her eyes from his darkening glare. "I mean, Master Ash."

"I thought not." Ash looked at the third rider. "Apprentice Terrence, is all well?"

Terrence lowered his hood, glancing skywards with a troubled expression as he ran a hand through dirty blonde hair before giving his attention to Ash. "I am not sure, Master. Something doesn't feel right." In response to his master's expectant silence, he hesitantly replied, "It's like something is draining the life from everything here."

Amelana made a disdainful gesture. "Nonsense! The only problem here is that these uncivilized, backwater villagers aren't advanced enough to build their roads above the ground, away from the filthy beasts." Terrence pressed his lips together, lowering his eyes.

"I did not ask for your opinion," Ash stated coldly, deep azure eyes flashing with annoyance in the sunlight filtering through the leafy canopy. The woman flushed deeper and looked away at the annoyed expression Ash directed at her.

Guiding his horse to join the young man, Ash stated with a kinder voice, "You have good instincts, Terrence. You're right." He looked away, scanning the thicker brush that only obscured a fraction of the huge roots that swelled like giant legs. "Something is awry in this area. Something that disrupts the natural order here."

Straightening with pride, Terrence opened his mouth to speak when Amelana huffed, "Master Ash, are you certain? Because I sense nothing at all, and you know *Avarians* are known for—"

Annoyed, Ash interrupted the woman. "Yes, I'm well aware of what the Avarians are known for. Or did you forget that my master and guardian was Bennu Avarian?"

The woman sensed the disgust in his voice. Dropping the petulance, Amelana asked in exaggerated, pleading tones, "Could you show me how to see what you see? You *are* my master, after all." She did not conceal her look of self-satisfaction when Ash turned his attention away from Terrence to her.

Sighing softly, Terrence tucked his hands in his mage robe sleeves briefly. Watching Ash focus his attention on trying to instruct Amelana, the apprentice shook his head, riding towards the rise they had been approaching to wait for the pair. The sight that greeted Terrence made the young man's blood run cold.

A wagon rested on its side, surrounded by several mutilated bodies, both human and beast. In the midst of it all, a single, one-eyed lupine savaged the body of a man, wrenching an arm free, shaking it viciously before flinging it aside to tug at the other arm.

At first shocked at the unexpected sight, the apprentice mage realized what was wrong. "It isn't eating him," Terrence whispered aloud to himself. He inhaled sharply when the creature, easily twice the size of a man, shifted to reveal a small, terrified child huddled against the bottom of the wagon behind the axle. Seeing Terrence, the child moved a little. He froze when the lupine raised its head, snarling.

"Master Ash!" Terrence yelled, drawing the attention of both his master and the creature. "Rabid lupine!" Grabbing the reins, he kept his horse from bolting in terror as the blood-covered lupine focused its attention on the intruder. He raised his hand, speaking the arcane words of magic that directed a burst of wind that blew the maddened animal back several yards.

Hearing the thunder of hooves behind him, Terrence did not wait, urging his horse forward towards the toppled wagon. The horse skidded to a halt, nervously prancing as the lupine staggered to its feet, shaking its head. "Come on!" Terrence urged the child, leaning down and extending his hand to him. "Hurry!"

The lupine fixed a malevolent glare on Terrence with its one good eye. The apprentice could almost feel its fetid breath, even though it was several measures away. He looked at the frozen child, and closed his pale blue eyes for a moment, expecting the beast to lunge onto him or his nervous horse.

Both lupine and humans flinched when Amelana's shrill scream filled the air. Making use of the distraction, Terrence willed the air behind the boy to push him close enough to catch him by the back of his tunic so he could pull him up. Keeping a firm grip on the boy and reins, Terrence raced the horse back towards his master.

With the maddened lupine pursuing his apprentice and the boy, Ash held both hands up, his voice harsh with the spell he gave voice to. Fur burst into flame, staggering the animal. It howled in enraged pain, but defiantly continued to follow.

Narrowing his eyes as the pressure in his skull increased painfully, Ash commanded the energy at the very heart of the matter around the animal. An embedded boulder shifted, shaking dirt loose as its shape altered and a stone spike erupted and impaled the lupine.

The lupine yowled, trapped in place by the bloodied shaft of rock protruding from its ribs. Despite the mortal wound, it was impossibly still alive. All three mages were taken aback by the look of intelligence behind its single eye as it raised its head to glower at them before the light of life finally faded and it went limp. The curl of smoke from the still smoldering animal appeared to curl against the breeze towards the deeper shadow near it.

With the child clinging to him, Terrence went to his master as Ash staggered a few steps and caught himself against his apprentice's horse. "Master? What...what was that? I have never seen an animal that...that took such pleasure in killing but not...not eating its kills. I thought it was rabid at first, but now..."

Swallowing hard against the pain the manipulation of the rock's fabric had caused him, Ash shook his head with care, pressing his fingers against his temples. "I do not know. But I have seen its like before."

Amelana inhaled sharply. "If that's how all lupines behave, then they should all be eliminated!" she proclaimed.

Ash squinted sideways at Amelana, scolding her. "That's not our way, Journeyman! It is as much our duty to protect the balance of the land as it is to protect our people. The lupines are part of the land." Taking a deep breath, he turned his attention to the devastation. "These lupines aren't the only creatures behaving strangely. We've tracked boars charging into villages, hawks diving at travelers, even forest cats abandoning their territories—all acting against their nature." His words stopped as he looked at his apprentice, expression hardening into an impassive mask.

Terrence hushed the child as he sobbed, tightening his hold on the young mage. Ash watched his apprentice for a moment, then looked at Amelana with displeasure. "Terrence, attend to the child." With reluctance, Ash turned to Amelana. "Journeyman, I will need your help in seeing to the deceased." He put a hand to his temple as the pressure of the magic backlash increased. "The chlayxin is especially sharp again."

Amelana stared in horror. "You want me to handle dead bodies? But I am senior! Terrence should be the one who-" She went silent at the hard look in Ash's deep azure eyes, nearly black with pain and irritation, swallowing nervously. "Y-yes, Master Ash," she said meekly, dismounting her horse and walking towards the bodies with keen reluctance.

Feeling a sense of guilt for the difficulty that Amelana gave Ash, Terrence spoke. "Master, perhaps it might be better if—" He fell silent when Ash shook his head.

"I'm convinced Amelana would only cause more trauma to that child," Ash muttered bitterly while watching the woman leave. "I fully trust you." With a reassuring hand on Terrence's knee, he continued with a tone full of patience and approval, "You did well, Apprentice. I'm proud of you."

Terrence flushed, squaring his shoulders with pride. He looked down at the trembling child he held. "Master? What now?"

"This is no anomaly. We're here because there have been enough reports about these strange happenings that Edai Magus Ellis Avarian insisted someone investigate." Ash continued to rub his temples. "And the rest of the Edai Tredecima agreed because they considered it a suitably menial task to occupy me, not because they had taken any of the warnings I had given seriously."

"But you're the Illaini Magus!" Terrence exclaimed, affronted on his master's behalf. "The goddess chose you Herself to serve all Forenta! You shouldn't be answering to—"

Ash managed a faint, affectionate smile for Terrence. "Perhaps not, Apprentice. However, being god-chosen doesn't change the fact that I'm still an unwanted orphan in the eyes of many. They simply cannot or will not accept a lowborn could be their equal, much less better than any of them."

The Illaini Magus sighed, shaking his head. "It's just as well we were here." Ash's expression grew troubled. "Something is definitely not right. I almost wasn't able to stop it." The senior mage ignored his apprentice's shocked expression. "It felt different from the others. Beyond the life energy that we Forentan mages have dominion over."

"But what else could it have been, Master?" Terrence wondered, soothingly stroking the child's hair until he had finally calmed. "The only other type of magic I know of is—" Light blue eyes widened as his voice lowered to a bare whisper. "Temporal?"

"Maybe so," Ash conceded. "Our main focus at the moment is laying these unfortunate souls to rest." He watched his journeyman with a hint of irritation as she moved aimlessly through the devastation, not contributing anything useful. "It seems Amelana can't handle such a task on her own without some direction," he grumbled. Turning back to Terrence, he said, "Gather whatever information you can from the boy so we can reunite him with his family. Afterwards, we can decide if contacting the Fortress of Time is necessary."

"The Edai Tredecima won't like it if the Guardians become involved," Terrence stated unnecessarily. "Especially the Se'edai Magus."

"That is not for you to concern yourself with, Apprentice," Ash said tersely, more irritated with the prospect of confronting the Forentan mage council's leader than Terrence's words. Sensing Terrence flinch at the censure in his voice, Ash closed his eyes a moment, regretting the sharpness of his words before he had to turn his attention to Amelana and her ineptitude.

Chapter Two

Dust motes, like tiny gold sparks, danced in the sunbeams illuminating the alcove. A woman with intricate braids of light brown hair sat on the ground before the alcove's central pool, her gaze fixed on its reflective surface. The sound of something crashing on the stone floor echoed down the corridor, causing her to jump and her turquoise eyes to widen.

Her tension was obvious. "Calm, Taylin." The shadowed figure moved into the light, lowering himself to one knee beside her. Brown hair streaked with gray fell forwards as the man placed a comforting hand on her shoulder. "You defeat yourself with your own doubts."

Taylin's cheeks flushed with shame, her gaze falling. "Dusvet Almek, I'm not sure I can scry water either. I can barely manage crystal." With a sad expression, she raised her eyes. "And my attempts to scry flame or wind leave me questioning whether I'm actually seeing anything, or simply projecting what I imagine I should see."

With a gentle smile and pat, Almek positioned himself to her right, near the pool. "Whispers of the past ride the air's currents; the future is glimpsed in the flicker of fire's light. Young Guardians of Time often neglect the present. Particularly those from Sevmana or Forenta."

A deep red flush rose on the woman's light tan cheeks. "I'm not *that* young, Dusvet," she said, nervously fiddling with her pale gray robes.

"Oh, do stop being so formal," Almek chided mildly. Two slashes of color, a vivid blue and a softer green, shimmered like polished metal where he touched his right cheek. "One day, the Timeless One will accept you as one of Her chosen, just as She had chosen me. You will earn your colors as I had."

Taylin argued, "I've already mastered healing magic. No one has ever possessed the ability to touch more than one type of magic energy."

Almek regarded Taylin with disapproval. "You've been listening to Unsvet Dremmen again." As the woman looked away, the Dusvet stated with strained patience, "You are *my* student, not his. And the Unseen deemed you worthy to continue your training in the temporal arts. Are you going to believe Dremmen over Our Lady's servants?" Taylin shook her head in silence, eyes averted.

Taking a deep breath to push his irritation with the other Guardian away, Almek took Taylin's hand, squeezing in reassuring encouragement. "I suspect others who were gifted in more than one talent existed over the centuries. But given only Guardians are blessed..." His smile faltered a little. "Or cursed with living longer than those who are not Guardians, those showing latent talent with temporal energies alongside other arts were never noticed."

"But you noticed it in me." Taylin's voice was hushed, her eyes staring at the water that shivered with the light touch of a breeze over its surface. "Even though I am just a healer."

Snorting, Almek shook his head once. "There is nothing 'just' about your strength as a healer, Guardian Adept." His voice took on a stern edge. "Tell me. Who else in the Zeridian Temple—or any healing temple—can mend bodies riddled with old, poorly healed wounds that others declare impossible? I watched you heal that child, who would not have survived to adulthood but for you."

"No one else can heal flawed and aged injuries as I can, Dusvet. But—"

"But nothing!" Almek's pale blue eyes flashed with his vehemence. "Most who have no ability to manipulate any energies cannot see their flow at all, save for when a strong healer works. Even a layman can see healing as a white glow. But you."

He turned her palm upwards. "When you turned from the fresh wounds to the old ones, your energy waxed from white to the blue only seen in lightning." He added more quietly, "Only seen in Guardians when we manipulate time on something we are in physical contact with." Releasing her hand, he waved towards the pool. "Now use the discipline you learned as a healer and quiet your mind." He paused for a moment as she settled. "Try again."

Obediently, Taylin turned her gaze towards the mirror-like surface of the pool, staring unblinkingly as she meditated.

Almek frowned as uncharacteristic tension lines appeared on the healer's expression after several minutes. He moved to her when outright terror filled Taylin's expression; the woman froze in fear as if she could not look away from what she saw. When the vision broke, she turned to flee.

Almek caught her, his hands steadying her trembling shoulders as she collapsed against him. Her sobs dampened the front of his robes while he waited, patient as stone. "Tell me what you saw," he murmured once her breathing steadied.

"I don't...I don't know," she stammered as she struggled to regain control of herself. "I saw...huge trees. So massive, it looked like evening, though I know...I know it was noon."

"It sounds like the forests of Forenta," Almek stated, his calm helping to soothe Taylin's terror. "What else?"

Swallowing, Taylin stepped away from Almek, wringing her hands nervously. "I saw a one-eyed wolf. A-A lupine. But it-it wasn't a lupine. It was something...horrible..." She shook her head sharply. "It...it attacked—" She covered her mouth with her hands, trying to repress her emotional reaction to the horror she had seen. "It tore them apart. The people. And it-it seemed to eat them. But not their bodies. It ate their...their souls!"

Almek's expression shifted from shock to grim understanding. "A temporal shifter," he murmured. Before he could elaborate further, the sound of heated voices echoing down the corridor pulled their focus away from the vision's implications.

"It isn't 'nothing,' Dremmen!" a male bellowed impatiently. "You have no right to—"

"The Dusvet Guardian will not be disturbed with your trivialities, Unsvet Jaison!" The responding male voice was higher pitched and nasal. A moment later, he grunted. "Unsvet Bella! How dare you touch me! Get back here this instant!"

A woman with olive skin and dark brown hair drawn back into snug braids appeared at the alcove entrance, looking over her shoulder in open defiance. Her gray garb was designed more for forest excursions than the traditional looser robes most Guardians wore. She reached up to adjust the unstrung bow strapped across her back.

"What will you do? You're an assistant, Dremmen, not the Dulain," Bella snapped, "and possess little to no real authority." She muttered sourly, "Goddess knows why Tyrsan keeps you around." As she faced Almek, the single, metallic sea-green line under her right eye—the mark of an Unsvet Guardian—flashed, mirroring the brilliance of her dark green eyes.

Almek put himself between Taylin and the alcove's archway as two others followed Bella. The two men scowled at each other while Bella stepped forward and bent her knee as she took Almek's hand, touching her forehead to its back. "Unsvet Bella," he greeted formally.

"Dusvet Almek," the woman replied as she straightened. The moment of serene formality was banished as she jabbed a finger towards the shorter, fairer of the two men. "That pompous ass is being impossible! Jaison has a legitimate reason to—"

Dremmen's seething bordered on incoherence. "You should be whipped for your disrespect and lack of decorum, Vodani," the fair man stated, crossing his arms. "Why the Dulain puts up with *you* is beyond me. If it were up to *me*—" The taller, darker man grabbed the smaller man's wrist in a merciless grip, scowling at him. The slash of orange that marked him as an Unsvet darkened to an ugly shade, catching the light against his dusky-hued skin. "Unsvet Jaison!"

Jaison shoved Dremmen away. "You will do nothing, or do you wish the Dusvet to learn of all your *other* little tricks?"

Dremmen's face blanched at the threat, his gaze darting to Almek's raised eyebrow before dropping to the stone floor. With an unintelligible mutter, he backed away and slipped out of the alcove.

"Jaison," Almek greeted as the younger man mimicked Bella's earlier gesture and bent his knee. "You shouldn't antagonize Dremmen. Either of you. He *will* make your lives more difficult if neither I nor Tyrsan are here to keep him in check."

"He already does, Dusvet," Bella said with a gusty sigh, waving her hand. "That Forentan-born ass was trying to keep Jaison from talking to you ever since you returned with your healer." The Vodani woman glanced at Taylin, then away dismissively. "He kept going on about propriety and how lowly we were in comparison with the only surviving two-color Guardian and—"

Almek frowned at the news. "I will speak with Dulain Unsvet Tyrsan about that. Dremmen needs to let go of his Forentan obsession with social hierarchy. It has no place among Guardians. Especially as you were both my students. Earning your colors does not suddenly end our ties to each other."

"Don't worry about it." With lips twisting into a rueful smile, Jaison shrugged one shoulder. "I grew up with prejudice, being a Vodani raised in Desantiva. At least the mundanes in the four territories of the Sundered Lands still see us as infallible."

The Dusvet sighed, shaking his head. "What was it you wished to see me about, Jaison?"

"The shadows in the river of time," Jaison replied simply.

Almek inhaled sharply. "You have finally seen them as well?"

"I have *been* seeing them, Dusvet." Jaison held his hands out to his sides. "Since shortly after you mentioned sensing the aberrations before you left on your last journey. It took me months to get past Dremmen to speak with the Dulain. Dremmen is of the mind that if *he* can't sense something, then it simply does not exist, and no one else should be bothered by falsehoods."

"And you, Bella?" Almek asked the Vodani woman as he studied her when she averted her eyes from his.

"I have not seen them. But I have sensed them." Bella's flippant demeanor became very serious. "But it's like trying to focus on something perpetually at the corner of your eye."

Almek pressed his lips together, pensive, his eyes falling on Taylin. He turned back towards the pool. "Come, Taylin. Share your vision with us."

"What?" Taylin went pale, staring at the older man. "B-but I can't...! I-I..." She turned away, hugging herself. "I'm afraid to see it again, Dusvet."

Bella tsked as she moved to sit across from Taylin's place by the pool. "Oh, come now. You're only an Adept Elite. A senior student. It couldn't be that bad. How horrible could it possibly be if you have not earned your colors yet!"

Jaison frowned as he studied Taylin and put a supportive, reassuring hand on the healer's shoulder. "Bella, shut up. You're acting like Dremmen now." The archer scowled at Jaison, but remained silent.

Taylin turned a grateful glance up to Jaison before taking a deep breath and returning to the pool. Kneeling, she extended her cupped hands to Almek, letting him cup hers and guide them into the cold water. "I just...I just have to remember? Even though what I saw is-is now in the past?"

Almek smiled. "Time is unique. Past, future, and present are conventions we mortals have to understand how it flows."

"We can use the essential elements to see any point in time, but it is through water that we can safely share our visions and memories with others." Jaison settled cross-legged with his hands on his knees, meeting Taylin's eyes as he spoke. "It's simply easier to see one facet of time through one than the others."

"Master's pet," Bella muttered affectionately to the other Unsvet, smiling more when he pointedly ignored her.

"Water is Her favored element," Almek said, letting the conversation continue so Taylin could relax more. "Because it resembles time so closely, able to flow in all directions, change its state, being subtle or not in its effects. It is that nature that allows us with Guardian talents to share memories."

Glancing at the Unsvets, Almek nodded before addressing Taylin again. "Now, share your memory with us of what you saw earlier, Taylin. Remember, it's merely a memory in time now." The pair of Unsvets slipped their hands into the pool and closed their eyes.

"Yes, Dusvet." Stilling her trembling, Taylin focused on the horrifying images. She jerked her hands away at the same moment she had during her original vision. Staring wide-eyed at the three, she felt a trace of gratitude that she was not alone in her terror. Jaison and Bella had pulled their hands out, looking pale as well.

"What in the hells...?" Bella whispered. "She's only an Adept. A student! I've been a Guardian for centuries, and I have seen *nothing* like..."

Jaison shook his head as if the physical motion could banish the lingering images. "Almek, that wasn't a normal time shifter. I can assure you." Soberly, he said, "No time shifter I've ever scried has ever *looked* at someone scrying. No one I know experienced that."

Almek, calmer than the others, removed his hands, pensive. "I had hoped it was only a vision of something less..." He sighed and went to Taylin, embracing her. "Never doubt your gifts," he said, his voice gentle but firm. "Your Guardian potential rivals your healing prowess. It simply awaits proper cultivation."

"I constantly struggle with scrying," Taylin confessed, glancing at the older man. "How could I possibly have a vision that would surprise even you?"

"It's easiest to see visions of those we have ties to," Almek answered as Taylin gently pushed away from him. "Perhaps you know someone from these visions...?" He made a thoughtful noise when she shook her head. "There must be a connection you haven't discovered yet."

"Do you think she's a fluke?" Bella fidgeted with her wrist bracer's lacing. "Or do you think there are others like her? Gifted in more than one talent?"

Almek rose slowly, stretching to ease his stiffness. "Considering that the aberrations have not only gained strength but also seem to have extended past the World Spine, I believe it's probable there are others with multiple gifts." He extended his hand to help Taylin stand. "The world aims for equilibrium, which is what we work to safeguard. If there's an imbalance, the universe will attempt to correct it. However, it's preferable to make sure the process isn't overly disruptive."

"What should we do now?" Jaison asked, looking up at the pair standing. "We don't even know where these anomalies are coming from. All we'd end up doing is fighting the symptoms, which won't solve anything."

"I must seek the wisdom of the Timeless One." The two Unsvets jumped to their feet in alarm, talking over each other in protest. "Silence!" Almek barked, frowning at them. "There is no other choice." He held up his hand before either could utter a sound, reassuring concession in his voice. "I will take Taylin with me."

Bella and Jaison subsided unhappily. The Vodani woman crossed her arms, drumming her fingers as she fixed Taylin with a hard look. "I hope she's as good as you say she is," Bella said as she turned on her heel, stalking out.

Jaison was less hostile towards Taylin, offering her a single nod of acceptance. The Vodani man turned his worry to his mentor. "Almek, you aren't as...young as you need to be to endure Her power. You only just returned to Fortress! Can you not...wait? Until you have recovered more...?"

"I have endured over five hundred years as a wanderer because She has named me her Sentinel, Jaison. Her servant has gifted me with more years than any wandering Guardian would normally see. For that blessing, I must accept the responsibility it was given for." Almek put his arm around Taylin to guide her out. "Everything will be fine, Jaison." Taylin glanced back at Jaison, worried and confused as they left the alcove.

Chapter Three

"WHAT IS THIS PLACE?" Taylin whispered as they emerged from the long tunnel into a cavernous chamber lit only by luminous lichens grown into the crevices around carvings of sea plants and creatures and the natural texture of gray stone, lending a surreal feeling of being underwater. She pressed her fingers behind her ears, declaring, "The walk felt endless!"

"This is the Timeless One's domain on the mortal plane." Almek tucked his hands into his sleeves. "Only Her chosen can locate it." The Dusvet brushed his fingers over the image of a dolphin with a faint, fond smile. "And She trusts me to bring only those who can be trusted into Her presence."

Taylin stopped short, her hand halfway through the motion to tuck a strand of hair back behind the braids looped from her temples. "You mean...I thought you were speaking, ah, figuratively. About seeking Her wisdom."

Almek arched an eyebrow, turning back. He studied Taylin for several long moments. After a time, his expression turned sad and affectionate. "Ah, my dear. Have so many lost sight of the gods' grace in our lives?"

"Dusvet?" Taylin blinked several times, suddenly feeling unaccountably ashamed.

The Guardian shook his head. "Never mind. Just sit here and remain silent." Taylin nodded, biting her lower lip as she sat on the bench. Her gaze moved from Almek to the central feature of the cavern.

Water fell from a crevice in the shadows above into the uplifted hands of a statue of a mermaid, posed as if to catch the falling liquid. The water coursed down her body where she sat at the edge of the pool; the black, mirrored surface of the water remained undisturbed by the flow. Almek stepped up the three steps to the side of the pool across from the statue and knelt, resting his hands on his legs.

The healer could not tell whether minutes or hours had passed, needing to call on the discipline of her training to keep from fidgeting. Turquoise eyes widened when the air seemed to shiver and a soft splash broke the oppressive silence. She clapped a hand over her mouth, stifling an inarticulate sound of surprise. Her heart pounded so loudly in her ears that she feared Almek could hear it.

A figure broke the water's surface—at first glance, she appeared to be a woman with flowing blue-green hair and alabaster skin. Then the light caught the shimmering scales where human legs should have been, revealing a powerful tail that rippled with blue, green, and violet as she emerged from the water and sat by the statue with liquid grace.

The mermaid's impassive features softened as a small smile touched her lips. "Much time has passed, Sentinel." Her voice, barely more than a whisper, carried easily to Taylin's ears. "I thought you'd forgotten us." The smile faded, replaced by a troubled worry. "You have grown old, my friend."

"Time does have that effect on my kind," Almek replied, his smile echoed in his voice. "For having seen over five hundred years, I think I am doing quite well."

The mermaid slipped off her perch to swim across the pool. She emerged and sat next to Almek, reaching out to touch his cheek. Webbed, impossibly long fingers traced the metallic blue and green patches of color below his right eye. "I dislike seeing how the years weigh upon you, dear one. As does She. Allow me to wash the years away again?" she asked in a hopeful tone.

Almek gently touched her porcelain white cheek with the back of his fingers, softly stroking her blue and green striped hair. "Oh, my dear Selina. If only I could be selfish enough to accept the offer now." Holding her hands, he added, "I am in dire need of assistance."

Selina's gaze moved from Almek to fix on Taylin, her expression devoid of warmth. "You have a new student. One already trained in the arts of molding flesh and bone. Taking one gifted in other arts as a student of time magicks would be unusual for any but you." She turned her gaze back to Almek. "Has she talent in the Old Ways? Is this why you turn away from my touch?"

Almek gave Taylin a reassuring look before returning his attention to the mermaid. "She has vast potential. But her touch is not yours. You know me better than that...I should hope."

Selina did not reply as her cool gaze raked over Taylin critically before she dove back into the pool, resurfacing onto her smooth perch across from Almek. "I do know you, Dusvet Guardian. You would not turn away my touch without good reason. Speak," she said, formal once more. "What do you require?"

"I seek the wisdom of the Timeless One," Almek replied firmly. "There are disturbances...like ripples caused by many pebbles tossed into a still lake. But I cannot find their source, and the ripples are not harmless. I fear the great balance is threatened. I need Her vision."

Selina tilted her head, puzzlement and worry marring her features. "What of your fellow Guardians? Seeking the source of these ripples and mending them...that is their purpose. Turning their backs on our Mistress's gifts is a dire insult."

"Many others cannot sense them. Perhaps because they bear only half our Mistress's blessings as Unsvets. They are like flickers of a candle flame at the corner of the eye. Easily doubted or dismissed as imagination." Almek held his hand out to Selina beseechingly. "I am the only remaining Dusvet Guardian. I have no one left I can consult. Some believe my many years have addled my mind."

"Addled?" Selina's calm demeanor broke with an angry frown. "They are fools to believe that!"

The mermaid calmed when Almek raised his hands, though a lingering irritation remained. Looking squarely at Selina, the man stated, "I have scried all the elements: crystal, water, flame, and wind. Nothing yields the knowledge to me. My students have sensed similarly, but again, the others think their devotion to me colors their visions." Almek leaned forward, desperation creeping into his voice. "The Timeless One's vision is unparalleled, and She never speaks lies. I must know whether visions speak truth or fallacy, to know where I must go next."

Selina frowned, glancing up at the statue. "What you ask...you know how dangerous it is to you. You nearly died once, and your body was younger by centuries. I do not wish you harmed, Almek." Crossing her arms, she shook her head. "No, I will not lose you to death by calling Her to share Her vision."

"If these disturbances are real...not merely the phantoms of an old man's addled mind...then they threaten every soul across the realms." Almek's weathered face softened as he reached towards the mermaid. "Selina, I would not ask if any other path remained. The fate of all rests upon this."

The mermaid did not reply, obviously troubled. After many long minutes of staring, she said in a harsh voice, "I will call Her. But I will not remain to watch you suffer!" Without another word, she dove into the pool, vanishing beneath its surface. Taylin rose, lips parted—but Almek lifted a hand, halting her unspoken question.

Reluctantly, the healer settled back in her seat, crossing her arms unhappily. A chill of outright fear stole through her as the statue across the pool moved, opening its eyes to reveal pitch black orbs that made Selina's almost emotionless indigo stare seem filled with warmth. Shedding the pallor of polished gray marble, the goddess slipped into the pool, settling on an unseen shelf beneath the surface that kept her aquatic half submerged.

"Step into the pool, my Sentinel," the imperious voice of the goddess commanded. "Give yourself unto the waters of Time. Let your life become Our life, your vision become Ours." Almek nodded obediently, rising to shed his clothing and step into the pool, the water coming to his waist.

Taylin sprang to her feet, her heart pounding in her chest, as the water twisted around Almek with the menacing precision of a monstrous serpent. It encased him from the waist up, forcing its way into his lungs with relentless determination. "Almek!" she screamed, panic clawing at her voice. The goddess remained indifferent, her gaze unfaltering, as if Almek's suffering was beneath her notice. Suddenly, another tendril of water shot out like a whip, striking Taylin with brutal force and hurling her across the room. She slammed into a column with a bone-rattling impact. Dazed and struggling to regain her senses, she fought through a foggy haze, powerless to stop the horrifying sight of Almek drowning before her eyes.

As the water flowed away, the Timeless One caught Almek as he collapsed. She gently laid his lifeless body beside the pool before returning to her place under the waterfall. As the Timeless One's body hardened into a statue once more, Selina returned, immediately going to Almek's side. Taking his face in both her hands, she pressed her lips to his in a long, desperate kiss. When she released him, he coughed weakly, unconscious, but alive. The mermaid turned her piercing stare onto Taylin.

The healer interpreted the look as permission to approach and rushed to Almek's other side, resting her hands on his brow and over his heart. Her hands glowed softly white, the color shifting to a pale blue in the dim light as she mended the damage to his lungs and the strain to his heart. A weary sigh escaped her as the glow faded. Sadly touching the new streaks of gray, Taylin murmured, "He is...whole. He will be weak for a few days." She closed her eyes, swallowing. "If he gives his healing the time it needs."

"You are very strong," Selina observed with approval in her voice. "And very gifted. No ordinary healer could have mended a wound from the Timeless One." She touched the back of Taylin's hand with light, cool fingers. "I understand now why he has taken you as his student. He was wise to bring you here."

Taylin murmured, "Had I known what he planned, I would have tried to talk him out of it. We cannot lose the last Dusvet!"

Selina looked at the unconscious man, her webbed fingers trailing through his silver-streaked hair. The pearlescent scales at her wrists caught the dim light as she leaned closer, her eyes reflecting the deep indigo of unfathomable ocean trenches. "Do not blame yourself. He is as stubborn as the tide. He knew the consequences of what he asked." Her melodic voice dropped to a whisper that rippled like water over stone. "He knew I would only have strength enough to restore his life—or his youth." Her lips, the color of sea foam at twilight, tightened with a hint of regret. "But not both."

"Why couldn't She—?" Taylin began to ask, then bit her tongue to silence her impudent question.

"Gods are not as free as mortals like to believe they are," Selina stated quietly. "Not even one of the Ancient Trinity. The laws of balance bind all—mighty and meek alike. He had to be strong enough to accept Her gift. He was, but he hovered between life and death. I could pull him back to life, but I could not do more."

"And I could mend the harm he suffered." Taylin sighed, closing her eyes for a moment before looking at Almek. She reached out to brush her fingers over his brow to reassure herself. "He is not age-addled," Taylin said, voice tight with restrained fire, as if arguing with those who accused the Dusvet Guardian of being mentally deficient.

"No, he knew he was not, despite the doubts that plagued him," Selina replied serenely, clasping Almek's limp hand in hers as both females sat vigil. "He never sought to prove anything to the other Guardians. He sought knowledge." Selina's expression was deeply troubled. "But She Who Rules Here...the Timeless One...even She could glimpse only shadows—fragments of what he has felt."

"It is...enough," Almek wheezed as he finally roused. "It is..." He shook his head as he let Taylin help him sit up; Selina drifted back and sank until the water touched her chin. "It defies explanation. Whatever disrupts the river of time...it is ancient. Old beyond imagination."

"What now?" Taylin asked. "If the others still will not believe you, what can you do? What can any of us do?"

"You must heal the Sundered Lands," Selina replied gravely.

"Heal the Sundered Lands...?" Taylin stared at the mermaid, then let out a bitter laugh, throwing her hands up in exasperation. "Why not ask for the moons and the stars to be strung on a necklace? The Great War left wounds too deep for any mortal hand to mend." Almek hushed Taylin, patting her shoulder in reassurance.

Selina's face remained impassive save for the subtle knitting of her brow. She glided towards the pool's edge where Almek sat, extending a webbed hand that held a small bottle encased in intricate silver wire. "This belongs with you now," she said, her voice like water over smooth stones. The vessel gleamed with an inner light as it passed from her hand to his. "Reserve it for when the first threads of the sundered tapestry rejoin—for only then can the greater weave be restored." Her cool fingers lingered on his weathered hand before she slipped beneath the water's surface without so much as a ripple.

In the silence after Selina's departure, the healer realized how rash she had been before the goddess and her handmaiden. "Dusvet," Taylin began, dropping her eyes in shame. "Forgive me. I meant no insult to—"

"Do not apologize, my dear. Selina is not human, but neither is she as cold as she seems. She and others of her kind serve as the bridge between us and our Mistress. She is not insulted, merely puzzled by our land-bound thoughts." Almek stumbled a few steps, leaning on Taylin. "Come. I promise I will rest to recover fully. But She has confirmed where we need to begin." He paused to catch his breath. "We must go to Forenta."

Chapter Four

"Dusvet," a deep voice rumbled from the arched doorway.

Almek looked up from the journal he wrote in, his pensive expression softening as he waved the bull of a man in. "I did not expect to see you so soon, Dulain Unsvet Tyrsan. "

The large man made an irritable sound as he entered, shutting the door behind him. He retrieved two glasses and a wine bottle from the small cabinet. "I suppose I should be grateful you did not think I was so heartless or callous that I would not come as soon as I heard of your...*adventure* with our Mistress."

"The duties of Sanctuary's caretaker leave little room for social calls." He accepted the offered glass, swirling the ruby liquid before taking a long sip. "Walking the tightrope between our traditionalists and the reformers must consume most of your waking hours."

"Just because you are Dusvet does not mean your welfare is not as much a part of my responsibility as the Unsvets and Adepts that call Sanctuary home." Tyrsan dropped into the chair opposite Almek. "Bella and Jaison are beside themselves with worry, and you know how difficult it is to unsettle the Vodani born. Hells, Jaison and Dremmen nearly came to blows—again—when the dolt implied your 'illness' was because of Bella and Jaison's 'needless worrying of an age-addled old man' in my presence." Draining half of his glass, he grumbled, "I was sorely tempted to beat him myself."

"Ah, yes. Jaison reflects his childhood raised among Desanti with that un-Vodani-like temper of his," Almek said mildly. Tilting his head, he regarded the younger man with less levity. "Has no one else proven fit to serve as your second?"

"Dremmen is unfortunately quite good at the job, and it keeps him where I can keep more of an eye on him." Pinching the bridge of his nose, Tyrsan said with strained patience, "You're trying to distract me from why I came here."

"Pity." Almek was unrepentant as he sat back, sipping his drink. "I nearly succeeded, too."

The Sevmanan man's dark complexion was tinged with barely contained anger. "Don't provoke me, Almek! I might have lived only around three hundred years compared to your five hundred, but I'm no fool." Tyrsan's gaze was intense as he locked eyes with Almek. "You've just come back from your recent travels, and the effects of being away from Sanctuary are clear even to the inexperienced."

"I'm just a little grayer at the temples. Hardly worth fussing over," Almek said. "No harm will come to me if I leave Sanctuary or the Fortress territory for another few years."

"I'm not so sure of that," Tyrsan stated, his voice grim. "I have scried the flames, and within all the paths I see, eventually your journey becomes...obscured." He shook his head. "I have seen nothing like it before, and it bothers me."

Almek waved a dismissive hand. "All the more reason I should go. Lives may depend on not delaying this journey."

With a feral growl, Tyrsan surged to his feet, slamming the table so hard it shuddered beneath the force of his hands. The light glinted off the metallic slash beneath his right eye, unmistakably marking him as an Unsvet Guardian. "To the hells with other's lives! It's *your* life I'm worried about!" He gestured vehemently towards the door. "You know damn well that Guardians cannot withstand the pull of time outside Fortress's territory without the need to return and recover within Our mistress's domain. The passage of time gnaws at us more fiercely there than it does here, and at your age, it will ravage you even more. Especially if you need to wield the temporal energies to any significant degree. Just seeking out the Timeless One has already harmed you." He pounded the table again with frustration. "I refuse to stand by and watch you recklessly squander your life!"

Almek lifted an eyebrow, unfazed. "I'm not doing anything carelessly, Tyrsan. You know my reasons."

"Then at least take Jaison with you. He is due to go out again to patrol Sevmana, anyway." Tyrsan emptied his glass and refilled it. "You should not be traveling with only a mere Adept who has not had formal training and is nowhere near earning her colors."

The Dusvet asked in deceptively bland tones, "So you feel my training would be inadequate for Taylin?"

Tyrsan scowled. "Stop putting words in my mouth, Almek. We've been friends ever since I came to Fortress."

"And you've done quite well for yourself...what was it you called yourself? An ignorant foot soldier?" Almek shook his head. "You were never that, not in the slightest. And even if you had been, you wouldn't have earned your place as the Dulain." With a weary smile, Almek continued, "Trust me a bit, Tyrsan. Taylin isn't your average Guardian candidate. She's already mastered her healing skills. Much of the formal training isn't different from training in any other discipline. She's got the discipline down. She just needs to learn to recognize and embrace time as she has with healing."

Tyrsan drummed his fingers on the table, clearly unhappy. "Fine. I won't argue with you. But you will not leave until you've at least recovered your strength from this latest brush with death. Understood?!"

Almek gave his brusque friend a warm smile. "Perfectly, Tyrsan. Now sit, would you? Tell me how it goes with Jaison's newest student. She's a Forentan, I hear? It's been more than fifty years since any have emerged from the northern forests."

"They're rather well matched," Tyrsan stated blandly. "She's as typical for Forenten as he is for Vodani. If you wish, I can have her brought to you to discuss the current temperament within Forenta's borders." Looking irritated, he added, "If you insist on heading to Forenta, you'll want to leave before the start of summer. The roads can become treacherous when the seasons cool. Most roads that connect Sanctuary to Sevmana are barely passable at all in the dead of winter."

Considering, Almek finally nodded. "Yes, I would like to speak with her. But for now, I'd prefer to catch up with an old friend who doesn't keep me perched on so high a pedestal as most." Tyrsan smirked, shaking his head as his anger slipped away.

CHAPTER FIVE

As they approached Forenta, the bald, rocky peaks of age-eroded mountains became obscured by the giant, ancient trees that rose like an ocean swell of deep, vibrant greens breaking against them. The canopy of the massive trees obscured the sky, dimming the light into twilight dimness well before the sun set. As true dusk approached, tiny motes of light appeared among the greenery.

Awed, Taylin stopped her horse to admire the sight. "It looks like the stars came down to sit in the branches! I never realized so many actually lived *in* the branches of the trees. I thought most lived close to the ground, just...surrounded by trees."

Almek chuckled in amusement, patiently waiting until Taylin got past her awe to resume the ride towards the main city woven between the great, green monoliths. "The forest floor houses only the boldest or the most unfortunate. Forenta is very rich in native magic, which affects all things that live here." Nudging his horse into a faster walk, he patted the mottled gray gelding's neck as it yielded and took hesitant steps onto the ramp that began the climb upwards to a wide bridge that crested the swollen roots of the silent giants.

A snapping twig drew Taylin's gaze downwards. Below the bridge, a trio of tri-tailed deer dashed beneath them. The animals were twice as massive as either her or Almek's horses. "If those are the deer, I would hate to see what preys upon them." As if on cue, five wolves that were just a hand smaller than their horses burst from the brush. "By Zeridis!" she cried, invoking the name of her temple's patron.

Almek looked bemused, with a touch of pity in his eyes. "From my past experiences in this territory, those lupine are less dangerous than most two-legged predators." He ignored Taylin's quizzical expression, his attention drawn forwards.

"Hold, foreigners!" a strident voice commanded in trade common. A guardsman dressed in black and gold emerged from the hollow of the tree they were approaching. "Identify yourselves and your business in Ithesra, capital of Forenta and home of the Edai Tredecima!" The 'or else' was clear as archers made themselves visible from various surrounding branches and walkways built into the tangle of trees.

Unhurried, Almek lowered his hood, offering a patient smile to the guardsman. Light glinted off the Guardian marks on his cheek, causing the other guardsmen to react, their aims faltering as they whispered in awe, "Guardian!" "Dusvet!"

The guardsman's demeanor changed dramatically as recognition set in. He nearly fell off his perch as he tried to wave the archers to lower their weapons and bow deeply in respect simultaneously. "Dusvet Guardian Almek! Forgive us! Word had not reached us you would arrive in Ithesra—"

"Forgive my negligence in sending word sufficiently ahead of my visit." The formality of Almek's words belied his lack of concern for his error in following Forentan protocols. "I could find no messenger who would have arrived well enough ahead of me before I arrived myself."

Once he recovered his composure, the guardsman hopped down several branches to the wooden bridge near the horses. He bowed to Almek once again, but seemed oblivious to Taylin's presence. "I understand, my lord. Tell me how Forenta may serve the esteemed Guardians of the Fortress of Time?"

"Ah, yes. My visit is purely a personal one." He raised his hand slightly before Taylin could utter a sound in argument, catching the sharp turn of her head and the weight of her pointed stare at his nonchalance.

The guardsman nodded once. "Of course, my lord. Naveene's Rest—" he began, when another interrupted in Forentan. Looking apologetic, he corrected himself. "Forgive me. One of the Great Families is celebrating a marriage. Only Visitors' Hollow has any space left for foreign-er, visitors." His glance at Taylin, while professional, was also disdainful. "The Sevmanan is with you, I presume?"

"Yes. Master Healer Taylin is my student," Almek confirmed, his voice edged with cool disapproval. "*And* a Guardian Adept."

The guardsman flinched at the underlying rebuke, pressed his lips into a thin line and squared his shoulders, but offered no apology. "Your mounts will be tended to. Come with me." A boy came to carry Almek's gear, but Taylin was left to manage her own.

The slight did not go unnoticed. Almek did not budge, forcing their escort to return for them. "I would appreciate if you would accord my student the same respect you so kindly show me. Whether or not she bears the Guardian's mark, the Timeless One does not take kindly to slights and offenses." Almek's distinct disapproval brought a flush to the guardsman's fair features.

"Of course, my lord. Please, forgive me." The guardsman snapped his fingers, and another boy emerged from the shadows of a nearby sentry post. He nimbly climbed down the trunk of the tree itself before hopping over to the main bridge. Only after Taylin's gear was claimed did Almek turn to follow the guardsman.

The boy carrying Taylin's gear winked at her, making a rude gesture at the guardsman's back before hurrying to catch up with the other boy. She coughed, hiding a small smile before she fell into step with Almek to continue the climb into the trees. "I never dreamed someone would be so rude to a Guardian of Fortress." Taylin whispered in Sevmanan to Almek. "Especially the Dusvet Guardian.!"

"Such treatment has grown increasingly frequent," Almek admitted, his voice low. "Forentan mages trace their lineage back to the First Sundering—they've always carried themselves with pride, but that pride has calcified into something harder towards outsiders." He glanced at a pair of passing locals, who stared openly at them. "Fortress maintains its ancient stance of non-interference with the four realms, even while Se'edai Magus Oberlain's suspicion of Guardians has festered these many decades. We don't impose our wills on those beyond Fortress's dominion."

"Why don't they? Impose their will, that is." Almek arched an eyebrow, and she coughed into her hand. "Not that I have a desire to punish anyone for...anything."

"The Fortress of Time has served the Timeless One since before the First Sundering. Regardless of some latent attitudes of what nation a Guardian was born to, Guardians serve all peoples, no matter what measure the lands use to order their social hierarchies."

"Perhaps they do not see Guardians as powerful because few have truly witnessed the meaning of temporal magic," Taylin said thoughtfully.

"Perhaps. I prefer not 'to flex my muscles' simply to earn respect." Almek offered a nod in greeting to several young people, who gasped and stared in awe at him as they passed. "And my longevity serves well enough. I've become a name passed through generations in the Sundered Lands, especially being the only Dusvet alive."

A broad terrace and natural overhang framed the entrance to Visitors' Hollow. Small windows and curved balconies dotted the massive trunk both above and below, marking the travelers' quarters carved within the living tree. Like most structures in Ithesra, Visitor's Hollow was hewn from the heartwood of its host, winding organically around the tree's central core. Its passageways followed the trunk's natural contours, rising and dipping with the concave and convex waves of the exterior bark.

When the guardsman led them into the main chamber, a hush fell over the crowded space. All eyes turned—shocked not simply by the sight of a Dusvet Guardian, but by his presence here in a business serving the lower classes. "If we had known you were coming," the guardsman said, clearly regretful, "Naveene would have assured you...and your student...had a place worthy of the Dusvet Guardian."

"This will do, I assure you." Almek offered a smile to the nervous girl who approached them. "Two rooms for us, please."

"Yes, my lord," the girl said, scampering off to talk to the headwoman of the establishment.

Another guardsman approached after their guide had departed, his posture impeccable as he bowed with practiced grace. "Lord Dusvet Guardian Almek Two-Tones," he intoned with reverence. "The Edai Tredecima extends their formal greetings and offers sincere regret that the full assembly cannot attend your arrival in proper measure."

The Guardian appraised the man, noting a physique shaped by a life far more 'hands on' than most upper class Forenten lived. "Thank you for your graciousness. What is your name, Captain?" Almek asked, his eyes falling to the sigil sewn into his tunic. "And a master mage, if I am not mistaken?"

The blue-eyed guardsman's serious expression faltered, and a smile warmed his demeanor. "Master Nolyn Lirai, captain of the Ithesra Guard, Lord Dusvet." He glanced at Taylin, his eyebrows going up in surprise as he noted the color of her clothing and the pendant she wore denoting her rank within her temple. "Word said you had a student and a master healer with you. I did not realize your student and the healer were one and the same." He added with some chagrin, "I did not realize it was possible."

"Master Healer Taylin of the Zeridian Temple." Taylin blushed as Nolyn took her hand, lightly kissing the back. "It's a pleasure to meet you, Master Nolyn."

"Forgive my guardsmen for their rudeness." Nolyn's lips twisted into a wry smile as he ran his fingers through light brown hair only a few shades darker than his skin. "My people are not especially renowned for their generosity towards outsiders, particularly when there have been...challenges of late." He glanced at the servant girl, who waved the two boys with Almek and Taylin's gear to follow her. "Might I have a moment of your time, Lord Dusvet, while your rooms are prepared for you?"

Almek inclined his head. "Of course." The three walked out onto the grand balcony, away from the ebb and flow of passing visitors.

Nolyn did not look at Almek, his eyes focused on a distant point in the depths of the trees. "Edai Magus Ellis Avarian wished me to relay his personal greetings—and a warning."

"I see," Almek said as he slipped his hands into his sleeves again, expression unchanged. "I believe I remember Master Ellis from my last visit to Forenta, and his twin brother Bennu. Fine men, both of them."

Smiling sadly, Nolyn said, "Unfortunately, Bennu has been gone these past fifteen years. He was a fine master, and I miss him incredibly." Taking a deep breath, Nolyn shook his head. "But that is not what I wish to speak to you about, Lord Dusvet."

"Please, do go on," Almek prompted, studying the Forentan man closely.

"I do not know what it was like when you last came to Forenta, but Edai Magus Ellis speaks of...better times. When the Edai Tredecima was...*moderately* more welcoming to Fortress's emissaries." Nolyn paused for a moment, then regarded Almek. "You will want to speak with the Illaini Magus before you depart."

Almek looked at Nolyn in mild surprise at the news and with no small amount of relief. "Your goddess has finally chosen a new Illaini Magus? It has been a concern of mine. She had not chosen another over the past three hundred years."

"Until fifteen years ago, we had no Illaini, no." Nolyn glanced over, silent until a group of people passed by to enter the main room. When they were gone, the man lowered his voice, his concern apparent. "Se'edai Magus Ysai Oberlain bears the same disdain for the Illaini Magus as she holds for Fortress."

Almek considered Nolyn for a time. "You do not trust the Edai Tredecima?" he stated more than asked.

Nolyn did not say a word, though his expression spoke volumes about his feelings. "*Ellis* is a fine man." His words took on a brisker tempo. "I expect Master Ellis will have sent a message summoning Illaini Magus Ash Andar back from the outer reaches of Forenta. It will take at least five days, barring unforeseen delays." He looked worried. "The Illaini Magus is a good man, Lord Dusvet, but he is a bit...blunt to the point of discomfort, at times."

"So, I should expect hostility from all directions?" Almek studied Nolyn.

Nolyn smiled wanly. "Not all of my people have forgotten the respect due Fortress...mostly an embarrassingly significant number of highborn. The others may be hostile because the Se'edai Magus is hostile towards Guardians of Time. The Illaini Magus is hostile towards most everyone equally due to...ah, *challenges* between social position by birth conflicting with social position by rank, rightly earned or divinely ordained. But he's got a good heart in there." He dropped his eyes to his hand, rubbing his thumb against a scar in his palm as he added under his breath, "Somewhere." Nolyn shrugged. "Just...try not to think ill of Ash Andar. Especially when you go into the tomb to meet with the Edai Tredecima."

"You dislike the Magus Academy?" Almek asked with some surprise.

"I dislike caverns, regardless of their beauty," Nolyn replied mildly. He glanced over towards the servant girl who approached, looking nervously between the guardsman captain and the Dusvet Guardian, and smiled a little. "It seems your rooms are ready. I will return in the morning to escort you and your lovely student to the Academy to meet with the Edai Tredecima. After you have had breakfast, of course. Best not to deal with...*challenges*...on an empty stomach."

"Thank you, Captain Nolyn Lirai. May the goddess keep you safe and bring you wisdom." Almek straightened and headed towards the waiting servant girl.

"Forenten do like to talk," Taylin muttered.

"It's what they don't say that troubles me."

Chapter Six

The ornate stone hallways of the Magus Academy echoed with the sounds of rustling robes and many footsteps as masters and students went about their daily routines. Taylin walked beside Almek, eyes wide as she drank in the grandeur. Colorful mosaics embedded into stone detailed the long history of the Forentan lands. Elegant script wound through the images like ribboned breath, though the healer could read none of it.

"Dusvet, this place is unlike anything I have ever seen!" she whispered in awe, reaching out to touch an emerald-colored crystal leaf on a column in the wide corridor. The faux vine wound from the floor to the high ceiling like a living thing. "This place appears naturally formed, not molded by artisans. As if it grew this way!"

"It is doubtful most of this occurred naturally," Almek replied mildly, inclining his head in greeting to passersby, who bowed deeply to him in respect. "Everyday life in Forenta is infused with magic. The artisans, no doubt, mage-trained."

The ceiling of the Majestic Hall was four levels high, as intricately designed as the hallways they had passed through. Ornate railings, filigreed with carvings so fine they whispered of lineage and history, lined the upper levels that passed along the outside of the massive chamber. A semicircle made of the darkest wood framed the rising sun pattern embedded into the floor, each ray's point ending at a council chair. In the heart of the brilliant gold sun was an image of the tree of life, a magnificent, sprawling, arboreal tapestry, its intricate branches intertwining like the threads of existence, each leaf representing a life woven in the rich fabric of the universe.

Of the thirteen seats on the mage council, only seven members were present. The man to the right of the center chair rose, offering a respectful bow to Almek. "Dusvet Almek Two-Tones of the Guardians of Fortress, on behalf of the Se'edai Magus and our absent Edai Magi, I offer our apology that the full Edai Tredecima could not greet you in kind."

Almek returned the bow. "No apology is needed, Edai Magus Ellis Avarian. I believed my presence here to be important and saw little use in sending word ahead—it would have arrived mere moments before I did, and changed nothing for those traveling from afar."

Taylin rolled her eyes and muttered, "Zeridis! Forentan love their words." She lowered her eyes at the slight elbow nudge from Almek. A sideways glance betrayed his amusement at her comment. The corners of his eyes crinkled.

Ellis settled back into his seat, resting his chin on the back of his hand as he studied the two visitors with speculative calm. "Dusvet, what brings you to our fair lands? I trust nothing is amiss?"

"I hope not," Almek replied, his voice measured. "But I felt compelled to see with my own eyes, to ease my thoughts. Word has reached Fortress of...shadows stalking the people of Forenta. If a formal request for aid was made, perhaps it was detained...or unaccountably diverted."

"You heard about...?" one mage blurted, eyes wide, "But no one was supposed to—" A sharp hiss from his neighbor silenced him. The circle of mages exchanged uneasy glances, a few frowning.

Another spoke, voice clipped. "Nothing that our own cannot manage, Dusvet Guardian."

"A few unruly beasts, perhaps, nothing more," a third added, waving a dismissive hand. "Forenta's bountiful magic does breed creatures that are much more robust than those beyond our borders. Fortress's presence is...unnecessary."

Almek's expression tightened. Before he could press further, Ellis rose, his face unreadable. "We thank you for your concern, Dusvet Guardian Almek Two-Tones. But Forenta's issues are best handled by our own." A soft tap of a carved hammer echoed through the chamber. "The Edai Tredecima is adjourned." Without another word, the seven mages filed out in formal silence.

Taylin gaped, her voice low and fierce. "They just dismissed you! I can't believe—" She stifled herself as Almek placed a steady hand on her arm, guiding her back towards the arched entryway.

"In Forenta," he murmured, "until a threat breaks the illusion in a manner none can deny, their leaders will often not acknowledge it. I haven't convinced Fortress of my worries either—not fully. I had hoped..." He paused in the hallway, rubbing his temples. His weariness was carved deeper than the surrounding stone.

"But the lack of respect they showed you, Dusvet—how could they?" Taylin tucked her hands in her sleeves, resisting the urge to strike anyone passing too near. "You are a Guardian! *The* Dusvet Guardian! Dismissal like that...it's sacrilegious!"

Almek offered a rueful smile. "The skills of a Forentan mage and Guardians do not appear dissimilar, so they do not hold the Guardians in as high of regard as the other nations, especially the most highly trained among them." He started walking, Taylin falling in step with him. "A certain degree of hostility has always existed between Forenta and the other nations. Fortress, in Forenta's eyes, is more nation than purpose."

"It is no excuse," Taylin muttered.

"Dusvet Guardian! Dusvet Guardian!" Two children dashed down the corridor towards them. Almek and Taylin stopped, turning to regard them. The pair of youths bent over with their hands on their knees as they tried to catch their breaths. "Thank you, Dusvet Guardian." The one who called looked extremely grateful that Almek stopped, straightening. "Master Ellis bids you join him in the upper east library." He added as an afterthought, "Your apprentice is invited, too."

Almek smiled and bowed slightly at the waist to both children. "Please relay to Edai Magus Ellis Avarian I and my student Guardian Adept Taylin would be pleased and honored to meet with him in the upper east library."

The boy nodded, inhaled deeply, and dashed back in the direction they had come from. The girl who stayed, appearing around eight or nine years old, gave a respectful bow. "Dusvet Guardian, I'll lead you and your student to Master Ellis." Moving at a slower pace, she kept sneaking glances at Taylin. "Are you truly both a Guardian apprentice *and* a master healer?" she inquired with genuine curiosity.

Taylin nodded, some of her irritation from earlier abating in the face of such a young child speaking to her. "I am both, yes."

Pale blue eyes went wide. "Wow! Really? We're always taught that people only ever have one talent ever their whole life. Which I always thought was silly—it makes little sense why someone couldn't have more than one," the child said.

When both Taylin and Almek's expressions reflected surprise, the girl blushed. "I'm not supposed to say things like that. Some of the masters switch my backside for being too pert. But Master Ellis says it's right to question because you can't learn if you don't ask about anything. And accepting gossip as truth is an affront to the goddess." Taylin couldn't help but giggle behind her hand at the exuberant girl.

Almek raised an eyebrow. "Master Ellis sounds like a very wise man. It's good of him to honor the teachings of Lady Forenta." He paused a moment. "Tell me, what is your name, child?"

"Oh, I'm Zoe. And Master Ellis is one of the very best masters. His brother was even better!" Whispering conspiratorially, Zoe said, "Master Bennu's last student became the Illaini Magus!"

Taylin blinked. "What is an Illaini Magus?"

Zoe looked at Taylin as if she'd sprouted a third arm. After a moment, she relaxed. "Oh, right. You're Sevmanan," she said, as if that neatly explained everything. "The Illaini Magus is the greatest of all the magi. They say he was chosen by the goddess Herself to learn all there is to know about magic and everything—and make sure Her teachings aren't forgotten."

Almek remained serene as Taylin bit her tongue against the slight dig regarding her nationality. "It's good to hear that another Illaini Magus has arisen. The last one I knew died of old age three hundred years ago. Perisi was quite pleasant."

Zoe's eyes went enormous. "You *met* the last Illaini Magus?! But you don't look that old!"

Almek chuckled warmly. "Trust me, dear child. I'm much older than I look." He answered her eager questions about the last Illaini Magus as they walked through the winding corridors towards one of the highest tiers of the Academy.

When they arrived before a pair of carved wooden doors, Zoe bowed deeply. "Thank you, Dusvet Almek. It was very pleasant to speak with you."

Almek bowed in return. "And thank you, Zoe, for being such an attentive listener. May the Goddess bless you." Zoe beamed and then opened the door, closing it quietly behind them.

Ellis stood beside one of the narrow windows in the room, its walls cloaked in book-filled shelves and low, scroll-lined racks that doubled as tables. He turned with a warm smile and stepped forward to embrace Almek. "Dusvet, it's a pleasure to see you again." Then he turned to Taylin, taking her hand and placing a courtly kiss upon it. "So this is the master turned student I've heard whispers about?" His eyes crinkled with charm. "It does an old man's heart good to be graced by such loveliness. Please, have a seat."

"An Edai Magus?" Almek asked lightly as he settled into a plush chair. "You have come far since I last visited Forenta. Weren't you a junior master then?" He glanced at Taylin and asked, "Would you be a dear and pour us drinks?"

Taylin nodded without hesitation, going to the cabinet Ellis indicated, As she prepared the glasses, she listened to the men's exchange.

Ellis chuckled, wistful. "My brother Bennu and I both—Goddess bless him. I've had my hands full since his death." He sighed. "If only I aged as gracefully as you, my friend. It feels strange to feel ancient and yet still a child in your presence."

"You are hardly a child. Then or now," Almek chided gently, accepting the glass Taylin handed him. "Young Zoe tells me Bennu's last student became an Illaini Magus. I had concerns. To have none for so long after Perisi's death troubled me."

"The goddess has always been sparing with whom She shares Her blessings." Ellis nodded with a slight grimace for the topic, accepting the glass Taylin handed him. "There have been fewer and fewer deserving over the years. But, that is a Forentan problem, not one to burden you with," Ellis demurred, waving a dismissive hand before leaning forwards. "I wanted to discuss your purpose in coming to Forenta."

Almek studied Ellis over the rim of his glass. "You're not going to chastize me for unnecessary worry, are you?"

Ellis snorted. "Hardly. But Se'edai Magus Ysai insists all is well within our borders. Many of the Edai follow her word without question. Others..." He shrugged. "Well, we do not argue openly. Public discord within the Edai Tredecima risks disrupting the careful balance Forenta has achieved."

Almek's gray eyes sharpened. "So you believe there's something more stirring?"

Ellis raised a hand, caution tempering his tone. "I suspect. The Illaini Magus has warned the council of a crisis looming in Forenta. But he brings only instinct and hunches, no tangible proof. And Ysai is...persuasive in dismissing such things." His lips pressed into a thin line. "To cast doubt on Her Chosen sets a troubling precedent. But he's young. And—" Ellis coughed discreetly. "Contrary."

Almek smiled faintly. "That sounds like one of Bennu's students."

Ellis's expression softened with pride. "Very much so. Wicked smart, dreadfully powerful. I sent word that you're here and wish to speak with him. If anyone can settle this mess, Dusvet—it's you. I hope you don't mind my presumption."

"You'd have me soothe him," Almek said mildly. "Convince him it's all just youthful imagination. I came *because* I believe there's something more than mere weather or beasts beneath this."

Color rose in Ellis's cheeks, and he cleared his throat, steering the conversation away. His smile returned, warm and intent, eyes sparkling with curiosity. "So, you're a master healer, are you, girl?"

Taylin blinked, caught off guard that he addressed her directly. "Er—yes, Edai Magus. I am one of the youngest master healers." Her voice steadied, shoulders squaring with pride. "And I'm the only one who can mend wounds past the time most healers can touch them."

"Can you heal the ravages of old age?" Ellis asked, half wistful, half teasing.

Taylin considered the question with utmost seriousness. "I'm not sure, Master Ellis. I've never tried." She lowered her gaze to her clasped hands. "Healing aged injuries is very draining. Growing old is regarded as a natural consequence of living. Even if I can, I don't know how much I could undo."

Ellis shook his head, laughing gently. "Oh, dear girl, I wouldn't ask you to make me young again. That's a Guardian's blessing to endure for so long, not mine." He sighed. "There are just things I'd have done differently and others I'll never get to do. But that is wind through the branches." He turned to Almek. "Still...it's rare, isn't it? A master of another art gifted with Guardian talent? Bennu and I debated endlessly about the possibility, but as we had never encountered it in reality, we accepted the prevailing belief of the impossibility."

Almek made a thoughtful noise as he drank. "A century ago, I would have said yes. But these days...These days I am not as certain as I had been." The Guardian tilted his head to one side, curious. "Is there a reason you ask?"

"Yes," Ellis replied slowly. "My reason for asking is the Illaini Magus. My twin brother's last apprentice anf journeyman, Ash Andar." Ellis rose, walking to the window to look outside. "He is a hostile, angry young man, but he has never been one to fabricate lies or fantasies. Not as Ysai has been insinuating since Bennu took him as his student. I attributed his natural strength and extraordinary abilities as the reason the goddess considered him worthy of Her blessing. But..."

He turned to regard Taylin. "We consider healing a cousin to Forentan magicks. A narrower focus. You brought with you a master healer turned temporal student, and it opened possibilities I would never have imagined. If my suspicions now are correct, I wonder if you would consider...handling Ash."

"You're afraid of him." Taylin's eyes widened at Almek's bluntness. "That he has both magus and Guardian magicks in significant measure."

"No!" Ellis turned back sharply. "I am afraid *for* him. I have seen for myself the results of untrained magic talent. It can twist and corrupt the one possessing it. Once the blight of corruption has sunk its roots too deeply, the only cure to prevent its spread is performing the morelmi. Ysai would only be too eager to find an excuse to perform it on him."

Almek explained to Taylin in hushed tones, "The morelmi severs the link between a living thing and the ability to embrace and control the energy of magic, leaving a barely living husk behind. Because it can be fatal to both the caster and the target, it is not done lightly." Looking at Ellis, he stated, "A corrupted version of the morelmi cast during the Great War between Forenta and Desantiva is considered the reason the lands sundered from two to four."

Ellis flushed, not meeting Almek's eyes at the Guardian's last statement. "I would not see that happen to my...Bennu's last student. Not to Her chosen." Ellis returned, sitting on the edge of his chair, urgency in his voice. "I ask not as one of the Edai Magi, Dusvet, but as an old man nearing his end of days. If he has the talent, as I suspect now, do what must be done. Train him. Suppress him. Whichever would be best. I don't want to give Ysai anymore reason to threaten him."

"Do you know when he will arrive?" Almek asked after a long silence.

Ellis looked down, closing his eyes. "I do not know if he even *will* arrive, Dusvet. We have never been on the best of terms since Bennu's death, so he is liable to ignore my messenger."

Almek pursed his lips and then nodded. "I will wait for as long as I am able. But then I must continue my journey. You understand."

Ellis nodded, managing a grateful smile. "It's all I have the right to ask of you. Thank you, Lord Dusvet."

Chapter Seven

Emerging from the upper rooms nestled within the massive tree of Travelers' Hollow, Taylin adjusted the soft gray robes that marked her as a Guardian Adept. Her fingers brushed the gold sigil of Zeridis at her neck—a familiar anchor amid the din. She scanned the main chamber, its crowded warmth lit by dozens of oil lamps that cast cheerful, smoky hues across clusters of Forentan and foreign patrons. The Forentan staff moved with practiced grace through the bustle.

Spotting Almek seated against the far wall near a knot of trader caravan workers—most of Sevmanan descent—Taylin headed towards him quickly. She met the hostile Forentan stares and the leering glances of foreigners with practiced disdain. Settling against the wall, she muttered, "Dusvet, it's been nearly two weeks. Why are we still here?"

"Because this is where we're meant to be," Almek replied, calm as candlelight. He signaled a serving girl to bring Taylin a glass of wine. "Relax, my dear. Our stay nears its end." He gestured towards the room. "You are a Guardian Adept. Observe. Learn. This, too, is a lesson."

Taylin turned her gaze to the newcomers entering the hollow. Travel-filthy men from various nations, three of whom broke off to sit alone while the rest poured through like a flood. They were coarse, loud—openly leering at the serving girls. Tension rippled as off-duty guards rose, subtly herding them away from Forentan patrons.. The rough caravan workers barked vulgar demands and slouched along the wall. Only the older women served them, enduring the pawing with stoic grace. "What could I possibly learn here?" Taylin muttered. "That caravan men are rude and disgusting?"

Almek's tone remained mild, but his words cut clean. "Perhaps learn to value the grace of those you've overlooked...those whose hospitality you once dismissed as expected of them or due to you because of your rank. But either way, seen as beneath you." She flinched at his words. "A Guardian serves all, Taylin. Regardless of station or personal opinion."

A sudden hush fell over the crowded inn, drawing everyone's attention towards the black-haired man standing in the entrance. His azure eyes swept the room, cold and precise. Nothing in the way the man was dressed overtly announced his status among the others. He wore heavy robes that were so dark a hue of forest green they were nearly black. Where others flashed rank or status in gaudy threads, his robes whispered power—shadow threaded with the colors of the forest. He bore only an intertwining knot of silver, gold, and copper in the shape of a tree that symbolized his status over his heart. But even without the emblem, his mere presence identified him as the Illaini Magus.

Two people flanked the man. One was an exquisite but haughty blond woman. The other was a young man, scarcely appearing as old as the most junior guardsmen. Both wore similarly styled, forest green robes, the boy's bare of symbols, the woman's with a symbol not as detailed as that of the man they followed.

The mage's dark eyes settled on Almek; he gestured his companions away. The young man bowed, obeying, and proceeded to a small, more isolated table. Conversely, the woman looked like she intended to take her master's arm before he waved her off a second time.

Taylin leaned close to the Dusvet, whispering, "I recognize him...he was in that terrible vision I had."

"Mm hm." Dusvet made a slight gesture to Taylin to remain silent.

The mage approached their table and bowed. His bow was shallow, almost perfunctory—a gesture of necessity, not reverence. "Lord Almek," he greeted in a low voice. "I am—"

"Illaini Magus Ash Andar," Almek finished for him. Taylin narrowed her eyes, cataloging the mage's form and movements with a healer's precision. "The stories of your skills and strength among your people are unparalleled. It is an honor to meet you." The sincerity of Almek's words seemed to unsettle the Forentan man.

Recovering his stoic composure, Ash spoke again. "Forgive me for not being here sooner. I was attending to a disturbance in a village some distance from here when I received word of your presence. I am grateful you have not yet left." The Illaini Magus's words were as stiff and formal as his posture.

"I thought you might have had other business that could not be rushed or dismissed," Almek replied. "Thus, I waited a little longer."

The grim man nodded in acknowledgment of Almek's words. "I would be grateful for the honor of speaking with you, Dusvet Guardian." His eyes flicked towards Taylin. He added, "Privately, without either of our students, of course."

"Of course." Almek looked at Taylin as he rose. "Considering the current patronage, my dear, feel free to return to our suite until my discussion with Magus Andar is completed."

Grateful for the release, Taylin waited only long enough for Almek and the Forentan mage to leave the main room before she moved to leave. The delay, however, was long enough to have drawn the attention of two of the coarser caravan ruffians, who slid into the seats on either side of her, blocking her escape.

"Ye sure be a pretty little thing." The less ugly of the two laughed as she slapped aside the hand that attempted to rest on her knee. "Spirited, too."

"I likes 'em spirited." The uglier one boldly tried reaching for her breast and was also slapped away. He glanced at the guardsmen, whose attentions were on those harassing Forenten. "An' no one protectin' her, neither, Bek." Leaning close, he loudly sniffed her hair. "She smells sweet. Bet she tastes sweet, too." He put a thick hand around her arm, pulling her towards him. "How's 'bout a little taste, eh?"

"Let go of me!" Taylin demanded, angry not only about these two thugs, but that the Forentan guardsmen were doing nothing to assist her. "Do you know what I am?"

The three men who had separated from the other caravan members approached Taylin's table. "Bek, Chok," the dark brown-haired Vodani man called cajolingly, a mandolin slung across his back. He was flanked by a pair of Sevmanen men, one monstrously huge with blunt features, the smaller man wiry in build with sharp features, both with the darker, dusky coloring of Gyspari. "Leave the pretty lady alone, hey? She's obviously got better taste in men than you two warthogs."

Taylin snapped, upset with the growing number of caravan men around her. "I can take care of myself, Vodani."

"There, ye see?" Chok crowed. "She don't want none of yer wussy junk. She be wantin' real men t' ride 'er hard and put 'er away wet. Don't ya, darlin'?" He reached for her lap, pawing at her.

Grimacing in disgust, Taylin pushed them away, hands on their faces. A black aura haloed where she touched them. They cried out in mortal agony, collapsing on the floor in a pair of writhing, smelly lumps. She stepped over one distastefully, her cheeks flushed with emotion. The main room fell silent, staring in shock. Guardsmen looked away, as if a scuffle between foreigners did not matter to them. Servants and patrons alike gave the Sevmanan healer a wide berth as she fled upstairs.

"Hey, Mureln, ye mind Emaris an' me take 'em outside t' play wit'?" the wiry man asked the Vodani, kicking one of the moaning men's sides ungently. Watching Taylin disappear up the stairs, he said, "Ye may want t' check on th' woman. Keep an eye on 'er. In case anyone else be thinkin' t' mess wi' her again."

The bard was barely listening, his eyes and attention fixed on Taylin. "Eh? Oh, of course. Have fun, Emil," Mureln replied cheerfully, hurrying to catch up to Taylin. He raised his hands in a peaceful gesture as she spun, her fingers curled with instinctive readiness, his sea-green eyes startled but steady. "Whoa! Hold up there, pretty lady. Only hoping to walk you safely to your room. No offense meant." He glanced over his shoulder meaningfully. "Those others will think you are fair game if you're alone."

Taylin snorted softly, lowering her hand and turning her back on Mureln, stalking upstairs. The Vodani did not hesitate and remained close on her heels. "My name is Mureln," he offered. "Master bard from Water's Resonance."

Taylin stopped abruptly and spun to face Mureln, the bard nearly running into her. She stared at him incredulously. "What is a Vodani master bard doing this far inland? Let alone traveling with those...those swine?"

Mureln shrugged. "Traveling with the caravan suited my needs." She turned away again, but her pace was less hurried. They reached a quiet landing carved into the living trunk—two small, curtained alcoves sectioned off with heavy brown and gold curtains. The stairs continued to spiral upwards into the massive tree trunk.

"I've not seen a healer as skilled as you outside of a temple in ages. What brings *you* to these incredibly cheerful lands?" She did not reply as she moved the curtain aside to her room and entered. Mureln paused only a moment before following her, letting the curtained wall fall closed behind him.

Taylin turned and stared at him in exasperation. "You aren't going to leave me alone, are you?" she asked rhetorically, his devilishly charming smile answering her. With an exasperated sigh, she stated, "Fine. I'm here with Dusvet Guardian Almek Two-Tones." She tugged open the curtains of the small window to allow fresh air inside.

Leaf-filtered sunlight brightened the deep reds and beige decorating the tiny room, somehow making it seem smaller than it already was. The bed was just wide enough for one person, and a single chair leaned against the wall across from it. She flopped onto the bed without decorum, covering her eyes with her arm, as if ignoring Mureln and everything else around her would make all of it go away.

"Are you a friend of the Dusvet Guardian?"

"I am his student."

Mureln arched an eyebrow. "But you are a master—"

"I know."

"Why would he—?"

"Would you just go away?" Taylin glared with impatience. "I don't need your protection."

"Oh, but you do," Mureln contradicted, abruptly serious. "I know it's draining for healers to use their skills. And given the average Hollow or Rest rarely gives in to the novelty of doors with locks, you might risk other unwanted visitors if you remain alone." He jerked his thumb over his shoulder in the general direction of the stairs.

Taylin sighed gustily. "Oh, very well. Stay if you insist. But I hope you enjoy hearing yourself talk, because I'm in no mood to chat right now."

Mureln chuckled, pulling his mandolin to the front and taking a seat on the chair. Strumming the strings, he played a quiet little song. "Oh, I'll not disturb you with my boring chatter, lovely Taylin. I think I shall practice instead. It's so much quieter in here." Both of the bard's eyebrows rose at some very choice Sevmanan vernacular the woman muttered under her breath. Very purposefully, he struck a loud, dissonant chord. His grin widened at her very unladylike response.

CHAPTER EIGHT

THE SERVANTS, UNUSED TO such august patrons at Visitors' Hollow, fell over themselves to prepare the table in the small, private room just off the main dining room. Both men were silent as they waited, each openly studying the other. The Illaini Magus ignored the young women's breathless fussing with patience only matched by the Dusvet Guardian himself.

The two looked towards the room's entryway at the sounds of agonized pain coming from the main room, the abrupt silence, then the growing hiss of whispers as the people in the main room overcame their initial shock. Ash arched an eyebrow in vague curiosity when Almek did not move. "I believe your student is having some trouble with the caravan thuggery contaminating the Hollow."

"As a master healer, Taylin can take care of herself," Almek explained simply. "She needs to understand the realities of the world outside of her temple's idealistic perspective." He took the bottle of wine before Ash could, pouring a glass of wine for himself. He then set the bottle aside to allow Ash to do the same for himself.

Ash held Almek's gaze before pouring. "You honor me. Few foreigners understand the intricacies of Forentan social traditions."

"Those of lower status pour for those of higher status," Almek stated as he raised his glass to Ash briefly before taking a sip. "Equals pour for themselves. Regardless of our ages, we are both the chosen mortal servants of our gods." He gestured towards the wine. "A charming tradition. It has been many decades since I was last within Forenta's borders. Not so long that I would have forgotten many of the enduring cultural particulars." The Guardian watched Ash unwaveringly, waiting for him to speak.

"I am," Ash began, and fell silent again, his eyes fixed on the liquid in his glass. "If you know of Forentan culture and of me, then you know I am—"

Almek waved a hand, cutting the younger man off, his words clipped. "I know of highborns, lowborns, and halfborns within Forenta's society. They are irrelevant to me because I'm not part of the social order here." Almek made a distasteful face. "You confuse them because you are the most gifted in generations despite the circumstances of your birth. They respect and disdain you as suits their moods." Almek shrugged one shoulder as Ash raised his eyes to regard him fixedly. "I am a Dusvet Guardian. I belong to all nations and to no nation. The basis of rank by birth and not ability bothers me as it contradicts my code."

Ash was silent for a time, thoughtful. "I suppose we are not dissimilar in that." The mage took a slow breath. "There have been...incidents...throughout Forenta. Things that have struck me as abnormal for reasons I cannot put my finger on. Things have happened I have barely righted. Or not been able to right at all. Even with strength and abilities that surpass any three mages from the Academy, I have found myself struggling." His eyes fell to his glass, expression troubled. "I am not strong enough to protect my people adequately."

Almek made a low, thoughtful sound. "You said you were delayed." Gray eyes studied the younger man. "What held you back?"

"The council will claim it was simply a rabid or diseased elder bear that attacked the Navar village." Ash's voice tightened. "But it wasn't right. Darkness clung to it. It possessed a greater awareness than any elder bear I'd ever encountered. It seemed...to enjoy killing." He shut his eyes. "I slew it, but barely."

As he spoke, Ash's hand tightened around the glass. "The Council dismisses my successes as merely my duty. They blame my failures..." The glass squealed, then cracked into many shards. Ash growled, ignoring the mingling of his blood and the spilled wine. "They call my victories obligation. My failures? Proof a lowborn orphan cannot be trusted." Ash's voice dropped to a harsh whisper. "They won't hear my warnings. That something dark lurks beneath these incidents."

"Interesting," Almek mused, watching Ash.

A frown creased the mage's face; his eyes reflected intense emotion. "...*Interesting?*"

"You're the third I've met possessing talent in another art, yet gifted with temporal resonance. It begs the question if there are not or have not been others." Almek extracted a cloth from the large pouch on his hip and tossed it to Ash, who was extracting glass from his palm. "I wonder how the Guardian Council overlooked so many strong potentials."

Ash's frown deepened; his thoughts drifted backwards. "I remember a Guardian from Forenta visiting the Academy when I was very young. But she had to speak with Se'edai Magus Ysai before she could tap any to go to Fortress. Then Ysai forbade Fortress from entering Forentan land at all." Ash grimaced—more at the memory than the pain—as another shard slipped free. "Ysai hasn't allowed anyone to leave for Fortress for as long as I can remember."

"There'd been a notable decline in Forentan recruits joining Fortress in recent decades." Almek's voice was half-thought, half-memory. He drummed his fingers on the table in a slow rhythm. "I wonder how many might have been overlooked—not for lack of potential, but because their gifts bloomed in other areas. Or worse, because someone decided they weren't worth cultivating." He fell silent for a time, gaze distant. "Perhaps we blinded ourselves," he murmured at last. "Believing that to touch one kind of energy meant you could not touch another. As if the gods had drawn clear boundaries across gifts, and we mortals had to honor divisions They never made."

The mage looked up, frowning at Almek as the meaning beyond his words sank in. "You believe I can manipulate both Guardian and Forentan magicks?" Almek nodded, watching Ash.

The mage was silent, lost in thought for several minutes before straightening. "I'm unsurprised," Ash stated with brisk self-confidence. "Guardian abilities are not very different from mages, and I *am* the best Forentan mage ever born." He set the last of the shards from his hand aside. He grimaced in pain as he forced the gashes in his hand closed, murmuring words of magic under his breath.

"Similar in appearance, but not the same." Almek twitched his fingers towards the pieces of glass. They pulled together and fused to make the broken glass whole, save for the streaks of blood now infused in the glass itself. "The significant difference between what a Guardian can do and what any other highly trained user of magicks can do is a matter of time."

Ash watched the shattered glass reform, eyes widening slightly. "You mean how long it takes to get trained?" Ash made a dismissive motion with his newly healed hand. "I doubt it would take me long. I have already mastered more of the Arts than most manage in their entire lifetimes." He looked surprised when Almek shook his head.

"No. A Guardian works with the energy of time itself. Most living things float along in time's currents, oblivious to the surrounding flow. A Guardian possesses the ability not only to perceive the currents, their rising and falling tides, but to affect them." Almek leaned forwards and stated in a low voice, "The simple fact that you sense what even some Unsvet Guardians do not, that you, untrained in time manipulation, have possibly been able to affect what most Guardians spend their lives training to do...this tells me you are more than merely a potential. You are at the same level as an Adept." Sitting back, Almek stated, "I would like you to be my student."

"Like the Sevmanan healer that travels with you?" Ash stated more than asked, considering. "All my life, I've sought to hone my skills. I'd be a fool to turn down such an offer." His voice cut off, but hinted at unspoken thoughts.

"But?" Almek prompted after an extended silence.

Ash's expression reflected annoyance. "The Se'edai had honor bound me to take my journeyman as my student. Granted, I could dismiss her, but keeping her has blocked the Se'edai Magus from causing me more aggravation. Ysai would probably bind more to me if she thought she could get away with it, but a master can determine the maximum number of students he is willing to be personally responsible for. I doubt she would let the chance to saddle me with worse pass. Even for the Dusvet Guardian. Perhaps especially for the Dusvet Guardian."

Drumming his fingers on the table, Ash added in a low voice, "And of my two students, I'd only be willing to dispense with one. They will need to come with me."

"No. I'll not have any follow me who didn't choose to do so themselves. Where I go will be too dangerous to demand it of someone unwilling to bear the burden." Almek's expression was especially grim.

Ash arched an eyebrow. "You are the Dusvet Guardian. Your word is law. Even more so than an Illaini Magus's word is supposed to be. Definitely more than a Se'edai Magus, no matter what Ysai wants to have others believe. You need only order it, and it would be done."

Almek irritably waved a hand. "Other Guardians may enjoy wielding such authority. Make potentials feel that the decision to walk the path of serving the Timeless One belongs to the teacher, not to the student. Making a potential believe they should be grateful for the Guardian finding them. That if they refused to follow their 'destiny' that the world would implode. Lording such over those without potential?" The Dusvet smacked the table for emphasis. "That is not my belief. The choice should always belong to the student, so their success or failure rests solely with their own desire to succeed. Otherwise, unwilling students taken away from their old lives would become resentful and dangerous. Those not students would be an even greater risk."

"The healing master chose to become Guardian Adept?" Ash studied Almek thoughtfully.

Almek nodded. "Taylin is my student because she chose to be, yes."

"And how did you determine she had the ability?"

The Dusvet Guardian did not allow his pleasure at Ash's guarded curiosity to reflect outwardly. "I witnessed it myself. You know successful healing is normally restricted to the time shortly after the injury occurred, and the more time that passes, the less likely anyone less than a master could succeed." Ash flinched, looking away but not before Almek noticed the flash of pain across the younger man's features. "Taylin could repair an old, poorly healed injury that would have killed the child she tended had it been left as it was."

Raising his eyes to Almek's, Ash studied the Dusvet. "You hadn't witnessed me doing anything, not even simple Forentan magicks. Yet you believe I...potentially...have this ability?"

"Several months ago, you encountered a lupine with one eye." Watching Ash's reaction, Almek continued in even tones. "It had attacked a wagon with several people. Only a small child remained alive. Your apprentice diverted it away to save the child." Before Ash could speak, Almek held up one hand. "The creature was not simply a rabid lupine. An entity known as a temporal shifter possessed it. A darkling as they are called outside of Fortress."

"A darkling...My master spoke of these things. Most consider them tales to frighten young children into obedience. Figments of the imagination."

"They are hardly tales, Illaini Magus, and definitely not figments. They are quite real. And only someone who wields temporal energies can impact these creatures." Almek sipped his wine, watching Ash. "I would teach you to harness that strength within you. Coupled with your already considerable strength in Forentan magic, you would be stronger than even me."

Ash opened his mouth, then shut it, frowning. "Guardians serve the Timeless One. I already serve the Great Mother." He held up his right hand. The image of twining ribbons of forest green and copper, both metallic as Almek's markings were, briefly appeared from the back of his hand to his elbow before fading from sight again.

Almek closed his eyes for a moment, then said in a low voice, "The Timeless One is one of the Ancient Trinity. Order, Chaos, and Time are senior to the other gods because their essences are woven throughout creation. Serving Her would not conflict with your duties to the Knowing One, but would expand them beyond the narrow focus of Forenta's borders."

Ash grimaced. "Her wisdom should never have been confined to only our land. It was meant to guide everyone to fulfill their life's purpose."

Before Ash could continue speaking, a tall man in black barged into the room. "Illaini Magus," he stated with a cold, lofty attitude. "Se'edai Magus Ysai Oberlain has received word that—" He looked at Almek, his words faltering as he paled. Less confidently, he continued. "You are forbidden from speaking with the Guardian. Forenta's sovereignty comes before the outdated traditions of kowtowing to outsiders."

"She *forbids*, Edai Magus Draustus Oberlain?" Ash leveled a hard look at the man. "She believes her authority supersedes that of the divine laws themselves?"

"The Se'edai Magus is the supreme authority of Forenta," the thin man stated flatly. "Fortress and the other nations are beneath our notice."

Ash looked at his palm, rubbing an old, star-shaped scar. "You allow your students to choose, Master Almek." Looking up at the Dusvet, the Illaini Magus stated, "I have chosen. And I can do no less than to emulate you and have my students choose to remain my students or seek other masters." Ash drew his knife and cut his finger, letting the blood pool at the tip. Before Almek could ask his intentions, Ash very deliberately drew a careful glyph onto the table.

Ysai's messenger stared in uncomprehending shock. "What do you think you are doing, Andar?" Draustus demanded. When he grabbed Ash's wrist, he was flung back against the wall, repelled by the potent field of magical energy being woven.

Ash stated in flat tones bordering defiance, "By my choice, I bind myself into your service, Almek Two-Tones, Dusvet Guardian of Fortress. I give you my Soul Oath to last until the end of this life and beyond."

"You fool! Do you have any idea what you are doing?!" the Edai Magus demanded. His advance stopped short after a step, backing away from the dark look in Ash's eyes. "If you had any family, they would all be punished for your disobedience, lowborn," he spat. "The Se'edai will hear of this." Following the dire promise, he departed.

Almek's eyes were wide as the depth of the spell sank in, feeling the ethereal tie solidify between them. "You have sworn your *life* to me...Ash, you need not have sworn so strongly."

"When dealing with the Se'edai and the rest of the Edai Magi, nothing less than everything will sway them. And this they cannot undo." As Ash completed the glyph, the bloody image hissed as it burned itself into the wood of the table. "My life. My soul. Belong to you, Master Almek."

Chapter Nine

THE DIN IN THE crowded common room fell to near silence when the Illaini Magus and Dusvet Guardian emerged from the private room. Excusing himself, Ash joined his waiting students. Almek almost collided with the bard stepping off the stairs.

Almek's eyes lit up with surprised delight. "Mureln Nadeesi! Are you a sight for sore eyes!"

Mureln shocked those watching as he laughed and grabbed Almek in a hearty embrace that the Guardian returned. "Almek! I heard rumors through the Gyspari clans you were out and about again!" He chided mildly, "But it's just Master Mureln now. You remember Vodani traditions. Masters have no family allegiances. Only the Forentan and Sevmanen masters keep their family ties." His disapproval of the tradition was apparent.

"I can see life has treated you well. And a master of the bardic arts?" Almek smiled. "I would love to speak more with you, but I need to check on my student—"

"Master Taylin will be down shortly." With a charming smile at Almek's surprised and then scolding expression, Mureln held up both hands. "I was a perfect gentleman with your pretty student, Almek. She just needed a nap after zinging a few idiots." Glancing behind him at the stairs, he sighed wistfully, "Lovely and strong."

"Mureln, behave yourself. And don't give me that innocent look. I've known you since you were a boy, and I can tell already you've lost none of the mischief."

The bard affected a comical expression of innocence as he teased, "I'm surprised you recognized me at all after all these years." He adjusted the mandolin on his back. "I was barely a man when we parted ways."

Almek snorted, turning to head towards the table that had remained empty since he left it earlier. "Are you thinking I'm age-addled, too?"

Mureln's jovial expression dissolved into one of consternation at the uncharacteristic sourness in Almek's voice. "What? No, of course not. But I *was* still a wet-behind-the-ears bardic student when you first came to Vodanya." He touched Almek's shoulder. "Who dares to call you age-addled? I'll take my mandolin up the side of their heads. Every last one of them."

The dire promise brought a wan smile to Almek's lips, and the Guardian shook his head. "No, no. It would be a pointless waste of a good instrument. Their heads are much too hard to do any good."

"*I'd* feel better," Mureln muttered like a petulant child, making Almek chuckle. Pleased to have lightened the Dusvet's soured mood, Mureln waved to one of the serving girls as they sat. He looked up as his companions rejoined him, brushing their hands on their hips. "Almek, meet Emil and Emaris of the Morlaiz clan. They've been my traveling companions for...what? Ten years now?"

Emil made a sound, waving a hand to the serving girl looking for him where he and Emaris had been waiting. Taking the drink and downing half of it, he shrugged nonchalantly. "We been keepin' 'is arse around t' count th' gold fer us." He wagged a finger at Mureln. "Don't go askin' me t' be doin' yer countin' job. Ain't that right, Emaris?"

The larger man nodded, looking Almek over and nodding once in greeting. "Emaris don't be meanin' no disrespect neither, Guardian. He jus' don't be much fer talkin', ye see. Hasn't made a sound since he were born." Taking the plate of food the girl brought him, he grabbed his spoon, waving it a bit. "Our boy Mureln, here. He been good t' us. Lots o' gold wi' him around."

Hiding his smile behind his hand as he idly rubbed his white-speckled beard, Almek nodded congenially. "It is a pleasure to meet you both. Mureln has always had a way of acquiring...unique companions. If I remember, there was this pretty girl he—"

Mureln cleared his throat. "There's no need to bring up the past." Seeing the open curiosity of the other two men, he wagged his finger at them. "Don't."

"Aw, but—!"

"No!" With comic annoyance, Mureln turned an accusatory glare on Almek. "Now see what you've started?!"

"Hm?" Almek asked innocently, eyebrows raised as he lifted his glass to his lips. The old man glanced across the room where Ash sat with his two students, observing their interaction.

"Dusvet Almek, forgive me. I—" Taylin stopped short when she realized who was sitting with him. "What are *you* doing here?" she asked incredulously.

"You have met Master Mureln. These are his companions, Emil and Emaris, wandering sons of the Morlaiz Gyspari clan." Both men stared at Almek in shock. "Don't assume everyone is oblivious to the Gyspari roads. Gyspari rarely travel separately from their clans. I know Mureln's taste in companions. He'd never align with anyone who'd have been banished, so you are wanderers." He winked. "Some of my best years were spent traveling with the clans."

Mureln stood and pulled out the empty chair for Taylin, waving an invitation for her to sit with a grand flourish. Annoyed, she sat, sliding her chair away from the bard and closer to Almek with a sniff.

The shriek of outrage from the Illaini Magus's journeyman drew all eyes to his table. "Now there be a happy girl," Emil muttered.

"Apparently, she is not pleased about the Illaini Magus choosing to become my student."

"Student?" Taylin and Mureln echoed in surprise.

"Almek, this is unusual, even for you. Taking on masters as students is one thing. But more than one student at a time?" Leaning forwards, Mureln whispered, "And one who is god-chosen?"

"You remember what I taught you when you were still my student, Mureln." Almek made a dismissive gesture. "Trust your instincts. You'll find what you need when you need it. And be where you need to be...when you need to be there."

"This surpasses mere intuition. Even I can tell that much." Mureln tore his eyes away from the minor scene the girl was causing. Even other Forentan were casting disdainful, disapproving looks over towards the blonde woman. "It *would* explain my restlessness for the past while."

Emil looked up from his meal, wiping his mouth with the back of his hand. "An' here I thought ye just needed t' get laid." Mureln snorted, smacking the back of Emil's head. "Hey! What?" Looking between Taylin and Mureln, the man rolled his eyes. "Oh, shards, ye still need to get laid, don't ye? I thought ye were goin' t' get with this pretty— Hey!" he exclaimed when the bard smacked him again, oblivious to Taylin's cheeks turning bright red. "Don't be gettin' on me about th' lack up here. Ye know these tree flowers got their legs clamped tighter than a noble's fingers on 'is coin." Emaris paused in his eating to belch loudly, earning Emil's attempt to outdo him.

"I can't take either of you anywhere civilized," Mureln lamented, waving a dismissive hand at the rough Sevmanen pair. He didn't look at Taylin as she averted her gaze and focused on her drink, her cheeks burning red. Mureln looked grim. "Seriously, Almek...what is going on?"

"I am not sure," Almek confessed. "Only a handful have sensed the wrongness that I have glimpsed. The other Guardians barely give me the consideration they used to. Sometimes it feels as though they simply humor me, but ultimately ignore me." Draining his glass, he said, "I went to the Timeless One to share Her vision."

Mureln jerked, his back stiff as he stared at Almek. Even Emil and Emaris went still, looking between the two men in silence, though they were more confused than shocked. "You did...what?"

Almek did not bother to repeat himself, knowing the bard had heard him the first time. "Even She could not clearly see, but She confirmed whatever is out there is not my imagination. But whatever 'it' is, it is beyond ancient." He met Mureln's gaze. "And She is afraid." In a quieter voice, the Dusvet pointed out, "You were my student once many years ago, Mureln."

"You know I did not choose my bardic training over that of a Guardian because..." Mureln's words drifted off, his expression the depths of apology and worry. The words began tumbling out of his mouth in a rush. "I just...I couldn't have lived without the music. Its call was too strong."

"Mureln," Almek stated emphatically to get him to stop speaking. "I never blamed you for your decision. If you need forgiveness, I forgave you long ago." Shaking his head, Almek's expression changed. "Perhaps what is out there will require Guardians with gifts beyond those we have always accepted," Almek stated. He took a long drink, unhappy. "I blame our own pride. The world seeks balance. If others had shown similar potential in uncommon talents, there must have been a need for them. If Guardians were turning a blind eye to that, then we failed in our duties."

The bard looked troubled. "I had always believed Guardians to be infallible. To have the clearest of visions and purest of purposes. Not to be petty and political like so many others are."

"Then, that corruption is a sign. Or it is something else. But regardless, it is a failure on my part for being blind to it for so long myself. But that is the past." He looked at Mureln. "It's now for me to mend things before they fall apart completely. I fear," Almek closed his eyes and whispered, "that it has grown beyond what I alone could manage." The Guardian extended his hand to the bard. "I asked you to be my student once, but the bardic call was stronger. Now, you have mastered your art, and your Sight is still strong. I ask you again...would you accept me as your teacher?"

"Almek, you were like a father to me when I was young." Mureln clasped Almek's offered hand in both of his, as if trying to impart his sincerity. "You don't even need to ask. I would share your path into the depths of all the hells, as your student or just as a friend. Though I'm afraid these lugs will tag along."

Almek smirked and shook his head, then looked at Emil and Emaris. Before he could speak, Emil scolded, "Don't be lookin' at us like that. We goes where Mureln goes. Always have." The wiry Gyspari smiled wickedly. "Besides, bet there be some fine money t' be made down in the hells. All them idiot nobles stuck on 'emselves gotta be there."

"No doubt about that," Taylin muttered. The three men looked sharply at her, then burst out laughing.

CHAPTER TEN

ASH'S EXPRESSION HARDENED AS he neared the table when Amelana jumped up, trying to loop an arm around his, purring in obsequious adoration. "Master Ash!"

"Sit down, Journeyman." Pushing her off firmly, Ash sat between his students. "There are things we must discuss."

The young man sat up straighter, looking at Ash in curious surprise. "Me too, Master?" Ash flinched as the young man's surprise at his inclusion only reminded him of how much he neglected him in favor of Amelana. He frowned as he glanced back towards Almek, seeing the easy camaraderie among the Guardian, the Vodani bard, and the two Gyspari. Looking away, he waved a hand to a server to bring drinks for them. "You both have a decision to make."

A crease of suspicion marred Amelana's delicate features. "What kind of decision?"

"You must choose whether you wish to remain with me or request new masters. I would make recommendations if you wish the latter," he said in a slightly gentler tone to Terrence as the young man's face fell. "I have sworn Soul Oath to Dusvet Guardian Almek Two-Tones. When he leaves Forenta, I will go with him. I cannot force you to leave Forenta because Master Almek forbids it." The man averted his gaze from Terrence, unable to look at his crestfallen expression.

"What do you mean, you are leaving Forenta?!" Amelana shrieked, both Ash and Terrence flinching at the shrillness of her voice. Ash rolled his eyes, crossing his arms while he waited for her nearly incoherent rant to run its course. "I do not want to leave Forenta! There is nothing those puerile little inferiors have that could *possibly* benefit me!"

"I said," Ash stated in measured tones, voice cold, "*I* will be traveling where Master Almek goes. You are no longer bound to me, Amelana. Either of you. You are free to petition the Edai Tredecima to attach you to someone who can finish your training here in Forenta." He flicked a glance at Amelana. "Or whatever would suit your temperament." The woman huffed and crossed her arms, turning her nose up. He looked at the young man. "Terrence, you have a considerable amount of promise. I'm sure Edai Magus Ellis would be delighted to have you as his apprentice."

"Master Ash," Terrence said slowly, both hands curling around his glass. "Your offer is...it means a lot that you have so much faith in me. But," he flicked a glance at the still huffing Amelana and quickly away again. "Having you as my master means more to me than anything in the world. You said learning requires testing yourself against the world." As Ash's lips twitched into a faint smile, Terrence sat up straighter, brushing the strand of dirty blond hair from his light blue eyes, his confidence growing. "Well, if you're stepping into the world to prove yourself, how could I not follow? I would like to join you."

Ash's lips curved a little more. "If that's what you want, I'll gladly continue your education while I learn, too."

"What?! You're going to take *him* with you? Not me?" Amelana sneered. Terrence flinched, eyes dropping at the woman's critical tones. "I'm your best student! He is nothing but a lowborn—"

"You are my *senior* student," Ash corrected, tones edged at her mention of 'lowborn.' "In magic, birthright means nothing without the skill or training to back it up. I have proven that myself, which is why you got yourself assigned to me. To gain the prestige of being the Illaini Magus's student." He narrowed his eyes. "Right now, you sound more like a prissy, spoiled brat instead of a disciplined mage student."

The woman flushed at the implication, but she gritted her teeth and pressed forward. "I gave up a great deal to become your student, Master Ash. They promised me—" She stopped as he raised his eyebrow at her. "You are honor bound to keep me until I earn the rank of master."

"I was never honor bound beyond keeping you for a year. I kept you because you're a member of my former master's family. Ysai can claim what she will. It's a waste of time arguing with her. Neither facts nor traditions move her." Narrowing his eyes, Ash removed her hand from his wrist. "I have sworn Soul Oath to the Dusvet. That supersedes anything the Edai Tredecima demands of me."

"Don't tell me you are not honor bound! Your word is your life! You taught me this. You gave your word! You said—"

"There are traditions that the Edai Tredecima easily brushes aside depending on its whims, but it cannot brush aside Soul Oath." Ash narrowed his eyes at the woman. "Choose to follow me, or choose to stay. Marry into a house with a station that suits you so you can play at those boorish social games you enjoy, if you tire of the work involved to become a master mage."

Her flush darkened to a furious crimson as she hissed, "You know I cannot, Master Ash."

Ash waved a dismissive hand. "I don't really care what you do, Journeyman Amelana Avarian. Don't imagine you...or the Se'edai, or any member of the Edai Tredecima...can sway what's already bound."

He looked to Terrence and said with a less harsh tone, "Speak to Dessa about preparing for traveling. When Lord Almek is ready, we will join him." Ash, pointedly avoiding making the same offer to Amelana, rose from the table. "Go make your preparations. Say your farewells to friends or family if you choose to follow me." Fixing a look at Amelana, he added, "Or stay there."

Terrence rose in haste, eager to flee Amelana's hateful stare.

Chapter Eleven

The heart of Ithesra comprised a wild tangle of bridges, broad branches, and winding walkways, all grown or built into the towering tree trunks that soared from the forest floor towards the sunlit canopy. Light filtered down in flickering patches of green-gold, dancing across bark, leaves, and paths.

Shelters and refuges clung to trunks like step-mushrooms or dangled boldly from high, heavy boughs. Bridges, from broad, steady structures to those gently swaying, and spiraling walkways curling along the outer surfaces of the silent giants, connected everything like an intricate web spun without symmetry. The younger, more agile forwent the safety of rails and steps, scaling craggy bark most times with rope and always with fearless ease. Their motion gave the ancient trees a quiet pulse of life—a breath shared between forest and folk.

After some discussion, Almek agreed he and his students would join the Illaini Magus at his private home to plan their journey ahead with considerably more privacy than the Hollow afforded. They followed wide, low paths through the arboreal sprawl, crossing Ithesra's northern border towards the eastern road leading to the Magus Academy's mountain retreat.

Descending the last bridge to the forest floor, the newcomers paused, awe-struck by the immense tree that housed the Magus's dwelling. Nestled within the tree's massive roots, the home rose from the living wood. Around it sprawled a verdant clearing, grasses thick and herb beds blooming in carefully tended rows, each tree root embraced by cultivated color.

Emil whistled low, echoing the wonder on every face. "Th' whole thing be yours alone, Mage?" He squinted upwards—once, twice, a third time—before stumbling back into Emaris. "Damn, man. How far up do it go?"

Ash gave him a wintry look and let the question hang. He gestured to the structure nestled against a tree opposite the entrance. "My stable can shelter the horses."

Barely masking his impatience, he waited as Mureln and the Gyspari companions tended to the mounts. The aloof mage flicked a glance at Taylin, who startled at the distant howl of wolves. "You need not fear," he said. "I have warded my home. No predator can cross its bounds."

Taylin blushed and lowered her gaze. "Thank you." Ash only shrugged and turned towards the blood red door.

She hesitated, looking towards Almek...but met Mureln's gaze instead. The bard offered a quiet smile and rested a reassuring hand on her shoulder. She blushed deeper, nearly matching the color of the door, and pulled away, hurrying after Ash to widen the space between herself and the Vodani man.

The lantern beside the door flared to life, soft blue-white magelight responding to Ash's silent will. The door opened with only the faintest squeal, and he led them inside.

Rich greens, warm golds, and deep woods filled the voluminous chamber, each hue woven into the structure's polished bones. The steady glow of candles and oil lamps softened the sharp blue-white flare of scattered magelight lanterns, wrapping the room in a cozy haze.

A delicate, fair-skinned woman dusting a vase turned with a bright smile meant for Ash...but her welcome faltered into panic as the motley company followed him inside. The vase slipped from her hands, shattering against the polished floor in a spray of porcelain. Clapping a hand to her mouth, she fled down the hall in silence.

Ash grimaced. "Dessa!"

"Not used to guests, is she?" Mureln murmured. "Or not used to foreigners?" He stepped towards the broken pieces, but Almek laid a hand on his shoulder and shook his head.

Ash clenched his teeth, glancing towards Almek before reining in the sharp reply. "We grew up together. She's mute."

"Then be kind to the young woman," Almek advised calmly. He raised his hands and focused. The scattered shards quivered, then pulled together in reverse, time folding the vase back into wholeness. As the porcelain knit together and settled, the Guardian bent to retrieve it with a faint smile. "It's clear she's not accustomed to visitors."

Ash strode to the archway where she'd vanished, voice taut with effort to keep his emotions leashed. "Dessa! Come out and meet my guests."

She emerged, eyes wide and frightened, trembling like a child braced for punishment.

But Ash's tone softened into something rare and unexpected. "Dessa, these are my guests." He named each one, noting their race...except for Almek, introduced only as a Dusvet Guardian. "I've given my Soul Oath to Master Almek," he told her gently. "He will be training me in Guardian arts."

Her stunned gaze met his, asking without sound. Ash nodded, answering the unspoken questions in kind, and brushed a stray strand of white-blond hair behind her ear.

Taylin broke the silence, her voice sharp with shock. "Oh, Zeridis!" Dessa flinched, retreating behind Ash as the healer stepped forward with an outstretched hand. Ignoring Ash's dark scowl and Almek's disapproving glance, Taylin fixed her eyes on the young woman. "Your throat—what happened? Who did that to you?"

Dessa turned away, shame flickering across her face as she raised trembling fingers to cover the horrific scar carved into her throat. Ash flushed at the question, his voice brusque and bitter. "Caravan guards. Foreigners. They tried to kill her...after they raped her." The pain of failure cut through the hate laced in his words. Dessa looked up and placed a steadying hand on his arm. He covered it gently. "I saved her life. But not her voice."

Taylin, free of judgment, extended her hand once more. "Please...I'm a healer. Let me help."

Ash studied her with glacial intensity, then drew Dessa close, whispering in Forentan. The group watched in silence as Taylin placed her hands over the scar.

Dessa gasped and stiffened. The pale white glow around Taylin's fingers flared bright blue—piercing, potent. Both women stood frozen in the glow for long moments until the connection fractured and sent them staggering backwards.

Ash caught Dessa before she could fall. Mureln rushed to Taylin's side, and she clung to him without thought.

Slowly, Dessa looked up at Ash, tears trailing down her cheeks. Her throat, once marred by the ugly gash, was smooth...newly whole. She swallowed several times, lips parting with effort. "A-Ash?" she whispered.

The mage stared at Taylin, stunned, then back to Dessa. "Shhh. Don't speak yet," he whispered, pressing his hand to her neck. "The healing is still fresh. There'll be time to speak later. Rest now." He led her through the archway towards her room, glancing over his shoulder at Taylin with a look no one could read.

Taylin choked on a sob, visibly shaken, her strength drained by the healing. Mureln tightened his grip around her, frowning. "Master Taylin...are you alright?"

She shook her head with a faint, trembling motion, fighting to reclaim composure. "Wrong," she whispered hoarsely. "The man...the one who hurt her..." She staggered two steps towards Almek, voice breaking. "Something...not right...it wasn't human. Not gone..." Her knees buckled, eyes rolling back as she collapsed. Mureln caught her just in time to keep her head from striking the corner of the table, cradling her close.

Almek knelt beside her as the bard held her. He touched Taylin's temple and closed his eyes, concern etched deep into his features...as if his will alone could revive her. He opened his eyes as Ash reappeared without Dessa. "She needs rest to restore her strength," he said. "I don't know what she saw. Hopefully, she can clarify her warning when she awakens."

Ash remained apart, arms folded, watching in silence. As Emaris stepped forward to lift the unconscious healer with ease, the mage's expression tightened. "I did not realize Sevmana could channel so much magic energy," he said tonelessly...a compliment in form, not in feeling.

Mureln leveled a scornful glare at the mage. "Perhaps if Forenta ceased being so narrow-minded and looked beyond its borders," he stated, voice edged with bittersweet mockery, "it would learn that others are not as inferior as it likes to believe."

The mage did not miss the insult. "Other *Forenten* are inferior to me," Ash stated, a dangerous edge in his voice. "Just as other races are inferior to Forenten, Vodani." Emil stepped quietly to Mureln's side, resting his hand on the hilt of his dagger. Tension mounted as glares sharpened...one breath from shattering into violence.

"Enough!" Almek snapped at the men. "There will be none of this!" He nodded to Emaris, who gently laid Taylin on the couch. "It wasn't just the healing that weakened her," the Guardian continued. "She is new to the manipulation of temporal energy."

Fixing a hard gaze on Ash, he continued, "To heal your Dessa, she risked herself—reaching farther than she's ever dared with forces barely understood. You, of all people, should grasp the risk." Though Ash and Mureln did not drop their glares, the heat of the looming fight faded.

"Taylin is the only healer known who can mend such old wounds...or injuries caused by whatever attacked that girl."

Ash looked away from Mureln, uncertainty flickering in his scowl. "It was a thrice-cursed Vodani-Sevmanan halfborn who slit her throat. I killed him myself."

Almek turned to him, eyes shifting from pale gray to storm-dark—five centuries of judgment brimming in their depths. Ash averted his eyes. "What you killed was not human. Or not entirely. That much Taylin was able to sense." He looked to Mureln and his companions. "Mureln, watch over Taylin." Then, to Ash, his voice flat, commanding.

"You and I need to speak. Now."

THE ILLAINI MAGUS'S PRIVATE study seemed cramped with all the shelves of books and racks of scrolls, despite being as large as the home's common room. Deep red cushions lined the heavy furniture; the magelight lamp that lit as soon as Ash entered barely gave sufficient light to see by from beyond the enormous chair behind the desk.

Almek crossed his arms, studying Ash as the mage closed the door to the room. "I realize you have become accustomed to being accorded a certain level of respect for your skills and your power." Almek paused for a heartbeat. "Or demanding respect. You earned it if the Knowing One chose you to serve Her. But I will not tolerate further disrespect from you towards my other students. Regardless of your achievements, as *my* students, you are all equals."

Ash gritted his teeth, unable to meet Almek's disapproving gaze. "The healer *has* impressed me," he allowed, tucking his hands into his sleeves as he spoke with cool formality. "The others—"

"You misunderstand me." Almek returned with a similar level of cool formality. "It does not matter who impressed you or how they impressed you. They are my students, as are you. And," he emphasized, "you have sworn your Soul Oath to me. Do not think I am unaware of what that means." Ash flinched. His lips pressed into a tight line, eyes lowering a fraction. "Yes, you are probably the most powerful of my students. It doesn't make you better than them. It makes you responsible for protecting them, just as you have been protecting Dessa all your life."

Ash's gaze snapped up, shocked by the turn. "What?"

Walking over to the small window, Almek pulled the curtain open. The breeze curled through the room, carrying the weight of memory and truth. After a long moment of silence as he scried the wind, he spoke, words soft and thoughtful. "You and Dessa were young when you both were attacked. Not even an acknowledged adept yet, because as children without families, they considered you inferior to those with better pedigrees. Your education in the Arts would have been minimal at best, if not for your Master Bennu—who took both you and Dessa as fosterlings under his roof."

"How can you kn—?" Ash's eyes widened as the old man laid bare his soul with unsettling ease. He fell silent when Almek raised a hand to silence him.

"Your attackers made you watch what they did to the others with you. To her," Almek continued. "And none of your own people came when you pleaded for help. The largest of them mocked you—called you weak. He reveled in your helplessness, then made you watch as he cut her throat."

Almek turned from the window, sorrow softening his gaze. "You called on the magic of your blood—called the trees themselves to strike them down. And afterwards, you mended Dessa's throat as best you could. No training. Only raw instinct...and the fierce drive to protect.

"You've worked with tireless determination," he said, "never again to be seen as weak. Or helpless." Almek tilted his head. "Or inferior." Ash averted his gaze from the clarity in the Guardian's eyes. "They would never have permitted you to become a Guardian," Almek said. "Not with your birth. They could never see past whatever unfortunate circumstances that left you an orphan. They feared you would fail...and reflect poorly on Forenta. So they denied you the chance."

He stepped forward, resting a hand on Ash's shoulder—fatherly, grounding. "How," he asked gently, "are you any different from those you disdain?"

Ash whispered, "How? How could you know?"

"To scry the wind is to glimpse the truth of the past," Almek replied. "But I have only ever been a Guardian. You...Taylin...Mureln...you're the first I've seen who can blend Guardian magicks with other gifts. You did it without guidance. Without training." He smiled thinly. "Had you been taught, you might've known Dessa's attacker was not wholly human."

"A darkling?" Ash asked, shocked. "I...killed a darkling before I was named Illaini?"

"Perhaps." Almek's voice was grave. "The vision was clouded. But what I saw bore the mark. Temporal shifters are parasites—slipping free of the time stream to puppeteer their hosts." He studied Ash's expression closely. "Are they common in Forenta?"

Ash did not answer. He crossed to a shelf and pulled out a thick, worn tome. "Most dismiss them as children's tales. Fables spun to explain misfortune." He laid the book reverently on the table, fingers tracing its cover. "But my master...he never believed they were fiction. He was old. Eccentric, they said. Easy to ignore."

His voice shifted to something brittle. "Dessa and he became my family, after I lost my first. One I couldn't protect. One I couldn't save."

Silence lingered for several heartbeats before Ash opened the tome to a sketch near the top of the page—a gray, ghostly humanoid with hollow eyes and stretching limbs. Its simplicity made it more terrifying. "The stories say they lurk deep in the wilderness," Ash murmured, "waiting in the shadows for travelers who walk alone." His finger slid across the elegant Forentan script.

"My master recorded accounts of those who returned changed. Kind souls turned cruel. Cruel ones grew monstrous. The more suffering they caused, the stronger they became, while those around them withered." His voice tightened. "Their children...always worse. My master believed they tainted other souls themselves. That even after death, their influence lingered...feeding on the pain they left behind."

Almek placed a hand over the page, eyes troubled. "Lingered..." Abruptly, he turned towards the door, his urgency startling the mage. "We must go to the girl. Now! Before it's too late."

Ash didn't hesitate. He asked no questions. He followed, hard on Almek's heels.

STANDING BEFORE A FULL-LENGTH mirror in her modest bedroom, Dessa traced her fingers over the flawless skin of her throat, entranced. The fresh wholeness seemed surreal. She startled as Ash and Almek burst through the door. Her wide-eyed fright melted into radiant joy.

"Ash!" She met him halfway, arms slipping around his waist with casual familiarity. Her pale blue eyes sparkled...so pure, so full of love. Ash held her protectively, his gaze sweeping the room with grim alertness. Used to his moods, her joy did not falter. "Oh, Ash! I can hardly believe it...It is like that day never happened!" Her voice rang light, sweet. "I can barely remember it now! Isn't it wonderful? It's as if I've been reborn!"

Ash's eyes went wide. The mirror surface darkened; twin red slits flared in its depth. "Dessa! Away from the mirror!" He yanked her behind him, raising his other hand to cast a spell. A burst of air surged into the glass.

The surface exploded, shards flying outwards...then abruptly froze mid-flight, suspended in time. Without warning, the slivers collapsed back into the wooden frame as if nothing had occurred. Dessa shrieked as the surface of the mirror rippled, a mirrored appendage striking the mage away and ensnaring her—like a mantis capturing a butterfly.

A dreadful voice hissed in their minds. *<For so long, I drank your pain...fed on your agony...as your soul bled without healing.>* Dessa struggled in the mirrored grip, horrified. Another glass-like limb caressed her—obscene and mocking. *<You were so delicious.>* She fought futilely, sinking into the glass as though it were water. *<Even better, his pain echoed through you.>* The eyes floated around behind her, as if examining the girl from various perspectives. *<It was so easy, learning his power's touch through you.>*

"Let me go!" Dessa begged, voice thin with fear. "Please!"

The voice growled as the red eyes brightened with virulent hatred. *<It was supposed to be only a matter of time. I was certain he would mate with you.>* The red slits flared, a hiss dripping malevolence. *<Given me a powerful body to anchor to your world. Then I could finally destroy him, and feed on you until I bled you dry of magic, too.>* Pain lanced through her as its grip closed like iron vines. *<It would have been perfect. But no. He had to be so noble. So careful. So* weak.*>* Snarling, it raised a pointed arm over the groaning mage as he pushed himself up weakly. *<He should have just taken you as I would have before he stopped me! I could have been darkborn! Free to hunt hidden among your naïve race.>*

Vivid blue energy shrouded the reflective monstrosity as Almek rested his hands on the mirror frame, the darkling shivering as it struggled in its grip. The Guardian grimaced, unable to subdue it. "Strong, Shifter. Stronger than I expected," Almek acknowledged.

The creature laughed evilly. *<Do you think I would have chosen a weak host, Guardian? This girl had more native-born magic than most of the pitiful excuses for mages that exist here. I had no need to take her fully to be able to feed.>* It laughed, eyes raking her like broken glass. *<I have been feeding on them both for years.>* Focusing, Almek narrowed his eyes and tugged; the mirror creature rippled as Dessa almost slipped from its grasp. It snarled. *<You think to free her, Guardian?>* Mirrored coils closed around Dessa tighter. *<You cannot have her. I will not allow it!>*

Almek extended a hand to touch its surface, stopping when a silvered arm ending in a sharp point hovered over Dessa's eye. The woman froze in wide-eyed panic. "I won't allow you to endure, Darkling," the Guardian promised, moving his hands slowly. The mirror rippled as Almek forced it and Dessa apart. "You will feed no more here."

Ash looked up just as Dessa broke free. She started towards him—then froze mid-step. A mirrored spike burst through her chest, the darkling's last act of defiance. A heartbeat after, the Guardian's power dominated and crushed it out of existence...too late. Ash caught her as she staggered forwards, easing her down to the ground, cradling her. "Dessa," he whispered, voice cracking with grief.

Having arrived in time to see the confrontation but unable to do more than watch, Mureln was at Almek's elbow, lending him support as the Guardian staggered. The bard looked down at the mage and dying woman and glanced at the ashen-faced Guardian. "Should I get Taylin...?"

Appearing to have aged years in mere minutes, Almek bowed his head, eyes closed in quiet grief. "Taylin is still too weak. She spent all her strength severing the darkling's tie to the girl. Were she conscious enough to try healing a temporally caused injury of this magnitude again, it might end her."

Sightless eyes stared ahead as Dessa reached out. "Ash? Where are you?" Ash clasped the outstretched hand, squeezing it tightly as he held it over his heart. "Oh, Ash," she whispered. "Thank the goddess...you are still alive...I feared...it had killed you, too..."

Ash choked. "Hold on, Dessa. The healer—"

Dessa shook her head slightly, shaking. "I know...it is...too late for me, Ash..." She swallowed, her voice growing weaker. "Ash...please...do not blame...yourself..." Her breaths grew shallower as her life faded. "It was never...your fault..."

"Dessa," the man whispered harshly. "Don't leave me."

"I have...always...loved you...Ash..."

"I know." Bowing his head, Ash held Dessa's lifeless body tighter. "I know."

MURELN POURED SEVERAL GLASSES of the strongest alcohol he could find, handing them out liberally. He paused beside Ash, who stared into the fire, unmoving. "Drink," the bard said softly. "It will help." When Ash didn't respond, Mureln leaned closer, whispered something, and squeezed his shoulder. Ash closed his eyes, then reached for the glass and drained it. Mureln refilled it before moving on to Almek.

Almek sat facing the fire, rubbing his face with one weary hand. "Never in my five hundred years have I encountered a non-corporeal temporal shifter on this side of the barrier so strong." He shook his head. "It's not normal for one to endure this long without a host. Or to gain so much strength." He hesitated. "Or...hadn't been."

Curled on the couch, wrapped in a blanket, Taylin looked pale as moonlight. She pulled her gaze from Ash and turned to Almek, her voice thin. "Forgive me, Dusvet. If I hadn't—"

Almek raised a hand, gentle, but tired. "Don't blame yourself," he said. "Temporal shifters are difficult to perceive once they've claimed a host. Even fully trained Guardians struggle." He glanced down, voice softer. "Even me." Mureln reached out, touching Almek's arm with concern. His eyes searched the Guardian's face. "Usually," Almek said, "they can only be seen when they control their host outright. The longer they linger, the more arrogant they become. That's when they reveal themselves."

"But this one hadn't," Mureln pointed out. "It just...leeched magic? From the girl? And the mage?"

Almek nodded, drained his glass and passed it back. "It's nearly impossible to recognize a time shifter's presence when it first takes a host. The early signs are subtle. Only later do they show...the traces that betray what they truly are."

He glanced towards Ash. "As long as it had been here, if it had inhabited her, I would have seen it the moment I crossed the threshold.

No doubt, Ash, it kept itself outside her...because it knew you would recognize it. One day, inevitably." The mage turned away, grimacing.

The Guardian sighed heavily. "It was Taylin who sensed it. Through the healing." He looked down, voice heavy. "Healing the wound severed its link to her. Taylin tried to tell us."

"It's my fault." Ash's voice came quiet, jagged. "I should have seen—"

"If fault exists, it lies with me." Almek rubbed his brow. "I had assumed nothing so brazen would dare live so close to one with Guardian sight. Non-corporeal time shifters are more bestial, often slipping out of the River of Time more by accident than design. I did not believe one like that could endure so long without a host."

Ash looked up, face pale and drawn. "It spoke of...mating."

Almek nodded, rubbing his cheek. "Yes. They are called darkborn. Temporal shifters—darklings—who take a host at the moment of conception. Before the soul joins the physical vessel."

The reaction within the group was one of revulsion and confusion. "Human souls are not unlike temporal shifters," Almek said. "Both exist outside our reality in the River of Time." He waited for the murmurs to subside before continuing. "Souls are timeless. What lives outside of our reality does not grow or change. The physical body is an anchor—a vessel for learning and experience. Some temporal beings, such as humans, join with the physical world at conception. For us, reincarnation is a natural phenomenon."

Emil frowned, rubbing the back of his neck. "So, what be th' difference b'tween these shifter things and anythin' else born?"

Almek took his refilled glass back from Mureln. He looked less gray, but no less haggard. "It's not so much the difference between darkborn and those born normally," he said as he chose his words with care. "For humans and those like them, soul-binding to flesh is a process developed across untold ages."

He gestured vaguely towards the fire. "In the River of Time, like in our world, there are predators and prey, scavengers and parasites. Guardians exist to protect this plane from what slips through...by accident or by intent." Almek sagged into his chair. "If they cannot be dislodged, they must be destroyed. But if a temporal shifter becomes darkborn...they are nearly impossible to detect until much, much later. And after considerable harm has been wrought."

Taylin's voice was small. "So everyone who feeds off others' misery is...one of these darkborn?" Taylin wondered, troubled.

"Alas, no," Almek said, offering a sad smile. "Some people feed on pain to feel powerful. That weakness makes it easier for shifters to remain undetected. Were it not for the physical form rejecting them over time...they could devastate everything."

Silence settled over the room. Then Ash spoke, voice low and steady. "I want to take Dessa to the only place I've ever known peace. So her soul can be at ease." He looked to Almek. "Then...we can go wherever you deem necessary, Master Almek."

The others turned to the Guardian. After a long moment, Almek nodded. "There's time enough for our journey to begin. We'll accompany you." Ash looked from one face to the next, nodding in silent gratitude.

Chapter Twelve

Cheerful birdsong filled the air as the group gathered outside of Ash's home. Horses milled about, cropping the grasses and nosing at the carefully tended plants. Terrence held the reins of Ash's mount, his expression nearly as devastated as Ash's had been. He impatiently rubbed his eyes using the heel of his hand.

Mureln approached him with quiet concern. "You okay, lad?"

Terrence nodded, swallowing hard. "Miss Dessa was always...kind to me. Even when I ruined supper. A few times." He gave a shaky smile. "She never got mad."

Amelana snorted. "She was soft. A sound beating would've taught you better." She turned her nose up at Mureln's disapproving look. Her voice soured. "I never understood why Master Ash kept only that woman around. He has the right to dozens of proper servants." Icy silence fell. Every eye turned to her, chill and condemning. She seemed oblivious. But when Ash emerged, she stopped speaking. Her expression twisted with disdain at the sight of the precious silk enshrouding the dead woman.

The ever-silent Emaris stepped forward, kneeling to offer Ash a leg up. Ash accepted the help, nodding his gratitude. Amelana rode around to join him, eyes flicking towards the body. "Master Ash," she said. "You should have that Sevmanan brute carry her. It is beneath you to bear a lowborn." Ash turned to her slowly; the look he gave her was dark, quiet, final. She prudently drew back and remained silent.

The perpetual twilight of the forest floor suited the mood as the group rode among the monstrous roots of Forenta's ancient trees along a meandering path. So when they broke through thick brush into a grassy glade open to the sky, the sudden light surprised them. Golden sunlight poured into the clearing. Bright flowering vines draped over the remains of a fallen tree at its center, and a cloud of songbirds and what appeared to be oversized insects burst skywards as the horses pushed through the leafy veil.

Terrence gasped, speaking before he could stop himself. "What is this place? I did not know..."

"Few do," Ash said, eyes forward. He guided his horse with one hand, still holding Dessa's body close with the other. "It's a protected place. Only those blessed by the Great Mother can find it."

"Protected by wha-?" Taylin failed to smother a squeak of fright as her eyes met the gaze of a small tree sprite. The tiny humanoid creature crossed her arms, scowling at the healer as her dragonfly-like wings buzzed.

More of the colorful creatures appeared, flitting through the air and inspecting the group with varying expressions, none welcoming. The one glaring at Taylin flew to Ash, landing at the edge of his saddle, her expression morphing to sadness. "All Mother not able helping you," she said sadly. "Life already slipped away. Is nothing but shell now."

"I know, Li." Ash offered his palm. The sprite stepped onto it. "I want Dessa to know peace and beauty in her death rest."

Li nodded. "All Mother would deny you nothing," it said in hushed tones. "But others...not sure if welcoming them—"

Almek watched, bemused, as the tiny winged figures clustered around him, chittering like birds, their voices bright with excitement. An especially small sprite flitted close and pointed at the metallic patches of color on his face. "Of course you may," Almek said gently. The moment the creature touched his Guardian marks, delight rippled through the others; sprites darted forward in gleeful flutters to do the same.

Ash glanced over just as the sprite in his hand stirred with the others' joyousness. Li's demeanor shifted instantly. "You have brought two-color?" she said, wings buzzing. "Many cycles passed since one visited. All Mother must see him!" She launched into the air, zipping over to Almek with commanding urgency. Scolding the others sharply, she scattered the cloud of sprites like petals in a sudden breeze. "You are not same two-color coming from before," she said firmly, settling on Almek's outstretched palm. "But not matter. She will want to see you."

Almek tilted his head, offering a finger in greeting. "No, I have never been here. There are no others but me now." Li buzzed in troubled thought, wings shimmering. "But I would be honored if my students and their companions could accompany us."

Li darted off again, zipping about the glade in a flurry of bossy commands. The sprites circled overhead, then descended in a spiral towards a dense curtain of flowering vines cascading from the fallen tree's crown. With swift precision, they peeled the vines back to reveal a passageway. "Four-legs must stay," Li said with authority. "We will take good care of four-legs."

Mureln walked to the entrance and peered through, then around the ancient tree. "This is not possible..."

Li zipped to hover in front of his nose, finger wagging with fierce conviction. "All things possible if know how. But know how you not need for you to see All Mother." She pointed imperiously down the passage that sloped towards what appeared to be a high cliff over-looking a sea bluff. "She waits. No making Her wait longer. Go! Now!"

Ash stepped forward, still cradling Dessa. Mureln muttered. "Shards! Bossy things come in small packages." The mage glanced at him, unable to suppress a faint smile.

⁕ ⁕ ⁕

THE TUNNEL APPEARED SHORT but proved deceptively long. The sprites dropped the vine curtain, leaving the only light within the passage coming from the distant exit. From the back of the group, Amelana's petulant voice shattered the silence with her litany of complaints. "We have been walking forever! Are we there yet? I can't see anything but this Sevmanan brute's back!"

Emil snorted and muttered loudly, "I need t' be wit'out a woman fer a lot longer b'fore I be desperate enough t' look at that one." Those nearest the wiry man fought to swallow their laughter, espe-cially when Amelana started demanding to know what everyone was discussing. The laughing stopped as soon as they stepped out of the tunnel onto the wide stone floor of a massive basin, staring in awe at the sight before them.

Soaring cliffs—painted in streaks of color—towered above the basin's wide stone floor, facing the sea. Framed by the cliff face was an immense tree that dwarfed any they had seen in the Forentan capital. Roots, like giant arms, cascaded over juts of rock, framing giant natural steps. Opposite the tree, the horizon was a flat blue line that shimmered in the sun, the distant sound of crashing waves hinting at a long drop from the ledge.

As if the marvel had long ceased to amaze him, Ash did not stop to stare in wonder. He walked towards a low, flat rock across from the tunnel along the cliff face. With the utmost care, he laid Dessa on it, resting his hand on her forehead for a long moment as he knelt by her.

"We mourn with you, Ash Andar," a soft voice using the royal 'we' whispered in the breeze, startling the others to look towards its source. Seated on the lowest of the roots, a woman regarded Ash with a maternal sadness. Delicate and willowy, the dryad seemed carved from polished wood, save for large, deep brown eyes. "We will protect her spirit in our branches until she has healed enough to return."

Ash looked upwards towards the woman, his face a still mask of discipline. "Naiya. Thank you." He approached her and sank to one knee with subservient respect.

"Rise, Ash Andar." Naiya rested her delicate hand atop his head as a mother would comfort a child. "Ease your heart knowing We are proud of you, always." She turned her head to regard the others. "It is unexpected that you bring Us a Dusvet Guardian." She turned to address Almek. "We are very relieved to know you live. The silence from all our siblings has greatly troubled Us. There are so many mortal voices now beyond Our domain; it makes it difficult to separate a few from so many to reach out discreetly. I have only heard the whispers of the Singing One, and She remains aloof."

Almek approached, though he did not kneel as the mage had, instead offering his palm to the woman. "My mentor Salais spoke of meeting you before her death. But after Illaini Magus Perisi died, I knew no one who spoke for you." He sighed. "Losing the Dusvets resulted in the loss of substantial amounts of knowledge over the centuries."

Naiya frowned, the branches of the massive tree above rustling, as she tilted her head. "Then you truly are the last? This is unexpected. And troublesome." She rose, walking up the root a pace, beckoning for Almek and his students to follow her. "Grave danger looms. Not only for the present, but the future as well." She paused to glance over her shoulder. "Unsvet Guardians have neither the vision, strength, nor balance of energies. We are uncertain a single Dusvet will be strong enough."

"Do you know what we are facing?" Almek stepped closer, hope flickering behind his question. "I sought the vision of the Timeless One, but even She could not see clearly what preys upon us." He looked towards Dessa's body down below. "What we faced felt more like foot soldiers than minds behind the cruelty."

Naiya stepped onto the soft soil of the next higher step, circling the group, eyes sharp with quiet judgment. "Unfortunately, We cannot say. We know that whatever it is, it is being very careful. The Knowing One is dimly aware of its presence. Outside and inside of time, it knows the currents enough to conceal its own ripples."

Almek frowned, looking towards the ocean's horizon. "What of the Seeing One?"

"We do not know where He is." Naiya rested her cheek upon the root, as if drawing solace...or offering it. "He has been silent for a very long time. We had hoped He only rested, as He likes to do. But it has been too long and We cannot find Him. We do not believe Him dead, but that He is beyond Our reach worries Us." She stood straight, waving a hand towards the tree. "Her grief has only been eased watching Her son Ash mature."

"Wait." Mureln stepped forward, disbelief cutting through his voice. "The Knowing One...is the tree, not you?"

Naiya looked highly amused, coming to Mureln to put a hand over his heart lightly. "Have your people not spoke of the Tree of Knowledge? There is much truth within the old stories you have so diligently learned, Master Bard of Water's Resonance. I am Naiya, Her voice." Mild surprise colored her features as she looked to Mureln. "He has the Vision. But barely trained. It is unexpected that a Dusvet would so poorly train his students."

"I have only recently taken them as my students. It seems even the Guardians of Fortress failed to consider the possibility of one person being able to touch more than a single energy." Almek shook his head bitterly. "Most have their other gifts discovered well before a Guardian appears to encounter them."

"Guardians had been present in Forenta in the years before Ash was taken into the Academy of Magic," Naiya pointed out.

Almek looked at Ash. "I believe they thought he was too lowborn to succeed and would shame the Forentan people. Even recently, they attempted to forbid his accepting my offer to teach him."

Naiya's expression darkened, and the ground seemed to tingle as the tree shuddered. "Lowborn?! What is his birth to Us, who chose him as Our Illaini? How dare they insult Us! We who have protected and sheltered them from their enemies?" Roots erupted from the soil, coiling around Terrence and Amelana with righteous fury. "They will all be punished, starting with these two! Ash is Our Illaini! Our son!"

Ash grabbed Naiya's shoulders, shaking her in urgency. "Naiya! Mother! Release them! They are my students!"

She looked at him, her visage terrible in her own and the goddess's fury. "They have caused Our Illaini pain! Why should they not all suffer? Have *you* forgiven them?"

"Not all of them caused me pain," Ash stated firmly. "I have sworn to protect the Forentan people. Your *children*, Mother! That includes them. It is for me to deal with, not You. Please. Release them."

Naiya stared at Ash for a long moment before the roots released Terrence and Amelana, letting them fall into the soft dirt, gasping for breath. "For you alone, We will spare them. But know this, Ash of Andar. Our love for you runs deeper than root or stone. We will not be so forgiving in the future." Naiya returned to the root, climbing back onto it. Her eerie gaze settled on Almek. "We wish there was more We could offer to help you, Dusvet. But We..." She paused a moment. "We are afraid. We very much need your help."

The humans looked between each other in dismayed shock. The bard blurted, "But you are...a god. You are so much more powerful than any of us mere mortals." Mureln's puzzlement spoke for all but Almek. "What can *we* possibly do that a god could not?"

The branches creaked as they moved, drawing all eyes towards the towering trunk. Naiya nodded and returned her gaze to the gathered. "Understand. It required balance for the Creator and the Destroyer to create the world. Each strength demands a weakness. Each weakness, its countering strength. When there are too many plants, there must be more plant eaters. When there are too many plant eaters, there must be predators. When there is too much life, there must be death to prevent inevitable suffering. It is part of the sacred balance.

"So it is with power. Each of Us Old Ones pays a price for Our power. We are the Knowing One. Our roots reach into time itself. Even to preserve Our self, We cannot simply—how do mortals say it?—speak bluntly of what can be learned for one's self. We can only reveal hints of what We know so others, who have the greatest flexibility, may learn for themselves."

Naiya reached down to rest her hand on the root's surface and said softly in a gentler voice, "She cannot leave this place, Dusvet. And she mourns. Her three siblings...brothers and sister...have been missing for a long time."

Almek frowned, looking down as he thought deeply. "Her brothers...I know the Ancient Trinity of the Creator, the Destroyer, and the Timeless One, are more parental than sibling. Their children...You, the Seeing One, the Singing one...only one identifies as male." He looked perplexed. "Who...who is the fourth?"

Naiya's expression was deeply apologetic. "She will not permit me to speak further. Forgive me, Dusvet. Forgive Her. Her shame..." The dryad paused a moment, shaking her head, then squared her shoulders resolutely, her voice resuming the duality quality when the Knowing One spoke through her. "Our shame is as old as the sundered lands. To speak of it endangers the balance. We cannot speak more, else We will have spoken too much." Naiya approached Almek, taking his hands in hers. "It is for you to discover. The road ahead is perilous. But the world depends on your success..." She glanced at the other humans. "And theirs."

Turning from Almek, the Dryad looked to the Illaini Magus. "Ash Andar," Naiya said with maternal affection, the young master mage approaching and taking her offered hands in his. "Your path has always been your own. Know We are always with you, no matter how distant your path takes you from Us."

The mage nodded, though melancholy had settled on his features. "I have always known, Mother. I will not fail You."

Naiya cupped his face in her hands with maternal sadness. "Do not fail *yourself,* My son."

Chapter Thirteen

THE TREES DIMINISHED IN size and number as the group approached the borders of the port city of Corast. The thunder of hooves waned, matching the bard's fading piping until they came to a stop on a rise that overlooked the wide valley. A glittering ribbon of ocean blue traced the valley's far edge.

Terrence caressed his mare's neck, thumping her shoulder. "They are barely winded, and we have ridden at a dead run all day! I have never seen such magic before, Master Mureln!" His excitement at the discovery of a gift not born of Forenta glittered in his eyes.

Mureln smiled as he tended to his twin flute before stowing it away. "It is not magic," he corrected, sounding exhausted. "Vodani have none as Forenten and Sevmanen do."

The young man looked puzzled, tilting his head. "But how then? It is obvious your music had some effect."

Emil chuckled as he rode over to Mureln, offering him a bottle. "Ye no' need be worryin' about it, lad. It be a Vodani thing. Bards always bringin' inspiration t' all around 'em. Even th' beasts." The wiry Gyspari guffawed at Mureln's expression when he took a long swig from the bottle. "Ye should be use ta Gyspari brew by now, Mureln!" The bard offered a rude gesture, the Gyspari laughing.

Apart from the others, Ash reached up for the forest sprite riding on his shoulder, the small creature forlorn. "Li not like you leaving Forenta," she complained, hugging his finger as he stroked her hair gently. "Too far for Li to follow."

Ash nodded. "I know. But I go where my master goes, Li."

"You will come home?" she asked hopefully, sitting forwards on her knees, her expression begging.

Unable to be anything but honest, Ash replied, "Perhaps someday, Li. Thank you," he said quietly, resting the back of his finger against her cheek, the tiny sprite hugging it tightly. "You always found me when I needed to be found. Now it is my turn to find what is needed." Cradling the sprite in his hands, Ash walked over to a rosebush and gently sat Li on it. "Guard Mother well, my friend." As he returned to his horse, Li keened, a high, mournful trill, before vanishing into the forest.

"So, what now?" Emil asked curiously. "Can't exactly be askin' 'round bout these shifter things. People'll either think we're nuts and try an' stone the madness outta us or panic, which looks like is th' effect these things want in th' first place." He glanced at Emaris. "An' so far, ain't been much fer gold t' be had."

"I would have thought you found plenty of gold when you went through the box in the kitchen," Ash stated tonelessly, eyes fixed forward. When Emil stammered denials, Ash shrugged one shoulder. "It matters not. I used to put money for Dessa to use at the market in it. She won't be needing it anymore." Though he stated his words without inflection, the others looked away from the mage.

Amelana urged her horse closer, though the beasts made intimacy impossible. "Oh, Ash..." The mage leveled a disdainful look at her and she smoothly corrected herself. "Master Ash, you should not let the death of that servant girl bother you so much." She reached towards him. "After all, you still have me—" Her voice and motion towards him both froze when his expression did not change.

"Ow!" Emil's exclamation disrupted the interplay between Amelana and Ash, the smaller man rubbing his shoulder, glaring at his massive companion. "Why did ya hit me like that for?" he demanded. "Damned near broke me arm, ya big lunk! I was just makin' an observation 'bout..." He glanced at Ash and Amelana and coughed. "Oh, er. Yeah. That's why. Ne'ermind."

"Master Bard," Ash called as he joined Mureln and his Sevmanen companions. "A moment of your time?" Mureln waved Emil and Emaris on, guiding his horse nearer to Ash. "I have ridden horses all my life. Some spells can drive beasts beyond their endurance, but the price is often their lives."

Neutrally, Mureln nodded. "I am aware of those, yes. My people possess no magic as you or Sevmanen possess. I assure you." Giving Ash a cool look, he stated, "We are no threat to your dominion," Mureln said, voice clipped with restrained indignation.

"Dominion...?" Ash frowned in puzzlement before the implication dawned on him. "Sevmanen have minor gifts as well. I wouldn't take offense at your people if they shared gifts like ours, Master Mureln." Ash pulled his horse around gently to face towards the others, his eyes moving over them as he spoke.

"Then you are unique among your kind, Master Ash." Mureln's words were clipped. "Can we get to the heart of what you want quickly? Regardless of my helping the horses extend their endurance range, the ride was long, and I am concerned about Almek. He is not a young man."

Ash pressed his lips together at the chiding, fixing his gaze on the Dusvet Guardian, Taylin hovering near him. "I once believed tales of bardic power were exaggerated—fanciful babbling of foreigners. But as my apprentice noticed, the horses are barely winded." The mage arched an eyebrow at the bard. "You are smiling."

Mureln's smile widened as he thumped the broad neck of his mount. "Yes, I am." Urging his horse to rejoin the others, he asked simply, "Do you believe there is nothing else besides Forenta's magic in the world? Nothing beyond her borders?" Ash opened his mouth to answer, then shut it again, frowning thoughtfully as he followed the bard to rejoin the others.

"Ye have never been outside Forenta's borders?" Emil was incredulous as the apprentice mage turned bright red. The Gyspari tsked and shook his head. "A right shame. There be a lot of interestin' things, 'specially th' farther south ye go."

"You recommended a place here in Corast." Almek looked towards Mureln. "Do you still believe that's our course?"

The bard looked amused. "You always said not to second-guess intuition. Has that changed now?" With the confidence born of a longtime master, Mureln waved a hand forwards. "Besides, if I'm wrong, the travel will be far easier along the coast than inland. Let's go before that gods-awful brew of Emil's wears off and I fall asleep where I stand. I've not had to move so many at once for years." Almek chuckled and headed down the road towards the distant gathering of buildings that marked the port town.

Residing on the border of Forenta and Vodanya, the scent of Corast had a strange and unique quality. The salty air of the ocean mingled with the crisp scent of trees. The half circle harbor was crowded with vessels of all sizes, from tiny two-man skiffs to large merchant ships and even one massive Vodani vessel called a *maternasi* that housed an entire clan, all vying for space along the many finger-like, floating piers that reached out into the cool waters.

Along the road, orchards and fields fanned out from the heart of Corast, all neat and ordered. Deeper into Corast, humans, beasts of burden, and massive wagons piled high with crates and barrels choked the wide streets. Unlike most towns and cities, Corast was without a central market, but it did not lack for commerce. It appeared as if every building bore a sign showing some type of business housed there. Merchants who were not local or had no building of their own hawked their wares from carts or wagons.

News of the Dusvet Guardian's arrival rippled through the market, and many vendors' attention focused on him in the hopes they could win the bragging rights for his business. With the realization that the Illaini Magus was traveling with the Dusvet, their efforts seemed to double.

"Corast has grown since I was last here with Bennu." Ash frowned slightly. "Much is now unfamiliar to me."

Mureln chuckled, content to allow his horse to navigate the sea of humanity that flowed around them. "Change always flourishes where a significant population of Vodani exists," the bard said mildly. "The wandering spirit guides us. Some more so than others." Pausing a moment, he tossed a coin to a flower vendor, then turned and offered the flower he bought to Taylin with a flourish. He smiled when she blushed, accepting the blossom. Standing up in his saddle, Mureln scanned the streets ahead of them. "Should luck favor us, the inn I have in mind will have space for us for some days."

Emil perked up with interest. "The Rusty Pelican?" he asked hopefully, a teasing tone in his voice.

Mureln looked at Emil sideways. "You know Mia'll gut you where you stand without remorse if she hears you call her place that." He looked to Almek. "The place is called The Silver Seagull. It's a very popular inn with locals and transients alike, though catering more to the affluent." Looking at Emil meaningfully, he added, "Not like the dives Emil likes to frequent."

"Hey! I gots t' make a livin' somehow," Emil countered. "Them high brow places are always so prissy. Never have any good games of chance goin' a'tall."

Mureln snorted softly. "They have games, they just don't want *your* light fingers anywhere near their well-heeled patrons." Taylin coughed, covering her smile behind her hand. Her amusement only increased at the sorrowful expression Emil tried to garner sympathy with.

"I have never seen so many foreigners at once, Master Ash!" Terrence said in wonder. He watched several Forentan and Vodani men working together to move large crates from the back of a wagon and carry them into a building. The ease between them—Vodani and Forentan alike—was unlike anything he'd seen in Ithesra. "And everyone seems to work side by side no matter if they are Vodani or Forentan," he said in fascination. "I did not think that was possible!"

"Oh, please. You *would* find that interesting," Amelana sneered condescendingly, the young Forentan apprentice flinching at her mocking tones. "The Forentan here are mere lowborn laborers who clearly have forgotten their place." Her horse pranced back as a pair of children dashed in front of it, forcing her to focus her attention on keeping her seat. "Stupid animal! Just step on them next time!" Ash said nothing, narrowing his eyes slightly. Terrence glanced up at his master's reassuring hand on his arm, squaring his shoulders.

A LOUD, CLEAR VOICE cut through the normal cacophony of the city as the group approached the huge establishment bearing a sign with a silver seabird. "Mureln!" A buxom Vodani woman emerged from the side entrance of The Silver Seagull Inn, holding her arms wide in welcome. "You are a sight for sore eyes!" The woman barely gave the bard time to dismount before she threw her arms around him, kissing him soundly on the cheeks. She looked over Mureln's shoulder to scan the others with him. "Are those two land rats of yours still following you around?"

"Aw, we be glad t' see ye, too, Mia," Emil drawled as he dismounted, holding his arms wide to the woman.

Mia held her hands up in a warding gesture. "I only just earned back the coin you snitched the last time you visited, Emil. You just keep your hands to yourself."

Emil feigned mock innocence. "Mia, I'm hurt! How could you say such a thing about me? Ow!" Emil looked up at Emaris. "Will ye stop hittin' me, Emaris?!" Mia laughed merrily, giving the huge man a hug as well. Emaris easily lifted her from the ground, earning a cheery scolding from Mia for man-handling.

Sparkling sea blue eyes examined the others as they dismounted. "I see you've found others to follow you around, you rogue," Mia said teasingly to Mureln, who merely shrugged helplessly, winking at her. "You always were one to travel with such motley groups." Mia gave each person an openly scrutinizing examination until she got to Almek. Her eyes went wide in amazement. Dropping her gaze, she fell to her knees with reverence. "By the spring tides! Forgive me, Dusvet Guardian! I meant no disrespect—!"

The Guardian glanced as attention grew on them from those nearby. Almek leaned down, gently pulling the woman back to her feet. "Please, there's no need to kneel to me, Mia."

Flustered, Mia babbled incoherently before she finally started barking orders to some stable hands peering from the adjoining stables. "Get out here and take our honored guests' mounts, you lazy boys! And make sure their belongings are taken to the top floor suites. Come, come!" Turning to the group, she shooed them like a mother would small children. "You must be starving! Do you Forentan never eat?! Look at this child! He's naught but skin and bones!" she exclaimed, pushing Terrence in ahead of her. "This simply will not do at all, it will not. Cara! Set the big table! These people are faint with hunger! Mikal, prepare rooms for the Dusvet Guardian and his companions!" Terrence's wide-eyed glance begged silently for rescue, but Mia was already sweeping him inside.

"Ah, yes." Mureln coughed a bit, scratching behind his ear with chagrin. "That's my little sister Mia. You get used to her."

Chapter Fourteen

THOUGH THE AWE OF having both Dusvet Guardian and Illaini Magus had not eased completely, after a few days, life returned to some semblance of normalcy for the Silver Seagull. Wrought-iron chandeliers hung from the high ceiling, brightening the dark wood interior. Cheerful serving girls dressed in bright colors moved among the crowded tables with trays laden with food and drink, laughing as they passed by the master bard as he circulated among the patrons.

Taking it upon herself to attend to Almek and his companions, Mia chattered as she wiped down the table as they ate while Mureln sang for the supper crowd. "Oh, no, no. Mureln and I weren't born here. He was born and raised at Water's Resonance. I was born on our clan's *maternasi*." She chuckled with amusement. "Vodani usually aren't born on dry land. We're born wanderers, moving where the tides take us." She picked up a wicker-wrapped bottle and topped off glasses. "We used to pearl dive at Water's Resonance when we were children until he felt the *a'alisna*. The wanderlust."

"I am glad to meet one of Mureln's siblings at long last." Almek raised his glass to her respectfully. "He had always spoken fondly of you."

Having gotten past the paralyzing awe she had for the man, Mia still blushed at the Guardian's words. "Mureln had mentioned meeting you years ago in his messages to me. I thought he was telling tales." She watched the Vodani bard conversing with a couple of sailors. He then sang, his tune sorrowful and sweet, hushing the area, drawing every listener. Her affectionate smile softened her brisk demeanor. "I am so very glad he wasn't."

"If Vodani wander so much, how could you have kept in touch?" Terrence wondered with curiosity untainted by any prejudice, eyes wide. "How do you find each other, with everyone always moving from place to place? They would not know where you were, and they might not be where you last remembered them." Emil looked at Terrence in confusion, opening his mouth to speak until Emaris elbowed him into silence again.

Drawing out a necklace, Mia held up a blue-green mottled stone wrapped in green-tinted copper. "This is a trifold stone. They're found in some of the deepest diving waters around the many Vodani islands." She smiled in memory. "It was one of my tasks to find one for my adulthood trials. They are broken into a minimum of three pieces, and one piece is put on an arrowhawk."

"Arrowhawk?" the curious apprentice asked. Mia pointed to the corner where a sleek black bird of prey streaked with blue wing markings sat on a perch, preening between its toes and ignoring all around it. Affixed to its leg was a band of leather with similar small stones wrapped in copper wire.

"Vodani have been raising them for generations. They are ever faithful companions, like your landwalker dogs." Mia didn't seem to notice the expressions of the Forenten and Sevmanen at the nickname. "When you have a piece of trifold, you can find the other pieces if you focus. Once practiced at it, you can focus on a specific piece or many. Either you are drawn to it, or it is drawn to you."

"That is interesting!" Terrence looked excitedly to Ash. "Master Ash, I never knew such magic existed outside of Forenta!" Turning to Mia, he asked eagerly, "Is it easy to get trifold stones or arrowhawks? How long does it take to train the birds?"

Mia's smile vanished as she clenched the stone, inexplicably cold suddenly, as she gave Ash a hostile look. "The trifold stones are not anything you Forentan will be stealing away from the Vodani, I can promise you that. And you can just forget the idea of owning an arrowhawk. You landwalkers do well enough with your own means of sending messages without stealing ours." In a huff, she disappeared back into the kitchen, leaving the party looking at each other in bewilderment.

Blinking at the three Forenten, Taylin looked to Almek, confused. "What was that about? Did I miss something?"

Amelana leaned closer to Ash, putting a comforting hand on the troubled mage's arm. "Don't let that obnoxious Vodani creature upset you, Master Ash. If it were real magic these peasants had, it would already belong to Forenta. She is merely being overdramatic because she envies our power and their utter lack."

Returning for a break from entertaining the other patrons, Mureln rejoined the group, reversing a chair and sitting. Resting one arm across the chair back, he reached for his waiting glass. The look he gave the Forentan woman was cool and impassive, though naked criticism filled his voice. "I suggest you stay very near your master, Journeyman Mage Amelana Avarian, if that is the attitude you will wear on your sleeve." Draining the glass, he reached for the bottle. "There are few other races that hold any love for those born of Forenta overall, much less Forentan mages. Many an arrogant traveler has vanished near the waterways."

"Are you threatening me, Vodani?" Amelana demanded, her air of superiority earning eye rolls from the Sevmanen around the table.

Ash's frown focused on Amelana and her attitude. "Journeyman Amelana, I don't care what you want to believe of the average people of other nations. But you *will* respect the masters of their crafts." Ash picked her hand off his arm. "Especially Master Almek's students. Else, you can return to your family right now." The woman turned brilliant red, dropping her eyes and drawing back.

Mureln met the mage's eyes and studied him for a moment before a small smile touched his lips and he respectfully nodded to the Forentan man. Ash's nod was almost imperceptible as he returned the gesture.

The bard drained his glass a second time, refilling it before speaking again. "Ah, I have missed trade port gossip." He sighed wistfully. "I could spend a phase of the greater moon just catching up with all the new tales alone. But." Mureln became more serious as he looked at Almek. "Of all the stories drifting through, one unsettles me." He took another long sip. "There's news out of Desantiva."

Almek blinked several times. "That *is* quite unusual. It would be too much to hope it was merely an anomaly."

"Forgive me, Dusvet Almek," Terrence interrupted. "I don't understand why news from Desantiva would be important. It is a barren land with nothing left there."

Mureln explained to Ash's puzzled apprentice. "It's unusual if for no other reason, hearing anything out of Desantiva this far from that land is virtually unheard of." He said more to himself, "Hearing any news of the tribes beyond Home Port's territory is nearly unheard of unless you're in port there."

"Tribes?" Taylin echoed in surprise. "I did not know anyone still lived there. I thought Desantiva was left empty. Lifeless wastelands nothing could survive in since the Great War."

Mureln shook his head, bitterness in his words. "Oh, no. Believe me, my lovely healer. The Desanti people are still there, they simply don't leave the confines of their territory's borders. But they are extremely mistrusting of the other races. Barely trust the Vodani, and we are cousins to them. They barely permit my people to know much about them."

"No doubt they are bestial savages." Amelana sniffed critically. "What use is news from a wasteland?" Mureln's normally easygoing expression hardened, but he held his tongue. The journeyman mage silenced herself when Ash leveled a warning look at her.

"Go on, Mureln," Almek encouraged, a faint frown creasing his brow. "Unusual or not, if the story caught your attention, there is a reason."

Mureln nodded. "Something has riled the Desanti, but the details are unclear. They're such a mystery to my people, they are not sure what the Desanti are saying when they talk. What I *could* determine is that one of their tribes was wiped out, and whatever did it also took out nearly a dozen of their Swordanzen."

"Swor-what?" Emil asked.

"Swordanzen." Mureln's voice dropped to nearly a whisper as he took a long sip of wine. Setting the glass down, he rubbed his cheek tiredly. "Warriors who could face a dozen Sevmanen soldiers alone and walk away unscathed. When they fight together—which is rare—the fiercest beasts would flee before them. Even gods would think twice before crossing paths with a group of them. The desert folk have a saying: 'Death comes on two legs when the Swordanzen hunt.'"

"I always heard that th' warrior people were mercilessly bloodthirsty an' ruthless. Maybe it was jus' some war 'mongst themselves, nothin' more'n that," Emil hypothesized. Mureln shook his head. "Why not?"

"I don't know much about Swordanzen. As secretive as the Desanti are, the Swordanzen are an enigma even among their own. What I learned of them when I was there is they are considered Desantiva's protectors and they are accorded a respect that is like that of a master and priest combined." He waited until he had at least Almek and Ash's full attention again. "They are solitary by nature and work together only when the situation is dire enough to require it." He sighed softly. "The story going around says none of the tribe survived and only one Swordanzen. So much loss has gotten them rather shaken up."

Almek leaned back, frowning in thought as he contemplated the implications behind the rumors. "I cannot believe it is a mere coincidence to hear news like this." He considered some more before straightening in his chair. "We must travel to Desantiva and find this Swordanzen," Almek decided. "And get more details than gossip tales will yield us."

Ash spoke up with keen reluctance. "Master Almek, Desanti and Forenten had been mortal enemies since long before the Great War. Forenten presence on Desantiva's soil might put you and the others in grave danger."

"Don't worry," Almek assured. "It has been perhaps fifty years since I was last in Desantiva, but the Desanti are, if nothing else, sticklers about their honor and traditions. The Desanti hold a deep reverence for the Guardians, and you are my student." He smiled wanly at Ash. "They will not *welcome* you with open arms, but they will not bring harm."

Mureln looked towards the ceiling, murmuring to himself as he counted, his thumb moving along the fingertips of one hand. "If we leave within the next few days, we can arrive in Desantiva at the start of the Time of Gathering. It should increase the odds of the rest of our survival."

"Time of Gathering?" Ash echoed, the question in his voice plain.

Explaining as much to Ash as to the rest of the group, Mureln stated, "It's a traditional time of peace when all the tribes gather in their only city of First Home."

With as much reassurance as he could muster, Mureln continued explaining the soundness of his reasoning. "It will also be the best chance of locating this lone Swordanzen while all the tribes are gathered. Desanti forbid those not of the tribes beyond First Home's borders. Almek can find out what he needs to know, and we'll be gone before you know it. It'll be fine!" Others showed skepticism, but did not dispute.

CHAPTER FIFTEEN

THE INHOSPITABLE NATURE OF Desantiva became more apparent as the ship sailed closer to the jagged coastline. As if the rest of the mainland had ostracized Desantiva from the rest of the continent, a wide, turbulent sea separated Desantiva from the northern mainland, pushing against the swift ship's approach.

"There's no place more hospitable to make port?" Ash asked as he stood with Mureln along the bow of the ship, watching the anemic city of Home Port come into view.

The bard shook his head, expression grim. "The Desanti allow Home Port to exist because it was where the Vodani were born during the Great War. Only ignorant Sevmanen pirates, raiders, or the most unfortunate dare attempt to touch land along the Desanti coastline." In answer to the silent, raised eyebrow of the mage, the bard explained, "The Desanti are rabidly hostile towards *all* outsiders, even Vodani, if they step outside the permitted areas." He traced his finger along the grain of the wood by his arm. "They will ruthlessly tear apart trespassing ships for salvage."

"What happens to those aboard the ships?"

"They leave nothing to waste, Master Ash. Prisoners are fed to the beasts that serve them." Ash opened his mouth to speak, then shut it again, silently watching the shore near as he pondered Mureln's words.

The coast of Desantiva was a jagged line of tan and brown rock. The navigator proved his worth, avoiding the ghostly, underground fingers of rock that lay just beneath the waves, threatening to gut the ship before they finally pulled into the tiny port. Unlike the bustling border town port of Corast, Home Port had only a single dock made of rough hewn stone, and a handful of buildings scattered around it.

Taylin looked around as sailors led their horses down the walkway from their ship, squinting in the harsh noon sunlight. "I only see...Vodani here. Aren't there any Desanti who live here? Or others who come to trade?"

Mureln shook his head, lips pressed together and eyes narrowed slightly as if he were fighting a growing headache. "Home Port is the ancient home of the Vodani people. It is our only remaining tie to our Desanti ancestors. The Desanti only allow foreigners and Guardians within First Home's borders." The bard and the dockmaster exchanged grim, silent nods of greeting as they passed. "Outlanders are unwelcome. Home Port is Vodani territory."

Ash frowned at Mureln. "Master Almek wishes to go to First Home and take us with him."

The bard shrugged. "They should make an exception for the Dusvet Guardian."

Terrence blinked at Mureln. "The way you speak, it's as if there is a difference between foreigners and outlanders. It's the same thing, isn't it?" The bard merely shook his head, teeth clenched tightly.

Emil tugged his mount along, looking at the locals they passed going towards the visitor's inn. "Fer all th' years I been travelin' wi' ye around Sevmanan and Vodani territories, I ain't never seen such serious Vodani. Haven't seen a single smile among 'em yet." Squinting at Mureln, he added, "And not any from you, neither. Not since we got here. Cheer up, lad," the mercenary scolded, receiving an irritable wave to silence from the bard.

Offering no apologies for his atypical, hostile behavior, Mureln led the group to a small building on the outskirts of the settlement. "All Vodani make a pilgrimage here at least once in their lives." He offered a few coins to a boy who opened the gate of a shaded corral where the horses were led. "So we can share in the pain of our ancestors and remind our Desanti cousins they will not be forgotten." He touched a worn sun symbol carved into the wall by the inn entrance. "No matter how hard they try to be forgotten." He stepped inside to speak with the innkeeper about arrangements.

"Such bitterness and pain," Taylin said softly. "It's as if it comes from the rocks themselves. I have felt nothing like it. It is so old. Like...an echo. Oh, Dusvet!" The Guardian put a comforting arm around her, holding her for a time. Even he looked pained. "I don't know if I can bear to stay in this joyless land."

"Shhh. Be strong, Taylin. Be strong," Almek murmured reassuringly, like a father to a child.

Amelana pushed past a Vodani girl coming out of the inn impatiently. "Out of my way! The heat out here is miserable."

"Ain't th' only thing miserable here," Emil said sourly. He looked at Ash. "I hope th' bitch be good fer somethin', Mage, 'cause she sure ain't good company." Muttering, he and Emaris filed in after Amelana. "If'n it weren't fer Mureln, I'd as soon chew m' own leg off t' get away from 'er." Ash scowled, remaining silent.

"We will not linger here any longer than necessary," Almek assured. "Once we have provisions, we will set out for First Home."

Chapter Sixteen

THE ROAD WAS LITTLE more than an expanse of rock eroded by centuries of feet wearing it smooth. Around them, rocks ranging in size from fists to that of large ships littered the landscape. The longer the travelers looked, the seemingly unchanging browns revealed a richness of color beneath the dust that covered everything.

As if bearing testament to a tenacious will to survive, they noticed plants. Strange tiny trees twisted from the winds, bushes almost completely stripped of most of their leaves, strange plants resembling green stumps, gnarled and needle-crowned, and long threadlike grasses grew among the rocks, defying the desolation that loomed over the travelers.

"This place is so...empty," Terrence whispered. He could not mask the horror he felt witnessing the wasteland. "How can anyone live here?"

Taylin squeaked as she pulled her horse up short, staring at a nearby rock. "I saw something move!"

Mureln glanced over his shoulder. "There are a surprising number of things capable of enduring this hell, but they're often hidden from sight." He looked ahead as the ground flanking the sides of the road rose up, the road following the course of a ravine. "And it is very dangerous."

As if to prove the truth of the bard's words, several spears with shafts made from a bone-like material decoratively wrapped in dyed leather impaled the ground in front of several of the horses. The alarmed animals reared up, spreading their panic to the others and forcing their riders to struggle to get them under control. Silent, dark-skinned figures rose from behind stone and shadow, their weapons trained without a word.

The one nearest the party stood up from his perch, unconcerned about a counterattack. Given the many warriors with weapons around them, he had little need to worry. He did not need to with the others with him. The man growled in heavily accented trade common. "What reason do you dare taint our lands, Outlanders? Have you come seeking death?"

Almek reached up slowly with both hands to lower his hood, impassively regarding the warrior. The warrior's eyes went wide as the sun glinted off the metallic markings on the Guardian's cheek. "Almek Two-Tones!" Barking orders to the others, the awe spread to the half-concealed warriors, but none lowered their weapons even the slightest. Their aim shifted away from the Guardian and Vodani to focus only on the Forentan and Sevmanan members. "Your return to our lands honors us, Lord Almek." With disapproving harshness, he demanded, "But why have you brought this filth?"

"They are my students." Calmly, Almek spoke firmly without lowering his gaze from the warrior. "I have urgent need to see your elders. I request safe passage for myself and for my students." With a practiced formality, he said, "On the honor of my ancestors, I offer my life that my students will bring no harm to Desantiva."

The man nimbly hopped down the nearly vertical rock face to the road with enviable agility. He walked among the party, studying them each with dark, narrowed eyes. He stopped when he came to Ash, his scowl deepening. Ash silently returned the gaze without expression.

Minutes passed, neither man looking down or away. "You trust your life to this vile get of the defilers?" The venom in his tone amplified the Desanti's skepticism, who appeared ready to kill the mage at Almek's command.

"I trust him with my life," Almek replied unhesitatingly. "Yes."

Growling under his breath, the man turned his back on Ash to return to Almek. He pointed down the road with his spear. "Stay on the road. If even one strays, all will die. If anyone threatens Desantiva, all will die."

Accepting the edicts, Almek nodded once. "Understood, Warrior."

Satisfied, the warrior returned to his perch atop the ravine wall to speak to the other Desanti. The decision was received poorly, many loudly arguing with their leader with sharp gestures made towards the group, especially towards the three Forentan.

The leader responded with stern decisiveness in his native language, gesturing sharply with his spear towards Almek. Reluctantly, the others backed down. Everyone except the leader and one other man disappeared into the surroundings once more. Though the warriors had vanished from view, an unsettling awareness lingered in the air, a palpable tension that hinted at their continued watchfulness. The leader addressed Almek as the second man made his way down the ravine wall. "Proceed. Warrior Radisen na'Citali will accompany you." With those words, he too melted into the landscape.

Almek inclined his head to the displeased warrior that joined them. Radisen raised his eyes to fix a hard stare on Almek in silence. His eyes were a startling light, golden brown verging on true gold that contrasted with his dark brown complexion and black hair. After a time, he finally nodded once, turning on his heel to walk down the road at a swift pace. Almek quickly urged his horse to follow. The others hurried to do the same, murmuring only when they felt they were far enough away.

"Savage animals." Amelana was flushed, overheated from the merciless sun beating down.

"You might do well to shut up, Journeyman Amelana," Mureln pointed out sharply. "Desanti tempers are short and violent, and they would love nothing more than a reason to kill a Forentan."

She sniffed and mumbled, "As if they could."

The group traveled for several more hours on the ravine road, the heat growing increasingly unbearable as the sun crested its path in the sky. It was not long before they were jumping at shadows, certain there were murderous warriors hiding along the way. Radisen walked in silence, ignoring any attempt to engage him in conversation, even from Almek.

"I really hope there be some worth t' stickin' our necks out in this gods forsaken land," Emil stated unhappily, wiping his face with a rag. "Iffin the Desanti don't kills us, I bet th' sun'll do it fer them." He squinted up at the cloudless sky and fiercely intense sun. "Gods, it's killin' me."

Though stoically silent, the Forenten were looking the worst of the group. Dressed as if they were in their far cooler northern lands, the heat was taking a toll on them.

"Master Ash." Terrence's voice was weak, and his eyes were glazed. Ash looked over at Terrence, frowning with concern. "I-I am not feeling very well..." Before the mage could say a word in response, the younger man sagged forwards.

With lightning swiftness, the master caught his apprentice before he fell off his horse. "Taylin!" Ash called sharply, bringing the group to an abrupt halt.

The healer looked over her shoulder, and then wheeled her horse around and rode back to them, heedless of the threat of hidden desert warriors. Frowning, she reached over and touched the young man's forehead. "He needs to be cooled down," Taylin stated with urgency in her voice. "If this goes on too much longer, it could do him irreparable harm, or kill him altogether." Both Illaini Magus and healer worked to get the heavier robes off the young man.

Almek tried speaking to the impassive Desanti warrior, insisting he had to help the boy, but Radisen just blinked at him, unmoved.

Annoyed, Mureln took a deep breath, and spoke with Radisen in his native tongue, including several hand gestures that suggested dire promises. The man grudgingly removed his own waterskin, taking a sip from it himself before tossing it to the bard. Radisen spoke curtly, making a gesture with his spear down the road.

Mureln handed the waterskin to Taylin, who dampened a towel to wipe the young man's brow, then with Ash's help, got him to drink some of the water. Terrence roused, coughing as he made a face.

"Radisen says First Home is just ahead. He will take us to the..." Mureln considered the words and translated, "visitor's area. It'll be cooler and there will be access to water. It won't be much longer."

"Think ye ken hang on, lad?" Emil asked. He received a weak nod and faint smile in reply.

"Better not be much longer," Ash stated in a low voice, his icy glare meeting the hateful one of the Desanti warrior.

Chapter Seventeen

The wide valley of First Home dominated the view as the group emerged from the ravine road. A sea of colorful tents and pavilions surrounded the carved face of the huge central butte. Brilliantly colored banners and ribbons fluttered in the scorching desert winds. They could hear loud voices and the calls of unfamiliar animals, the sounds of song and music mingling through it all.

Radisen guided the travelers through one of the winding roads between the pavilions. The Desanti they passed all turned to watch the travelers with open hostility. Occasionally, hateful shouts would follow them. The warrior spoke curtly with another man, then vanished into the forest of tents without a word, now that his duty to the Dusvet Guardian was complete.

"Welcome t' Desantiva," Emil said dryly as young children took the horses to a neighboring pavilion to be tended to and the humans were guided to the one they would stay in.

Mureln shook his head at Radisen's departure before he gave the pavilion a critical assessment. "I am surprised they gave us such nice quarters." Rubbing the heavy canvas between his fingers, Mureln said more to Almek than anyone else, "No doubt for your benefit, Almek. Last time I was here, I had to share some overcrowded quarters with Vodani traders."

"Nice?!" Amelana put her hands on her hips in critical outrage. "It's a tent! Peasants live in tents, not highborns. What kind of privacy can you have in a tent? None!"

Almek allowed the door flap to fall. "That there are separated sleeping areas is about all the privacy the Desanti would afford foreigners like us. Be grateful for this much, Journeyman Amelana."

"No," Mureln stated flatly.

Almek blinked, then nodded at the bard's curt correction. "Ah yes, I forgot myself." The others looked confused.

"Permit me to clarify." The bard fixed the others with a hard look, his patience strained. "Almek is a Guardian and the Desanti welcome him only because of the colors that mark him with his status. *I* am a foreigner." Mureln ignored the startled expressions at his uncharacteristic behavior. "Because the Desanti recognize the Vodani as ancient relatives, but no longer as one of them. The *rest* of you are outlanders. You are defilers, the unforgiven descendants of those who desecrated this land, making it into the wasteland it is now."

Undaunted by the looks the others gave him, Mureln stated with an edge to his voice, "And if it weren't for the strict tradition of peace during the Time of Gathering *and* being Almek's students combined, they would have fed the rest of you to the beasts by now." He looked directly at Amelana as he gave his advice. "So I strongly advise you to shut your damned mouths and respect our hosts before you end up a footnote in the histories of your own peoples."

Having only known the bard to be easygoing, Mureln's terseness shocked them, even his Sevmanan friends surprised. Ignoring their stares, the bard turned and walked towards the tent's sleeping area and jerked back the curtain divider to one of the private areas. "I am going to take a nap. Desanti do little until the sun sets and the land cools. There won't be anything of interest happening until then. I suggest the rest of you do the same."

Almek cleared his throat. "For all his bluntness today, Mureln speaks the truth. These are Desanti lands, and we should be respectful." Amelana huffed, crossing her arms as she looked away. "And we should rest while we can. We're all worn out from the journey here."

Ash pushed Amelana off as she walked with him towards the sleeping areas. "I suggest you share an area with the healer, Journeyman. It would be *proper*, don't you agree?" Amelana was stunned speechless, oblivious to Taylin's grimace of distaste. Ash did not wait for her to recover or for Taylin to protest, heading to the sleeping area the bard had disappeared into.

Ignoring the prospect of sharing space with the journeyman mage, Taylin pulled Terrence aside, her voice kind to the young man, "Come over here and we'll see about getting you back in a better state, hm? Emil, see if they have left us anything edible. And some water, please."

"'Course, Healer." The sharp-featured man joined them agreeably. "Yer lookin' whiter 'n a ghost, lad." He patted Terrence's shoulder. "Be fine if'n ye were a ghost, but as ya ain't..." Terrence chuckled weakly, flushing at the mercenary's teasing.

Satisfied his apprentice was going to be well cared for, Ash paused in the entrance to the sleeping area for only a moment before entering fully, letting the divider fall back in place.

STRIPPED DOWN TO JUST his trousers, Mureln had flopped onto his sleeping mat in the half he had claimed, arm thrown over his eyes to block the sunlight that made the roof and walls of the pavilion glow. He concealed his attempts to ignore Ash's presence poorly, not speaking nor moving to acknowledge him.

Dropping his gear on the floor, the mage laid out his own sleeping mat, removed his robe, and sat down to tug off his boots. Ash kept his voice low as he spoke. "Of everyone, I would not have expected *you* to lose your temper."

Mureln looked up at Ash in surprise at the unexpected sympathy from the Forentan Illaini Magus, and then resumed lying back with his arm over his eyes again. "Of everyone, I would have expected you to have lost it *long* before now."

Methodically folding his robe carefully, Ash replied blandly, "I assume you are speaking of my journeyman."

The corner of the bard's lips curled ever so slightly. "She must be particularly gifted for you to put up with her attitude." Mureln lifted his arm slightly to observe Ash's expression with curiosity.

The silence hung for some time after Mureln's comment, Ash frowning. "I don't expect her to attain mastery." Ash sat his clothing on the low table provided to keep them off the ground. "I have considerably more hope for my apprentice. Terrence had shown significant promise early in his education."

Shifting to prop himself up on his elbow, Mureln frowned in puzzlement. "Then why keep her as a student? She obviously does not respect her own arts, much less those of anyone else." Ash remained silent as he stared at a point on the ground, holding an ornate pendant that showed his rank. Finally..."Ahhh. I see."

Ash narrowed his eyes at the Vodani as if trying to determine if the bard mocked him. "Even if she is a very minor member, the Avarian family is well placed. They have significant influence on matters of student assignments."

Mureln blinked. "You're Illaini Magus. You don't choose your own apprentices?"

"We're Forentan. If for no other reason, it makes the matter more complicated." The mage shrugged one shoulder. "By tradition, no one can order a master into a marriage contract without his consent. They can, however, prevent an apprentice from being taken if said well placed family insists that their own family member be assigned as well in the hopes the master would change his mind about marital matters."

The bard watched Ash, his expression empty of criticism or judgment. Ash looked away as he tugged off his shirt. "Amelana has no shame. And," Ash sighed a little. "She is convenient."

Mureln shrugged. "You deserve better." The bard quirked a smile when Ash looked at him with mild surprise. Mureln gestured towards the sleeping mat. "Get what rest you can in this infernal heat. Life picks up considerably when the land cools." Laying back with his arm over his eyes again, Mureln yawned. "It'll be educational." He smiled at Ash's snort.

CHAPTER EIGHTEEN

"ELDER VERRIS NA'ZHEKALI IS honored you have blessed Desantiva with your presence once again, Dusvet Guardian Almek Two-Tones." Ornate beading and dyed leather cords braided together decorated the dark-skinned young woman's pale brown leather halter top and short paneled skirt. She offered a warm smile to Almek as she rose from her bow, white teeth bright against her dark skin. "He wishes you to meet him at the Hall of Remembrance at your convenience."

"Your Elder Verris is very kind," Almek replied with a smile. "Will my students be permitted to explore the area unescorted while I am speaking with Verris? I don't wish our visit to be an inconvenience at this time of celebration, but I also don't wish my students to waste the opportunity to observe your people."

The girl's smile faded to one of guarded curiosity as Almek addressed his students' welfare. "Your students will come to no harm should they choose to leave the tent because it is the Time of Gathering." She added, "But should they leave this valley, their lives are forfeit. The elders have decreed it so."

"Do you require my attendance, Master Almek?" Ash ignored the dark look the Desanti girl gave him, more menacing than the one his journeyman shot him.

Almek shook his head. "No. I wish to speak to Elder Verris alone. The rest of you..." He waved a hand. "There is much to learn here. Keep your eyes open and stay out of trouble." He turned to the Desanti girl. "Let us go, Tia." She nodded and led Almek out.

"Stay out o' trouble," Emil muttered in echo. Once Almek and the girl were gone, Emil clapped and rubbed his hands together in eager anticipation. He looked up at his brother. "C'mon, Emaris, these desert folk has t' know 'bout toss stones or somethin' wi' gambling." The big man snorted and followed Emil out of the tent.

Taylin was hesitant to leave. "I want to watch over Terrence a little longer. He is mostly recovered, but dehydration is not something my touch alone can heal." The sickly pale young man looked down in shame, starting to apologize. "Shush, I will hear no apologies for something so out of your control. This land is harsh, and you are unused to it. It could have happened to anyone. Come." She led him to the low table surrounded by huge pillows, taking a piece of fruit and handing it to him, ordering him to eat. He smiled a little as he sat on a pillow and took a bite.

Amelana sniffed critically as she watched Terrence and Taylin and stated loftily, "I want nothing to do with these savage dogs." Without another word, she flounced off to the sleeping area she shared with Taylin.

Mureln shook out his wide-brimmed hat and put it atop his head, adjusting it before heading outside. He stopped short at a shrill voice speaking in Forentan. The bard paused, looking over his shoulder. Amelana held onto Ash's arm, preventing him from following the bard.

In response to her strident protest, the mage said absolutely nothing, simply staring at her with displeasure. When she finally went quiet, he said something to her in a low voice, removing her hands from his arm. Mureln hurriedly turned away and went outside.

⬥⸱⸱⸱⸱⸱⸱⸱⸱ ⟆ᲫᲿ ⸱⸱⸱⸱⸱⸱⸱⸱⬥

ASH EMERGED SHORTLY, LOOKING around. Spotting Mureln, he joined him. "You do not need to spare my pride so much, Bard. I am not ashamed of my journeyman's behavior." He pulled his hood up as they walked. "I *am* irritated that she cannot see the embarrassment she brings to her family and our people."

"Forenten are a fascinating people." The bard's dry comment elicited a curious look from the mage.

"Explain," Ash stated, and then added in nearly forgotten courtesy, "Please."

"Ah, well. Your people are well known for being..." Mureln paused, searching for the diplomatic word, opting for blunt honesty. "Elegantly condescending."

Ash almost smiled. "You are definitely not Forentan. My people would dance around the truth for days and still never address it directly...if they could help it. It is refreshing to speak with someone who can get to the point within my lifetime," the mage admitted. "My master used to tell me I was too direct for my own good." Mureln chuckled quietly. "You said all Vodani come to the city your people originated from at least once in their lives. Have you been here in this Desanti city before?"

"Twice." Mureln looked skywards in silence for a moment. "Once, when I was a boy. Once after I attained my mastery. Returning becomes harder each time, yet the longing remains constant."

"Even though being here obviously causes you genuine pain?" Ash's voice held something more than clinical curiosity.

Mureln opened his mouth to snap back, and then closed it again, jaw muscles twitching. "Do you Forenten feel anything from your land?" he finally asked in a low voice. "Do you feel the life that flows through each and every part of it? Do you feel it not as a master pulling and pushing the threads, but because you are a small thread of that intricate fabric?"

The bard looked at Ash, his eyes holding a haunted look in their depths. "Can you imagine hearing the echoes of the screams when the life was ripped out of the heart of the land itself during the ancient Great War?" Having no words to offer, Ash simply shook his head, his attention fixed on the bard. "Even though the ocean waves offer the Vodani solace and peace, we return to this land. To Desantiva. So we do not forget where we came from." Looking away, he half growled, "Nor forget who caused it."

Ash started to say something, and then stopped, frowning. "Is that why you hate my people? Because of what my ancestors had done?"

Looking back in surprise, Mureln shook his head. "Stars above, I don't hate your people, Illaini Magus. Even if while we are here, my instincts are to scream curses at you, your students...even my friends and the healer. It is an unforgivable weakness to allow our instincts to dominate us." Eyes forward, the olive-skinned Vodani fell silent.

The mage broke the awkward silence between them after several minutes. "When my master took me as his apprentice, he taught me about the Great War between Forenta and Desantiva. But he was unlike many other masters. He did not take pride in our victory over the savages who threatened to destroy us, as most of my people do." Ash folded his hands into the sleeves of his robe, looking down at the bedrock smoothed to a dull gleam from untold numbers of feet that had trod upon it.

"Master Bennu said our triumph was our greatest shame. He said a victory is no victory if what it takes to win makes you little better than what you defeated. I don't feel what you do, though I can tell there is something...different in the rocks themselves." Ash paused, searching for the words. "But I appreciate you are feeling genuine pain, and my ancestors caused it. I never really understood what he meant until now."

Mureln had turned to regard the mage's hooded profile as they walked towards the central market, the volume of voices—human and beast—and a boisterous cacophony of music growing. "I think I would have liked your master. He sounds like he was a wise man."

The full impact of the market noise hit them when they came out of the quieter road into the chaos that was the central market. The aisles were wide enough to admit three northern wagons abreast, and still Desanti of all ages and appearances crowded the space. Laughing children chased each other around the adults moving at a methodical pace. Merchants bellowed over the noise, trying to outshout one another.

After several moments, Ash finally realized what bothered him. "Why are they speaking trade common? Given there are only Desanti or Vodani who speak Desanti here?"

"Tradition." Mureln shrugged one shoulder. "It had always seemed odd to me, too. But believe me. I was grateful when I was a boy first learning to speak Desanti."

The Desanti appeared as a beautifully diverse group, their skin tones varying dramatically from lighter shades of brown to hues nearly as deep as pitch black. Most of them boasted dark hair and eyes, but among them were individuals with light brown locks kissed by the sun, creating a striking contrast. As the sun set, the majority had abandoned the protective robes they wore against the day's relentless heat, opting instead for a variety of garments. Some were clad in simple tunics and trousers, while others wore only loincloths, leaving little to the imagination and disregarding conventional notions of modesty, regardless of gender. The mage took note, observing that only a scant few appeared older than either of them, a detail that intrigued him as he glanced around the vibrant assembly.

The dark Desanti natives scrutinized the two men, most scowling at them, especially at the mage. Some regarded them with an odd, open, childlike curiosity. A few recognized Mureln, greeting him with exuberance. Generally, the Desanti conversed only in their native tongue, reserving trade common for commerce alone. Remaining stoically near the bard, Ash considered for the first time what foreigners to Forenta must have felt like. Relegated to the minority, he discovered it felt extremely uncomfortable.

Angry shouts drew everyone's attention, most of the Desanti excitedly running off to witness whatever the source of the furor was. Ash moved closer to Mureln's side, in case they might blame whatever was the issue on his presence. "What is that all about?"

"Nothing that concerns us at all," the bard reassured. He looked keenly interested in following the Desanti as well, ever curious. "It's a mating dispute, from the sounds of it."

Ash drew back from the sea of people moving in their direction as the source of conflict moved towards them, biting back a comment about animalistic savages. "Considering your interest, I assume this is not a normal occurrence?"

"Not of this nature." Mureln stood on his toes as if he could catch a glimpse of the source of the commotion. Seeing the throng was coming their way suddenly faster, he pulled Ash further back along one stall to get out of the way. "Not only are there two men vying for the same woman, the woman is a Swordanzen."

The familiar, well-muscled warrior named Radisen, clad in an ornate loincloth and decorative leather pieces on his arms, erupted from the wall of people as they moved aside to let him stumble backwards. Following him, another Desanti, who could have rivaled Emaris with his massive build, stalked after him. "The woman is mine, dog!" the bigger man bellowed in trade common, as if their conflict was a trade dispute.

Radisen regained his balance and took an aggressive stance, but did not lay a hand on any of the many weapons he wore. "You have no right to her, Sumalen! The elders gave *me* the right to win Storm il'Thandar!"

While Radisen irritated Ash, something about Sumalen deeply bothered the mage, something beyond the mere fact that he was Desanti. He put a hand on Mureln's shoulder to get his attention, but the Vodani hushed him as the pace of the confrontation was escalating rapidly.

A woman's voice rang clearly from near Mureln and Ash, drawing all eyes. Those around her bowed to her with deference, and backed away, clearing the surrounding area. "The elders can talk all they want. In this matter, they have no voice."

Ash's gaze settled on the woman. Where other Desanti women wore revealing garments, she had chosen practicality—a plain leather skirt and close-fitting half-tunic the color of sun-bleached sand that made her copper skin seem to glow. One bare shoulder revealed a stark black tattoo depicting an eagle in mid-dive. As his eyes lingered, he noticed old scars crisscrossing her skin and fresh bandages spotted with blood, deepening his frown.

Though smaller than either Desanti male, she carried herself with unmistakable strength. Her green-gold eyes glinted like a hawk's as she spoke. "The elders cannot offer what isn't theirs to give. Neither of you has any claim on me. I've won my right to stand outside tribal mating customs." Her gaze hardened as she fixed it on the first challenger. "Radisen, you know this."

Sumalen spat to one side in derision. "A Swordanzen woman. *Men* are the warriors. Women are to be claimed by the strong!" He took two steps, advancing on Storm, who glared at him as if daring him to try touching her.

Without warning or thought, Ash moved to stand between Storm and the two men. Silence fell as the Desanti stared in shock at a Forentan, of all people, getting in the middle of the mating challenge. "The woman said no," he stated coldly. "Leave."

Time itself seemed to stop as the Desanti considered the mage. Finally, both suitors stalked away, and the crowd melted away with them in disappointment, now that the spectacle was over.

As he watched the antagonists leave, Ash was unprepared for the iron-hard grasp on his lower arm as the Desanti woman dragged him around to face her. "I do not need anyone to protect me, defiler," Storm hissed. "I especially do not need the likes of *you* protecting me. Stay out of matters that do not concern you." The woman shoved him away from her and stalked off into the crowd that scattered away from her path.

Ash scowled after her, absently rubbing his arm. "Are you alright?" Mureln asked in quiet concern.

"Ungrateful savage," the mage growled under his breath.

Mureln looked exasperated. "Don't you understand? She is a Swordanzen. You are lucky she didn't kill you. You are fortunate *none* of them tried to kill you." He looked askance at Ash. "What the hell possessed you to get in the middle of that?"

Ash gave a dismissive sniff, letting Mureln guide them out of the market and away from the chattering Desanti staring and pointing at him, some amazed. Others were less charitable. "No Desanti savage could harm a Forentan mage."

Biting back harsher words, Mureln said in clipped tones, "You keep telling yourself that, Forentan." Ash flicked a sideways glance at the bard, surprised at his tone and words, and fell silent.

Ash finally broke the silence between them. "Perhaps it would be best if I returned to the hostel tent for now." Mureln did not hesitate to agree, leading Ash far enough so the mage would not get lost.

ASH RETREATED TO THE privacy of his sleeping area, ignoring his journeyman's petulant complaints about not getting any time with him. Creating a dim, glowing ball of magelight, Ash pulled his sleeve up to examine his arm. He was equally surprised and unsurprised to see darkening bruises left behind by the woman's merciless grip.

'Do you Forentan feel anything from your land?' Mureln's words echoed in his mind unbidden. Ash frowned to himself as he raised his head. "If Vodani feel the echoes of the past," he wondered to himself, his words slow, "is it possible Desanti feel it more so?" After a moment, he shook his head sharply. "Impossible." He covered the bruises with his hand, willing them gone with his magic. But he could not will away the shadow of doubt clouding his thoughts or the vision of a pair of fierce green-gold eyes that reflected absolutely no fear of him in their depths.

Chapter Nineteen

Sound reverberated from the soaring, vaulted ceilings of the ornately adorned Hall of Remembrance, nestled within the colossal butte that served as the foundation of First Home. Intricate ancient mosaics adorned the walls, each depicting tales of long-forgotten histories, painstakingly embedded into the rugged stonework. The flickering light of torches cast dancing shadows, making the still images seem to come alive in a mesmerizing dance of light and shadow. The floor was a breathtaking tapestry of tiles, arranged in an intricate pattern that spiraled outwards from a magnificent fountain at the center, from which flowed the purest, coolest water, its gentle sound adding to the serene ambiance of the hall.

Studying the fanciful images, Almek contemplated the similarities between the Forentan academy and this Desanti place, sighing. He murmured to himself, "So alike, yet so different."

He approached one image, reaching to touch the stone around a dragon. Chains shackled the creature, its mouth open in a scream as flames haloed its silhouetted form. Blood red slashes across its flanks reflected deep wounds. Around it, tiny depictions scattered around the dragon showed humans and beasts in various stages of dying. He did not turn to look at the person approaching behind him. "This is ancient."

"It is the first made in the Hall of Remembrance." A man appearing about sixty years old approached, his weathered, dark brown skin looking like old leather. He regarded the image as he stood next to Almek. "It represents the rage and pain that our ancestors felt when the defilers tried to destroy us. But we were strong and endured."

Almek turned and smiled, offering the Desanti man a bow. "Elder Verris. It pleases me to know that the desert children not only endure, but thrive." He glanced at the image again thoughtfully, and then gave the Desanti man his full attention.

"You honor us, Lord Almek." Verris bowed, lowering his eyes respectfully. "As you requested, I have sent for the surviving Swordanzen of the Vi'disa tribe extinction." He smiled warmly up at the Guardian. "My grandfather told me about your last visit to our lands. Many of the younger generation had hoped to bear witness to your presence someday, myself included."

"Your grandfather?" Almek stopped short, frowning some as he thought back, doubting his memory. "It has not been so long since I have been here. Perhaps only forty years at the most." Verris' laughter puzzled and intrigued the Guardian.

"Lord Almek, you honor me in considering me one of the honored ancients of our people, but I will have seen only forty summers myself this cycle." Verris chuckled and waved expansively towards the starry mosaic on the ceiling, a trio of comets haloed by smaller shooting stars forever racing across the depicted heavens. "Our lives are much like the warriors of heaven. They are bright and courageous."

Almek considered the images, troubled. "And short-lived," the Guardian murmured sadly.

"Do not pity us, Lord Almek. We do not mourn our brief lives as you might think. We Desanti see our shorter lives as flames that burn all the brighter for their brevity." Verris's mild voice took on a pride edged in defiance. "Our survival is our victory over the defilers. They thought to destroy us. Destroy the land we called our own."

Verris's expression hardened, though a small, mirthless smile touched his lips. "While it displeases many, it pleases *me* the defilers are here in First Home." Holding his arms out, he said proudly, "They can bear witness to their ancestors' failure. They will not find it easy when they come again to strike us down."

"The Great War is over, Verris. They will not come again as they did before." Resting a comforting, calming hand on Verris' shoulder, Almek blinked at the ripple of energy he sensed through the contact. "You have Guardian talent!"

Verris shrugged dismissively at the revelation. "We are a nation of warriors, my lord. Survival depends on anticipating your opponent. It is whispered that the greatest among us can see through time itself."

"The survivor?" Almek asked hopefully, even more intrigued.

Though he straightened with pride, Verris's voice hinted at a paternal ache and sadness. "Yes, my lord. She—"

"...She?"

Verris smiled. "Yes, my lord. She. My granddaughter. The only Githalin Swordanzen of our generation. Claimed as Thandar the Golden's own."

"Who will not tolerate your constantly trying to defy tradition to convince me to accept a season mating dance, Grandfather." Storm spoke conversationally as she approached, pushing a strand of bronze hair streaked with vivid red and bright blond back in the leather headband. She placed a light kiss on the older man's cheek. "Radisen and Sumalen are lucky it is the Time of Gathering. But if they push too far, I *will* kill them." To Almek, she offered a respectful nod, but did not lower her eyes in subservience as Verris had earlier.

Verris frowned at the slight. "Show Lord Almek Two-Tones respect, Storm!" he scolded. Gaze cool but annoyed, Storm dropped a hand to the hilt of one of her many bladed weapons, Verris echoing the gesture.

Almek quickly spoke to diffuse the impending violent confrontation. "It is quite all right, Elder Verris. I take no insult from one who is as obviously skilled as she is lovely." Almek was pleased to cause a faint blush to appear on Storm's cheeks as he caught her hand to kiss the back of her knuckles. Verris grumbled, but agreed to Almek's denial of any insult, still glowering at the Swordanzen woman.

"You wished to speak of the Vi'disa tribe." She turned to Verris. "I would speak with Lord Almek alone."

The depths of pain reflected in her eyes, echoed in her voice, quelled any protests from her grandfather. "Of course, Githalin Swordanzen." Bowing deeply, the older man excused himself quietly and left.

Almek studied the proud young warrior for a long moment, taking note of the bandages around her middle and her thigh, deep red with fresh blood. "Child, you still bleed from the fight? How long has it been?"

"Perhaps two phases of the greater moon." Storm shrugged, unconcerned. "It is not the first time I have encountered *dinnais*, and I must still answer challenges made to me." She did offer in reassurance, "My wounds will be healed by the next moon phase since I can defer challenges during this time."

"I meant the wounds on your spirit as well, Storm il'Thandar." His voice was quiet, gentle concern clear.

Storm closed her eyes, looking away. "I wish I could say I knew they will heal, eventually. I have found little solace in knowing the evil was stopped." Briefly, she appeared to resemble an improbably young girl burdened with an excess of responsibility, rather than an experienced warrior.

Almek repressed the urge to hug the young woman in comfort, recognizing her determined pride to prove herself strong. "Please. Tell me what happened."

"I do not know how the Vi'disa came to be afflicted with the *dinnais*. I sensed the wrongness and gathered those Swordanzen nearest me. We arrived too late to save anyone from the tribe. The touch of the *dinnais* had corrupted even the youngest." A single tear escaped her closed eyes. "I was the only one left after the adults of the tribe were dispatched...to attend to the tainted younglings. And then honor the dead by building their pyres to set their souls free to rejoin the warriors of heaven." Barely audible, she hissed, "All but the shell the *dinnais* inhabited. Its victim became its prison."

Almek's eyes widened as her words sank in. "Storm il'Thandar, would you share your memories with me, so I may know what you know, as you know it?"

Storm hesitated. Finally, she asked, "How?"

"It's an ancient technique of the Guardians. Allow me to teach you." She followed him to the fountain, sitting with him on its broad edge. Taking her hands, he reached into the pool, cupping her hands in his in the pure cold water of the fountain. "Think on those memories. Focus on them as if they were happening right now. Let the waters of time reflect the past to the present."

Almek inhaled sharply, taken aback by the vividness of the memories that exploded into his consciousness. Not only did she share the vision of her memory, but all the other senses with terrifying clarity. The scent of burning tents mingled with the smell of smoldering flesh and spilled blood. Unnatural shrieks split the air. The *dinnais* was obvious, its host haloed with an ugly darkness that turned the stomach.

Between it and the many Swordanzen, the Vi'disa came at them, puppeted by the *dinnais*. Not only had the adults attacked, but the elders, women heavy with unborn, and young children also swarmed the warriors. The tribesmen fought with unnatural skill and strength. While the Swordanzen were skilled, they were vulnerable, hesitant to slaughter attackers who were victims as well. Their hesitation doomed them.

Every cut Storm received burned, but still she fought on. Once the able Vi'disa were removed, the remaining few Swordanzen advanced on the *dinnais*. The others fell one by one, mortally wounded. When Storm would have followed them, a Swordanzen man found some last reservoir of strength to jump between her and the *dinnais* and take her death blow. Storm subdued the monster finally, but not in time to save any others.

She knelt by the dying warrior whose sacrifice saved her, cradling his head. He offered a wan smile to her, reaching up to wipe away a tear. "Do not waste tears on us, my beautiful, fierce Storm," he whispered. "Better to die fighting than linger too long and die weak and decayed."

She clasped his extended hand, holding it tight and pressing it against her heart. Blocking out all else, she focused on his touch, his scent, the pulse of his weakening heartbeat. It slowed, beat by beat, until finally there was nothing but a whisper as his soul escaped the confines of its shell. His death made all her other injuries negligible in comparison. Her scream of loss echoed into the desert night. No one was alive to hear.

Almek cringed as her memories of having to slay infants tainted by the *dinnais's* touch, of far too many bodies on funeral pyres. A desire to join the fallen almost overwhelmed the will to survive that was the core strength of the Desanti race.

It was several minutes after the memories faded before Almek could find his voice. "You have...suffered so much, Storm. Had I..." he swallowed. "Had I only known, I might have been able—"

"You bear no blame, Lord Almek." Storm pulled her hands from his, letting the water run back into the pool. "It is Swordanzen duty to protect Desantiva from all of its enemies, and an honor to die fulfilling our life's purpose."

He shook his head sharply, expression grim. "No, Storm. What you faced was a temporal shifter, the responsibility of Fortress. They are called darklings in the North. They are enemies to all humans, not only Desanti, and they are the responsibility of Guardians. It is also the purpose of Guardians to find the gifted and train them. Until I heard of the Vi'disa tribe's extinction, I had not truly realized we had abandoned Desantiva so completely..." He shook his head. "That is unforgivable, my dear. No words of apology can express my regret to you and your people."

At a loss, Storm was uncertain what to say. Finally, she asked, "Do the memories help you, my lord? Will their deaths not be in vain?"

"They help, but they are not enough. I must see the place for myself." Storm paled several shades as she tensed, prompting Almek to catch her hand to keep her from fleeing him. He could feel her trembling through their touch. "Please, Storm. Had you had the training of Guardians...as all of your strongly gifted should have...you would have seen the traces I need to see. But your memories are seen through untrained eyes, and no amount of training now will remedy that. Even imprisoned, a shifter can be a danger to the unaware. It needs to be dispatched for good to protect your people."

Storm was silent for a long while. "You brought students. They would be joining you?" she stated more than asked.

"Yes." His reply was simple, without inflection.

A scowl marred the young woman's features. "You count defilers and their get as your students," Storm said accusingly. "No outlanders are permitted beyond the borders of First Home. They are unwelcome." Almek said nothing. They both knew the necessity, and the uselessness of arguing over that necessity. Finally, she sighed. "I will convince the Council of Elders of the need so they can pass word to the tribes. I will secure the necessary supplies for your numbers." He released her hand as she rose.

Almek drew back startled as Storm abruptly drew the long, two-edged blade from its sheath, and held it up, studying the point briefly. In a fluid motion, she offered the blade to him, hilt first, the point pressed against the spot just beneath her sternum. Without thinking, he grabbed the hilt. "I give you my life in service to you, Lord Almek Two-Tones, until the day you need me no longer."

"Storm, you do not need to—"

"If you do not find me acceptable, kill me." Storm watched Almek knowingly as he tried either to let go of the sword or move the point away and found himself unable to do either. "You must accept or reject Blood Oath, Lord Almek. The Heart of Desantiva will allow you no other choice."

"But why? I never asked you to—"

Storm regarded Almek coldly. "You brought defilers into my homeland, the sworn enemy of my people. You must accept my oath if you want both them and me to live. The Elders will have no power to deny you access to our lands if you have my oath." She paused for a moment. "Nor will I kill your defiler students myself, unless you so order it."

Almek grimaced and nodded reluctantly. "Very well. I accept your Blood Oath, Storm il'Thandar." As soon as Almek had spoken the words of acceptance, he could move the blade away. He regarded the blade in his hand for a moment before reversing it as she had and handing it back to her.

Storm slid the blade back into its sheath with a ritualistic motion and then offered a slight bow to Almek. "I will see you again within three days once I have arranged for supplies for the journey, Lord Almek. May Thandar's wings shade you."

Chapter Twenty

Mureln roused from fitful sleep, blinking in disorientation as he pushed himself up. He glanced at Ash briefly, suppressing a flash of envy at the mage's peaceful slumber. Consciously hearing the quiet sobbing that had roused him, the bard pushed himself to his feet and went into the common area of the pavilion, looking around in concern.

Seated on one of the large pillows at the main table where they shared the meals provided by their hosts, Taylin sat with her face buried in her arms, shoulders shaking. She jumped when Mureln put a hand on her shoulder. "Master Bard," she said with formality, sniffing and wiping her eyes hastily.

"Master Healer." Mureln did not smile; his eyes filled with worry for the woman. "Are you alright? You should sleep to recover your strength from the journey here and acclimating to the heat. Terrence has recovered completely thanks to your careful attention."

Taylin sniffed critically, casting a dark look over her shoulder. "I would rather be staked naked under a hornet's nest than share the same space as that heartless woman."

Mureln's lips twitched in a slight smile. "That which does not kill us makes us stronger," he quipped, winning a half-hearted chuckle and exhausted smile from the healer. He brushed her cheek with one finger lightly. "That's better." Reaching over for cups and an ornate glass bottle, he poured water for each of them. "But I don't believe the likes of that Forentan woman could bring you to tears. You are far stronger than that." Gently pressing the cup into her hands, he looked into her eyes for a long moment. Inhaling sharply, he said in the barest of whispers, "You feel it, too. Don't you?"

Taylin bristled. "Feel what? I don't know what you're talking about."

"The Desanti call it *Psia Re*. My people call it the ancestral agony. Born as a result of the Great War." He looked down at the stone table inset with a myriad of pieces of colored glass or stone. "All of Desanti blood feel it, including my people. No one knows what it is exactly." He sighed. "Just that the memory of it is the first from birth and the last at death."

"I am neither Vodani nor Desanti," Taylin pointed out after sipping the water.

"I know. That is why I am...curious." He did not meet her eyes as he spoke. "No one from the North has ever felt it in the known histories. But then," he said slowly, reaching to take one of her hands gently, studying it while his calloused thumb rubbed the back lightly. "No healers from the North have ever come to Desantiva, either. Especially not one of your caliber."

After several minutes, Taylin pulled her hand away from him, unsettled. Nervously reaching up to tuck her hair behind her ear, she asked, "So? What should my being a healer matter?"

"Tell me." Setting his cup aside, he pulled out his knife, contemplating it a moment. He got to his feet, walking several steps out of her reach and resting the blade in his palm. "If I would cut myself, would you feel my pain without touching me?"

"Are you crazy?! What are you doing?" Taylin asked in alarm, though not so loud as to wake anyone. "Put that thing away!" She flinched as he dragged the blade across his palm, cutting deeply.

Grimacing, he held his bloody palm upwards, looking fixedly at her. "Can you feel my pain?" He backed away from her as she tried to reach for him. "Answer me!"

"Yes, of course!" Taylin snapped at him. "Even if I close my eyes, your pain all but glows in my mind's eye. Now stop being foolish and let me heal that, you idiot!" She snatched his hand in both of hers, closing her eyes as she willed the sliced flesh to knit. He half closed his eyes as the healing energy flowed through her touch, the pain muffled to near nonexistence.

Capturing her hands in his, he stepped close to her, their eyes meeting. "Don't you see? You feel the ancestral agony of Desantiva. You feel the echoes of the ancient pain from so long ago." Taylin tried to pull away, but he would not release her. "Beautiful healer, let me help you quiet the roar of pain that torments you."

Panicked, Taylin tried to pull away from the bard as he pulled her against him. Gently, but firmly, he put a hand at the back of her head and pressed his lips against her forehead. She struggled a moment more, then went still, letting him hold her. When he finally released her, he offered an apologetic smile. "It-it is...quieter," she admitted. "What did you—?"

"I touched my soul to yours just enough to mute the ancestral pain to protect you."

"You-you can do that?" Her eyes were wide. "I always thought only a healer could—"

"Making people feel things is not the only thing a master bard can do. We can blunt them, too. Music conveys our will, shares our soul with many without physical contact. But the stronger the mind, the harder it is without actual physical contact." Looking weary, Mureln went over, finishing his water. "You didn't believe it was the *Psia Re* tormenting you. If I had told you my intentions, would you have believed me? Or allowed me to quiet the *Psia Re*?" He did not wait for her answer, walking unsteadily towards his sleeping area again. "You should be able to rest now, Master Healer. Even sharing space with that Forentan woman."

"Master Bard," Taylin called softly. Mureln paused with the partition half drawn back, looking over his shoulder. She hesitated a moment, then spoke shyly. "Thank you." Mureln merely smiled and disappeared behind the canvas.

Chapter Twenty-One

After the twilight meal, the group had settled in to relax before heading out for the central market. Mureln, Emil, and Emaris remained at the table, starting an idle game of toss stones. Amelana and Ash were in his sleeping area, the journeyman insisting she needed to speak with her master privately, though the muffled noises coming from the far sleeping area had little to do with magic or any real discussion.

Left to his own devices, Terrence watched the other men and finally approached. "Excuse me," he interrupted, three sets of eyes turning to regard him. "What are you doing?"

"We be gamblin', lad." Emil offered a toothy grin. At Terrence's quizzical look, he clarified, "Games o' chance where money be won or lost. Ye have those up in yer trees, don't ye?"

Terrence considered for a moment, then his eyes lit up as he understood. "Oh! I participated in many activities that focused on the factor of unpredictability when I was a child, but they are forbidden in the Academy as being exercises beneath the principles of higher learning." Emil stared blankly at Terrence long enough to make Mureln start coughing to cover his laughter.

"He said mages aren't allowed to gamble," the bard translated helpfully. Mureln laughed outright when Emil punched him in the arm.

"I knew that's what he said!" Looking to Terrence, Emil asked, "Ye want t' try a game o' toss stone? I promise I'll go easy on ye."

Terrence looked at the three six-sided stones longingly. "I do not think I can. Apprentices have no money of their own." He looked towards the back and made a face. "And Master Ash would not wish to be interrupted right now."

"Oh, don't ye worry, lad! Emaris has plenty. He'll spot ye some money." Emaris regarded his brother with surprise and annoyance at the 'magnanimous' gesture. "C'mon, Em-boy, help th' lad out. Ye know ye'll win it back from me anyways." Sighing heavily, the huge man took out his pouch and got out five coins, sliding them over to Terrence, who sat next to Mureln.

Terrence offered grave thanks to Emaris, lowering his eyes respectfully. Emaris grunted, but his expression softened. The young man looked at Emil expectantly. "Okay! So, since yer only jus' cuttin' yer teeth on toss stones, we'll start wi' one o' th' easier variations." Sliding a coin out, he waved for Terrence to put one of his own with it. "Now, this game be called tri-toss. We take turns tossin' th' stones 'til one of us be gettin' three th' same." Scooping up the small objects, he shook them in his hands, blew on them, and then gently tossed them onto the table. None of the upwards faces matched. "Yer toss."

Gingerly, Terrence picked up the three dice, studying them speculatively a moment before attempting to mimic Emil's toss, down to blowing on them. Three single dots faced upwards. Terrence looked up at Emil uncertainly as Mureln started coughing into his hand again, and the faintest of smiles touched the corners of Emaris's mouth. "That is good, isn't it?"

Emil blinked several times. "Well, yeah, that be a winner. So ye get t' take th' pot." At Terrence's blank look, he pushed both coins to him. "Th' pot. Th' bet. Them be yer winnin's." Pushing two coins out, he declared, "That be called b'ginners luck, when ye win th' first time out. It ne'er holds out."

"If beginner's luck doesn't hold out, then why would I want to bet again?" The young Forentan was oblivious to the other two men's growing amusement.

The skinny warrior cleared his throat. "Ah, well, ye never know when b'ginner's luck will give out, so ye might win s'more still. An' ye has t' match challengin' bets." Terrence's coins joined Emil's. "Good! Now, it be yer turn t' start th' toss—" Emil went silent as the three faces came up the same again, four dots each. "Aw, ye must be shitten me..." Emil gave Terrence a strained but encouraging smile. "Th' lady of luck be favorin' ye, lad."

Mureln put a hand on Terrence's shoulder, whispering in his ear. With a soft, "Oh, okay," the young mage put a single coin out, Emil matching it. Emil's toss was a loss. But this time, so was Terrence's.

Emil brightened. "That's more like it. Now then! When no one wins th' first toss, ye add more to th' pot, and I'll match ye, and we tosses again."

The young Forentan eagerly rolled the dice, completely unflustered as all his coins were ending up in the pot. Emil tossed first, only two of the three faces matching. Terrence pushed the last coins to the pile, and picked up the dice, rattling them in his cupped hands. "Now, since yer out of money, we'll figure out what ye can bet—" Emil gaped as the three faces came up, each with five dots.

Terrence looked up at Emil, concerned. "Master Emil? Does this mean I win? Master Emil?" he called several times as Emil simply stared in disbelief. He looked in puzzlement between Mureln and Emaris, who began laughing so hard tears came to their eyes. Mureln could only mutely nod as he pulled the mound of coins towards Terrence for the bewildered young man.

After several more glances between the other men, Terrence solemnly separated five coins and offered them to Emaris. "I believe I owe you this, Master Emaris." Pleased, Emaris patted Terrence's shoulder with rough affection, the Forentan wincing at the well-intended thumping.

Recovering after several minutes, Emil said, "Mureln, we gotta take this lad with us t' the gamblin' roosts back home. We can clean 'em out!" Emil looked at Terrence with renewed eagerness. "Let's see how good ye are with a more complicated game!"

Terrence glanced sideways at Mureln, who nonchalantly touched his finger to his temple and winked. Turning back to Emil, Terrence replied eagerly, "I would enjoy that very much, Master Emil, thank you."

Emil wrinkled his nose. "Master? Me? Gods, you Forentan are so uptight. Ye are an adult, ain't ye? We gotta find ye a lass who'll curl yer toes." Terrence turned bright red, averting his eyes. "Trust me, they ain't all like that bitch yer master keeps."

Terrence did not meet anyone's eyes as he busily stacked his coins in front of him. "I am, ah, very happy to know that, mas-, ah, Emil, sir." He said with such fervor, all three men just chuckled, patting his shoulder with sympathy.

CHAPTER TWENTY-TWO

THE PAVILION WAS SILENT as the sun finally sank below the horizon. The bard and mercenaries had taken Terrence with them to explore desert gambling. Taylin had accompanied Almek to speak further with the Desanti elders. The distant sounds of celebrations drifted through the evening air.

Ash lay on his back, staring at the ceiling, lost in his thoughts. Amelana leaned over, half resting on him, tracing circles across his chest. "Ash," she purred as her golden blond hair cascaded down her back and across his chest. "You are still so tense." She kissed him, but he did not respond. "What is on your mind, Ash?"

"My thoughts are my own, Journeyman," he stated without inflection.

She sighed dramatically. "Do you still dwell on that dead servant girl of yours?" Heedless of the darkening expression on the Illaini Magus's face, Amelana said carelessly, "She was barely worth keeping as a servant. Holding onto grief for a lowborn such as her is beneath you. You should be happy you could be rid of her." Sliding her hand down his side to his hip, she purred, "What good are cold memories when you have me to keep you warm?"

The mage growled, shoving the naked girl off and sitting up. He closed his hand on her throat, glaring into her eyes. "If you ever speak of Dessa again, I will send you home marked as the tramp you are." Shoving her away, he glared, barely restraining from striking her. "Get your clothing. Leave me." Wide-eyed, Amelana obeyed, tripping over herself.

Alone, Ash sighed and lay back again. He created a privacy barrier with the wave of a hand, the invisible wall that kept sounds from penetrating it brought him utter silence. "Dessa." His whispered voice carried a hint of desperation as he closed his eyes. The sight in his mind's eye was not that of the gentle girl he had known nearly all his life, who had forgiven him for his inability to protect her when he could never forgive himself.

His foremost thought concerned the Desanti woman, Storm. Ash growled. "Be gone from my thoughts, Swordanzen!" The scene of Dessa's rape from his youth and the scene from the Desanti market inexplicably played themselves together in his mind. He shook his head sharply as he pushed himself to a sitting position, pressing the heels of his hands against his temples. "I will allow no one to taint Dessa's memory. Least of all an ungrateful savage like you!" Restless, he got dressed, dispelled the barrier, and stalked out of the pavilion.

Not caring where he was going, Ash walked deeper into the darkness, away from the sounds of large numbers of people. Eventually, he came to a place lush with greenery. Strange, gnarled trees stretched spindly limbs to the sky, ferns huddling around their trunks. Though incomparably foreign to anything he had ever known, the plants soothed his mind, giving him a modicum of peace. He went deeper into this unexpected refuge of greenery, finding a rock by the wide pool of water in the oasis's center to sit on. He sighed, staring at the reflection of the waxing moons rippling with the gentle evening breeze.

A familiar, bitter voice disturbed the mage's tranquility. "Did you purposely choose this place, defiler, or did fate guide your feet here to disrupt my peace?" A great cat's purr touched Storm's weary voice. Studying him for a long time, the irritation radiating from her subsided. "I see. You seek solace from your own shadows pursuing you."

Unable to ignore her presence, bothered by her keen and unwanted insight, Ash glanced over at the woman seated amongst the tall ferns near the rock he had sat on. He frowned as he studied her with more objectivity, noticing the stained bandages she wore. "You are injured. Was it one of those men who harmed you? That one called Sumalen?" Remembering the feeling of something unnameable bothering him about the large Desanti, Ash's voice got a harsher, almost protective, edge to it. "You should have your wounds tended to."

Storm appeared taken aback, opening her green-gold eyes to study him. "I am surprised it matters to you, treewalker."

"It doesn't," he snapped—then faltered, the concern he'd tried to bury betraying him. He looked back towards the water. "I simply wondered if that brute was the one who injured you." His mind made an intuitive leap when he looked at her. "You are the Swordanzen that Master Almek wished to meet." The woman was still and silent, though she opened her eyes again to study him through narrowed slits. "He told us you are taking us to the site where you encountered the darkling."

Still, Storm said nothing. Her eyes closed again, legs crossed, hands resting on her knees. But he could see the tension across her shoulders. After several minutes of silence, she stated, "The elders are informing the tribes that Lord Almek and his students are permitted to go beyond First Home, so the tribes won't kill you on sight." After a moment, she spoke again, but with visceral pleasure edging her chill tones. "Elder Verris wants you defilers to bear witness to your ancestral failure."

Ash's eyes narrowed to slits. "Failure?"

Storm opened her eyes to meet his. "Our people still live." Ash ground his teeth at the bitter words. "Do you revel in seeing what your defiler ancestors had done? How they ripped the very life from the land? Nearly every beast and green, growing thing gone. The life from not only warriors, but elders and infants and even the unborn, leaving us to suffer? Does it anger you to discover they were not strong enough to destroy all of Desantiva completely?

"Perhaps knowing we Desanti are not as weak as you convinced yourselves we were sits in the pit of your stomach like pieces of broken glass, cutting you inside a thousand times. Maybe you believe that one day we might come to exact justice for your ancestors' crimes against the gods." Green-gold eyes narrowed as she insinuated, "It torments you with unreasoning fear, doesn't it?"

"Do not presume to know my thoughts, Swordanzen," Ash growled harshly. "You know nothing about what I think."

Rising with lithe suppleness, Storm stretched, unconcerned about the underlying threat behind his words, or that he could see the deep red of blood on her bandages from the wounds that continued to bleed. She leveled a hard look at the mage. "Lord Almek Two-Tones thinks you are worthy of serving him." Her voice was mocking and derisive. Turning to walk into the darkness, her voice drifted back. "You better be, defiler."

Chapter Twenty-Three

Ash returned to the pavilion as the sky glowed with the false dawn. The bard, the Gyspari mercenaries, and his apprentice had returned already, Emil proudly showing off a strange knife to Taylin and Almek. "It be called obsidian. Th' whole thing be carved from it." Though the light glinted off the facets, the black of the glassy obsidian seemed to hold greedily onto the light, a deeper black than any of the northern folk had seen before.

Mureln dismissed the matter with a casual wave of his hand. "I still say you got lucky. The gods must watch over idiots."

Emil grinned toothily, waving the blade around with the grace of one well-trained in wielding knives. "I may be an idiot, but I still won this pretty fair 'n square. So ye not be needin' t' worry some angry merchant be goin' t' chase us down or nothin.'"

"I have never seen anyone able to throw knives so well." Terrence's enthusiasm was as boundless as it was innocent. "I think you even impressed the Desanti. It was like they danced across your fingers."

"Ah, m'boy, nimble fingers be good fer many things." Emil winked. "Ye can ask many of th' girls who been with me over th' years."

"And a few of their husbands," Mureln drawled, this time avoiding Emil's fist to his arm. "Don't listen to this lout for advice about women, Terrence. He has been slapped more times than there are blades of grass on the plains."

Emil looked affronted. "Just b'cause I can't charm th' balls off a bull like ye can, Mureln, ain't no reason t' be talkin' bad 'bout me." He glared up at Emaris. "An' you quit yer grinnin', ye big lunk! Yer s'posed t' back me up!" The men laughed at the skinny mercenary, who humphed and crossed his arms in a pout.

Mureln glanced at the mage as the man paused by their shared sleeping area, meeting his eyes. Nodding slightly to the silent request, Mureln turned to his companions. "I'm going to go shake the sand out of my britches before the morning meal is brought. Make sure you bottomless pits leave some food for me when it arrives." Emil waved Mureln off, drawing Terrence over to the common table to talk about 'real' women. Mureln shook his head, following the mage into the private area.

As soon as the bard entered, Ash waved his hand. The sounds outside of their area went silent, not even Emil's loud and descriptive exaggerations audible. Mureln nodded, expression thoughtful, as he dropped to sit on his sleeping mat. "Remarkable privacy barrier. It is a rare gift to use your Northern magic without speaking. I'm impressed."

The mage made a disagreeable sound as he removed his outer robes, dismissing the compliment. After several more moments, he spoke, his words slow and measured. "Tell me, Bard. Why do you not judge me as everyone else seems to do?"

Mureln pulled off his boots, tipping one after the other to pour out the fine grains that had gotten inside, then removed his socks to shake out the sand from them and brush the remaining irritants off his feet. "We all judge each other, Illaini Magus," he said with a shrug. "It is the nature of humans to judge, for good or ill."

"Do not play Forentan philosophy games with me, Bard. I don't have the temper for it right now. You know what I am asking you." Sitting across from each other, Ash fixed Mureln with an intense gaze. "These desert folk look at me as if I were one of the ancients who had wielded the forbidden magicks of the Great War. Your own sister looked at me as if I were a murderer, though I had never even met her before and done no harm to her. They look at me thus for no other reason than because I am Forentan." He looked at Mureln again. "Everyone but you. Why?"

Any hint of levity faded from Mureln's expression. He sat in silence, weighing his words carefully before speaking. "When I travel between the realms, I carry stories like precious gems in a pouch," he said finally. "Each one must shine with its own truth, not clouded by my fingerprints upon it. A master bard must remain untainted by prejudice."

He looked down at his hand, rubbing his thumb along the calluses of his fingertips. "The moment I allow my own prejudices to color a tale, I've failed my calling. People often resent my neutrality, but they would despise me if they sensed I bent their truths to match my own beliefs...or worse, tailored them solely to please an audience. Once such a deception is discovered, nothing I would say would be believed. Once lost, such trust cannot be restored."

"The Desanti judge everyone as their enemy," Ash observed bitterly.

"You must try to see the world from their point of view, Andar." Ash looked up at Mureln with a puzzled frown. "For all their bravado, deep in their hearts, they are afraid. They are terrified of disappearing entirely from the face of the Sundered Lands. Their lives are harsh beyond anything you or I could comprehend. Since the Great War, their numbers are..." He pressed his lips together and waved a hand. "Every Desanti alive is here for the Time of Gathering. Barely the population of a single small city up north."

The mage blinked, his anger evaporating into shock. "...All of them?"

"All of them," Mureln confirmed. "They are nomads because they cannot remain in one place for long. The land struggles to sustain what numbers they have. Once every few years, the tribes come together in peace. Some will go with another tribe to strengthen the bloodlines. And then they will separate again to wander the land in smaller groups. Almek was lucky that the timing of his journey coincided with this event. So are the rest of us."

"You said the Vodani are cousins to the Desanti," Ash stated, his question implied.

"There are many traits the Vodani and Desanti share in common. Desanti are fiercely protective of the land they call home; thus, they must wander, else they could overstress the life that clings to the land. The Vodani are those Desanti who felt the call of home in Vodanya's waves. All Vodani are wanderers. Our spirits move as the tides, urging us to new places, new experiences, and ensuring the waters are not overstressed by fishing or other activities. We shared what the mages had wrought on the warriors in the last battle until the sundering split Desantiva and Vodanya was born."

"So you became a bard because of your wandering spirit?"

Mureln chuckled. "Perhaps in a way, yes. Ever since I was a boy, I have been curious about the other lands. The other peoples. I was Almek's student when I was barely a man. Until the music called to me. When the music called, I answered. The first stories I learned from the Desanti only made me hungrier to experience the truth for myself. Everyone has their secrets; learning the truths behind the facades allows me to navigate more treacherous tides, perhaps help bring peace to those in conflict. The most basic truths are shared across all parts of every society."

"And what are these truths you found?" Ash's tone held less contempt than it might just a few minutes before.

Mureln quirked a faint smile. "I learned many things. I learned perceptions are born of a grain of truth, but what we see on the surface may run through to the core, or may only be an illusion in the mind's eye." He regarded Ash, waiting for the mage to consider his words.

"Do you see a murderer when you look at me?" Ash asked simply, his eyes fixed on the belt in his hands, squeezed to conceal his agitation.

The bard blinked at the unexpected question. "I see a man capable of murder, but not a murderer. I see a man who was once confident he knew everything he needed to know of the world beyond his homeland and discovered it is much, much more complicated than he expected." He was silent for a time. "When I first met you, I thought you were an arrogant bastard who dismissed everyone else as worthless and beneath him."

Flinching, the mage could not deny the accuracy of Mureln's initial observations. "And now?" Ash's voice was barely audible despite the privacy barrier that cordoned off sounds from both sides.

"I see a man who built walls around his heart to protect himself from hurt. Who tried to become strong enough to protect those he cared about, to control everything so it would all be safe, and had his entire world crash around him when he discovered that utter control was still beyond his grasp." Pausing, the bard continued in a gentle voice.

"You look at your past with fresh eyes, and you question yourself. You look at your people's past and realize what they have tried to forget. You look at the future and realize it isn't as clear as you thought it was...and that you are not strong enough to protect everyone alone."

Ash's face colored at Mureln's blunt and accurate honesty. He looked away to conceal some of his shame from the Vodani. "I am weak."

"Weak? Hardly." Mureln's clipped tones drew Ash to look up at him again. "What your people want is not so much control but predictability. You want the world nice and ordered. And you fooled yourself into believing you had finally achieved that elusive order and predictability. But you learned the world was neither, and someone you cared about suffered for that mistake. You strove to strengthen yourself, and still it was not enough to protect Dessa."

"And you Vodani don't want the same thing?" Ash asked, deflecting the focus away from himself. "Control over your world?"

Mureln could not help but chuckle. "Ah, I suppose in a sense we do. But we live within the embrace of the oceans. There is no power greater, and while some of us are gifted enough to influence the tides and storms, we accept we cannot stop them. Instead, we learn how to adjust to their comings and goings." He sighed, expression sad. "And sometimes, no matter the skill, the precautions, we cannot prevent the inevitable. The world simply is not predictable. But we rather like it that way."

Ash frowned. "Why would you like unpredictability? It brings nothing but pain and grief."

Mureln gave the mage a measured look. "Life comprises both pleasure and pain...and both shape us. Success is sweeter when we've risked failure. Moreso when we have known failure on a visceral level. Each day is precious because it may be our last. And I'd rather die here and now, having truly lived, than survive for centuries knowing what to expect." The bard studied him for several moments. "Something happened tonight," he said, inviting the mage to speak.

"I encountered the Swordanzen that will guide Master Almek into the desert. The woman Storm il'Thandar." Mureln sat bolt upright, staring at Ash as he fell silent. The mage's jaw muscles jumped as he clenched his teeth.

"You are still whole," Mureln said gently after a beat, trying to give Ash a positive point. "I take that as...promising. She didn't try to kill you on sight."

The mage remained unresponsive, his eyes focused elsewhere. "She's still bleeding from the injuries she sustained in the encounter that brought us here." Mureln was about to say something but hesitated. There was an intriguing note in Ash's voice—an unexpected hint of concern for the Desanti woman. He studied the mage's profile intently.

Ash looked away. "She gave her word...Master Almek and his students...won't be killed for leaving First Home."

His tone held no doubt, which further piqued Mureln's curiosity. He narrowed his eyes. "She said something else." The mage pressed his lips together. "Something that cut deep."

"My thoughts are my own, Bard," Ash gritted out. Try as he might, he could not repress the frustration that bubbled up, erupting in a burst of hissed seething. "She said I'm no different from those who..." His fists clenched. "No different from my ancestors who slaughtered hers. What they did was wrong! If I could undo it...Not even these savages deserved..."

The muscles along Mureln's back relaxed as understanding settled in. "You're a son of your ancestors, Ash Andar. Yes, to my Desanti kin, that makes you a murderer. They judge through memory, not mercy. It's safer to mistrust than to lose everything they've fought for.

"But you're not the people from the past. I judge you as you are now. I do not see a murderer." He rose, standing over the silent mage. "What I see is a solitary man who chose to be alone. And suffers for that choice."

Chapter Twenty-Four

THE MORNING SUN WAS high in the sky when the group emerged with their gear, squinting and not entirely awake. "Master Almek?" Terrence asked, yawning. "Why are we leaving now? Not even the Desanti are awake."

Almek smiled in sympathy. "The Elders recommended it would be best to depart before the tribes are fully awake. Desanti obey their elders to a fault, but he does not want to tempt fate by giving them the chance to...try to get around the edict of safe passage for us. Especially with the Time of Gathering nearing its end. By the time we return, the tribes should be well scattered, and our guide will help us avoid them."

"Where is my horse?" Amelana demanded to know as she huffed. "I swear, if these dogs have eaten my horse, I will—!"

"You will what?" Storm emerged from a path, leading a danger-ous-looking reptilian creature that resembled a horse only in purpose. Long horns capped with gleaming bronze caught the light as it lowered its head, angling its horns menacingly towards the Forentan woman. "Shhh, drizar," the woman crooned affectionately to the animal. The animal relaxed, snorting and digging at the ground, striking sparks with his metal shod claws. Young handlers led similar beasts, all saddled with gear and supplies strapped to the backs of the saddles. These other beasts, however, while equally evil looking, were considerably less massive and much more docile than Storm's mount.

"Our horses are being taken to the Vodani city to be cared for there until we return," Almek assured the Forentan woman. "It is wiser to use mounts adapted for survival in this land. The extremes here would probably kill the horses, and I doubt you'd want to walk." He looked to his animal as its handler offered him its reins. "They are called drizzen."

With just a gentle touch, the drizar lowered himself to the ground, al-lowing Storm to climb onto his back. She waited calmly as the handlers instructed the non-Desanti on how to control the creatures. Suddenly, the drizar let out a piercing shriek, startling both humans and drizzen as he sprang to his feet, revealing his long teeth. All eyes turned to see two other Desanti approaching on their mounts, clad in travel robes with their faces covered to protect against the elements, hiding their identities.

Storm put herself and her mount between the two men and the rest of the group. Her harsh words were clipped, and the gestures that she made were unquestionably threatening. The men growled back at her, disputing whatever she told them.

Mureln frowned and muttered from where he waited near Ash, "I recognize those voices." Ash made a noise of agreement in his throat, scowling at the larger of the two newcomers.

Almek joined Storm, regarding the men. "You will speak where all understand, or you will depart," he stated flatly.

The men unwound the fabric covering their faces, the smaller of the two offering a grudging respect to the Dusvet. "Lord Almek Two-Tones," Radisen greeted. "Excuse our intrusion. My and Sumalen's business with Storm is unrelated to you."

"Storm has sworn Blood Oath to me," Almek returned flatly. Radisen shot a look at the scowling woman. "If your business interferes with her, then your business relates to me."

The two men were silent, unhappily considering Almek's words. Sumalen growled. "We come with. It would not be right to allow our desert flower to travel among outlanders unprotected."

Storm narrowed her eyes, bristling. "I should rip your throat out right here for your continued insults," she snarled, her hands snapping to the hilts of her paired single-edged blades. She froze when Almek put his hand on her wrist.

"It is still the Time of Gathering. I'll not have you breaking your traditions, Githalin Swordanzen." Almek watched her profile intently. "So long as their presence does not interfere with our task, I am unconcerned."

Releasing her weapons, Storm made a disgusted, dismissive gesture, pulling her beast around sharply. She spoke to no one as she ranted, riding a short distance away. But considering the surprised expressions of the two men and the coughing and blushing of the young drizzen handlers, the others could guess something of what she was saying.

Ash observed Mureln, whose expression revealed amusement mixed with fascination. Feeling the mage's eyes on him, Mureln glanced over.

"I have heard colorful cursing before, but this is quite educational. I don't think any of it is even physically possible."

"I see." Ash turned his impassive gaze towards the Desanti woman again.

Mureln chuckled as he adjusted the cowl of his desert robe's hood, putting the face wrap around his neck loosely to allow him to pull it up later. "I wouldn't want to get on her bad side. Especially when nothing restrains her from acting."

Amelana rode up between Mureln and Ash, roughly pulling her drizzen to a stop. "Desanti dogs," she growled. "They are a bunch of animals." She subsided when Ash gave her a dark, meaningful look.

THE GROUP WAS SILENT as they followed Storm along a road that led out of the valley of First Home. They paused on the ridge as the woman stopped her animal to look back. Drawing her two-edged sword, she held it up in a salute, murmuring something in another tongue before lowering her eyes. She then slid the blade back and wheeled around. The other drizzen followed the larger beast without their riders' urging.

"What be that about?" Emil wondered curiously, glancing back the way they came, then towards Storm up front.

Even Mureln was perplexed. "I don't know. I have never heard that tongue before."

"It is a Swordanzen ritual of farewell," Radisen stated tonelessly as he passed near enough to the Sevmanen and Vodani to hear them. "She asked the Totani to watch over the people in her absence."

"But what language did she speak?" Mureln looked at Storm's back. "I thought I had learned all the languages. But that sounded...old."

"It is the holy language of the Swordanzen." Before Mureln could ask more, Radisen spurred his drizzen forward to ride nearer to Storm and Sumalen. The bard narrowed his eyes, thoughtful.

By noon, the heat from the sun was scorching, and the light was blinding. The welcomed relief of the setting sun was short-lived. Within a few more hours, the sun sank below the horizon, the land cast in the twin moons' silvery blue glow. The day's warmth seemed to vanish with the sun, bitterly chill breezes blowing around the travelers.

Almek pulled gloves on and urged his drizzen up next to Storm. Unhappily, Sumalen and Radisen fell back out of respect for the Guardian. "How long until we reach our destination?"

"Three, perhaps four days if we encounter nothing to delay us." Storm pulled her face wrap down, looking towards Almek. "I could make it there alone within two, but none of your outlander students could manage the pace or the terrain."

The Guardian nodded, giving her his complete trust. After a moment of silence, he glanced over his shoulder at the pair of Desanti men. "Your suitors are persistent."

Storm looked sideways at Almek. "You were not entirely truthful to the elders. Not all the outlanders are your students," she replied, avoiding the topic of Radisen and Sumalen.

"You noticed that, did you?" Almek was bemused. "I suspected you were quicker than you let on. I let the warriors who challenged us assume they were. The elders accepted their assumptions as fact. I thought it prudent to let them continue believing so."

"Understandable." Storm shrugged. "And wise. We Desanti prefer things to be simple. To get around the edict not to attack your students, they would claim they thought they were attacking a tagalong." Carefully, she maneuvered her mount around a small rock protrusion. "Know my oath extends only to your true students, Lord Almek. I will not protect the others. Especially not defilers. That I must protect any at all is insult enough."

"Storm." Almek watched her as he spoke with muted emphasis. "Losing any here would distract my students from our purpose. It would please me if you would include everyone in your protection."

The woman made a face. "You ask much of me, Lord Almek."

"No more than I know you can give, Storm."

Sighing, rolling her eyes, Storm agreed. "Very well, my lord, if it is your desire, then I shall protect them all." She paused. "Even the defilers' get."

Almek shook his head, flicking a glance over his shoulder towards the Forentan contingent. Balancing the pride and egos of the mage and the Swordanzen was an unexpected challenge. He changed the topic. "The drizzen you ride. It looks like a fine animal. Is it a different breed from ours?"

A small smile touched Storm's lips as she looked at the beast fondly who bobbed his head, as if knowing he was being discussed. "Not at all, Lord Almek. The ones gifted to you and your students are females or males that failed to mature. My companion is a drizar. A full male." She reached forward to scratch a patch of hair on the beast's neck. "Finding a wild drizzen to be a companion is a test of the Swordanzen. I am the only one to succeed in winning the heart of a drizar."

"It must have been difficult to tame him."

"Tame?" Storm looked at Almek in surprise. "My lord, Swordanzen do not tame their companions. Taming breaks the spirit. Necessary for those untrained to handle the true spirit of the land. But it would be an atrocity for a Swordanzen to break the spirit of a brother or sister creature. Besides, no one can tame a drizar. No tribe has any as part of its herd."

"Ah, I see." He glanced over his shoulder. "I must make use of the time of our journey and give my students more instruction."

Storm smiled faintly as she pulled her face wrap back in place. "Do not worry, my lord. I will not permit Radisen or Sumalen to distract me from my duty to you."

Almek nodded and dropped back. Almost immediately, the two Desanti men flanked Storm. Unhappy, he sighed as he fell in beside Taylin.

"There is something different about those two men, Master Almek," Taylin commented. "But...I am not sure what."

"Each race has a special...quality to it." Almek studied the Desanti for an extended period. "But even in my five hundred years, I have learned little about the Desanti." Taylin looked over at him in astonishment. "I am now seeing the prices their people have paid in the time since the lands sundered that I and other Guardians have carelessly overlooked."

Taylin frowned, studying the backs of the three Desanti in the front. "Prices?"

Almek nodded. "I used to be a weaponsmith's apprentice when I was a boy. It was not nearly as fine an art then as it has become now." He sighed wistfully. "I still remember some of my first attempts. One blade was too soft. It bent when hitting a hard surface, proving ineffective.

"Another blade was hard and sharp. But brittle. It withstood nearly all things, but when it came into contact with something equally hard, it proved to be too brittle and shattered." He looked at Storm again. "The men are difficult to see clearly. I cannot read our Swordanzen at all. Not because I don't have the ability." Taylin blinked in surprise at Almek. "But because she does not allow it."

"She can do that?" Taylin whispered in awe. "Is she a-a Guardian?"

"Yes. No." Almek frowned. "The world provides when there is a void. Not only did the Desanti shut out everyone from their lands—including Guardians of Time—they shut themselves in it. But what Guardians protect against knows no borders. The Desanti must have forged themselves into weapons to survive and protect Desantiva from the likes of temporal shifters, whether they knew them as such. But Storm is something more, even among them."

"She frightens me," Taylin confessed, looking ashamed.

"She should," Almek replied crisply. "The Desanti nicknamed the desert at the hottest part of the day the Forge. She is no meek desert flower. Storm is a weapon forged and tested, but I have not yet determined her mettle." He smiled at the healer. "Now then, we should continue your lessons." Taylin looked relieved to get her mind off the troublesome topic of the Desanti.

Chapter Twenty-Five

THE JOURNEY STRETCHED ENDLESSLY through Desantiva's frigid darkness, where breath crystallized into glittering clouds and fingertips numbed within minutes. Twin moons—one jade-tinged, one amber—cast their competing light across terrain that rose and fell like a petrified ocean. Obsidian crags and knife-edged ridges jutting skywards like the spines of buried leviathans, vast swells of sand frozen mid-heave. The hardy drizzen, their scales glittering with frost, followed the full male drizar whose metal-capped horns caught moonlight as he tossed his head, releasing challenges that sliced through the silence—a sound between a falcon's cry and metal scraping stone. From the distant darkness came answering calls, haunting echoes that made the group's skin prickle.

Despite the day's scorching emptiness, the desert now teemed with nocturnal life—six-legged lizards scuttled between rocks, luminescent beetles pulsed with blue-green light, and somewhere, unseen predators with yellow eyes tracked the travelers from shadowed crevices. Strange animals emerged into the chill darkness, their alien songs of mating and challenge weaving a discordant symphony. The day-loving humans had long fallen silent; even Storm's pair of suitors who dogged her were subdued, their proud shoulders hunched as they clutched desert robes close about them.

As the sun cast its soft glow on the horizon, the subtle changes in their surroundings they missed stood out. Taylin spoke of what occupied everyone's thoughts. "My gods," she breathed. "This land makes where we started seem lush!"

Incredulously, Emil peered at his scaly, fur-patched mount and squinted. "Is this thing eatin' rocks?"

"Drizzen eat whatever they can find." Storm brought her mount to a stop, reaching forward to thump the broad neck. The drizar snorted as he stopped short, pawing the ground, and bobbing his head arrogantly.

The other drizzen, as if following some unspoken command, all came to an abrupt dead stop in unison, pawing the ground as they snuffed around in their continuous hunt for food. If not rocks, they took mouthfuls of sand and chewed that. "We will stop here for the day."

"Are you mad, woman?" Sumalen demanded with a snarl, trying to kick his animal to move towards the Swordanzen. The animal bucked in refusal, forcing him to slide off to the ground, bringing a darker color to his already anger-flushed face. He stalked towards Storm. "*You* were the one who started this foolish journey. You want to stop now?! We are losing precious travel time!"

Storm's mount sidled away from Sumalen as she drew one of her single-edged blades, holding it pointed at his heart. "It is not your decision when or where we stop. It is mine. The outlanders cannot endure Desantiva's days without rest." Her expression was hard and unflinching. "Even Desanti are not foolish enough to challenge the heat of the Forge often."

"If they cannot keep up, let them lie where they drop!" Radisen growled, glaring at the three Forentan. "They are not our responsibility."

"They are *my* responsibility." Eyes narrowed, Storm stated tonelessly, "*You* were not invited. If you intend to remain, you will do as I say. Otherwise, you have only two choices left to you. Leave. Now. Or die, and I will feed you to the drizzen to nourish them and stretch our supplies further." The rest of the group watched the interaction with varying degrees of interest, curiosity, or disgust. The silence stretched out until the drizar shrilled in challenge, angling his metal-capped horns at the men.

Holding their hands up, both backed down, sullenly going to the pack animals to drag off the large sun shelter. Emil and Emaris, used to similar travel, dismounted to help them.

Mureln shook his head and commented to his brothers-in-arms, "It's like watching two male dogs encountering the same bitch in heat." Emil cleared his throat, pointing behind Mureln after the bard's droll observation. The Vodani's eyes widened as he glanced over his shoulder. Coughing, Mureln turned to face Storm. "Er, no insult intended, Githalin Swordanzen." He held his hands up in a gesture of surrender.

A barely perceptible smile touched Storm's lips, though it did not reach her eyes. "Once you have your gear, turn the drizzen loose so they can forage. They will stay near my drizar, and he will remain in sight of me." The wicked beast lowered his head, as docile as a gelding, to allow

Storm to remove his head harness. He remained where he stood until Storm made a gesture away, and he turned to bound like a northern deer.

At the far end of the group, the Forenten were having considerable difficulty with their mounts. None of the creatures would hold still long enough to permit them a safe dismount, nor did any remember the commands to make the beasts lower themselves to the ground. "Senior Apprentice Terrence," Amelana ordered sharply. "Get over here and hold this mangy beast still!"

"I would if I could, Journeyman." Exasperated with Amelana's complete self-centeredness, Terrence struggled to hold on to his unruly drizzen. The animal bucked, forcing the young man to wrap his arms around the thick neck to keep his seat and not be thrown onto the sharp rocks surrounding them.

While not having complete success, Ash's years of horsemanship aided in keeping his animal under some semblance of control. Angling his beast to move alongside his apprentice's, Ash leaned over to grab the head harness of Terrence's drizzen. The drizzen hissed at the mage, a wad of spit spattering on Ash's cheek. Silent and grim, Ash said nothing, his hold secure and forcing the animal to calmness. Terrence gratefully slid off and grabbed his gear, backing away from the baleful creature before it kicked him.

Before Amelana could shrill demands at the young man to assist her now, Mureln went over to Amelana and her unhappy beast, crooning a soothing song. Almost at once, the drizzen calmed, its ears flicking forward. Taking hold of the harness, Mureln said cheerfully, "Come on and get down, princess. You have been nominated to take the first turn to prepare the morning meal. Hop to it!"

Amelana's eyes widened with indignant outrage. "What?! How dare you order me around, you-you Vodani peasant!" Without a groom to assist her, and the Vodani not getting the animal to lower itself, Amelana's dismount possessed a decided lack of grace. The snickering from the pair of Sevmanan Gyspari only added to her sense of personal insult. "Do you know who I am?"

"There are many words that describe you, defiler." Storm approached to assist with the drizzen. Given her attention to the animals, they rated more concern than the humans to the Desanti woman. She removed the harness and saddle from Terrence's animal, tossing him the beast's gear before sending it off after the drizar.

Storm repeated her actions for Amelana; her 'toss' compelled the Forentan woman to stagger back because of the blow. "If you do not want to cook, you do not have to eat either." The expression Storm leveled on Amelana almost begged the Forentan woman to give the Swordanzen reason to draw a weapon on her.

The two women glared in silence for the space of a heartbeat. "Master Ash!" Amelana whirled to the mage before he and the bard had completed removing the mage's gear from his mount. Dropping her gear, she clutched his arm. "You won't let that Desanti dog talk to me like that, will you?"

Unprepared for Amelana's sudden simpering plea, Ash took a few steps back to regain his balance, glaring down at her flushed, upturned face, unmoved by her plight. The mage's silence continued until Amelana turned a deeper red that had little reason to do with the rising sun.

Finally, Amelana drew away, murmuring apologies to Ash for her outburst as she stooped to gather her dropped belongings, and then turned towards the shelter. She cast hateful glares at the snickering mercenaries, throwing her hair over her shoulder as her subservient posture regained its air of superiority.

Mureln flicked a look between Storm and Ash as the pair fixed each other with hate-filled stares. He noticed Terrence staring wide-eyed between them and threw an arm around the young man's shoulders. "Hey, lad, have you ever played Vodani toss stone?" he asked, drawing him away towards the shelter.

"No, sir." Terrence kept looking over his shoulder at Ash with worried uncertainty as Mureln drew him away. "I know only the games Master Emil taught me and a few of the Desanti games. The Desanti ones were much more complicated than I expected..." The young man's voice drifted away, leaving the Forentan Magus and Desanti Swordanzen to face each other in silence for many long minutes.

Ash finally broke the silence, his voice pitched low and only just loud enough for the woman to hear. The warning was plain in his words. "In the future, do not speak to my student with such impudence, Desanti."

The mere arching of a single eyebrow shifted Storm's demeanor from hostile to dangerous. She took a step forward, measured and slow, much like a predator circling prey. "Or what, Treewalker?" she asked with a deceptively mild purr. Her movements were casual, so unlike the snake-strike swiftness he witnessed in the First Home market. The hairs on the back of his neck stood up at the growing sense of danger with her deliberate movements. "You would dare to bring harm to one of the Dusvet Guardian's students?"

Scowling in response to Storm's words and circling advance, Ash crossed his arms and stood his ground, following her movements only with his eyes. "Your importance to Master Almek is minimal at best, Desanti. If it exists at all."

"Really." Cold eyes raked over the Forentan as she approached. "Your arrogance will be your death, Treewalker, and I will mourn only that I could not kill you with my hand!" she hissed as she stopped nose to nose in front of him. She was close enough that he could feel her body heat radiating like the heat of a fire. She was visibly restraining the urge to strike him.

"Storm! Ash!" Almek called, his sky-gray eyes fixed on the pair.

Despite the Guardian's invitation lacking any rebuke, both recoiled from one another, as though physically struck. Storm backed away from Ash several steps before turning her back on him. The mage waited a heartbeat before following her. "Yes, Lord Almek?" "Yes, Master Almek?" they said in unison.

Almek's hand rested on a small outcropping of rock on one of the many natural, human-sized stone pillars that littered the landscape. While the Guardian ignored the others, this one drew Almek's complete attention. "What is this?" The nondescript reddish-orange stone was one of many around the encampment. "There is a familiar...resonance..."

"It is *A'tyrna Ulan*," Storm answered with matter-of-fact reverence. "There are no words for it in trade common." She lowered her eyes in uncharacteristic embarrassment at the apologetic confession. "The histories say they are the anchors that keep Desantiva alive. There are only six *A'tyrna Ulan*. They are from the..." She frowned, searching for the words. "...From the Before Time."

"'Before Time?'" Ash blurted questioningly before he could censor himself. His curiosity overpowered his disdain for the Desanti and their lands. Eyes on the rock, he started reaching for it. "The resonance seems—?"

"No!" Storm snarled. One hand latched onto Ash's wrist in a merciless grip. "You will not desecrate the *A'tyrna Ulan* with your filthy touch, defiler!" Ash grimaced, struggling not to show weakness in the face of an unmistakable promise of something much worse than death.

"Storm!" Almek barked, finally penetrating the woman's haze of rage with the third repetition of her name. "Release him!" With teeth bared, Storm was unmoved by the order. Taking a deep breath, Almek stated in toneless harshness, "By your Blood Oath, Storm Il'Thandar, you *will* release him!"

The woman flinched as if Almek had struck her. Releasing Ash abruptly, Storm turned away, making a strangled sound as if in pain, stalking away into the desert several measures. She did not stop until she was nearly out of sight of the camp.

Ash glared at the woman's back before turning his attention to his wrist. Muttering, he pulled the sleeve back to reveal bruises that were already darkening. "Stupid—"

"Don't antagonize her." Almek put his hand on Ash's shoulder, his voice quiet and paternal. "Her Blood Oath is akin to your Soul Oath." The old man made a face. "I asked neither of you to give your lives in your service to me. But don't think I'm not prepared to use your oaths to demand obedience. I won't allow either of you to die over your racial pride. Do you understand me?"

"Yes, Master Almek." Ash ducked his head, meek as a scolded dog. He tugged his sleeve down, careful to hide the second injury he received from the deceptively slight woman.

Satisfied, Almek turned back to the rock. "Tell me what you sense from the *A'tyrna Ulan*."

Nodding, Ash reached out again, but stopped short of touching the craggy surface. His eyes closed for quite a while before he spoke. "It's ancient." Surprise and reverence filled his voice. "I have felt nothing like it before...but it seems...familiar at the same time." He opened his eyes, searching the desert for the woman. "How could she even sense anything? Desanti have no magic to—"

Almek smiled a little. "Do not underestimate the Swordanzen, my dear Illaini Magus. Or the Desanti people. Perhaps there is more to learn here than you thought, hm?" Ash blinked at Almek, staring at him. "Come, my boy. The sun is becoming unbearable. And it looks like you will need to prove your pretty student has not poisoned the rations."

CHAPTER TWENTY-SIX

BY MIDDAY, THE SUN shone down with blinding intensity, feeling even hotter now than in the days since they had arrived in Desantiva. The fierce desert heat had subdued even Amelana's unceasing complaints and criticisms. Most of the travelers had fallen into a dead sleep of utter exhaustion, leaving the camp quiet. Even Storm's suitors eventually gave up their never-ending badgering and slept.

Ash sat apart from everyone, attempting to use meditation to ignore the heat. Opening his eyes halfway, he roused to a thirst he could no longer suppress. Unfamiliar lethargy dragged on him as he struggled to get to his feet. Eyes fixed on the water skins, he staggered several steps.

The next thing Ash knew, he was sitting once more, with something pressing against his lips. Even though the liquid was sharply bitter, he couldn't stop himself from grabbing the waterskin and drinking greedily. He fought to keep the source of water as it was pulled away. Shame at his desperation and lack of self-control finally penetrated raw instinct, hearing Storm speaking to him.

"You will make yourself sick if you drink too much too fast, treewalker." Storm's voice sounded odd to him. Somewhere in the back of his mind, he realized her voice was missing the hatred and hostility he had grown accustomed to.

He squinted up at her, blinking to force his eyes to focus on her. "What—?" Ash rasped, pausing to swallow and try speaking again. "What...what is in...the water?"

"Desert herbs used to help cut thirst." Storm helped him drink from the waterskin again, but only allowing him a few swallows. She smirked. "This is my personal waterskin. I am not trying to poison you." She glanced over her shoulder towards the sleepers. "Nor will I mention your...moment of weakness to anyone."

Grunting, Ash said grudgingly, "Thank you." He was not expecting much for his expression of gratitude, but the growl of insult surprised him. He narrowed his gaze at the woman as she spoke scoldingly.

"Do not thank me, defiler. If not for my oath to Lord Almek, I would sooner see you and all your kind dead than help you survive in this land of *your* making." She looked away, fists balled as she forced herself back to calmness again.

Once she had reclaimed her self-control, Storm leaned closer, tugging at the outer belt of his heavy robes. "Thandar's talons, you outlanders and your clothing. You will cook yourself to death with all these layers trapping the heat against you." As soon as she loosened and tugged the heavy garment off, Ash sighed in relief, closing his eyes. "Drink. You are overheated."

Ash did not offer any words of gratitude this time. Storm remained silent, ignoring his intense eyes studying her as she sat with him until he was fully recovered. When she rose, he caught her by the wrist. Ignoring her stiffening at his touch, he waited until she looked at him. "Your suitors—"

"Are no concern of yours," Storm replied in clipped tones.

The mage pressed his lips together in annoyance, his voice equally clipped. "If they interfere with Master Almek's journey, they are my concern."

Storm fixed Ash with a hard look. "You stay out of my personal matters, and I will not interfere with you and your slut." The mage flinched, opening his mouth to deny the implication, feeling his sunburned face flush. "I am not blind, treewalker. Nor do I care. You obviously do not keep her for her sweet personality, and my drizar has more mage talent than she has.

"It matters nothing to me who you prong. She is not a true student of Lord Almek. My responsibility to protect Forenten begins and ends with you, no matter if Lord Almek wishes otherwise. He is too kind to accept the fact that trusting your kind only ends in pain and death."

Looking down, Ash let his hand drop away as Storm stood, his thoughts muddled from the heat and unexpectedly troubled by Storm's blunt—and partially accurate—observations. Her flat voice cut though his thoughts. "Finish the water. Then get some rest. We will be resuming the journey at sunset."

Chapter Twenty-Seven

THE GROUP SETTLED INTO nighttime travel and daytime rest after three days. Mureln regaled Taylin with romantic songs from all the lands he had traveled. When she turned her nose up at them, sunburned cheeks flushed with embarrassment at the attention, he crooned the bawdiest of bawdy songs to the hoots and howls of his mercenary companions. Terrence failed miserably at maintaining the typical aloofness Ash displayed and laughed with the mercenaries, especially when Almek would lean over to whisper something in his ear that made the young man turn as bright red as Taylin.

"Heathens," Amelana stated with lofty criticism. She glanced over at Ash when there was no reaction. "Master Ash, have you heard anything I said?"

"You have not stopped talking since we left Forenta and have yet to say anything worthwhile." Ash's eyes remained directed forward. "It is a waste of time and energy that you could better use to complete your preparations for your mastery trials."

"Master Ash!" Amelana gasped in shock. "How can you say such a thing?! If we were home, you wouldn't—"

"We are no longer in Forenta, Journeyman." He let his statement sink in before continuing. "Achieving mastery is something you trained for throughout your life." Ash glanced at her, voice bland. "Is it not?" The Forentan woman humphed and spurred her drizzen ahead of her master.

The shrill cry of the drizar cut through the air, and the rest of the animals came to an abrupt stop. The rest of the group grumbled, still not accustomed to the herd mind that overrode human direction. "There is a spring here," Storm called. "We will refill the skins and water the animals before we find a place to make camp."

Emil dropped from his beast's back. "Why not make camp here?" Sitting on a broad, lichen-covered rock encircled by vines, he threw his arms out. "More shade; there's plenty of water. It be a little piece of heaven." Emaris, as silent as Emil was boisterous, simply crossed his thick arms, shaking his head at his friend. "What is it yer people call it? An oasis?" Storm said nothing, the critical expression in her eyes as cutting as a knife.

While everyone eagerly refilled waterskins and watered the drizzen, most of the travelers took the opportunity to relax in the small, rock-littered desert oasis. As the sky lightened with the approaching dawn, many wondered why Storm wouldn't make the call to make camp. However, no one was willing to challenge the Swordanzen woman, either.

Taylin lowered the voluminous hood of her travel-dingy robes, her clear turquoise gaze scanning the milling group. Frowning, she approached Almek, resting a hand on his arm. "Dusvet Almek," she murmured, the concern in her voice drawing Mureln and Ash's attentions as well. "Do the Desanti seem to be behaving...strangely?" The three men followed the healer's gaze to the far edge of the oasis.

The Desanti men were not hounding Storm as they had every waking moment since before the group departed First Home, as had become typical. All three had weapons drawn, eyes scanning the area. "Well, this is the first real oasis we have encountered," Mureln speculated uncertainly. "Perhaps they are just...standing guard?"

"Those two have not taken a turn at watch yet," Almek observed about Radisen and Sumalen, frowning as he, too, looked around for what anomaly caused such uncharacteristic cooperation between the woman and her rival suitors. "I doubt their animosity would change without cause."

"What in th' hells—?!" Emil's exclamation drew everyone's atten-tion. One vine surrounding the rock Emil sat on arrested his attempt to jerk away, encircling his wrist. More 'vines' came to life, lashing around the Sevmanan's body.

"*Sendarli*!" Mureln pulled Taylin behind him instinctively, though they were far enough out of reach. He grabbed Almek by the arm to keep him from going to Emil. "No, Dusvet!"

The old man scowled at Mureln. "I won't stand by and watch the man die, Mureln. He's your friend!"

Mureln shook his head, expression contorted with grief. "There's nothing that can be done, Dusvet. Weapons cannot harm *sendarli*, they are too strong and have too many arms." Almek tried to take another step forward; the bard kept his hold firm. They were shocked as Storm raced by with no weapons in her hands.

Emil's struggles were weakening as the tentacles tightened around his chest and throat. He jerked in surprise when Storm appeared at his side, using her arm to block a dripping white tentacle that was about to lash onto him. As it wrapped around the metal guard on her wrist, everyone heard the hiss of acid. With her free hand, she clawed at the tentacle around Emil's throat. "Emaris! His obsidian knife! Use it!"

The gigantic man did not hesitate to obey the Swordanzen or question how she knew of the object, saving his bewilderment for later. He yanked the pouch off Emil's hip and ripped it open to pull out the ornamental stone blade. Holding the small object awkwardly in his massive hand, he jabbed at the tentacle around his neck. It jerked, oozing greenish blood, and loosened its hold. Though it did not fully release Emil, its other tentacles remained well out of reach.

Ash's expression was hard and unreadable; his eyes locked on Storm, ignoring Amelana as she clung to his arm until her words finally penetrated his consciousness. "Finally, we will be rid of that annoying thief and stupid Desanti bitch." With a grimace, the mage shoved Amelana away from him and strode to the three struggling for Emil's and Storm's lives, remembering Almek's admonishment of his responsibility to protect his fellow students. "Master Ash! What are you doing?" He ignored the alarm in Amelana's voice.

"Get ready," Ash told the three as he rested his hands on the thickest of the tentacles around Emil. Before Storm could utter a sound of protest, the crackle of pure energy danced along the monster. The electrical attack jolted the three humans in contact with the *sendarli*. Emaris recovered first, able to pull Emil free, and staggered back to Taylin, who immediately began healing the blue-faced, barely conscious man. Storm nearly collapsed, but was not yet free. Her face had a sickly bluish-gray cast, her breathing labored.

Ash pressed his lips together, displeased the woman seemed overly sensitive to the energy in the spell. "I can do it again. But it might kill you."

"Do it," Storm rasped. "Rather die quick by a defiler's hand than suffer eternity in a *sendarli* gut."

The mage hesitated a moment before nodding. Closing his hands around the thickest tentacle remaining, he closed his eyes. He focused on directing most of the power away from Storm and towards the *sendarli's* body. The thing uttered a spine-chilling shriek as it suddenly withdrew all of its arms, its convulsions unburying its entire form. The slug-like monstrosity curled in on itself like a dying insect.

Ash's grim, satisfied smile disappeared as Storm staggered back a half step with a choked gurgling noise, falling to one knee. He instinctively caught her before she collapsed. There was no time to dwell on the bewildering physical lurch of his heart at the sight of Storm approaching death. "Taylin!" he called, the healer by Storm's side before Ash finished saying her name.

Taylin squeaked in shock as a sword point appeared between her and Storm. Radisen scowled at the woman. "You will not touch her!"

"She's still alive!" Taylin argued, her surprise giving way to anger at the interruption. "I can save her life!"

Radisen growled. "Swordanzen do not use healers, outlander! We live or die by the will of the Totani and our own strength!"

Emaris charged Radisen like a bull and shoved him away. Taylin wasted no time watching the distraction, putting her hands on Storm's brow and heart. She looked up at Ash in accusation. "Release her from your magic, Forentan!" she ordered coldly.

Ash scowled, less at the lack of respect than at the order itself, the implications perplexing. He put his hand on Storm's bare shoulder. He could sense the energy of his magic coiling within the woman like an evil serpent. The pattern was inexplicably warped, barely recognizable as his own doing. The mage closed his eyes, focusing on untangling the unexpected results of his spell.

The moment Ash cleansed the lingering magical energy, Storm gasped, sitting bolt upright, her eyes wild with confusion. She shoved everyone away from her as she staggered to her feet. The drizar appeared as if he had been summoned, letting her lean on him for support. He curled his head around her to touch his chin to her lower back protectively as he glared balefully at the humans, baring his wickedly long, sharp teeth.

"What the hell just happened?" the bard asked no one in particular as he assisted Taylin to her feet and pulled her close, giving Radisen a dark look. Having spent a great deal of herself to heal Emil, the healer rested her head on Mureln's shoulder with a sigh, leaning into his strength.

Unrepentant, Radisen met glare for glare. "Healers are forbidden to Desanti. Especially to the Swordanzen. We live and die by the will of the Totani and our strength alone. To use healers breeds complacency and weakness and goes against the edicts of the Heart of Desantiva. I honored Swordanzen teachings. You taint them!"

"Finish." Storm wearily dragged herself onto her drizar's back, too tired to do more than lean against his neck. "Must camp soon." Not a single person uttered a word about camping in this oasis again, gathering the scattered waterskins and securing the drizzen.

Terrence approached Ash, expression troubled. "Master Ash, I have never seen...what happened to the Desanti woman? I do not understand."

Ash placed a hand on Terrence's shoulder in silent reassurance. "I don't know, Terrence. It's something I intend to understand before we leave these forsaken lands." Behind him, Amelana glared.

Chapter Twenty-Eight

There was a noticeable shift in how Storm's suitors viewed the Swordanzen woman, and the difference between the Desanti men's behavior towards her became more prominent. It was most obvious when the group stopped to set up camp at the border between the sand wastes and the ravines that lay in the distance. Radisen offered an almost reverent, if grudging, respect. Mutual understanding, acceptance, previously absent, bloomed between them despite exchanging no words.

In contrast, indignant rage all but oozed from every pore of Sumalen. He stalked towards Storm, stopping when Radisen stepped in his path, his bone spear held at the ready. "Enough of this foolishness," Sumalen growled, shoving at Radisen; the smaller warrior stood his ground. "Out of my way! Swordanzen is a man's art. It is time someone took her in hand and reminded her of her place."

Barely recovered from the encounter with the *sendarli*, Storm dismounted and turned with a soul weariness that was painful to witness. "Come, Sumalen. Let us finish this." She gave Radisen an imperceptible nod at the questioning look he gave her over his shoulder.

Sumalen surged forward, shoving Radisen to the side. Storm did not move, waiting for him with her hands at her sides, eyes unfocused. His hand grabbed at emptiness. Before he could do more than blink, Storm drove her knee into his stomach, driving the wind from his lungs, then struck the base of his neck with her elbow. The staggered Sumalen stubbornly kept coming at her. She rewarded him by twisting his arm behind his back. The dull, wet sound of his shoulder separating from its socket was clearly audible before he howled in agony.

The Desanti woman's voice was chill with formality. "I am Githalin Swordanzen. By Swordanzen tradition, I am outside the rules of tribal mating traditions because Swordanzen belong to all tribes and to none." She jerked his arm up harder behind him. "Ignoring the mark of the

Totani I bear, you denied I was Swordanzen out of pride. You wished tribal rituals followed. I have granted you your wish."

Her voice held no pity as she shoved him away, his face hitting the dirt. "I have answered your challenge for mating rights. Your defeat has been witnessed." She shoved him away from herself with a foot to his lower back as he attempted to push himself to his feet. "Remove yourself from my presence, or die by my hand."

"This is not over, woman." Wheezing, half bent over, Sumalen glowered at Storm even as he left, the rest of the travelers coming closer to the Swordanzen. The drizar herded his drizzen alone over to the man. Sumalen shied away from the fang-bared drizar.

Storm remained unmoved by Sumalen's threat, waiting until the man vanished from view over the dunes where they originated. Radisen jumped forward to catch Storm by the elbow, keeping her on her feet. "You must rest," he muttered in broken Swordanzen. "Your injuries—"

"Sumalen was not the only enemy I have in this camp," Storm murmured in return. "I cannot rest while there still may be challenges made to me."

Radisen shook his head. "I may not have been Named, but I never turned my back on Swordanzen honor. You have my promise. I will allow no harm to come to you. Especially not from the defilers." She looked at him sideways in silence, and then eventually nodded. As Storm finally lay on her sleeping mat, Radisen sketched a salute to Almek as he took the watch position near the Desanti woman, guarding the camp only by virtue of the fact he was guarding Storm.

"Well, that was...interesting," Mureln said, breaking the utter silence that had settled on the group. Offering an innocent expression to the shocked ones turned to him, he held up his hands. "What?" Uneasy laughter shed the last of the paralysis, and the remaining travelers settled in to wait for sunset.

SITTING APART IN MEDITATION as usual, Ash's nearly closed eyes rested on the Desanti pair. He had folded his heavy outer robe neatly and placed it next to him, the water skin with Storm's mark resting atop it. So fixated on studying the Desanti pair, the master mage did not notice Amelana until she touched him.

"Master Ash," Amelana crooned in Forentan. "It was so brave how you to save that Sevmanan mercenary. The healer is oddly fond of him." Pressing herself against him, she slid her hand inside his tunic.

Ash pushed Amelana away, regarding her with narrowed eyes. "Restrain yourself."

Affronted, Amelana said petulantly, "What's the matter, Master Ash." Boldly leaning against his back, her hands slid around his waist to his lap. "You always liked it when I—" She stopped when he caught her wrist, forcing it and her away again. Deterred only for a moment, she pulled her hand out of his, slid it around his waist, embracing him from behind. "You are tense. Let me help you relax."

"Not here," Ash stated flatly, aware of Radisen's eyes—unnaturally gold in the sunlight—watching them. As Amelana's hands deftly slipped under his belt, he clenched his teeth, trying to suppress the very reactions she so easily aroused. "It is impro—"

Amelana laughed softly. "Why worry about propriety out here? No one here but the Dusvet is important, and he's sleeping." Nuzzling his neck, she murmured, "It never bothered you before when lowborns could see—"

Unable to restrain any reaction, Ash grabbed Amelana's wrists, all but throwing her to the ground, pinning her wrists above her head. He looked down at her, and any desire he felt died in a wash of disgust. For her and for himself.

Ash growled. "I said. Not. Here. You are a journeyman mage. *My student.*" Releasing her, he stood up. "Prostitutes behave with more self-respect than you. If you continue acting like this, I promise you, Avarian or not, I will ensure you will be marked with disgrace." He gestured away sharply. "Go!"

Amelana pushed herself up, cheeks burning as she pulled her robes shut and scurried over to her sleeping mat. Ash looked over towards the Desanti to see Radisen averting his gaze from the mage. Unaccountably bothered that the Desanti man had witnessed the incident, Ash growled inwardly.

Chapter Twenty-Nine

The wind lamented as it blew across the arid land with biting sand caught in the currents. A bittersweet scent also touched the air, making everyone uneasy. Storm brought her drizar to a halt at the crest of a rise, staring out in the distance.

"Are we there yet?" Terrence wondered aloud as the others came up beside Storm, also stopping. When he caught up, his jaw dropped. "Oh, by the gods..."

"It-it's horrible." Taylin averted her gaze, unable to linger on it, squeezing her eyes shut. Feeling a touch on her arm, she looked up into Mureln's equally pained eyes. She took a deep breath, squaring her shoulders to face what lay ahead.

Though several months had passed since the death of the Vi'disa tribe, the dark shadows of the half-burned pyres and fallen tents lingered under the dust that had blown over them like a mourning shroud. Grimly, Almek angled his drizzen to go down the slope to the site of the massacre, the others following him.

Ash did not follow the Guardian, studying the Swordanzen from the corner of his eye, frowning. She had not blinked since he started watching her stare at the devastation before them. "Swordanzen." He scrutinized the woman, focusing his gaze when she did not respond. "Swordanzen!"

Storm finally blinked, but did not otherwise acknowledge the mage. Neither the pallor nor haunted look left her eyes as the drizar started moving. Ash pressed his lips together, unsure why the Desanti's feelings concerned him more than the horrific devastation of the tribe. Shaking his head in a futile effort to dismiss his emotions, he followed the drizar into the field of death.

Nothing had disturbed the dead. The horror was so severe that neither scavengers nor insects dared trespass. Blackened bodies had been laid out, their arms crossed. The full range of the deceaseds' ages amplified the horror. "Oh, gods," Taylin whispered, clapping her hands over her mouth as she saw the infants all clustered together. Mureln put his hand on the healer's shoulder, his own jaw muscles jumping with tension.

"There was not enough fuel to burn them all properly. Their drizzen had perished or fled. I do not know." Storm's voice was so empty of any emotion no one could bear to look at her. She pointed to the single body, shriveled from weeks in the sun, untouched by fire. "The source of the taint is there."

"You did not burn the body," Almek stated without criticism, studying the corpse before looking back to the Swordanzen woman.

Storm's voice was distant. "To burn the body is to set the soul free. Too many lost their lives. I would not permit it freedom." She closed her eyes. "I could do nothing else. It was unlike any *dinnais* I had encountered before. Someone had to tell the other tribes of their loss. Warn them to avoid this place in their wanderings."

Almek frowned, nodding once before approaching the corpse. He raised his hand. The body twitched, and an unearthly shriek split the air, unsettling the drizzen. The desiccated body moved as if alive. Soon though, the body collapsed into a pile of dusty bones and a ghostly shadow separated itself from the body, trapped within the Guardian's power. Its eyes—white, glowing points of light—fixed on Almek, widening in surprise.

"Guardian!" The thing hissed as it writhed. "How can a Guardian be here?!"

"How is irrelevant." Terse, Almek shifted his hands, the shadowy thing shrieking in pain. "You will hunt no more, Shifter."

The shadow writhed, begging. "No! Do not destroy Dzee! Dzee can help you!" Almek started closing his hands, the power squeezing the thing. Struggling, the shifter yelled in desperation, "Dzee can tell the Guardian who sent Dzee and others here to hunt!"

The words brought everyone up short, even Almek pausing. "Who?"

"Guardian must promise not to destroy Dzee! Do not destroy! Then Dzee help!"

Storm glared, drawing her paired single-edged blades, stalking towards the thing. "Do not listen to it, Lord Almek! It must be destroyed!" The shadow hissed, trying to flee the approaching woman.

"Hold, Swordanzen!" Almek barked. Storm froze, only the shiver of light on the blades betraying her emotions. He turned towards the creature. "You know I cannot set you free, parasite. You do not belong on this plane."

"Guardian, Dzee was born here. Born when Desantiva green. The one that sent Dzee told Dzee could stay. But Dzee had to feed to have the energy to remain." The thing hung its head in shame. "Dzee did not like hurting anyone. But it was the only way Dzee could stay. To go home."

Almek considered for several long moments, and then lowered his hands. Joyfully, Dzee hissed, then arrowed for Terrence. Before anyone could react, the entity's shadow entered the young Forentan man through his mouth.

Terrence gasped and then clutched his throat, falling to his knees with wide eyes. Storm growled, raising her swords to behead the Forentan apprentice. "No!" Ash grabbed her arm as simultaneously Almek yelled, "Hold!"

Terrence panted as his struggle ended, and he looked up, his pale blue eyes turned dark black. "Guardian freed Dzee. Dzee will help Guardian. The boy is strong. He has a pure heart. And he has strong energy. Plenty enough for Dzee to stay and harm no more. Dzee..." Shaking his head, Dzee-Terrence's words became less broken. "I...will not hurt the boy. I promise."

Dzee-Terrence looked at Ash. "I only want to go home." In the hollow of Terrence's throat, a faceted gem had formed, with a soft glow in its center. The young mage touched the smoky jewel. "He says he created this so I may sleep. I have...very much wanted to rest. Not to have to...kill. I have been gone...for so very long."

Dzee-Terrence looked at the Swordanzen woman. "I thank you, Warrior, for holding your strike. You allow me a chance at redemption." Looking weary, Dzee-Terrence's shoulders sagged a little. "Beware, Warrior. The darkborn is coming for you." The young Forentan looked up, his eyes returning to their normal pale blue. "I sleep now. I will not hurt him." The gem at Terrence's throat darkened as his eyes cleared and resumed their pale blue color.

No one moved, uncertain of what to do. Terrence touched his temple, voice rasping. "M-Master Ash. You...you do not need t-to worry. It...Dzee...I don't know how to explain. It is strange. I can...I can sense it there. Like feeling someone standing close behind me."

Ash moved to his apprentice, kneeling by him as he took him by the arm to help him stay upright. "It does not control you?"

Terrence shook his head. "No, Master." He touched the gem at his throat. "It asked me for help so it could stay without feeding as it had before. It told me." Swallowing several times, he closed his eyes, shaking his head. "With somewhere it can stay and rest, it does not need to feed as it had. It really..." Looking up at Storm, Terrence said, "Dzee really is very sorry, Swordanzen. It did not know any other way. It is so desperate to stay. But...It needed..." He looked away shamefully. "It needed life energy and a physical form to anchor itself. Desanti...have little of that energy to spare and no access to it outside themselves."

Storm clenched her swords so tight, her fingers were white with blood loss. Looking at Almek with an expression of utter betrayal, she made an inarticulate guttural noise and turned away. Radisen tried to offer a comforting hand on her shoulder, but she only shoved him out of her way.

She stopped in front of the group of nine bodies, each with a two-edged blade similar to the one that Storm carried driven into the ground at their feet. Throwing her single-edged swords down, Storm fell to her hands and knees in front of the ninth body. Putting both hands around the half-buried sword's hilt, she bowed her head for a moment, and then screamed with such pain and grief, even Amelana paled and looked away.

Radisen bowed his head, a single tear coursing down his cheek. Almek studied Radisen. "You cry?" the Guardian half stated, the question of why behind his words. "She doesn't."

"Desanti do not waste water, not even tears. To shed tears for yourself is a sign of weakness, but for another it is a tribute to their sacrifice and their loss," Radisen said in a gruff voice. "Storm has shed her tears already for her Swordanzen brothers and sisters."

"You cry for the Vi'disa and the lost Swordanzen?" the Guardian prompted.

"No. I cry for her. For your hand in her betrayal of her Swordanzen vows, Guardian." Almek scowled, but fell silent at Radisen's words. "The pain of not being able to avenge the deaths of two tribes and nine brothers and sisters of the blade is a pain I cannot imagine."

Mureln frowned, trading looks with Taylin and the two mercenaries. "...*Two* tribes?"

"Of course. You could not know; you are not one of the people." Radisen wiped the single tear from his cheek. "Storm was the only survivor of her birth tribe and has never found their killer. To protect the people and prevent prolonged suffering, she killed the remaining members of the Vi'disa tribe, including infants. She could not save even one because the touch of the *dinnais* had corrupted them. If they had not perished in the Forge before encountering others, they would have spread the corruption." The Desanti man shook his head. "You cannot understand her pain."

Almek considered Storm for a moment, then looked to Emil and Emaris. "Find somewhere upwind to set up camp. I must consider what to do from here." Eyes looked at the Swordanzen, then quickly away.

Ash hung back as the others followed the two Sevmanan mercenaries, watching Storm. With quiet purpose, he walked over to her and waited. Certain her throat was all but bleeding from the intensity of her agonized screaming, he said, "This nonsense is not serving any purpose, Swordanzen."

Storm swung around with a snarl to glare at Ash. "Go away, treewalker."

"No." The mage spoke without inflection. "This distraction is not serving Master Almek. Stop it."

Storm's eyes dilated in surprise, and then turned nearly black in fury as she lurched to her feet, her knife blade against his throat. "I should kill you, defiler," she hissed, her words pitched for his ears alone.

"But you won't." Ash remained impassive in the face of her maddened rage. "You won't because you gave Blood Oath to the Dusvet Guardian. You knew," he continued, ignoring the bite of cold metal against his throat as the blade pressed closer. "You knew the oath would be needed to control your impulses."

"What do you know of my oath, treewalker? You spit on all things Desanti."

The mage met her gaze without flinching. "Because I did the same. I swore my life to Master Almek, and he uses my oath against me, just as he had used it against you." His words penetrated the rage, and he felt her falter with uncertainty. He waited. Finally, she lowered the blade and closed her eyes, turning away. "Can you go on?"

"I must. I have no choice." Her voice was so raw, Ash winced hearing it. She returned the knife to its sheath, retrieved her paired single-edged blades, and walked towards the camp.

THE OTHERS HAD SECURED the shelter and finished caring for the animals as the sun had reached halfway to its zenith. Tired from the long emotional day, no one noticed the raiders until it was too late.

The raiders quickly subdued the outlanders with odd precision, striking the Forenten and Guardian in the head, grabbing or beating the others into submission before they could react.

Except for the Swordanzen. Storm reacted with preternatural speed, dispatching three of the raiders before the largest of them got her attention. Her eyes went wide. "Sumalen!"

The man smiled, licking his lips as he looked her over. "I told you it was not over. Now, you are mine and will learn who your true master is!"

"No one owns me." She bared her teeth in a feral snarl. "I will see you dead first." Her advance halted as a raider dragged Almek over, blood in his white hair, wobbling on his feet in disorientation.

"Oh, I think I *do* own you, because I own *him*." Sumalen purred as he walked around and stood close behind her, reaching around to cup her chin in his massive hand. "I had been hunting for you for a long time, my lovely desert flower. I was not sure until now it was you." He licked her ear. "I could sense your strength even as a child, but after I killed your tribe, you still managed to hide yourself from me."

Her eyes went wide, clenching her swords tighter, but remaining frozen as she stared at Almek. As if she needed to see him to remember her oath. "Now put your swords away, my desert flower. You will breed me an army, and then we will finish where those Forentan bastards failed." Fighting instinct, Storm obeyed, the blades returned to their sheaths. "With the seed of this body planted in yours, my brothers and sisters will be unstoppable!"

Mureln looked up sharply at those words and whispered in horror. "Darkborn!" He looked over at Ash, hearing the mage groan. "Come on, Andar. Wake up!" he hissed.

Sumalen laughed at the bard as the raiders dragged the subdued and tied prisoners to a place outside of the shelter, tossing them there like sacks. "So much for the power of Fortress and the outlands. I will take pleasure in making your deaths a long, long time in coming."

Grabbing Storm by the arm, Sumalen dragged her to the pavilion. The sound of the woman being struck hard enough to be thrown to the ground panicked the others.

"He's going to kill her!" Taylin whispered, horrified.

"To the hells with the Desanti bitch," Amelana exclaimed. "They're going to kill us!" One raider rewarded Amelana's panic by cuffing the woman in the head and coldly snarling, "Shut up, bitch. I'll have you and the Sevmanan woman after the master is done with you both."

"Storm," Ash whispered desperately when she fell, their shoulders touching briefly through the heavy canvas. He tried to focus, but his head swam from the blow to his head. He struggled against the bindings on his wrists when he heard Sumalen throw her to the ground again, and the memory of his co-mingled vision of Storm with Dessa's rape roused unreasoning panic. "No! Storm!" he choked.

"Easy, Mage." Emil put a hand on the mage's shoulder. Blood oozed from the mercenary's wrists in his efforts to free himself. He kept his voice pitched low as he kept the oblivious guards in the corner of his eye. "I'll cut ye loose, but don't let on too soon we're free or those bastards'll kill us all now. Storm's tough. She'll be fine." Carefully, the mercenary watched the raiders as he sawed at the deceptively thin ropes. "What in th' hells are these made from?" he grumbled.

The sounds inside the shelter changed subtly, and a gurgling sound followed by a heavy thump spoke of death. They all looked up to see Storm standing at the entrance, with an unholy look in one eye, the other swollen mostly shut. Blood smeared her arms, fingers curled like claws. She looked at the pulsing lump of flesh in her hand—a human heart—then flung it away.

With purpose, she pulled the twin single-edged blades Sumalen had been too arrogant to take from her. She spoke a few words in the Swordanzen tongue. Radisen reacted with shock. He argued, then words failed him when he met her eye. He lowered his gaze and nodded. His subdued acquiescence satisfied her.

She turned her gaze to the raiders. A surreal, unsettling metamorphosis washed over the woman—cuts closed, swelling subsided, bruises faded. Suddenly, she moved as if she were fully rested and uninjured, advancing on the raiders who were rooting through the supplies. Five fell before the raiders could mobilize.

The thunder of a stampede drew the attention of the prisoners and distracted the raiders as both the travelers' and raiders' drizzen swarmed the encampment, led by the drizar. "Get the others on the drizzen, bard." Radisen grabbed his own sword and bodily blocked one raider trying to strike a final blow on the Guardian. With a roaring battle cry not unlike Storm's, he fought with the same moves as the Githalin Swordanzen, if not as swift or precise. Emaris and Emil joined him, the three men giving the others time to mount and flee.

"What about Storm?" Emil asked as the last of Almek's group fled. The raiders, diminished by a third already, had already dismissed the prisoners, determined to take down the Swordanzen.

"Just go." Radisen grabbed the reins of his own drizzen, looking over his shoulder at Storm, her drizar fighting at her side, stomping and goring with impunity. "Go! Lord Almek needs us more than she does!" The two mercenaries spurred their animals into a dead run. The Desanti man hung back to make sure none of the raiders followed, watching Storm's deadly dance. "Farewell, Storm il'Thandar," he murmured sadly before turning away.

RADISEN FINALLY CAUGHT UP to the rest of the group, the new and old drizzen milling nervously nearby the half shelter of tall rocks. "Where is Storm?" Almek asked, waving Taylin away irritably from healing the gash on his temple.

The Desanti man was grim. "If she is not dead yet, she will be soon." The others reacted in alarm.

"You *abandoned* her?" Mureln asked incredulously.

Radisen snarled at Mureln. "I had no choice! She demanded it. She dances the Final Dance. Once begun, it will only end with her death. I will not dishonor her sacrifice by dying myself." He closed his eyes in grief. "Before she began, she told me to take her place with you, Lord Almek."

Ash just blinked at Radisen as if not comprehending his words, a raw sense of fear in the pit of his stomach. "Master Almek charged me with protecting his students." Ash kicked his mount hard. The drizzen shrilled as it lunged into a dead run back to the Vi'disa deathlands.

"Mage! Stop!" Radisen called desperately. "Come back! Do not dishonor her sacrifice with your death!"

ASH WHISPERED WORDS OF magic to force his mount to keep going despite its exhaustion. Finally, he could sense its heart burst as it stumbled and fell. The mage tumbled off with the practice of years of horse riding, rolling to his feet. Disoriented, he searched for Storm, and when he finally located her, he could not help but stare.

Bleeding from dozens of cuts, Storm moved with the same fluidity as during her occasional solitary practices. The desperate raiders had long since abandoned their arrogant superiority about a woman's ability to fight, desperate to survive. The drizar kept several penned in. Knowing that there would be no escape from the Swordanzen unless she was dead kept the men from fleeing into the desert. Fighting was their only chance to survive.

But even when they got past the deadly flashing blades that cut the air with an eerie hum, they could not break the pattern of Storm's dance. Strikes that should have felled her or at least made her falter closed to thin lines. Shrieking in defiance, the drizar stomped those raiders that twitched even a little after they fell.

Shaking off his momentary paralysis, Ash ran to Storm. He froze as the red and silver blade arced towards his throat, shifting to slide by, leaving him unhurt. She spun away from him. The mage pivoted, standing back to back with her.

He cast a spell that blasted a hole in one of the attacker's chests, giving the others pause before advancing on either of them.

"Fool." Her trade common was thick with her Desanti accent. "Almek needs you. You must live!"

"So must you," Ash returned sharply. Focusing through the pain in his head, he extended his power into the ground itself. Rock came alive, fingers of granite jutting up, closing around the remaining raiders, and crushed them to death.

The abrupt silence was deafening. Recovering from a moment of paralysis, Ash turned to Storm, intending to bind her wounds, abnormally shallow given how they were made. "Put your swords down. It's over."

Storm's copper complexion had turned a sickly gray. She stared wide-eyed at the display of the mage's power. "I-I never knew...how...powerful..." Without warning, the swords fell from her hands with a clatter as convulsions seized the Swordanzen woman, her eyes rolling back in her head.

Ash caught her reflexively, eyes wide in shock when it felt as though iron bands squeezed his heart. He eased her to the ground, cradling her head in his lap to keep her from cracking her skull on the unforgiving ground as she thrashed uncontrollably. "Storm! Storm, it's over! Storm!" He started raising his hand to attack a missed raider at the sound of thundering drizzen feet and saw it was Radisen. Dismissing the Desanti man, Ash turned his attention back to the dying woman. "Storm!" he called helplessly.

Radisen slid off his drizzen and knelt on one knee by the pair. He placed a hand on Storm's brow, the convulsions weakening as she did. "There is nothing to be done." The Desanti begged the mage, "Do not let her die in shame." He offered his own knife to the Forentan. "Make it quick!"

"No!" Laying his hand along her cheek, Ash said intensely, "I will not lose you, too! Not like Dessa."

The power Ash called on glowed with a painful blue-white intensity, his voice a continuous rasping murmur, willing Storm to live. Radisen watched in awe at a battle more intense than the one just ended, unable to look away.

It was impossible to tell how much time had passed, but finally the convulsions eased and stopped. The mage sagged forward weakly. Radisen put an uncertain hand on the Forentan's shoulder, helping him sit up. Ash was sickly white, panting as he finally opened his eyes, looking down at Storm.

The Desanti man inhaled sharply as he felt Storm's pulse at her throat. "She lives!" Radisen whispered in deep reverence. "You saved a Swordanzen from the Final Dance!" Lowering his eyes, his respect was untarnished. "Lord Ash, you have performed a miracle!" He reached for bandages to start binding Storm's wounds.

Ash barely heard Radisen's words, eyes only for Storm as he put a shaking hand along her cheek. He watched as the injuries that had been suppressed blossomed like grotesque flowers. "I heard stories," he whispered to himself. "Of mages who pushed themselves so far, they died from the effort." Swallowing against the lump in his throat as he watched Storm's eye swell shut again. "I thought it was a sign of weakness. Until now." Shaking his head, he stated, "Do not praise me, Radisen." Ash's whispery voice was heavy with shame. "She...she may yet die."

"But she may live," the dark-skinned man countered, taking Storm in his arms and helping Ash to stand. "Take my drizzen, Lord Ash. She will bear you willingly." The Forentan man could only nod, dragging himself onto the skittish beast's back.

Fighting to remain conscious, Ash looked over as the drizar fell in beside Radisen as he carried Storm's inert form while walking between the animals. "Why don't you ride Storm's drizar?"

"A Swordanzen's drizzen is a lifelong companion, and none are tamed. The ties that bind them to each other are soul to soul. Without her conscious permission, I'd end up like him." They walked past a dead man, his entrails spread out in a grotesque fan.

Ash nodded, focusing on just keeping his seat on the scaly beast. "I see." He closed his eyes against the feel of the Swordanzen's wounded, agonized spirit he had entrapped, raging like a wild animal throwing itself against the bars of its cage.

Chapter Thirty

The rest of the travelers took shelter in a shallow, cave-like depression in the large spur of windblown rock. The sun had sunk below the horizon by the time the three finally caught up with them. Emaris and Emil ran to the Desanti man, who was ready to collapse, having walked the entire way on foot. Emaris took Storm while Emil lent the Desanti his shoulder.

Taylin went to Storm immediately. She placed her hands on the woman's forehead, then gasped, stumbling back and looking at Ash in horror. "What have you done?" The mage could only look away in shame, too exhausted to conceal his emotions.

Everyone reacted in surprise as Radisen lurched towards Ash in his defense. Emil had to move quickly to get his shoulder back under the Desanti man as he staggered between the healer and mage. "Lord Ash saved a Swordanzen from the Final Dance. No Swordanzen has ever survived the Final Dance. You should honor him, not revile him!"

Mureln looked sharply at Ash when he heard the mage whisper harshly, "There is no honor in what I have done."

Before the bard could go to Ash, Amelana appeared at his side, fawning and fretting over him. Terrence was no less worried about his master, but his quiet strength was obviously more welcome than Amelana's hysteria, the master mage leaning on his apprentice as he brushed Amelana away.

Almek knelt by Storm and touched her brow; he grimaced. "Taylin, do what you can for her body. Anything else..." He shook his head. "Only time will tell." He looked to the bard. "Watch over them, Mureln. I will return with the others to cleanse the place and collect what supplies we can. Without our Swordanzen," Almek looked to Radisen and said firmly, "either of our Swordanzen, we won't survive without supplies."

"Lord Almek." On the verge of collapsing from exhaustion, Radisen was torn between honor and shame. "I am...not Swordanzen. The Totani never granted me my Name." He confessed, "I did not pass my final trial."

"In my eyes, you reflect the strength and honor of a true Warrior. Rest now, Radisen. We will need you." Grim, humbled, the Desanti man lowered his eyes and nodded once.

Terrence removed his outer robe and folded it, offering it to Radisen. The Desanti and Forentan looked at each other for several moments before Radisen nodded once, accepting the offered robe, and lay with the folded garment under his head.

"I am not leaving Ash!" Amelana stubbornly knelt by the mage, who sat holding his head that ached from more than physical injury or exhaustion. "He needs me!"

Almek glared at the girl. "You can serve your master more by assisting me than hovering over him here. He needs rest, and I need your mage skills to ensure those who attacked us are properly taken care of." Amelana frowned thoughtfully as she got to her feet. Almek put a hand on her elbow, steering her away. "We will not be long in returning," he assured her.

Terrence rolled his eyes as he fell in with Emil and Emaris, the two mercenaries putting a hand on the young Forentan's back.

"Ye sure that thing ain't hurtin' ye, lad?" Emil worriedly eyed the crystal at the apprentice's throat as he held Terrence's drizzen for him.

The young man nodded. "Dzee is keeping its promise and sleeping." He admitted, "It does feel like it sleeps with one eye open, so to speak. It lets me know things it thinks I need to know." He sighed as he looked around the desolate landscape, putting a comforting hand on the jewel at his throat.

AFTER ALMEK AND HALF the group departed, Mureln sat on a low rock around the small fire pit. He played his mandolin quietly while Taylin worked on Storm, Radisen, and Ash. The music first aided in giving her strength to finish her work, then soothed her when she finished. After she fell into a sound sleep, Mureln looked over at Ash as the mage pushed himself to his feet and staggered over to sit by Storm. He rested his hand on her bare, tattooed shoulder, propping the other on his raised knee. He rested his head on his forearm, but it was obvious he was not asleep.

"You should rest, too," Mureln told Ash.

"I don't deserve rest." Ash's agonized voice broke with the turmoil of emotion. "I've committed an unforgivable atrocity." Closing his eyes, he looked away in shame. "In one act, I became the exact man I had hated my entire life. The man I swore I would never become. I used my power to take another human's free will away from her."

Mureln frowned, studying Ash. "Atrocity? You saved a life from being carelessly thrown aside."

"It was not careless," Ash murmured with his head still bowed. "I realized that only after I bound her soul. She made the decision with deliberate purpose. It was her means to fulfill her oath to Master Almek, to protect his students, and to avenge the murder of her birth tribe." He raised his eyes to regard the bard, so filled with despair, Mureln was taken aback. "To finally be able to rest, free of the pain of loss, of failure, of being alone. And I stole that decision from her. Forced her to continue suffering."

The bard studied the mage, frowning. "She is fighting you," he stated as he suddenly understood. "She wants to die that much?"

"She does. But...I can't let her go," Ash admitted. "I don't know why. She is just a Desanti. But I can't release her. I won't let her go. She must live. She must!" Mureln was shocked, never having seen such an open intensity of emotion in the Forentan mage about anyone or anything. That a Desanti cracked the wall of Ash's rigid front of impassivity amazed the bard. "But how can I ask her to live? I know her pain. I have lived with it for so long, believing no others could possibly know it. But she knows. She has lived it, too. How could I ask her to continue to bear the suffering she had quietly endured for so long? The suffering I dismissed in the name of serving Almek?"

"The same way you ask it of yourself, Illaini Magus." Mureln's simple statement drew Ash's attention. "You dismissed her suffering because you could imagine no one knowing the pain that you do." He looked towards Storm, waving a hand towards her. "Now you burden yourself not only with your own suffering, but with hers as well." Putting a hand on Ash's shoulder, Mureln said intently, "You tied her to you to hold her here. She can hear only you right now. You are the only one who can ease some of her pain, and your own, by sharing it. You are not alone, and neither is she. Show her this."

Ash closed his eyes after staring at Mureln for a time, sighing heavily, nodding. As the bard respectfully put himself at a distance to give the two some shred of privacy, the mage regarded the unconscious woman, brushing her cheek with the back of his fingers.

"Storm," he said for her ears alone. Words crowded themselves in his mind—long-winded prose, threats, cajoling—but they all rang hollow and meaningless. "I am...sorry I must ask you to delay the rest you so very much deserve. But know..."

He swallowed hard. "Know that your family's murderer is dead. And the other deaths...they will not be in vain. They led to discovering...there is a greater danger to all our peoples. You are needed, Swordanzen. By your oaths to Lord Almek and to your own people, you need to live."

Without warning, blinding pain shot through the mage's mind. He felt as if someone had stabbed him in the head with a knife as the tie between him and Storm shattered. He clutched his head, gritting his teeth as he struggled to find her before she slipped away forever. A familiar pressure on his wrist, not as crushing as he remembered, drew his attention. As his vision cleared, he found himself looking into Storm's eyes.

Her eyes, so filled with grief, fury, shame, and emotions he could not name, made Ash feel ill. "I cannot forgive you." He could almost feel how tender her recently healed throat was through her voice. Not expecting gratitude or forgiveness, her following words shook him even more. "But I understand why."

MURELN LOOKED UP WHEN the drizar called to the approaching drizzen as Almek and the others returned. He sighed and pushed himself to his feet, moving to intercept them before they reached where the others slept. When Amelana's expression changed, he grimaced and braced himself.

"Why is that *creature* next to Master Ash?!" Amelana's shrill indignation startled Radisen and Taylin awake. Thankfully, Storm and Ash were far too exhausted to rouse. Amelana slid off her drizzen, ready to run over to her master. Mureln blocked the outraged woman's advance.

"Ash needs to recover his strength, Journeyman Amelana," the bard stated in icy tones, arms crossed. "If you wish to question where *he* chose to sleep, be my guest and go wake him. I am sure he will be so *very* pleased to have his decisions questioned by you."

The woman froze, torn between going to her master and staying away. Ultimately, she chose the latter, but Mureln noticed her hateful look.

The bard jumped when Emil slapped a hand on his shoulder. "Yer lucky ye still have yer nads! Swear that'n makes 'em shrivel." He sighed dramatically. "I don't even look at th' healer no more having been around that Forentan ice queen."

"The healer is grateful," Taylin said dryly, rubbing her eyes as she joined the two men. Emil smiled winningly at her and bowed, laughing quietly at Mureln's elbow in his ribs. She looked up into Mureln's eyes. "How long was I asleep?"

Mureln smiled gently, reaching up to tuck a tendril of hair back behind Taylin's ear. "It will be morning soon. Are you rested?"

"Mostly. I would have preferred not to have been startled out of a sound sleep by a shrieking banshee." She looked down shyly at his gentle gesture. "I am glad you finally convinced Ash to sleep."

"I didn't. She did." He nodded towards Storm. He shook his head, stopping Taylin's question. "It is...complicated." He took Taylin's hand, kissing her knuckles lightly, retaining it in his as he drew her towards Almek. "I have only the energy to stay awake a little longer."

Almek had sat by the small fire, holding his hands towards the meager heat it produced. He glanced up at Mureln and Taylin as they joined him. "I trust it went well?" Mureln asked simply.

"Our mage and Swordanzen were very thorough. It doesn't appear there was anyone left who might follow us. And Sumalen's been handled," the Guardian stated in such a flat tone, the pair shuddered. "Amelana took particular pleasure with the raiders after I pointed out they were the ones who hurt her, though her efforts were...lackluster. I had Terrence finish burning the bodies of the dead Vi'disa and Swordanzen. He, at least, reflects proper training."

The pride at Almek's praise did nothing to dampen the quiet awe in Terrence's voice. "The ground absorbed their swords and knives when fire fully consumed their bodies." Mureln and Taylin blinked in surprise.

Radisen did not look up from where he sat nearby, his expression drawn. "Desanti sacred blades are gifts from the Totani themselves. They are divinely wrought." He drew his knife and sighed. "We call them Naming Blades. When a Desanti earns his adult name, he receives a knife. When he earns his Swordanzen name, he receives the sword. When we die, they return to the earth we are all born from."

Mureln mused. "I noticed all adult Desanti wore a knife. I never really thought about why they were so significant to your people, though." He considered the Desanti man. "You have not earned your Swordanzen name." Radisen shook his head, closing his eyes. "Do Swordanzen go by their...adult names once they are Named?"

"If they wish it. Most do not. To be accepted by the Totani to bear the Swordanzen Blade is an honor and a responsibility." Anticipating the question, Radisen stated, "No one knows Storm's adult name."

"What?" Taylin blinked. "No one? Why not?"

Radisen raised his eyes to regard Taylin, the Sevmanan healer shuddering at the look in their depths. "She was a Named Swordanzen before she was fully an adult."

Almek coughed, changing the subject as he looked to Mureln. "I sense our Swordanzen is whole again. All went well after we left?"

Mureln pressed his lips together. "Not...exactly. Whatever Ash had done to keep her alive..." Taylin closed her eyes, hugging herself. The bard put a comforting arm around her. "It had affected them both. He had to hold her to life until she willingly stayed." He looked over his shoulder at the sleeping pair. "I've never seen souls so burdened as theirs, Almek. It doesn't seem right."

"Sacrifices were made to reach their skill level as fast as they had. By any standard, they are young for their demonstrated abilities." Almek closed his eyes wearily. "Radisen, if you are able, I'd like you to take the next watch." The Desanti man nodded, pushing himself to his feet. "Let those two rest for as long as they allow themselves. Mureln, you too. You've done enough without respite."

"But where are we going to go from here?" Taylin asked. "There is nothing..."

"Storm knows where we need to go. When she is ready, she will guide us." Almek smiled wanly. "I have every faith in her."

Chapter Thirty-One

IN THE DAYS THAT had passed since the desert raiders' attack, Storm had remained silent and withdrawn into herself. Radisen took on Storm's duties with deep reverence, along with a personal responsibility for protecting her. Though his eyes held deep worry and sadness for the woman, he also had the deepest faith in her to recover. The others were doubtful she had the capacity for speech any longer.

"Almek, we cannot wait much longer," Mureln said to the Guardian. "We are running out of supplies, none of us are at our best, and we can't ask Radisen to shoulder more responsibility than he already bears. I know you want to give Storm more time, but there's none left to spare."

The Guardian sighed, closing his eyes. "I know, Mureln. But we cannot leave Desantiva yet. We still must help Dzee. Storm is the only one who knows where it needs to be."

Radisen was silent as the Guardian discussed the situation with his students, eyes lowered. Knowing that while they included him because he held Storm's place, he felt sorely lacking. "Storm is still here." He looked up at Almek, feeling the eyes of the others on him. "She can guide us through the drizar."

Ash narrowed his eyes, studying the Desanti man. "You are serious."

"Yes, Lord Ash, very serious." Radisen glanced between the others, then towards Storm, then returned his attention to them. "If she knows where to go, she will get us there through her tie to the drizar. The bond they share is one of legends."

Taylin pursed her lips. "It sounds insane, to be honest. But we can't stay here. And if nothing else, I'm sure the beast would at least guide us to the nearest source of water, which we desperately need to replenish soon."

"I suppose it explains where the Desanti wandering nature comes from," Ash said without inflection, looking towards Storm. "The need to find...resources." He sighed, closing his eyes.

"Regardless, I think it is worth trying." Almek turned to the Desanti man. "Radisen...do you think any of the raiders' drizzen that followed the drizar back would be suitable to replace Ash's mount?"

He rose, shaking his head while observing the milling animals. "Lord Ash can use my drizzen. She will behave. Those beasts are ill-trained. Too dangerous for a novice handler. I will use one of them."

"It will be high sun soon. A few hours of heat will be harsh, but I think it's best to get moving." The others nodded in agreement with Almek's decision and headed back to the main camp to pack up.

As soon as she settled onto the drizar, he snorted and strode unerringly south, the other animals falling in line. It gave the rest of the group hope they would at least find somewhere far more hospitable than being so close to the Vi'disa lands.

After they were underway, the Desanti man regarded the silent woman's profile. "Storm," Radisen said in the Swordanzen tongue after several hours. "The others are worried about you. So am I." After a longer silence, he sighed. "I wish I knew what was bothering you."

She was silent for so long, Radisen expected she would remain oblivious to anyone's presence. He masked his shock when she answered. "I gave my Blood Oath to the man who allows the Vi'disa killer to live." Storm's voice was rough with disuse, her eyes fixed forward. "It lives among us in the only defiler I could have tolerated. What do you think is bothering me?"

Radisen's brow creased as he contemplated a response. "Trust in Lord Almek. His wisdom spans more years than I can count. He said—"

"I know what he said," Storm growled. "It is all I can do to hold my rage back, to hold on to my honor." She clenched her teeth in frustration. "What little honor remains from breaking the pattern of the Final Dance. Having a healer mend my wounds instead of proving myself strong enough myself."

The Desanti man frowned. "There was no honor lost. Lord Ash is as bound to Lord Almek as you. As is the healer. They consider you one of them. Having spent time with these outlanders, I see they do not regard death as we do. There is little difference between dying well and dying poorly in their eyes. To them, death is abominable. You did not break the pattern. Healer Taylin and Lord Ash had. *He* nearly died to save you."

"Why?" Storm asked helplessly. "Lord Almek needs him more than me. I've seen Forentan power. It is so much more than ours, Radisen. So very much more."

From behind them, Terrence spoke clearly to the Desanti pair. What shocked them was the language the Forentan apprentice mage spoke—he spoke flawless Swordanzen. "Honored Warrior, how may I earn your trust to quell your fury?"

Storm wheeled the drizar around, the beast snorting as he bucked, slashing at the air with his horns in response to his mistress. "You speak the holy tongue?! How is this possible?"

Dzee-Terrence lowered his dark eyes subserviently. "Honored Warrior, I speak the holy tongue because I was one of the Great Ones in the Before Time."

Radisen stared, blinking in disbelief. "You were Totani?!"

"Totani?" Storm whispered, stricken. "I fought...Totani? Almost...I almost...killed..." She clenched her fists, wracked with a turmoil of emotions she could barely restrain.

Terrence started looking drawn, as he would whenever Dzee became agitated. "Yes, I am Totani! Honored one," Dzee-Terrence implored. "I must return to our Lord Father. But I recognize nothing here. It has been so very long. You know how to find the way. Please, I need your help." As Dzee receded into sleep, it whispered, "Please...He needs me. I must return to Him."

Ash put a hand on Terrence's shoulder as the young man sagged, clinging to his mount, looking between him and the Desanti. "What is going on?"

Mureln studied the two desert warriors. Radisen looked to Storm for an explanation, shocked and worried. The bard could find no words to describe how unsettled Storm looked. Mureln moved his drizzen between Almek and the Desanti woman, blocking the Guardian from going to her. "Look at her eyes, Almek," the bard said quietly as the old man opened his mouth to chide him. "She's in a dangerous mood." Almek nodded reluctantly.

Terrence pushed himself up, looking at Storm with worry. "She-she is in shock. I-I don't know what Dzee said to her—"

"You lie," Amelana accused. "You know exactly what was said. You protect that *thing* you picked up." Flushing at Amelana's accusation, the young man did not cower at her sharp words as he once might have. He squared his shoulders, blue eyes cold and defiant.

"Silence, Journeyman!" Ash snapped at the Forentan woman, his eyes never leaving Storm. He waved Radisen away, the tall man nodding and backing his mount a short distance. As Ash neared, Storm lashed out, a flash of silver between them. The mage did not defend himself, grimacing as he held a hand over his bleeding chest. Her blade cut through his clothing and skin as easily as if through water. "Get out of here," he ordered the others. At their hesitation, he shouted, "Out of sight! Now!" They waited only a heartbeat longer before riding ahead in the pass and around the bend.

Ash dismounted, the Swordanzen mirroring his motions and dropping lightly to the ground. Suppressing the urge to unleash his power on her, he allowed her to find release through her attack on him. She was fast, the mage unable to keep up with a speed born of the madness that gripped her. Yet none of her blows did more than make shallow cuts. All he could do was force the slices in his garments to knit shut.

When it reached the point that he felt it was enough, he attempted to stop her. Only through sheer luck he caught her by the wrist. He held tight, restraining her. She struggled, her rage draining into tremors until she fell to her knees, her body trembling with quiet, tearless sobbing. He knelt with her, cupping her chin in his hand, gently turning her face upwards. "Storm," he murmured.

"You-you let me cut you," she whispered. "Why?"

"You were distressed. I didn't know another way to share your burden than to let you lash out." Looking into her eyes, he brushed the escaped tendrils of hair out of her face. "So young...you are so young to bear all of this alone."

Storm frowned, pushing his hand away. "Do not pity me, treewalker! I am not young. I have seen twenty summers!"

Ash frowned at that. "Only...twenty? I thought...I thought you were older than that."

"Your defiler ancestors failed to destroy us in the Great War. But we have paid the price every generation, watching those around us die." Storm moved to push herself to her feet, then collapsed to her knees again, unable to summon the anger that had fueled her. "So much sooner than you outlanders."

Ash rested a hand on her shoulder. "Why do you try to bear this alone? Master Almek, or the bard—"

"A Swordanzen must be strong. Must prove themselves worthy. Must answer all challenges to prove they are not weak, or die in the attempt. It is tradition."

"Then it is wrong." She looked up at him, bristling. "I followed Master Almek because I wanted to learn more, to be stronger than I already was. To learn...is all I have ever wanted." She was still as stone, only the breeze shifting her hair. "But I did not expect to learn...exactly what my ancestors had truly done to this land. To your people."

"This land of death...it does not please you," Storm stated, as if finally realizing it. "But not because your ancestors failed."

He shook his head, looking down. "No. Because no matter their reasons, nothing could have justified...this." Ash grabbed a handful of coarse sand, letting it spill from his fingers.

Storm put her hand beneath his, catching the sand before releasing it to the earth. "Swordanzen are sworn to protect the balance," she finally said softly, not meeting his eyes. "We pass on the knowledge, language, and traditions to the next generations while we live."

Ash opened his mouth, then shut it again, watching and listening attentively. "Githalin Swordanzen...We are not like other Swordanzen. Other Swordanzen can choose to put down their swords and become Tyluri. Swordanzen trainers. But not the Githalin. It is our duty to protect and to serve the Heart of Desantiva until we die."

Suspecting the answer, Ash asked carefully, "How old were you when you began your training?"

"After my tribe died during my sixth summer."

Ash flinched as so very much about the Swordanzen woman became clear. "Storm." She waited in silence, expression quizzical and wary. After long moments of searching, he finally found the words. "Please. Trust me."

She did not reply immediately, lowering her eyes in thought. "You should have the healer attend to your wounds." She got to her feet, purpose in her movements. Turning away from him, she walked a few paces, her back to him. "I must...meditate on the words spoken here."

Ash reached towards her, then looked at his hand, which was covered in blood. He had not realized how much she had hurt him until he finally let it seep into his consciousness. "You are right," he agreed without inflection. "Don't be too long. We need to find shelter soon." She only nodded, back remaining towards him.

AMELANA KEPT TRYING TO get past Radisen and finally shouted, "How can you leave Master Ash alone with that killer bitch?! Can't you tell he's sick? Letting her attack him?" Radisen was unmoved, scowling at the Forentan woman. Emil and Emaris joined the Desanti man, running interference whenever Amelana tried to go around Radisen and back up the path to where the Illaini Magus and Githalin Swordanzen were.

Almek drew Terrence aside. "Lad, how much do you know of what Dzee knows?"

Guarded silence met the question. "I'm not sure, Master Almek. It's very confusing, you see." Terrence rubbed his temple. "Dzee...its...her...memories are not very clear."

Mureln arched an eyebrow. "Her? Dzee is female?"

Terrence turned bright red under the sunburn on his cheeks. "Well, I am...I mean, she just feels...well. Female. I don't really know." He looked between the bard and the Guardian. "When we met the Knowing One in Forenta, there was a-a feel of age. It was as if I could feel the number of years that the Knowing One had seen. How many Naiya had seen. Dzee is younger than the Knowing One, but she feels...as old as Naiya. Maybe older. Something very wrong had happened to her. That I am very sure of. But she doesn't want to let me know. To protect me. And to hide her shame."

Almek looked surprised and impressed. "It's been many years since I heard someone say something of that nature. Sensing the age of a soul." He frowned a little as he narrowed his gaze at Terrence. "I rarely miss the talent of a Potential."

A faint smile played at the edges of Terrence's mouth. "Honestly, sir, I believe learning from Master Ash plays a role in it. He pushes me to challenge my limits, emphasizing that everyone interacts with magic differently. He urges me to trust my instincts when encountering situations not covered at the Magus Academy. Plus, I wanted to prove I was superior to..." he looked back at the ongoing chaos further up the path. "Ah..."

Taylin said dryly, "That journeyman of his?"

Terrence's grin widened as he nodded. The smile faded a moment later as he turned his gaze back up the trail, worry in his eyes. "You don't think the Swordanzen will kill him...do you?"

"No, she will not kill him." Almek's certainty helped Terrence relax. "I think our Illaini Magus is figuring out how to deal with our Swordanzen's pride and temper."

"Master Ash!" Amelana finally got past the three men to run to the Forentan mage as he rejoined them, her expression more offended than horrified. "What did that whore do to you?!"

Radisen frowned, leaning over to Emil and whispering to him. "Means a woman who has sex fer money." Emaris grabbed Radisen's sword arm, looking askance at Emil. "What? He asked!"

Ash gave Amelana a disdainful look. "Get out of my way, Journeyman. I would prefer not to bleed to death." Taylin went to Ash's other side, shooting a scathing look at the Forentan woman, who flounced off in a huff. Ash let Taylin guide him to the side, forcing himself to relax as the healer began her work.

"Illaini Magus Ash, is *she* all right?" Taylin asked in a low voice.

Ash pressed his lips together in silence for a few moments. "I don't know. I hope so."

When the drizar rejoined the group, everyone looked up. Storm was grim, but no longer lost in her thoughts. She had wound a strip of cloth around her hand; red soaked it. "We need to ride quickly to reach shelter. The rage winds are coming."

Chapter Thirty-Two

THEY HAD RIDDEN WITH relentless determination for the better part of a day, their path leading them towards the imposing cliffs of the mountainous foothills. Behind them, the sky morphed into a canvas of ominous darkness, dominated by looming clouds of dust and sand so vast they seemed to touch the heavens, humbling in their sheer enormity. The eerie roar of the winds, which had started as a gentle whisper, steadily amplified into a menacing crescendo as the formidable wall of sand drew ever closer.

The winds, with alarming swiftness, had intensified, transforming the air into a swirling tempest of sand that lashed out like a thousand tiny, cutting knives. In response to this growing threat, the travelers secured ropes between each of the drizzen, trusting implicitly in the sure-footed drizar and the guiding force of Storm to lead them to safety. They moved with urgency, aware that the blowing sands threatened to scour the very flesh from their bones. With determination, they pulled the cowls of their travel robes tightly down over their faces, a feeble yet necessary defense against the merciless onslaught of the storm.

Abruptly, they felt the wind die, though they could still hear it, howling like a demon. One by one, they cautiously unwrapped their faces to look at their surroundings. The group gazed in astonishment to realize they were in a monstrous cavern that other travelers had sought shelter within before them. The cavern floor was smooth of any stones or pebbles, rocks had been arranged in fire rings, and there were even some piles of dried bones or drizzen dung favored by the Desanti for their fires had been left for future travelers. Towards the back, a deep, spring-fed pool offered respite from the arid land without.

"I have never seen a storm like that in my entire life." Almek shook the sand from his robes. He fixed a look on Storm. "You could tell it was coming?" She shrugged one shoulder.

Radisen smiled as he dropped from his drizzen, setting it loose in the ring of taller rocks that served as a crude corral. "To be Desanti is to be a child of the land. To be Swordanzen is to be one with the land, to be able to sense the rage winds when they come."

Withdrawn, Storm looked towards the cavern's entrance with a concerned expression. But she was half listening to the others talk, her voice muted but carrying clearly in the massive cavern. "The rage winds come from the Heart of Desantiva, when the pain and the grief of the land is awakened."

"How long do they last?" Mureln shrugged at her quizzical expression over his curiosity and implied familiarity with the phenomenon. "It reminds me of some of the extreme storms from Vodanya. There is a terrible beauty about them. Such massive, unstoppable power."

Storm shrugged. "Hours. Days. Legends say the first ones would last months." Walking towards the entrance, she studied the wall of sand and dirt racing past. "This one will take several days to exhaust its energy."

"Days?!" Amelana exclaimed. "We will be stuck here for days? What are we supposed to do for days?!" Various displays of disgust and annoyance rippled through the travelers as the Forentan woman began one of her typical rants.

Ash put his hand on her shoulder, speaking softly. Amelana's eyes rolled back, and she sagged unconscious, her ranting cut short. He caught her, scooping her up in his arms. He looked down at her in annoyance. "You can sleep and be silent if you will not be productive. Terrence! Your help, please." His apprentice nodded, a huge smile all but splitting his face as he pulled Amelana's gear off her drizzen and followed his master to lay the woman's sleeping place out.

"That be a useful trick," Emil observed. "Wonder if'n th' mage can teach it t' me."

"You can't teach old dogs new tricks, my friend," Mureln said cheerfully. He laughed, ducking a rock flung at him. He went over to Taylin and sketched a deep bow to her, making her blush. "My lady, may I assist you?" Shyly, she nodded, both of them reaching for the gear on her drizzen's saddle.

While the others set up camp, Radisen and Storm prowled the depths of the caverns to ensure the group would be secure until the sandstorm passed. By the time the group had finished and settled around a campfire, the Desanti pair returned, carrying several small animals unlucky enough to cross paths with the two warriors.

"I don't get why yer people don't live in places like this 'n," Emil said from his place as he watched over the cook fire.

"The land provides." Most of Storm's attention focused on inspecting her weapons. "But a tribe's needs would strip the land bare in its demand to survive. Moving allows the land to recover so it can provide for the tribe when they return."

Mureln strummed his mandolin, playing an idle tune. "It is much the same reason the Vodani clans are always on the move. If any area is overtaxed, the clans suffer for it if the region dies."

Terrence looked puzzled. "But some Vodani live on land. Does everyone wander? They don't have to, do they?"

Mureln shrugged. "It's in our blood, I suppose. Some few find places to anchor to, like my sister Mia. But most of us...there are always new horizons to explore." He offered the apprentice a smile. "We have done things this way for so long, it has become a part of us." He turned a rakish grin towards Taylin. "Why don't you dance for us, Healer?"

Taylin blushed deepened. "I-I don't think—" Her protests stopped when the bard played a complex refrain, her eyes lighting up. "Oh, that is my favorite dance! How did you know?" The bard grinned knowingly, winking at her as he continued the verse.

"Hey! Swordanzen!" Emil called after Taylin finished a lively dance composed of intricate step patterns. Storm looked up from her weapon maintenance, blinking at the Sevmanan. "You know any dances?"

"Of course. Dances are traditional," Storm replied mildly. "They tell the stories of our ancestors."

Emil and Emaris traded surprised, hopeful looks. "Would ye dance one of them dances we seen at yer First Home?"

Storm looked thoughtful, her expression turning to one of amusement when Radisen leaned over, suggesting several of the more provocative dances. "Show me one of your northern dances. Then perhaps I will. If it amuses me."

Quite agreeable to the exchange, the two men got to their feet, telling Mureln something in Sevmanen. The bard laughed outright at the suggestion and tapped the rhythm on the belly of his mandolin before launching into a fast-paced tune. By the time the drunken jig was done, Terrence and Taylin were laughing helplessly, holding their sides. Even Mureln had trouble keeping his fingers on the strings of his instrument because he laughed so hard. Radisen shook his head, unable to repress a grin. Neither Storm nor Ash smiled, though they seemed entertained.

As the two mercenaries flopped down, panting, Emil pointed out cheerfully, "Yer turn!"

Storm inclined her head in acknowledgment and began removing her many weapon belts, setting them aside ritually. Shedding her robe and other outer clothing, only the one shouldered half top and her loincloth remained. She told Mureln the rhythm to play, and the melody was simply 'sad and wistful.' Taking her twin single-edged blades, she padded barefoot over towards the space apart from the others.

Everyone fell silent, staring at the young Desanti woman. The difference between her and other Desanti women was somberly striking. Nothing about Storm was soft, skin taut over corded muscle, lined with scars both new and old that spoke of a hard, unforgiving life. Each move she made had purpose, sinuous like the stalking of a giant hunting cat.

Mureln jumped when Taylin elbowed him out of his paralysis. He coughed, turning red, and strummed the mandolin. Though the tune was simple, there was a haunting bittersweet quality to it as Storm danced one of the Desanti story dances.

Radisen's voice faltered mid-explanation of the story as Storm's blades cut silver arcs through the cavern's shadows. Her feet barely whispered against the stone floor, each deliberate step telling the tale of a warrior's desperate battle. Her spine arched like a drawn bow when she lunged, muscles coiling beneath scarred skin, then released in a fluid sweep that sent her twin blades singing through the air. Firelight caught the polished metal, transforming each weapon into a ribbon of molten silver and gold that framed her silhouette. Her eyes remained half closed, lost in the ancient rhythm, while sweat beaded along her collarbone and traced shimmering paths down her arms. When she finally stilled, with the last echoes of Mureln's melody hanging in the air, no one dared even breathe.

"I dinna know anyone could move like that..." Emil sighed blissfully. "I think I be in love." Emaris snorted, elbowing his brother hard. "Hey!"

Storm only smiled as she returned to dress and arm herself again. Quietly, while the others traded more songs and dances, she slipped away from the group, disappearing into the depths of the caverns again.

"Hey, where's Storm?" Taylin wondered, frowning a bit.

Radisen dismissed their concerns. "She will return in time. Swordanzen are solitary by nature and necessity." Accepting the explanation, the others returned to exchanging songs. Radisen was the only one to notice the Illaini Magus had disappeared soon after, smiling in satisfaction.

AFTER HAVING GONE DOWN several wrong corridors, Ash finally located Storm in a remote chamber of the catacomb of caverns, meditating on a large, flat rock, hands on her knees, eyes closed. He sat next to her without a word, just watching her in the glow of the small ball of magelight hovering overhead.

Her eyes remained shut, though the tension in her features eased slightly. "Your woman is going to squawk if she discovers you are purposefully seeking me out," Storm stated blandly.

Ash scowled. "She is not 'my woman.' She is only my student."

Opening her eyes, Storm cast a skeptical look at the man. "She would disagree." Ash grunted his opinion. Storm shrugged. "As you wish it."

"Why haven't you paired with Radisen?" Ash asked bluntly, watching her profile. "He seems like a fine warrior. And he certainly seems to care about you."

"I am Githalin Swordanzen."

"So?"

Her lips curved into a smile. "I had heard stories of Northerner's mating habits. Complex rituals of courtship and lifelong vows of love." She smirked. "We have idealistic stories of these things, but my people do not have time for such luxuries."

Ash frowned. "Luxuries?"

Green-gold eyes opened to regard Ash in silence before she spoke. "We Desanti have no time for love as you Northerners talk of it. We must bear as many children as we can, and we need our children to be born strong so they may survive. Thus, we choose our mates by their breeding potential, rarely for love. Parents often die before they see their children grown, so tribes raise all children together."

The mage considered. "You do not have orphans?" he stated more than asked, a vague hint of envy in his voice.

"We do not have a word that has the same meaning as your northern 'orphan.' We *do* have a word for children left without a tribe." She paused. "Cursed."

Ash blinked in surprise, envy fading. "That seems...extreme."

"When no one knows what caused a tribe to die, they can only assume it was a disease that the children may still carry. Or that bad spirits follow them." She looked away with a pained expression. "Cursed children are left to die to keep their scourge from infecting other tribes. It is what I spared the Vi'disa younglings—suffering until they crossed the blade because of predation, exposure, dehydration, or starvation. It is not something any Desanti would choose to do lightly. I would not have done it if there had been any other option for them."

Ash fell silent, studying her again. He frowned as he noted the number of scars, new and old. "You push yourself too hard. You should allow yourself to heal before you—"

"A Swordanzen must answer all challenges when they are made, no matter their condition, mage. That is our way." Storm regarded him. "Swordanzen belong to all tribes and to none. Why have I not paired with Radisen? Would that I could survive all the inevitable challenges and successfully bear a child, my child would be Cursed as I was because I would be dead long before they became an adult. I have no tribe who could claim it. And I told you once before. A Githalin Swordanzen cannot become Tyluri. I will be Githalin until death."

Ash was silent for a time. "Radisen trained as a Swordanzen." She nodded. "Yet he still tried to win you? Knowing this?"

"Githalin Swordanzen are very rare. Sometimes the Totani do not choose one for generations at a time. My people are not aware that it is permanent. Given many Swordanzen never live long enough to choose to put down their swords, it is not something I have bothered sharing with others." She sighed. "My grandfather, Elder Verris, was desperate to restore the tribe through me. Swordanzen rarely live over five summers from their Naming." Before he could ask, she said, "I have survived nearly six summers. My time is limited; why burden another life with my suffering?"

The silence between them lengthened until Storm finally spoke again. "What of you and your wo- your student? She seems as possessive as a harpy vulture over a fresh corpse."

Ash smirked at Storm's analogy and shrugged. "The Edai Tredecima could not force a marriage contract on me when I became an acknowledged master. But they could assign me students. Her family had enough influence to get her assigned to me by preventing my choice of Terrence until I agreed to take her as well. She has been trying to convince me to marry her so her family can claim control of me because I was lowborn."

It was Storm's turn to frown. "Barbaric." Ash could not help but smile at a Desanti calling Forentan customs barbaric. She tilted her head, leaning forward to look at him curiously. "I have never seen you smile before."

The mage considered his reply, and then shrugged. "I should not have intruded on your meditations." Beginning to rise, he paused at her hand resting on his forearm.

"Why?" she asked, eyes intent on him. "Our people are mortal enemies. You say your oath to Almek bound you to protect me. I can understand that. I was willing to die to save the rest of you. And you were willing to die to keep me from dying. But it does not bind you to show me kindness." When he remained silent, face turned away from her, her hand tightened slightly. "Tell me!"

"I don't know why," he confessed. "There's no logical reason that drives me."

"Logic?" Storm shook her head. "There is no logic where the heart is concerned, treewalker." This time, her words were more affectionate than her more familiar spitting of epithets. "And I know you are not heartless."

"What is it your heart tells you, Swordanzen?" he asked to divert attention from himself, discomfited.

Storm took her hand from his arm, resuming her meditative posture. "What my heart tells me is irrelevant. I will not live long enough for it to matter." He opened his mouth to speak. "You should return. Your harpy vulture will wake up soon." Ash grimaced at the thought and left without another word.

CHAPTER THIRTY-THREE

THE WINDSTORM RAGED FOR two days and only seemed to grow stronger. Almek's subdued students went about their lessons or personal training routines. Storm, who stood near the entrance to the cavern, watched the blowing sand deep in thought.

During the morning of the third day, Mureln was making the meal. He studied the Swordanzen after serving the others. He could not remember seeing her eat once since they took shelter, as she often disappeared during mealtimes, so he decided to remedy that and prepared a plate.

He sat next to Storm, offering the food to her. Frowning when she shook her head in refusal, he let his concern show in his soft voice. "Storm, you have to eat." She did not look at him, polishing her two-edged blade in silence. "When was the last time you ate?"

"A sevenday ago," she replied simply.

"Storm!" the bard scolded, drawing eyes to the pair. She narrowed her eyes and dug her fingernails into his leg where the others could not see. "Ow!" he hissed. She released him almost immediately, not intending the strike to be more than momentary. "Damn it, Storm, what was that for?"

"I know what Lord Almek seeks, even if he does not." Storm gazed out at the tempest with a fierce intensity that startled the bard. "I know what I must do, and I have hidden everything since I chose to give my oath to Lord Almek from my Totani Thandar, so only I am at fault. I must break my vows once more and bring outlanders before my people's ancient god, the Heart of Desantiva." She eyed the edge of the blade. "To honor Him, His suffering must be my suffering." She added, "Right or wrong, the laws are absolute. I will be punished."

"Storm," he said in sympathy, worry in his eyes.

"For as long as Desantiva has existed, the Heart of Desantiva has suffered as His children have suffered. I would do anything to ease His pain. Anything. All I can do is share it." She looked up as the ground started shaking, the only one not looking alarmed. "He is fully awake now. It is time."

Mureln rose quickly, putting a hand under her elbow inconspicuously to keep her from stumbling. She gave him a small smile, appreciating both the help and his effort to protect her pride.

"Lord Almek." Storm approached the wall of sand still blowing violently across the cavern entrance. The others looked bewildered and alarmed between the earthquake and Storm's odd behavior. She paused before the archway leading outside and looked back. "My drizar will watch over the others. It is time to leave for the Rumblelands. Home of the Heart of Desantiva."

Turning forward, she cut her palm, then waved her bloody hand in a wide arc. The sand parted like a curtain to a dark tunnel, with a dim red glow lighting the way. An unearthly bellow split the air, the ground shaking in echo. The others hesitated to follow, but when the ground seemed to buck under their feet, they hurried to catch up to her.

A wall of blinding, searing heat assaulted the travelers as they emerged onto the expansive volcanic plains. The air shimmered with the intensity of the heat, distorting the horizon. Red, glowing rivers of molten rock snaked through the dark, craggy landscape, resembling the veins of some colossal shattered glass sculpture. Jagged ridges jutted from the ground, emphasizing the chaotic and violent nature of the land, as if some massive force had ripped it asunder. Storm stood transfixed, her eyes wide and raw, as if they were open wounds exposed to the harshness of this unforgiving terrain.

As Mureln stepped foot onto the coarse, blood red volcanic rock, he faltered a step as a wave of fierce pain threatened to overwhelm him. He closed his eyes as he focused on suppressing the pain once more, much as Almek did. He heard the healer's whimper of pain, and the bard went to her, putting his arms around her to augment the block he'd created for her in First Home.

Radisen staggered, putting his hands to his head and falling to his knees in agony as he choked back a cry of pain. Emil and Emaris went to him, trying to determine what took him down. "What happened, man?" Emil asked. Emaris put his hand on his blade, scanning for a source of attack. Emil looked up at Almek. "We don't be seein' no injuries an' no attackers, Guardian."

Mureln grimaced, his own eyes narrowed. "It's the *Psia Re*." He put his hand on the Desanti man's shoulder for a moment. Radisen sagged at the abrupt relief. "The ancestral pain. All those of Desanti blood—or healer sensitives—feel it. Have ever since the lands sundered during the Great War." He managed a wan smile as Radisen put a grateful hand on Mureln's wrist and lurched to his feet again.

"I have never known it to be so strong." Almek narrowed his eyes as he suppressed the *Psia Re*.

The bard stated solemnly, "Our belief was wrong; the *Psia Re* was not merely an echo from antiquity." He shook his head, grimacing a bit. "It is more than that."

"Well, why isn't it affecting her?" Amelana demanded, pointing at Storm. Swordanzen gave no sign she heard the woman; instead, her gaze wandered far into the horizon, an infinite despondency in the depths of her eyes.

Ash approached Storm, about to touch her shoulder when she spoke. "It does not cripple me because this is where I called home after I became Cursed. It pales in comparison to the loss of my family."

The mage drew his hand back as if burned, looking at the barren landscape in horrified revulsion. "Storm," he began, uncertain what to say.

She looked over her shoulder but met no one's eyes. "Come. Be aware. Here, all can understand the heart's voice." The others looked bewildered as they realized she spoke the Swordanzen tongue but still understood her. "All tongues are equal in His domain. No false words can mask the truth." She turned forward and started walking down the only thing that resembled a path.

Heat radiated through the soles of their boots. Burning winds whipped around them, strong with the scent of sulfur. As they approached the entrance to a massive caldera, a large golden figure dove from the sky, striking Storm. The others froze in place, drawing weapons in preparation to fight. "No!" Storm shouted. She held up a hand, bloody from the rock she had fallen on. "Do not attack!"

The Swordanzen did not reach for her weapons, pulling herself to her feet without complaint and continuing forward. Again, the figure swooped down, striking Storm, and again she got to her feet, though a little slower, ignoring the alarmed voices of her companions.

The third time the creature struck her, Ash could see Storm's cheeks were wet with tears. Without a second thought, the mage raised his hands, speaking words of magic to create a barrier. The creature rebounded off an invisible wall that protected the fallen woman from its dive, several golden feathers fluttering loose. The gleaming figure of a great desert eagle screamed in fury as its strike was blocked, its wings kicking up dust and sand as it hovered over the fallen Swordanzen.

Radisen's eyes went wide, falling to his knees in awe. "Totani!" Prostrating himself, he could not bring himself to look on one of the divine servants of his people's god who was so obviously enraged. "Thandar, the Golden One!"

"How *dare* you?" the bird screamed, its shape melting to one of a half-bird, half-man, stalking towards her. "He gave you His trust! His love! And *this* is how you repay Him?!" He struck Storm in the head with the back of his fist. "You brought outlanders to witness His shame?!" Golden eyes rose to fix the group with hatred. "Defilers! Murderers!" His feathers half raised from the back of his head down his spine.

Terrence pushed past the two mercenaries who had put themselves between him and the strange creature, holding out his hands. "Stop!" he yelled in the Swordanzen tongue. "Stop this now, Thandar!"

The birdman froze, staring. He narrowed his golden eyes, straightening, though his fists remained balled up. "I know you!"

"Do not punish her. She is here because I asked her to bring me home." Waving a hand at Almek, Dzee-Terrence said, "And the Sentinel needed to come. To see. To know." Terrence walked forward, holding a hand up to Thandar, the birdman placing his palm against the young Forentan's. "You know her. She bears your mark! Do you truly believe *she* would have betrayed Him?"

With the Totani distracted, Ash rushed to Storm's side, his face contorted with worry. "Storm." He pulled her next to him. Weakly, she struggled against his effort to help her. "I'm here." Holding her fiercely tight, he gently stroked her hair, hushing her as she sobbed.

Thandar stared at Ash as if he had grown unnatural limbs and oozed putrescence. "The defiler protects His Daughter?"

"He is not like the others. Nor is this one." Dzee-Terrence gestured at himself. "Please, Thandar. We must see Him."

The birdman looked torn, staring at Ash, who held Storm in a protective embrace. Finally calming, he moved to the fallen woman and knelt by her, cupping her bruised cheek. "You should not have hidden so much from me, my Githalin. But I understand. No Githalin has ever been as strong as you. His heart aches for you from your pain." Looking up into Ash's eyes, Thandar stated, "Betray her, and no borders of time or space will protect you from my fury, Defiler."

"His name," Storm whispered in a pain-soaked voice, "is Ash Andar." Ash blinked in surprise, hearing his given name coming from the bristly Swordanzen woman's lips for the first time since they met.

Thandar grunted and rose. He circled each person in the group. Pausing before Mureln, he studied the Vodani. "Vodanya's waves crash against your soul, Spirit Singer. Do not let them break you." The bard blinked, opening his mouth to speak, but he could not produce a sound. He closed his eyes, hand along his right cheek.

Moving to Radisen, he stood over him. "Rise, Warrior." As Radisen did so, he dared to raise his eyes to meet Thandar's. "You have finally proven your worth, Warrior. Another has a claim on you, and if not for my Storm, I would claim you as my own."

The Sevmanen mercenaries received only brief appraisals and cursory, noncommittal grunts. Thandar spat at Amelana's feet and dismissed her. He paused by Taylin, blinking. "I have not seen a soul as fiercely gentle as my Githalin's is fierce since the Before Time. Do not fear using both edges of your blade to preserve the balance." Taylin opened her mouth to speak, but could find no words.

Finally, Thandar approached Almek and regarded the Dusvet Guardian. "You are still very young, Sentinel. I can see you knew nothing of this land. The echoes of the two-color Guardians had gone silent for so long, He worried none remained." Thandar made a satisfied noise. "It is good not all of your kind were destroyed."

Dzee-Terrence stepped nearer to Thandar, putting a hand on the bird man's arm. "We must see Him at once, Thandar. Our lord must know what comes. They are strong. But I am unsure if they are strong enough."

Thandar nodded, and his shape shifted back to the giant golden eagle. "Proceed. He awaits." He launched himself into the air and vanished over the rise they walked towards.

Ash put a hand on Storm's cheek, closing his eyes to 'see' and grimaced. "Stop concealing your suffering from me, Storm." She opened her eyes to look up at him, a wan half-smile on her lips. He sighed, knowing the futility of changing her habits. "Can you go on?"

"I have no choice." He cringed at her pain-soaked whisper. Reluctantly, she added, "But I need...help." Keeping his arm around her, he assisted her to her feet. The extent of the beating became apparent. The rock had cut her exposed skin in many places when she had fallen against it. Where she did not bleed out, dreadful bruises darkened the surface.

"You should let Taylin attend to you," Ash scolded in an even-toned voice for her ears only. "You can't even put weight on your leg."

"No." She took each step with painful determination. "What I suffer is nothing compared to what He suffers."

The caldera opened wide in front of them, and Ash would have stumbled at what he saw, but for his concern for Storm. The others reacted similarly.

In the heart of the bowl-like caldera, a massive dragon raged, its feet entrapped by giant chains. It tried to fly, its huge wings creating violent swirls of wind. The chains arrested the attempt with cruel abruptness; the creature crashed back onto its jagged rock bed. Blood streamed from around the shackles and where the rock cut its hide as it screamed its fury to the heavens.

As the others caught up with them, Storm spoke, exhaustion soaking her voice. "Lord Dusvet Guardian Almek Two-Tones. You stand before the Heart of Desantiva." She looked at the dragon and said in a choked voice, "Outlanders called Him the Raging One."

Terrence's eyes went wide as Dzee retreated. He put a hand over the gem at his throat in a comforting gesture. "That...He looks nothing like what Dzee remembers."

Choking back emotion, Taylin blinked back tears. "So much suffering," she whispered. "I can feel...what He feels...What He suffers. So much pain...I must help Him!"

Mureln pulled her back when she started stumbling towards the dragon without a second thought. "Taylin, no. It's too dangerous. You can't—"

"Such agony! I-I *must* do something..." The healer broke away from the bard before he could react. She ran towards the dragon, heedless of the danger, ducking sweeping wings. She reached the dragon in the brief pause between when he crashed to the ground and his lunge skyward and put both of her hands on his side, pouring blue-white healing energy into the ancient god.

His thrashing abruptly stopped, the dragon's eyes clearing of the haze of endless pain. Wings lowered as the tension eased. He looked down at his side as Taylin slid to her knees wearily. "Who are you?" the dragon demanded. "Outlander woman who dares risk death to ease My pain?"

"I-I am Taylin." The healer looked upwards to meet the dragon's eyes without fear, then lowered them again in respect. "Forgive me. I am not strong enough to do more."

The dragon lowered His head, His warm breath washing over her as He sniffed her. "You are one of the defilers' get. But not like those who imprisoned Me." The tip of His tail snaked around Taylin, helping her to her feet. "I am grateful to you, one called Taylin."

Putting too much weight on her already injured leg, Storm grimaced as she overbalanced and pulled at her broken ribs. She hissed between her teeth, wrapping her arm over the too-dark bruise on her side. Drawn out of his shocked stare at the dragon, Ash tightened his arm around Storm, keeping her on her feet as her knees buckled. "Storm!" he whispered, urgency in his voice.

At the same moment, the dragon god swung His head around, the sharp spines along His back rising as He growled, worry obvious in His voice. "Daughter! Where are you?!" Wings flared wide, echoing His emotions. As Ash helped Storm walk forward, the dragon's head pulled back in surprise. "Defiler! You *dare* touch My Daughter?" The dragon lunged forward, snapping at the mage. Only the chains held the dragon's maw just inches from His target.

Ash instinctively flinched, but did not flee. Storm looked at the mage, squeezing his hand as she pulled his support away. "I can stand alone, Mage. Do not anger Him further." Ash opened his mouth to argue, then shut it again. With keen reluctance, he released her and backed away.

Storm did indeed manage to stand without support for a moment. But the façade of strength evaporated, and Storm staggered forward to fall against the dragon's nose, resting her head against His hide, closing her eyes. "Father, forgive me. I didn't know what else to do."

With infinite care, the dragon lifted the Swordanzen, bringing her to His side, and gently depositing her by Taylin. "I know you tire, Healer. Draw strength from your heart and you will draw strength from Me. Ease My Daughter's pain."

Taylin looked up with wide eyes. "I thought healers were forbidden to Swordanzen." The words escaped before she could stop them.

Growling, the dragon looked down at the Forentan Illaini Magus. "That power from which you draw is all but gone from the weave of this land. But what *they* stole from Desantiva made Desantiva stronger." As the dragon looked down at Storm, His wings sagged. "For a price."

Along the wall of the caldera, as clouds of smoke moved from the face of the sun, light flickered off a cloudy block of crystal streaked with a rainbow of colors, a dark shape deep in the heart of it. Terrence stared wide-eyed at the large mound, walking over to it. Reaching out a shaking hand, he touched it, then drew back as if burned. "It is...Dzee." Looking up at Ash, Terrence said with a sense of panic, "Master Ash! It's Dzee! Her-her body is still alive!"

The dragon swung His head around with a snarl when He realized someone was near the crystal. Terrence dropped to his knees when the gaping maw threatened to drop on him. Dzee-Terrence called out, "Lord of my heart! Wait!"

"Dzee?" The dragon lowered His head. "My Light? You are here?" He lowered His head until His chin was just above the ground, staring at Terrence. "How is this possible? I could not find you. None of My children could find you. We searched for so long, but I would not believe you were gone. I could not give up hope you were not lost completely."

Terrence stood up, lowering his darkened eyes. "The...defiler that slew me, that led those who imprisoned and nearly killed you...she was a Shadowlord." Looking desperately afraid, Dzee-Terrence said, "I fear there was something...behind the war. Something darker. Someone."

The young mage hugged himself, shuddering a bit. Raising his eyes, they were clear blue again. "My Lord, when she was...nearly...killed, she said something...terrible...had captured her on the other side. It tried to feed on her and prevented her from returning to the physical plane sooner. She fought for a long time. When she got free, she was too weak to cross the boundaries between worlds and remain on this side."

He bit his lip, putting his hand over the gem in comfort. "Another used her desperation to return to you. She believed the only way she could remain on the mortal plane was to-to hunt and feed on the humans here. Those who survived...became tainted. Mindless, bestial husks and had to be killed to protect others."

Almek listened in silence to Terrence's words, then looked up at the dragon. "There is wrongness in all the lands, Great One. More and more destructive temporal shifters have crossed the Great Barrier. And I fear that there is corruption within the Guardians."

The dragon reared back, jerking the chains that imprisoned Him. The group ducked and braced themselves as the wind from His wings buffeted them. "Those My children trust...corrupt?!"

Almek lowered the arm from his eyes when the dragon's wings stopped fanning. "Aye, Great One. Those with talent in both the realm of guardians and their own native domains were not being trained because no one looked past one talent for another gift." Pausing a moment, he added, "Or they were dying young. Killed when they were too young to defend themselves."

The Raging One growled. "I have seen this phenomenon within My borders. Many strong younglings were taken before maturity. Thandar barely found My Daughter in time before those who took her tribe could have reached her." He looked over at Radisen, fixing him with an intense stare. "Others We would hide among the trusted. Let the world test them. Perhaps harder than We should have allowed."

"The world seeks balance and provides when there is need. I have suspected—because those of Guardian Sight alone were fading—that those strongly possessing another talent along with the Sight were being born." He waved a hand to the gathered. "I have taken it upon myself to find them. Train them."

"Good," the dragon rumbled, half folding his wings.

Hesitating a moment, Almek stated bluntly, "No Guardian has come from this land since before the ancient war, and that has left Fortress unsteady. But the Talent runs very strong among Your children." The implied criticism was not lost on anyone.

The dragon growled, lowering His head to glare at the old man. "Do not test me, Guardian! My children do what they need to survive. They were dying. Nearly extinct! No mere handful of warriors, no matter how skilled, would have been able to defend against the numbers the Outlanders still possessed."

"You kept the world out and your children withdrawn to preserve the balance." Almek crossed his arms, regarding the Desanti god. "Even Guardians were treated as outsiders. Such a complete severing of ties was unnecessary."

"You criticize *Me*?" The Raging One roared in anger. "That it was a Shadowlord who instigated the attack on Desantiva does not matter. *They* have always feared My children. *They* wished them all dead and gone." Looking fixedly at Amelana who looked like she would bolt any moment, the dragon hissed. "Ask the defilers. They are happy to pretend We do not exist. We are happy to let them believe the lies they tell themselves. The balance of energies remains secured, precarious as it is." He growled sullenly, "The imbalance would be worse if My children perish."

Unnoticed, Ash had moved to the crystalline mound, eyes fixed on the shape in the heart of it, and scried. In his mind's eye, he could see the shadows of the past, the war his ancestors brought to this one. Massive death and destruction, inflicted unexpectedly, hobbled the dragon, Who felt each one. Unable to kill a god, they crippled Him by ripping away one of His immortal servants and imprisoned Him in divinely wrought chains...created by His own sister, the Knowing One. That act sent ripples across the land of Desantiva that began reaching beyond Desantiva's borders. Only the greatest of sacrifices prevented the death that should have been assured.

"*A'tyrna Ulan*," Ash whispered, drawing all eyes to him. "They were dual bloods." Pale with the shock of understanding, he looked up at Almek. "The *A'tyrna Ulan* were children of a mage and a warrior." Struggling to speak, Ash explained, "To save Desantiva, they sacrificed themselves during the attack that would have utterly destroyed Desantiva by joining their essences of mage and warrior with the land, becoming part of it."

The mage looked at the crystal-encased body, struggling to come to terms with the truth his people had tried to forget. "The Knowing One...She was deceived into believing the warriors meant to destroy Her children, Her mages. Her shame...Her shame was nearly succeeding in killing Her own brother." He looked up at the dragon who watched him. The only movement was the lashing of the tip of His tail. "She allowed the warriors to become distant memories...because You wished it. And it was the only thing You would allow Her to do."

"She betrayed Me." The Raging One growled deep in his chest. "Betrayed My trust. Defiled My realm."

Terrence looked at Ash intently, sensing a sudden shift of energy around the mage. "Master...what are you doing?"

"I cannot undo the past." He dropped to his knees, putting both hands on the crystal. "But perhaps I can mend at least one rift." Humans, Totani, and god stared in wonder and awe as a brilliant blue-white glow enveloped the crystal tomb.

A rattling hiss from beyond the lip of the caldera drew the Guardian's attention upwards as several Totani converged on the dragon to defend him. One called out imperiously, "The shadows have breached the barrier again! Defend our Father!"

Almek put both arms out, blocking the others from rushing over to pull Ash away, his eyes going up to the lip of the cliff above them. "Protect Ash!" the Guardian ordered.

Grotesque serpentine creatures slithered down the wall, long, needle-like teeth promising pain and suffering. Radisen, Emil, and Emaris moved to stand between the mage and the monsters. Though the dark snakes were easy to slay, they kept coming like an endless tide. Behind the warriors' ranks, the bard, apprentice mage, and Guardian struck down those few slipping past the warriors.

The dragon bellowed and exhaled fire along the top of the wall, searing many of the monstrous things. Thandar and other half-humanoid, half-animal entities joined the battle to protect the handicapped dragon, but even then, the creatures kept coming, their numbers increasing as the daylight waned.

Terrence looked over his shoulder as if he had heard Ash call him, going to the mage deep in the casting of magic. "Master?" Terrence asked in uncertain worry as he knelt by the Illaini Magus. He gasped when Ash grabbed his apprentice's throat, trying to fight back at the unexpected attack as he felt his life force being pulled out of him. "Master!"

Ash jerked his hand away. Terrence gasped as the mage ripped the gem from his throat and slapped it onto the crystalline surface. The crystal tomb trembled, cracks appearing along its smooth facets. Ash grabbed Terrence and pulled him down, covering him with his body as the crystal exploded in a shower of crystal shards and brilliant light.

Everything stopped, time itself seeming to hold its breath as the dust cleared. Gingerly, a delicate half-woman, half-dragonlike creature the color of rainbows on silver picked herself up. She looked down at herself in wonder, then up, her expression turning malevolent. Raising her hands, she commanded, "Be gone!" A wave of white light exploded from her hands, and the shadow creatures evaporated, unable to withstand the purity of her power. "Never dare taint my Lord's land again," she growled.

The dragon stared, lowering His head to touch her with His nose. As she relaxed her stance and reached out to touch Him, He closed His eyes. "Dzee. My light."

"My Lord," she whispered. She bowed her head. "I am finally home."

"Master Ash?" Terrence sat up weakly, shaking his head to clear the ringing in his ears. He put his hand on Ash's shoulder. "Master?" He shook the unmoving man's shoulder, cold fear settling in the pit of his stomach. "Master!"

Chapter Thirty-Four

Groaning, Ash put a hand to his head as he awoke. He felt a hand restraining him from rising. Briefly he opened his eyes, hissing as he flung his arm over them. "Gods, so bright..."

"Forgive me," a soft voice said. After a pause, the sound of a spell spoken in an ancient dialect was barely audible. "There. It should be better now."

Carefully uncovering his eyes, the mage looked around at the chamber of blood red rock, all but one torch smoking from being extinguished abruptly. "Where am I? What happened?"

A surreal woman with draconic eyes and smooth rainbow-colored reptilian skin smiled at him in reassurance. "You are safe, Ash Andar." He frowned at her with a lack of recognition, blinking in puzzlement. "I am Dzee. You saved my life."

Ash was silent as he tried to clear the fog in his mind. "Dzee. You are Totani."

She smiled. "I am once more. Thanks to you." She closed her eyes and bowed at her waist, touching her palms together in supplication. "I am in your debt for making me whole."

He relaxed, shaking his head. Even the slightest movement sent pain stabbing through his skull, and he groaned again. Cool fingers brushed his forehead, and the pain eased. "There is...no debt." He took a deep breath, unable to find more words for the tangle of emotions that added to his pain and exhaustion-induced confusion.

Dzee smiled. "As you wish. Regardless, I am very grateful to you. The wound on my lord's heart when I was stolen from Him can finally begin to heal. And through Him, Desantiva can begin to heal from the wounds that have never stopped bleeding."

Ash's eyes snapped open at a familiar, painful lurch in his chest, and he sat up. "Storm!" Fighting through the pain that made his head swim and pushing against Dzee who tried to force him back down, the mage demanded, "Where is she?"

Dzee's reassurance rang hollow. "Storm rests right now." She put a hand on his cheek. "Relax, Ash Andar. You need to rest to recover."

Ash looked at Dzee through narrowed eyes. "No. Something is wrong. Where is she?" The dragon woman did not answer, hesitating. Ash grabbed her wrist, heedless that she was a divine servant of the Raging One. His azure eyes flashed with the intensity of his emotions. "Answer me! Where is Storm?! What's wrong with her?"

Dzee lowered her eyes with a sigh. "She remains with our Lord. The healer..." She shook her head. "Taylin is very skilled, but she cannot mend a wounded spirit." Ash stared at the rainbow-colored female. "Even before the war, before the First Sundering, those who became Desanti held tight to tradition and ritual. They are what the people lived and died by.

"Everything Storm knew. Everything she believed. It has changed too fast. Even if her actions were for Desantiva's benefit, for Him, they are still acts of betrayal she cannot forgive herself for, even if He has. She is beyond His reach to hear Him." Dzee closed her eyes in grief. "She has retreated into herself. She will not allow even our Lord to touch her heart."

"She is dying?" the mage asked incredulously. "After we have come so far? And with so much more that needs doing?"

"It is not that she is dying." Dzee chose her words carefully. "At least, she is not dying from any physical injury. Her body is whole. It is that...in her remorse, she does not *deserve* to live."

Ash looked down, pressing his lips together. Dzee put her hand under his chin, gently tilting his head up. She gazed into his eyes for a long moment. "Oh. I see now." After a time, she stood and offered her hand. "Come. I will take you to her."

The moment he put his hand in hers, a wash of soothing warmth flowed into him, restoring some of the strength he had spent saving her. The mage blinked as he followed the dragon woman, squinting when he emerged into the caldera again. He shook off Dzee's hand, determined to walk without help.

The dragon was subdued, curled around the unconscious Storm. His head lifted to regard the mage, and then settled on the ground again, heaving a sigh. Ash could barely look at the god's open grief.

"She is dying," the dragon said simply. "For all My power, I cannot save My Daughter's life because she does not wish to be saved."

Ash knelt by Storm, lowering his eyes respectfully. "In the short time I have known her, I have found her to be...incredibly willful and stubborn."

The mage had a sense of the dragon smiling. "Indeed." The dragon exhaled gustily. "So many of My children have passed from this world. Their lives so short and bright, like shooting stars in the heavens." Ash looked up as the dragon closed His eyes. "I had hoped it would not be so soon for her. Not like this."

"Is this my fault?" Ash asked bleakly, reaching out to touch her cheek tenderly with the back of his fingers. "When I pulled her back from the Final Dance? Used her honor to convince her to live on?"

The dragon opened His eyes, raising His head to narrow His gaze on the mage. Ash closed his eyes, hearing the spiny ridges bristle along the dragon's spine and the low rumble of a growl. "It was *you* who disrupted her pattern?" The mage only nodded once, bracing for whatever death loomed over him. "I thought she had understood...!"

Instinctively, Ash cringed, shielding Storm with his body as the dragon shrieked, the sound poignantly helpless and grief-stricken. The careless flailing touched neither mage nor Swordanzen, bringing them no harm. Totani came in their many forms, the human companions of the Swordanzen and mage joining them. None, however, dared to come within the Raging One's reach, save for Dzee.

"My lord, what is wrong?" Dzee flicked a look at Ash and Storm, looking perplexed. "She has not yet died. There is still a chance—"

"Patterns must be learned, ingrained, their purposes understood before they can be broken and new ones made." The Raging One bellowed inarticulate frustration. "But I never taught My daughter how to make new patterns. I ignored how very mortal she is!" He jerked back as if to launch Himself into the sky, and crashed down again as His shackles reached their unforgiving limit, narrowly missing Storm and Ash. The jagged rock gashed His hide mercilessly. "*My Daughter is broken because of Me*!"

The mage had no words, bearing witness to the god's grief for this far too young woman of the desert. Ash looked down at her, unable to deny the echo of those feelings within his own heart, the tightness in his chest knowing she was so close to death yet again. He gathered her into his arms, holding her close. "Storm," he said with desperation in his voice as he sought her mind and found only an unnatural, echoing emptiness. "Storm, please stop concealing your suffering from me."

Pressing his forehead against hers, he stopped short of willing her to obey, wishing he could reestablish the tie he had created when he last held her spirit to the world of the living, to find her before it was too late. Unbidden, a tear formed in his eye, escaping to roll down his cheek. "Please, Storm. Don't leave me alone."

The tear traced a trail through the dust on Ash's face and then fell soundlessly. The world vanished when the tear splashed onto her cheek, brilliant white light bathing his mind, the abrupt silence deafening. "What do *you* know of being alone, treewalker?" Storm's voice whispered in his ear. "Yours is a world filled with people. With life."

Ash straightened his shoulders, regarding the surrounding formless emptiness. "Just because there are people around you does not mean you cannot be alone, Swordanzen." He closed his eyes to the memory of himself as a boy, curled in a corner as he cried while cruel laughter drifted to his ears. "It can make it worse."

"It is different. *We* are different! You *chose* to remain alone." Hurt and accusation swirled around him. "I had no choice! I was Cursed. My family, my tribe! They died because of *me*."

"Nothing was your fault." Ash held onto his calmness in the face of her anger. "You were blessed, and the shadows sought to extinguish your light. The Totani would never have saved a Cursed child. The Raging One would never have claimed you as His Daughter if you were at fault. You know this!"

Storm's anger did not abate in the face of his cooler logic's truth. "It is the duty of Swordanzen to preserve the traditions, and I have broken them! I brought outlanders into His lands. Let them witness His shame. Allowed a healer to touch me! Swordanzen cannot have ties to others, and I gave my oath to the Guardian. There cannot be a choice between serving the Heart of Desantiva and any other."

"Is it wrong to change? When even the Heart of Desantiva wishes it?"

Ash closed his eyes, raising an arm to shield himself against the winds of Storm's frustration. As merciless and cutting as the sandstorm, the fury of her emotion whipped around him. "It goes against tradition! It is the responsibility of a master to keep the patterns whole and intact, and I *failed*."

"No," Ash stated firmly. "It is the responsibility of the student to master the patterns. It is the prerogative of the master to break them and create new ones when there is need." Ash could tell he had touched a nerve with the oppressive silence that hung in the air. "You are the best, are you not?"

"You know I am," Storm snapped back at him.

"Then it is time for you to make new patterns, Storm il'Thandar." The haze faded enough to reveal the battered spirit of the Desanti woman. She watched him with wary distrust and suspicion. "There is a new war. Bigger than that between mage and warrior. A Githalin Swordanzen is needed." He held his hand towards her, inviting her out of the shadows. "*You* are needed."

After many long moments, she finally took a step closer. Then she took another. Though her body was whole, her soul was battered, bruised, and bleeding. Storm fixed the man with a tired, wary gaze. "I betrayed my Father."

Seeing her made his heart ache, knowing his part in making her this way. "You know that is not true. You knew what needed to be done, even though it went against everything you were taught. You knew the patterns you had learned were insufficient." She stopped in her approach, narrowing her eyes at him. "Storm, you did what needed to be done *for* Him."

"I brought Him shame!" Storm countered, challenging him to deny the statement.

Ash tilted his head, regarding her in silence as he considered his reply. "You bear no shame. Your Father is very proud of you, Storm il'Thandar. He faults Himself for your pain."

Storm looked stricken, drawing away from him. "What? No, you lie! I-I have broken traditions! Allowed healers to touch me. Brought outlanders—"

Not about to let her go, Ash matched her steps away as he stepped towards her. "You know I don't lie."

Storm fidgeted, pacing. "But I-I do not...I cannot..." She turned away to hide her shame. "I am afraid. I do not deserve to live."

"You can't die, Storm il'Thandar."

"Why not? What does it matter to you? I am *nothing* compared to you!" She turned to face the mage, challenging him. "I saw your strength. You are powerful. You need no one. You have proven that those strong enough can stand alone."

"No, Storm." Though habit and pride begged him to agree with her words, he could not deny the truth he had denied for so long. He looked away in shame. "I...can't."

"What?" She stared at him, the honesty of his admission throwing her off her stride.

"I can't do this alone." The mage took advantage of the young woman's shock, forging ahead, taking step-by-step closer to her. "We are not that different, you and I." Ash met her eyes. "You are the only one...who understands. The pain of being isolated. Of being different. Of having lost family." A trace of uncertainty colored her eyes. After several long moments, she finally looked away. He held his hand out to her again, and she finally closed the remaining distance between them and accepted it.

The world without came rushing back. The mage sat up, looking down at the Desanti woman stirring in his arms. She glanced around in bewilderment. "Father?"

If the single word had been a shout, there would have been no difference. The dragon's violent thrashing stilled instantly. "Daughter?"

Storm barely noticed Ash helping her to her feet as she stumbled the few feet to the dragon's side, throwing her arms against the wall that was his chest. "Father, forgive me."

"Storm!" He curled around the woman protectively. "My beloved Daughter. I will forgive you only if you can forgive Me."

Ash looked away from the Raging One and his human daughter to see silvered rainbow feet next to him. He met Dzee's eyes and let her help him to his feet, leaning on her support. "What you have done for Desantiva does not erase everything that Desantiva has suffered at the hands of your ancestors, Ash Andar." The mage grimaced, looking down. Dzee gently turned his face towards hers again, smiling gently. "True healing always takes time. It is a beginning."

CHAPTER THIRTY-FIVE

IN THE FOLLOWING DAYS, the Raging One and his divine servants gave shelter to the travelers. Despite the inhospitable nature of the Rumblelands, the generosity of the entrapped god and his Totani knew few bounds. Save for Amelana who had been returned to the cavern to wait with the drizzen, the Totani fussed over the Dusvet Guardian and his students with an almost childlike fascination that bordered on maddening for the humans. They particularly focused on Terrence for having been Dzee's willing host, albeit after she claimed him.

But for the young Forentan mage apprentice who bridged the rift between warriors and mages, everything was a troubling tangle. One day, neither human nor Totani could find him. Surprisingly, none of the Totani seemed able to sense him, either.

"I do not understand how a mere human can obscure himself from us," the mountain cat Totani called Kailee complained, her tail lashing impatiently. "No one has been able to hide from us or our Lord since—" An elbow from one of the other Totani in human shape cut her words short. With ears flattened back, she snarled, but then went quiet.

Seated with the others around the low, flat rock serving as a table for the humans to eat at, Storm shrugged one shoulder. "He has a quick mind. I could always hide from you when you were being annoying. I warned you all you were getting as vexing as midges."

Thandar looked down at her with rather sad pride. "*You* are the Daughter of the Heart of Desantiva," he said as explanation. The birdman stood, stretching out his arms in preparation for taking his full bird form. "I will go search for Terrence."

Emil snapped his head up. "Let me take a turn lookin' fer 'im." He shrugged as all eyes turned towards him. "Iffin' he not wantin' t' be found by you Totani, he may not be thinkin' 'bout one of *us* lookin' fer 'im.

B'sides, I be needin' t' stretch m' legs." The Totani were silent, then grudgingly yielded to the mercenary's request.

ONCE HE WAS WELL away from the caldera, the Gyspari mercenary closed his eyes for several moments, then opened them again, studying the terrain. Satisfied, he headed out for one of the more treacherous hills. It did not take long for Emil to track the young man. He found Terrence sitting on a protrusion of blood red volcanic rock sheltered from the sky and from the valley, staring out over the desolation of the Rumblelands. He glanced at Emil, who scaled the steep incline as if he were part mountain goat, then turned his pensive gaze back to the distance.

"Lad, everybody be worried 'bout you. Even th' Totani, which is pretty impressive. Why are ye up here all by yerself?" Sitting next to the young man, the mercenary pointed out, "Ye need t' give me a chance t' win m' coin back, ye know." Nudging Terrence in the ribs with his elbow lightly, he added, "An' how often ye get th' chance t' play toss stones wi' divine servants, eh?"

"I'm sorry, Emil," Terrence apologized, sounding despondent. "I'm not in the mood for gambling today. Perhaps tomorrow."

Emil sighed, putting a hand on Terrence's shoulder. "Lad, somethin' be eatin' at ye." The Gyspari's voice turned droll. "Wi' all th' shit that's happened, I ain't surprised. It be a lot t' take in, even fer me an' Emaris, and we been travelin' fer longer than you been alive." He leaned forward to catch the young man's eye. "Might help figurin' things out if ye talk 'bout it."

Terrence closed his eyes, silent for a time. "When Dzee was in me, we...we shared memories. I saw how she remembered Desantiva." He bowed his head, clenching his fists. "It was so...beautiful. So full of life! As much as Forenta. Maybe even more because the Desanti truly were part of their land and allowed their land to flourish naturally. Not like my people, whose domination inhibits change and adaptation. Even the Rumblelands were not this desolate."

Troubled, Terrence looked down at his hands, digging nails against the rough rock. "Even if the one who nearly destroyed Dzee was a Shadowlord, the others...my *ancestors*...they were not. They followed either blindly or knowingly, and either way, it shouldn't have mattered. What my people did to Desantiva goes against everything...Just look at this place!" He looked at Emil imploringly. "How could we do all of this? How could we—?"

Emil shook his head. "Stop. Just stop right there, lad. It don't do no good t' take th' responsibility fer others' mistakes. T'was a different time. Ye don't know what the Desanti were like back then." He held up his hands to forestall Terrence's protest. "Not sayin' they deserved nothin' like this. But I could see how someone coulda duped yer ancestors inta believein' that th' warrior folk were out t' kill 'em all. Hells, ye seen them Desanti angry, yeah?"

"It's hard not to." Terrence looked out at the horizon again. "They seem very quick to anger as a people."

Emil chuckled. "Yeah, well, imagine there bein' a whole lot more of 'em. I might be shittin' m'self, too, if someone be tellin' me they're out fer m' blood. Be too easy to believe it be true." He poked the younger man's shoulder. "But that been their fault. Not yers. Not a'tall."

"But it was still wrong!"

"Hell, yeah, it was wrong! But th' fault not be yers." Emil grinned a little. "Gods, boy, ye helped a Totani t' live again. Ye already proved ye not be like them ones in th' past. There prolly be others of yer and yer master's mind who think what happened was wrong. Or at least could be convinced. Just...well. They be afraid t' speak up b'cause of people like that bitch journeyman of yer master's. Or they be happy ignorin' everything around 'em. Hoping all th' trouble will go away or at least it won't be them that will be bit in the arse."

Terrence sighed gustily, looking at the Gyspari with a helpless expression. "So, what should I do?"

Emil reached up to scratch behind his ear idly. "Well, I figure ye gots two choices. Ferget it an' go on like it ain't a problem, like them ones that be more like sheep. Or do what ye can t' help make it right again, like ye already done fer Dzee. There be a lot t' be fixed, ye know? Just don't be blamin' yerself fer it *needin'* t' be fixed."

Terrence considered the Sevmanan's words and finally offered a wan smile. "You are right." He sighed again, looking at the horizon. "I can't help but feel sorry for the Desanti for all they've had to suffer."

"Pfft!" Emil held up both hands in a warding gesture. "Dear gods, don't go an' pity them desert folks, lad! Not where they know it anyway. They ain't want none of that, I promise ye." He held out his hands as Terrence looked at him in surprise. "They be a strong people. Hafta be t' live here. They be proud t' ha' survived what most likely couldn't. It be a pretty damned impressive accomplishment. Ye pity 'em, and they will get riled up that ye think they ain't as good as ye fer their sufferin'. An' that'd likely start th' bad feelings b'tween yer peoples all over again."

Terrence frowned a bit. "That's...not going to be easy."

"Never said it would be, lad." Emil stood up, offering a hand to the younger man to pull him to his feet. "C'mon, b'fore th' Totani get impatient wi' me an' start trying t' hunt ye down. They are very infatuated wi' thems they like. And *you* they are *fascinated* with."

As they started down the steep incline, Terrence said, "You are a wise man, Emil."

The mercenary nearly lost his footing, looking back at the mage with a comical expression of horror. "Don't ye be goin' blabbin' anything like that around, lad! Mureln'll never let me live it down, and Emaris'll have a smirk on his face, and life'd be unbearable between th' two of them great louts."

Terrence looked amused. "It'll be our secret then."

Emil grinned back over his shoulder. "Yer a smart one, ye are, lad. Now 'bout that game ye owe me..."

CHAPTER THIRTY-SIX

THE COOLER BREEZES OF the coming nightfall gusted over Almek and his companions, minus Amelana and Storm, as they sat among the Totani in front of the Raging One. The brilliant panorama of colors in the sky was shifting to the deeper purples of the night sky. Tiny, jewel-like motes of light became visible, tiny glowing tracks breaking the stillness occasionally as a shooting star raced across the heavens.

Taylin smiled shyly as Mureln sat by her. He arched an eyebrow in amusement when she shifted to sit nearer to him, but said nothing. Her smile faded as she looked to the massive dragon, the rattle of his chains reminding them of his state. "Dusvet, I remember stories from my childhood about Shadowlords, but I thought they were just...make believe." Her cheeks colored at the grumbling of the Totani. "But even in the stories, no one described what they looked like. What were they?"

Almek ran his fingers through his hair, threaded with even more gray, considering his reply. "Part of an ancient secret society. Speaking of them was dangerous in itself. Even now, most will not discuss them for fear others like them will reappear."

The Raging One raised his head to regard Almek. "They are gone?"

Almek closed his eyes, expression pained as he remembered. "I very much hope so. For the sakes those who died to eliminate their threat to the great balance."

Taylin leaned forward, lips parting to pursue the subject, but froze when Mureln's hand covered hers. The bard's usual mirth had vanished, replaced by a gravity that stilled her questions. She swallowed, gathering her thoughts before shifting direction. "If Fate maintains balance as you've said," she ventured, eyes darting from Ash to Almek, "then why now? Why create dual talents when there were none during your battles with the Shadowlords? Surely they would have been more necessary then."

The dragon shifted uncomfortably on His bed of jagged rock. "It was not unheard of before the Great War. But it was exceedingly rare. Few can master multiple disciplines." Almek regarded the dragon with open shock. The god snorted. "Do not look so surprised, Sentinel. Since creation, all things have been the union of opposites, a balance of Order, Chaos, and Time." He stretched his wings fully, blotting the sky briefly. "Even Us gods."

Ash rubbed a star-shaped scar on the palm of his hand, frowning pensively. "What changed that we are needed now?"

Almek looked troubled. "I wonder if it was not a matter of potentials not being born, but simply that we Guardians were not looking for them, nor encouraging the pursuit of learning other arts." He looked at the mage and said grimly, "Or some agency killed potentials because they could see their promise before others and sought to eliminate them." The comment caused a ripple of unease. The Totani squirmed in shame as the Raging One growled deep in His chest, the glow in His eyes flaring brighter as He fixed a critical glare on them.

"Strings are definitely being pulled," Mureln agreed. "However, I don't think everyone is dancing to the intended tune. Forenta and Desantiva always seem to be the major focus." He looked over at Taylin, grim. "I think the only reason Sevmanen and Vodani have not been so tainted is we are considered...lesser than our cousins."

Thandar stretched his wings wide, flipping them to his back with a snap. "Many of the Vodani skills you had described are facets of Swordanzen arts. But the shorter lives and considerable amount of knowledge to master make it impossible for Swordanzen to attain the mastery Vodani have."

"I think it must be the same for the Sevmanen, cousins to the Forenten as they are." In her humanoid form, Dzee raised sad eyes up to the dragon. "Those who attacked Desantiva stripped the land of the part of the life force that was my heart. If not for Terrence..." She looked away in shame. "I will never forgive myself for the pain I brought You, my Lord."

The Raging One growled, spines along His back rising. But when He lowered His head to bump Dzee, His touch was loving and gentle. "I have already forgiven you, My light." She covered her face with her hands, leaning against His cheek.

Kailee mrowred unhappily as she hopped down from her perch to the ground near Thandar. "So, we face a battle with an unknown evil that has an unknown purpose and unknown resources with a decided lack of those trained to have any hope of survival." The sand-gray mountain lion stretched, raking slashes in the stone with her claws. "And our Lord imprisoned by one of His own. This bodes well." The cat's sarcasm was thick in her voice. She hissed at Thandar when he smacked her haunches with one wing.

"How can it be that He cannot free himself?" Taylin wondered, drawing dark looks from the Totani. She flinched a little, but continued. "The Raging One must be as powerful as the Timeless One or the Knowing One. What could prevent Him from just...breaking the chains that imprison him?"

Standing stiffly, still suffering from the lingering aches resulting from Dzee's restoration, Ash slowly approached the dragon god, putting a hand on the cuff of the nearest shackle. "The laws of magic bind Him." He looked up to regard the god, others looking between the two in amazement at the mage's confidence in approaching Him. "The Knowing One...She must have feared You meant to kill Her, but She could not bring Herself to kill You, Her own brother, despite Her belief You would kill Her."

The dragon growled in irritation, jerking back on the chains. "I never intended to kill Her. I still do not despite My suffering. She is My sister!" He lifted the foot, the massive links rattling dissonantly. "Yet they still hold."

"All binding spells require both the binder and the bound to agree on the fundamental purpose of the binding." He closed his eyes, studying the structure of the massive chains. After several moments, he sighed as he lowered his hands and stepped back. "She cast it with the belief You wanted to *hurt* Her." Ash paused a moment. "The moment it was cast, You *did* want to hurt Her." He gazed up challengingly. "You still *do* want to hurt Her, and She still believes You do."

"Of course I want to hurt Her!" the dragon bellowed, beating the air with His wings as He pulled against His restraints. "I have suffered thousands of years unable to move from this place of torture, unable to go to My children when they need Me! Because of *Her*! Yes! I want to hurt Her! I *want* Her to know My suffering!" He seethed, steam rising from His nostrils. "*Wanting* to do something does not mean I must. I demand nothing of My children I do not practice Myself. I know My nature. Self-control is required; otherwise, the risk of harm to what is innocent is too high."

"Then You will never be free, Father." Storm appeared, startling dragon, Totani, and humans alike. "And neither will Desantiva until you forgive Her."

"Forgive? Forgive She who imprisoned Me?!" The dragon swung His head down, nose a hand's breadth away from the Githalin Swordanzen. Storm did not flinch, did not cross her arms in judgment. She simply stood there. "You ask too much of Me, Daughter."

"No more than I know You can give, Father." The dragon roared to the heavens in frustration. Storm looked down, shoulders sagging. She looked towards Ash. "If the spell cannot be undone because Father will not stop wanting to harm His sister, would it be enough if His sister could be convinced He would not harm Her?"

Ash considered for a moment and nodded. "It might. But She would have to believe it without suspicion. All She knows is His pain and anger. She cannot come here Herself and hear His words, and obviously, He cannot go to Her." He looked at the Raging One, pressing his lips together. "I am loathe to deceive Her. But things must change."

"There would be no deception. I will go to Her and speak on my Father's behalf."

The dragon was stunned into silence, the eyes of the Raging One and all the Totani suddenly falling onto the young woman. "Leave Desantiva? You would leave Desantiva, Daughter?"

"I love You, Father. For You, I would suffer an eternity of torment if it would end Yours." She went to him, resting her cheek on His leg. "Something must change. As things are now, Your suffering causes the land to continue to bleed."

Ash watched Storm, his expression unreadable. Meeting Almek's eyes, he waved the Dusvet Guardian over to him. "I need your help." He whispered to the Guardian, the older man nodding in agreement. While the Totani and dragon were distracted, the two approached the god's resting place, filled with jagged rocks that offered no comfort or peace, endlessly cutting into His hide. Focusing together, the Guardian and his mage student forced the will of time on the rocks, the jagged points wearing away until nothing but a smoothed, shallow pit of black and red sand remained. The dragon went almost limp, eyes half closing at the easing of the once inescapable torture.

Almek nodded in approval to Ash as teacher to student. "Your instincts serve you well, Ash." He looked to the dragon. "We cannot undo the bindings, Raging One. But we wished to bring You some small comfort."

"Thank you." The dragon closed His eyes, relaxed for the first time in centuries. "I will...try to do as Storm asks of Me. But I can make no promises." Ash and Almek nodded, returning to the others of their traveling group. He looked at the young Desanti woman. "You need not leave, Daughter. Stay with Me. I will be free in time."

"I must go, Father. If You can be freed sooner, while I am still alive to know You are free, I must go."

The dragon heaved a sigh. "Very well." He raised His head and looked at Dzee.

Nodding to Him, Dzee turned to the group. "You came to De-santiva knowing only something was wrong, despite the history of enmity the people have held towards all outsiders, and have helped to mend the land. Desantiva wishes you to know We are grateful to you and accept you as siblings to Our children." Growing like glowing vines, blades emerged from the ground at the feet of all but Radisen. "Take these so the children of Desantiva know you are accepted and welcomed here. May the strength of your hearts protect you."

Before Dzee could turn to Radisen, the mountain lion leaped between them, snarling at the other Totani. "Do not steal what is mine, Dzee! You know I claim him!"

Dzee snorted, waving a dismissive hand. "Then stop playing your games, Kailee. I have no patience for them." Kailee snarled at Dzee's back. Dzee, back remaining to the lioness, waved a dismissive hand.

Radisen took a half step back as the snarling mountain lion turned back towards him. "Foolish child. You gave up when you did not pass your Naming trial instead of trying to prove yourself worthy!" Calming, the Totani's hackles lowered, her voice reflecting pride. "But when our Lord's Daughter needed you, you selflessly stepped up to be what you have always been, despite being without your Name." The lion crouched and sprang on Radisen, looking as if she meant to rip his throat out. He gasped as claws ripped off his tunic's shoulder, revealing the silhouette of a mountain cat mid-attack.

Kailee licked his cheek. "Don't be so foolish again, Skyfire." The lion sprang back off of Radisen, a gleaming two-edged short sword much like Storm's resting by him with an ornate sheath. On either side, a pair of single-edged blades rested as well.

Storm offered a hand to Radisen, smiling knowingly. "Welcome, Githalin Swordanzen Skyfire il'Kailee."

Dizzily putting a hand to his head, Skyfire cleared his throat. "If I'd known what being Githalin entailed, I would never have envied you, Storm."

The others chuckled as Storm laughed outright. "Such is the price we pay for the love of our Totani." She looked at Thandar with deep affection, then at the dragon with an unconditional love touched with sadness.

Chapter Thirty-Seven

Even the non-Desanti noticed a change in the land the moment they began the journey back to First Home. Subtle at first, a distinct increase in plant life became noticeable, lurking around the many rocks. Not visibly but no less noticeable, there was a certain air of peace they had not known since they stepped onto Desantiva's shores.

With the Time of Gathering long over, the valley of First Home was desolate. Only the age-worn paths hinted at the massive community that had been there only weeks earlier. A handful of Desanti remained, tending the meager fields near the oases that dotted the valley, serving those for whom the nomadic life had become too harsh.

Verris na'Zhekali was the first of the elders to come out to welcome Almek and his outlander students. He skidded to a stop when he saw Skyfire standing by Storm, his jaw dropping in shock. "You...you are..."

The Desanti man stepped forward, bowing to Verris and the other Desanti gathering before them, all staring in awed shock. "Githalin Swordanzen Skyfire il'Kailee." He sounded like he was still getting used to his new name and title, standing with pride.

Storm looked smug. "I told you, Grandfather. A Swordanzen cannot be anything than what they are." She gave Skyfire the gentlest smile any of her companions had seen yet. "He has earned his Name and more. He is *th'yala* to me."

"I, er, well...ahem." Verris looked lost for a moment, as all the hopes he had for Storm slipped from his fingers. "The tribes...are blessed to have you both guarding us all."

Smile fading, Storm chose her words with care. "The tribes won't have us for long. We must leave Desantiva with Lord Almek." The surrounding Desanti went wide-eyed and pale at her words. She added, "Both of us."

The elders, attendants, and guardsmen shook off their paralysis all at once, all speaking and moving animatedly. "What?!" "You cannot leave!"

"Desanti do not leave Desantiva!" They turned hateful, accusatory glares on Almek and his students. Despite the risks of facing Almek, the guardsmen drew weapons, as if killing him and his outlander students would prevent their Swordanzen's departure. Even the attendants started reaching for their knives.

Storm and Skyfire responded by drawing their own twin blades, standing in front of Almek. Facing two Githalin Swordanzen gave the Desanti pause. "Look at them! They bear sacred Naming blades. They mark them as accepted by the Heart. Even two of the treewalkers!" Her words were clipped as she held one sword out, pointing towards Ash and Terrence. Her voice turned scathing. "Can you not feel the change in the *Psia Re*? How it has eased? Have you not seen the changes in the land?! They were balms to Desantiva's oldest scars." The other Desanti hesitated, trading confused looks as their weapons lowered.

Leveling her piercing green-gold eyes on Verris, she stated, "You cannot stop me, Grandfather. I will not allow it. I know things you do not. You do not understand that I *must* do this. Desantiva's continued survival depends upon this journey."

The elderly man stared at her for a long moment before his shoulders sagged. He cupped her cheeks in his hands. "Your eyes are so old, dear child. I have only ever wanted to spare you suffering and erase your curse to restore our tribe."

Sheathing her weapons, Storm smiled sadly. "I know, Grandfather. But the challenge line in the sand has been drawn, and I must stand to meet what opposes me, else all the Swordanzen in history will not be enough to save Desantiva." She covered his hands with hers, gently pulling them away. "It is my duty."

"I will accompany her, Elder." Skyfire's voice was filled with a quiet confidence that had been absent before. He put his hand on her shoulder, meeting her eyes with an understanding affection. "I would never abandon Storm to the whims of the outlands."

Verris sighed and nodded. "Very well. Tia, have food and drink brought to the dining hall." He waved to Almek and his students to follow him. "Come. Tell us what we must know. We will do what we can to prepare the tribes for the trials that come." His voice had a wry resignation. "There had not been a Githalin for two generations before Storm. We endured before, we can do so again." He looked at Storm and Skyfire. "It is our duty as Desanti to protect the land."

THE EARLY MORNING SUNLIGHT flashed off the bronze metal shod horns of the drizar as he led the line of drizzen towards Home Port. His shrill cry announcing himself turned the heads of the Vodani tending to the small patches of food plants. The surprised Vodani stared in childlike wonder at the sight of the full male drizzen, running to the edge of the road to get a closer look.

As though drawn by some unheard call, Vodani of all ages emerged, lining the road, offering respectful bows to the two Swordanzen who rode side by side. The nearer the group got, the more excitement rippled through the Vodani population. At the edge of the town, they dismounted. The Desanti who had accompanied them took the drizzen to return to First Home, save for the two belonging to the Githalin Swordanzen.

Once Almek arranged with the Vodani captain who would take them and their horses back to the mainland, the group waited at the main tavern. Far cooler outside than in, they sat in the open air shielded by a heavy tarp overhang. The pair of Desanti sat apart from Almek and his students, shoulder to shoulder, drinking the water brought to them.

Skyfire glanced over at the Vodani still hovering outside, chattering to one another as they pointed to the two warriors. He bumped her shoulder to get her attention, speaking more fluently in Swordanzen since his bonding to Kailee. "Doesn't it bother you? Having all their eyes on you like this?"

Storm shrugged with indifference. "People have stared at me all my life. When I sense no ill intent, I ignore it. Vodani are cousins of the people after all. They see us as kin." She eyed the water in her cup with a sigh. "It will not be as benevolent when we cross the Great Water. *We* will be the Outlanders in the defilers' lands."

Skyfire reached for her hand, squeezing it. "Then we will be an oasis of sanity among them." She could not help laughing, returning the affection, raising her cup to him.

Seated at a table further back from the Desanti pair, Almek and the rest of his group sat together, keeping an eye on the two Swordanzen. Mureln glanced over at Ash, who had returned to his silent brooding since they had departed the Rumblelands. The bard followed Ash's unwavering stare towards the Desanti pair.

Intrigued, the bard avoided baiting the Illaini Magus. "Seeing her smile is good. Like a heavy weight has finally been lifted from her shoulders." When there was absolutely no response, the bard reached over and poured wine, putting the cup in front of the mage, who ignored it.

Taylin leaned closer to Mureln, whispering in his ear, "I thought he was ill-tempered before." She flinched when Ash turned his hard look on her, hiding behind Mureln.

Mureln patted Taylin's hand, giving Ash a disapproving look. "Seriously, Ash, you're going to draw attention if you don't stop staring daggers at everyone."

The mage snorted in response but shifted in his seat, taking up the cup of wine to sip. He looked down at the liquid critically. "This is extremely bitter."

"Aye, it is. But there isn't much in Desantiva that isn't bitter." Mureln gave Ash a sidelong look. "And yes, I am talking about you, too." Only the clenching of his teeth and tightening of his hold on the cup reflected the Forentan mage's emotions.

A young Vodani boy trotted up to Almek's table, bowing deeply. "Lord Almek, the *Wave Dancer* will be ready to depart soon. But we are having some...ah...troubles with the drizzen." He glanced towards the Swordanzen and said, "The drizar has tried to gore everyone who gets near him! And he keeps protecting the female so no one can reach her, either."

Looking amused, Storm pushed herself to her feet, Skyfire following her lead. "Allow me to assist. The drizar gets nervous around large numbers of people."

"Lady Storm, if that is nervous, I sure hate to see what angry is!" the boy said emphatically.

"You are very wise," Storm told him, her matter-of-fact tone showing she was completely serious and not mocking or teasing. The boy looked confused as she walked by, glancing at Skyfire. The Githalin man gave the boy an approving smile and nod; the youngster squared his shoulders.

The local Vodani once more stopped whatever they were doing to gather near the docks as Storm led the way to the *Wave Dancer*. Several men and women stood around the drizar and drizzen pair, but not near enough for the angered beast to reach with paw or horn. Skyfire's calmer mount was no less dead set against walking up the narrow plank to be put in the hold with the rest of the horses.

The drizar was in an attack stance, snorting and striking sparks on the dock's stone surface with his sharp, metal-clad claws. Faint gouges scored the ancient stone. The gleaming bronze caps on his horns were slashes of reflected sunlight as he swung his head about when one sailor tried to get near him.

Without a hint of fear, Storm approached the beast, making soothing noises. No one could hear her words, but the change was profound. With ears turned forward, the drizar went from murderous madness to sedate. He nibbled on her shoulder as she petted his neck. Turning, she started up the wooden walkway.

The drizar did not hesitate, bounding after her, making the board bend so hard it threatened to break, springing to the deck beside his human. Soon after, the female drizzen followed Skyfire, wary but obedient and far more sedate. The Vodani, delighted, cheered the spectacle. No doubt, Mureln told the others as they followed the drizzen, the stories of the first Swordanzen taking to the seas would be all over Vodanya before sunset.

"I suppose it takes an animal to talk to an animal," Amelana muttered under her breath. She gasped in pain, staring at Ash, who glared at her for a long moment before releasing the merciless hold he had on her arm, shoving her forward to board.

Having reassured the crew that the pair of reptilian mounts would sleep for days once they had their fill of food, Storm and Skyfire emerged from below deck. They walked to the starboard side of the ship, opposite the dock, and looked down into water deeper than any within the Desantiva territory.

Skyfire recognized the change in Storm, going to her side. Putting a hand on her shoulder, he whispered in reassurance to no avail. She shook her head sharply, fingernails digging into the wood.

"Is there a problem?" Ash joined the two, hands tucked in his mage robe sleeves. Though he spoke to them both, his eyes were only for Storm.

Skyfire looked between the two before he finally stated in a low voice barely audible to the Forentan. "A Swordanzen cannot show fear. We have...never seen water so deep as this, Lord Ash." He flicked a glance at Storm's hands. "She cannot let go of the rail."

Ash considered Storm, noticing her cheeks had darkened as Skyfire explained her weakness. Turning his back to the water, the mage leaned against the rail, crossing his arms as he watched the crew prepare to set sail. After a moment, he lightly touched the back of her hand. "Storm. Relax."

"Easy for you to say," she hissed through gritted teeth. "*You* can probably swim like a fish and breathe water."

Ash blinked at the outrageous, childlike accusation of water breathing. Unable to help himself, he smiled, crossing his arms again. "Actually, no, I cannot swim, nor can I breathe water. I should probably learn someday, but there has been no need."

Storm looked at Ash sideways for several heartbeats. "You are annoying." She closed her eyes, took a deep breath, and wrenched her hands off the rail. Muttering something in Desanti, she stalked down to her and Skyfire's shared cabin below. Ash glanced at Skyfire for a translation.

"You do not want to know." Reflecting his own nervousness, the Desanti man glanced at the water uneasily. "It isn't physically possible anyway." Clearing his throat, he excused himself and followed Storm, ducking through the doorway leading below decks.

Chapter Thirty-Eight

ONCE THE SHIP WAS underway, things quickly fell into a routine with the Vodani sailors. Their passengers kept to their small cabins until later in the evening when the ship's cook had the evening meal prepared. As the group settled at the table to eat, Emil looked around curiously. "Where be our Desanti? I wanted t' see if we could convince Storm t' dance again. Ow!" He glared at Emaris. "M' ribs are not made fer yer elbows, ye lout."

Amelana smiled with faux sweetness. "Oh, I doubt we'll see the Desanti at all. They've been in their room since we left." She leaned on Ash, slipping her arm through his. "Making all sorts of uncivilized noises." Pushing Amelana off his arm, Ash gritted his teeth but said nothing, reaching for the wineskin and a mug.

"It's called vomiting, and if you would prefer our Swordanzen to vomit into your lap, I am sure they would be *happy* to oblige you, Journeyman," Taylin said acerbically, emphasizing the rank and earning a dark look from the Forentan woman. "Perhaps you can demonstrate what civilized vomiting is like sometime, hm?" After Amelana turned her nose up and looked away from the healer, Taylin turned to Mureln and Almek, irritation yielding to concern. "I *am* worried about them. Neither seemed the type to...hide away like this."

Mureln chuckled, his easygoing demeanor reassuring to the other two. "The first time aboard an ocean ship is often upsetting to those who've only walked the land. I will go check on them. Now that we are under way, none of us need worry about impeding the shiphands. I am certain they will feel better once they get some fresh air." He pushed himself to his feet, leaning close to Taylin to brush the back of her hand, smiling as he turned away when her cheeks colored.

The bard paused outside the Swordanzen's room, listening. Nodding to himself, he knocked on the door. "Go away," Storm called curtly.

"Sorry, I can't do that." Mureln pushed the door open and walked in on two of the most miserable people he had ever seen. Closing the door behind him, he reached down for a small stool. "Trees are not as green as you two," he quipped, though his voice held the tenor of worry.

Rolling her eyes up in exasperation to regard Mureln, Storm rested her head against the wall. "I know *you* would not come to gloat over our misery." Swallowing hard, she put her head back down on her arms. "What do you want?"

"How do you Vodani endure this constant moving and the smell?" Skyfire asked mournfully. "Kailee's tail, my stomach."

Mureln sat on the stool between their narrow bunks. "Not every Vodani born endures the waves gracefully. We learned a few tricks over the generations. Here." He reached for Skyfire's arm and pressed his fingers against the inside of his wrist.

After a few moments, the Desanti man blinked several times. "I feel...better." He looked at his wrist. "What did you do?"

Mureln smiled a little. "There are certain pressure points that help with the seasickness. Once you get your sea legs, you'll feel better." He knew better than to reach for Storm, simply holding his hand out to her and waiting.

The young woman eyed him warily, glancing at Skyfire and back before relenting and offering her hand to the Vodani. She sighed with relief and offered the man a grateful smile. "Thank you."

Mureln waved off their gratitude. "I wouldn't suggest eating anything more than bread and watered-down wine until you have fully acclimated to the ship. Getting some fresh air would help, too. I know it's heavy with salt, but trust me, there are much worse odors on the waters."

The Swordanzen woman stood and stretched gingerly. "I would like to see the sun again. Now that I do not need to worry about ending up curled in a corner like an abused animal trying to keep my stomach inside." She grinned at Skyfire. "We should explore...Just this room alone! Have you ever seen so much wood in one place, Skyfire?"

Mureln chuckled and shook his head as he left them. "Amazing," he murmured to himself. "How two hardened warriors could possess such unblemished innocence..." His smile faded as he realized a problem, looking back over his shoulder a moment. "They *are* little more than children. Two dangerous ones headed to lands hostile to their people." After he rejoined the others, he reassured them that the two desert folk were fine and would likely be seen more often in the near future.

Almek considered the silent bard as the others chattered amongst themselves. "Mureln," he said quietly in Vodani. "Something is bothering you."

Glancing to see if any of the sailors were nearby, and satisfied there were none, Mureln looked back to Almek. "Do you realize how young our two Desanti are?"

"Everyone is young to me, my friend." Almek and the others looked up as the sailors delightedly welcomed their Desanti cousins when they appeared, drawing the pair over to their tables. The two looked surprised but amused as the Vodani chattered to them in Desanti, asking for stories. Skyfire deferred to Storm, who obliged the sailors. Her audience sat raptly attentive as she settled into the storytelling. "She's pretty good. Perhaps she should train as a bard," Almek teased.

Mureln arched an eyebrow. "Perhaps. And *I* should take up needle-craft and sew pretty flowers on your robes," he replied drolly.

Almek snorted and then laughed quietly. "You are a most irreverent student." The bard merely winked, knowing the Dusvet Guardian appreciated not being set apart or on so high of a pedestal. They both watched Storm, Skyfire leaning on the wall behind her, an ever-protective shadow. "Sometimes it's hard to remember precisely how few years they have seen. They act more mature than some elders I have known."

"I do not think it is so much a matter of the number of years they have seen, but their sheer...inexperience," the bard stated, trying to find the words that did not make the Desanti's flaws seem a criticism of them.

Almek looked from the two Desanti to study the Vodani bard's profile. "You're worried about them."

"I am...and I'm not. I'm not sure who I am worried about more," Mureln confessed. "Them, or those who might try to take advantage of their naïveté. They are children of the Raging One. Their hearts lead before their minds. Gods, you've seen Storm's temper already. I'm sure Skyfire has one of his own, given how Kailee Named him. Our master mage has certainly endured it often enough." He shook his head. "I worry about the first time someone tries anything that comes across as even vaguely threatening or challenging, whether or not it was intended that way. The mainland does not take kindly to minced idiots." He paused. "Deserving or not."

"Point taken. I will speak with them privately." The two looked up when the sailors suddenly burst out laughing, chuckling as Storm swatted Skyfire's arm for the peculiar expression he made. "You are right," the Guardian admitted. "A child's innocence with a warrior's training is a dangerous pairing to leave unbridled."

Chapter Thirty-Nine

DAYS PASSED, AND THE two Desanti not only acclimated to their new environment but thrived, learning everything they could. One of the older sailors took Skyfire under his wing, teaching the young man how to climb rigging and handle the ropes. The speed he took to sea craft earned him the admiration of the Vodani.

Storm, much more reclusive, kept more to herself. When she was not picking the brains of the captain or helmsman, she was climbing the ropes, walking along the rails, or perched on one of the highest crossbeams on the masts, staring out into the distance.

During the evening meal on the twelfth day at sea, Storm was missing from the gathering. When asked, Skyfire shrugged and pointed upwards. "She has been up there all day today. She'll be back down when she's ready." He grinned widely at Almek. "I know better than to interrupt her when she gets in these moods."

"Her presence would be helpful." Almek broke off a piece of bread to eat with his stew. "There is much to prepare before we make landfall. I would prefer that we start sooner rather than later."

Mureln offered a cup of mead to Taylin with exaggerated flourish, the woman accepting with all due solemnity before grinning at him. The bard looked over his shoulder at Almek. "I confess, Almek, I have to agree with Radisen—forgive me—*Skyfire*. Storm lives up to her name, and I need all my fingers for my craft."

Looking bemused at the deference to Storm's temper, Ash pushed himself to his feet, detaching Amelana from his arm. "I'll inform her you wish to discuss plans for when we reach the mainland, Master Almek."

"But Ash—*Master* Ash," Amelana corrected herself when Ash leveled a dark, critical gaze on her, "you've barely eaten anything. Can't it wait? And you were going to give me lessons after—"

Ash replied distractedly, "I'm not hungry, Journeyman. We'll continue your lessons later this evening."

Almek reached out to catch Ash's arm, his gray eyes filled with concern. "Don't push her too hard," Almek told Ash in a low voice. "There's plenty of time to plan if she's not ready." The mage nodded, hurrying to leave before anyone delayed him further.

Ash emerged onto the deck, taking a deep breath of the clean sea air gratefully. Squinting, he searched the tops of the masts to find where the Desanti woman was this time. He spotted her sitting atop the furled top-gallant's crossbeam. Removing his outer robe and boots so he wore only his tunic and trousers, he scaled the ropes with the ease of a lifetime of having lived in the high trees of Forenta.

Storm glanced over when he reached her, then turned her eyes back out to the horizon. "I can understand why you dislike the mess hall. It's unbearably close with so many." He settled on the other side of the mast, then studied her. "Master Almek was looking for you." Still, she stared out into the distance, silent. "What are you doing up here?" His voice held only uncritical curiosity, which finally elicited a silent response. He followed her finger when she pointed into the distance. He saw small figures rising and falling against the horizon. Mentally estimating the distance and what the size of the things were, he made a sound that reflected he was impressed. "What are they?"

"The Vodani call them whales." Her voice barely carried over the wind. "The captain says they are animals that are as big as this ship. Some bigger! And there are smaller ones like them they call dolphins." Her eyes never wavered from the animals, her expression impossible to read. "There is so much life in the Great Water. But the sailors say it can feel as lonely and desolate as the desert. I cannot believe the Vodani cannot see how filled with life it is."

Ash looked at the whales for a moment longer before giving Storm his complete attention. He watched her as she spoke, not interrupting. He waited until her words finally trailed off. "There is nothing wrong with feeling overwhelmed. There are many things you are not used to," he told her, drawing her attention away from the horizon. "I felt the same when I came to Desantiva."

"There isn't anything in my land to be overwhelmed by." The acute bitterness in her voice surprised Ash. "Listening to Mureln and the Sevmanen talk—even the Vodani—a tiny city in the north has as much life as all of Desantiva."

"There is more in Desantiva than you realize is there," he countered, surprising her. "One day, Desantiva will heal from the wounds it has suffered for so long."

Storm shook her head, raising a hand to brush a tendril of hair that the wind blew loose from its confines. "I will never see that day. Healing will take a very long time, and the scars will always remain." She looked at a very old scar on the back of her arm. "They always do."

Ash reached over, brushing the scar with his fingertips. "Taylin could probably heal that if you wished."

Storm merely smiled, and Ash would have sworn her smile had an almost innocent shyness. "You should return to your journeyman." At his consternated expression from the unexpected response, she asked, "Can't you sense her glaring daggers up here? She has been pacing like a small thundercloud down there since shortly after you climbed up here."

Ash glanced down and, sure enough, the Forentan woman was walking in circles below, occasionally yelling at sailors to get out of her way. He shrugged. "She can wait. I prefer your company to her incessant, brainless chatter."

"She lacks patience," Storm observed, not bothering to look down. Looking back towards the horizon, she fell silent for a time. "Is she typical of Outlanders?"

Heaving a resigned sigh, Ash nodded. "Unfortunately, some of them, yes. Thankfully, not all are like her. Most are content to ignore things so long as it does not interfere with their daily lives."

Nodding, Storm pondered for several more moments. "She seems to be an unusual choice of student for you."

Ash frowned, asking in harsher tones than he intended, "What do you mean?"

Storm smiled at the man's bristling at the implied insult. "She does not apply herself to her training. She does not give anyone the respect they deserve. She especially gives you little to no respect. She is petty and spiteful and has a completely unwarranted jealousy towards me. You do not think highly of her, I think. I would have believed you'd have chosen a higher caliber of a student like you had with Terrence."

Ash blinked several times and made a face. "Amelana was assigned to me by the Edai Tredecima...the council of mages...as a journeyman because the second highest ranking Edai Magus is of the Avarian family. To get Terrence as my apprentice, I had to agree to take her as well." He could sense the confusion of the Desanti woman. "Master mages do not have the complete freedom Swordanzen have, especially if they are lowborn, not highborn."

"Lowborn?" she echoed. "Highborn? I do not understand these terms." The whales forgotten, Storm gave her complete attention to Ash, a slight frown marring her features. "Explain to me, please. I want to understand so that I do not embarrass Lord Almek."

Ash's smile turned rueful, having to explain something often indirectly spoken of in his homeland, if discussed at all. "Family status in Forenta is based on how old the family is. How rich, how much power ancestors had before, and how much now. If you are born into a well placed family, you are highborn. If you are born into a family not as strong or powerful—or you have no family at all—you are lowborn. Many lower-born families try to marry their children into higher-born families to raise their own statuses. Or highborn families will attempt to claim particularly strong lowborn as their own to have control over them."

Storm looked insulted. "You are judged just by how you were born? You do not have to earn your place? Or prove you are worthy?" The mage did not bother to answer. "That makes no sense. How does that keep the blood strong?"

"It used to. When the highborn families had the best and most powerful mages among their numbers. Families would match their strongest children with the strongest of other houses, and that would usually produce even stronger children. Now..." his voice drifted off and he shrugged. "I'm not sure."

Storm leveled a narrow-eyed gaze at the Forentan man as she considered his words. He could tell the moment she understood the underlying facts behind them. "She considers you beneath her. Despite your skills and power and her obvious lack of them." Storm snorted. "Stupid bitch. You would have better breeding with a lame drizzen."

Ash regarded the Desanti woman with quiet admiration and murmured, "What do you mean Amelana's jealousy is *completely* unwarranted?" Storm looked confused and had opened her mouth to speak when something distracted their attention downwards at the same moment. The ship abruptly listed, forcing the two to grab onto the ropes on the mast to keep their seats.

Her reaction a heartbeat before his own did not escape the mage. "You could sense that?" Ash looked down at the surrounding water. "There is something else here."

"Something large is near..." Storm clung white-knuckled to the mast. "There! See the dark shape in the water?" At the moment she took to point to the shadow underwater, the ship listed to the other side, and she lost her grip. Ash lunged to grab her wrist. His grip was secure, but before she could find purchase on the mast, something jolted the ship again and she slipped from his grasp. She hit the water feet first and disappeared beneath the surface. Without hesitation, he dove after her near where she disappeared.

In the cold, silent underwater world, it took a moment for Ash to get his bearings, and then to locate Storm. He got behind her and put an arm around her waist. Holding her tight, he pulled her upwards, the two gasping for air as they broke the surface.

Coughing water out of her lungs, Storm wheezed. "I thought...I thought you could not...could not s-swim."

"I can't," he said in her ear, holding her tight against him. "I can just about keep my head above water."

"Liar," she coughed, trying to laugh to hide her absolute terror. They both looked downwards as something snaked around them, jerking them underwater.

The world fell into an eerie silence once more as they were dragged beneath the waves; sunlight danced and glimmered on the water's surface high above. Through the murky depths, they glimpsed the creature assaulting their ship—a massive, shadowy form with countless writhing arms, a formidable beak, and eyes as vast as the ocean itself. It inexorably drew them towards its gaping maw.

At the same moment, Storm jabbed her two-edged blade into the nearest eye, and Ash cast a spell that sent a shockwave into the thing. The water went black as the monster fled, wounded and unprepared for such dangerous prey. A flailing tentacle knocked the wind out of both as it fled.

Finding his bearings, Ash kept his arm around Storm and kicked back towards the surface. His lungs screamed for oxygen, but he focused on getting back to the air above. He gasped, coughing up black water.

Storm hung in his embrace, unmoving. He lifted her head up, patting her cheek. "Storm," he wheezed, desperate for a response. "Storm, wake up. Answer me!"

"Lord Ash!" Skyfire yelled from somewhere above them. "Mureln! Lord Almek! They are over here!"

"Storm," Ash begged the woman who was not breathing. "Come on! Don't give up on me now." He grabbed the rope the sailors threw down to them, wrapping it around them both.

He would not release Storm when they were pulled aboard, laying her on the deck, touching her cheek. "She isn't breathing," he said. "Storm!" He shoved someone trying to get near and felt his arm caught in a firm grip.

Mureln shook the mage a little to get his attention. "Turn her onto her side. We need to get the water out of her lungs." The mage nodded, letting the bard help shift Storm. The change of position helped the woman cough up inky water. Unconscious, she still held the two-edged blade in her hand in a death grip. It took both Skyfire and Mureln to force her to release the blade. Though unconscious, she relaxed the moment Skyfire returned it to its snug sheath.

"Come on, let's get you below," Mureln said. Skyfire gathered Storm in his arms as Mureln put his shoulder under Ash to keep the man on his feet.

Taylin blocked Amelana from following. "You will stay away until they have recovered, Journeyman. They need rest, and you will give neither any."

Amelana scowled, starting to shove past Taylin. "Get out of my way, Sevmanan bi—" the Forentan woman began when she gasped in shock and then screamed in pain, collapsing into a miserable, quivering ball.

"I said," Taylin stated coldly, her fingers curled like claws and haloed in shadow from the anti-healing magic she used, "stay away. Next time, I will do worse than just cause you pain." The healer spun on her heel, leaving the woman collapsed on the deck. Neither Almek's students nor the *Wave Dancer's* sailors bothered to even look at the Forentan woman.

THE SOUND OF STORM'S weak coughing roused Ash from fitful slumber. Squinting as he tried to focus in the dim light, he saw the Desanti woman in the bunk across from him, curled on her side in a fetal position. Her breath came in wheezing gasps between the coughs wracking her body.

"Storm!" The mage was shocked at how weak his own voice sounded to him.

He looked at the hand placed on his shoulder, a sense of grateful reassurance in the touch, then up to see Skyfire. "Lord Ash. It is good to see you awaken finally. We have worried about how much of the black water you swallowed."

Ash closed his eyes, putting a hand to his head, feeling as though the room were spinning. "Black water?"

"The Vodani call the thing that attacked the ship a kraken. They say when the beasts are alarmed, they send out a cloud of black venom into the water to keep their attackers from following." Skyfire reached over to rest a hand on Storm's head, worried. "The ink from smaller versions called squid only irritates. Large amounts can be...fatal." Shaking his head sharply to dislodge more worrying thoughts, he spoke more briskly. "You lost consciousness shortly after we brought you below."

"How long?" Ash reached deep to find the strength to push himself to sit up, keeping his hand on his head, and grateful the Desanti man did not force him back down to rest.

"You were unconscious for four days."

"Storm?"

Skyfire's silence drew Ash to look closely at his grim visage. The Desanti shook his head. "She wakes up...now and then. The coughing drains whatever strength she recovers." Before Ash could speak, Skyfire continued. "Mureln said we are heading to a place called Water's Resonance. They have medicines that will help you and Storm."

"How long?" Ash looked at Storm, her sickly pallor worrisome.

"The ship's weather wisdom has done what she can to keep the winds strong. They are hoping we reach it in the next day or two." Skyfire looked from Storm back to Ash. "You should rest, Lord Ash. You need your strength."

"I'm fine," Ash argued before a wracking cough seized him. Skyfire rested a hand upon his shoulder, as if he could will strength to the mage. When it finally eased some, Ash looked embarrassed. "Thank you."

"No, Lord Ash. Thank *you* for keeping her alive. Again." Skyfire paused a moment, embarrassment creasing his features. "I am...not ready to stand in her place. Not to stand and face your god on behalf of ours." The Desanti man smiled wanly.

"Mage," Storm whispered weakly.

"Shhh." Skyfire dipped a cloth in a bowl of water, placing the cool damp cloth on her brow, murmuring reassuringly. "He is here, Storm. He is safe." The reassurance calmed the fever-stricken woman.

Ash tilted his head, looking at her. "She calls for me?"

"And you for her. You both keep trying to find each other." Skyfire's expression was unhappy. "We brought you to Storm's and my room. We tried taking you to your own." Ash looked quizzically at the Desanti. Skyfire said darkly, "We must take turns standing watch to ensure you both can rest. It is easier when you are together."

"Amelana," Ash said tonelessly. Skyfire nodded. Both men started when a fit of coughing overwhelmed the Desanti woman again, leaving her even weaker than before, breathing shallow and with a trickle of blackish blood appearing at the corner of her mouth. "Taylin cannot heal her?"

"Taylin says healers can mend the body, but have no power over things like alcohol or poisons. She does what she can to mend the damage, but the black water is in your blood. The Vodani on this ship say the body can purge it...but with as much as you both got in you, it will kill you before you do." He dabbed the blood from Storm's cheek. "Mureln says the Vodani medicine at Water's Resonance is the only thing that can draw the black water out of your bodies quickly and completely." Listening to Storm's weak wheezing, he got to his feet. "I will go get the healer. Storm is worse than before."

As the door closed, Ash turned at the sound of his name. With only the need to reassure her, he moved to sit on the floor by Storm, taking her reaching hand in his and felt much of her tension ease. "Shhh. I'm here, Storm."

"Ash?" She opened fever-hazed eyes. "Ash, I am afraid. I cannot...I cannot breathe."

"I'm here," he said reassuringly, clasping her trembling hand tighter and resting his head on his other arm. He wasn't sure how much time had passed when he noticed others in the room. There was some argument about getting Ash back in the bed, but it ended with a note of resignation. A moment later, Ash felt a blanket draped around him.

CHAPTER FORTY

LIKE THE ESSENCE OF rainbows captured in watery crystal, the violet spires of Water's Resonance reached into the sky like delicate needles. Grand arches over the water dwarfed the many Vodani ships that docked within and without the strange island's embrace. Much like at Home Port in Desantiva, Vodani crowded balconies above the cavernous harbor to glimpse the unusual visitors, particularly the Desanti.

A willowy woman hurried to the group as they disembarked on the main landing, touching Ash's cheek, then Storm's. "Come, come! There is no time to waste!" She led the group into wide halls, waving her hands imperiously at the gawking Vodani, scolding them in an almost musical voice. The Vodani dispersed like a parting sea.

"Tulis, quickly." The woman pointed to an ornate couch for Skyfire to lay Storm on, Terrence guiding a barely coherent Ash to a similarly designed chair. Sending the pair's companions out, she crouched by Ash, offering him a crystalline glass filled with an odd, shimmering liquid. "Drink." She spoke in a tone that brooked no disobedience. Holding the glass for him, she would not lower it until it was empty.

Ash grimaced, feeling strange as the liquid seemed to sit in the pit of his stomach like a heavy weight. He wanted to ask questions, fighting the urge to gag, feeling as if his stomach was being ripped from his body.

"The purging will be harder on her," the woman said. "She has a great deal of dark water in her. Stay with her, Tulis. It will be especially harsh."

"Of course, Ilsa."

Without warning, Ash felt his stomach rebel after untold long minutes, unable to stop himself from vomiting. He was dimly aware of a comforting hand on his back and a basin placed in front of him. After what seemed an eternity, his stomach kept heaving though he had nothing more to purge. Eventually, the spasms finally eased, leaving Ash drained. He wiped his mouth with the back of his hand and stared at the smear of blood-stained blackness.

He looked up when Storm was caught in the throes of vomiting; the sounds made his own insides twist. By the time she was done, she curled in a ball on her knees, the dry sobs he was familiar with tearing at her more than the dry heaves left after the purging. The unknown man gathered Storm in his arms to lay her on the couch. "Storm!" He struggled against the unfamiliar woman's restraint, trying to get to Storm's side.

Gentle music seeped into Ash's consciousness, and he felt himself being drawn towards the oblivion of sleep. The mage shook his head, fighting the lethargy, determined to get to Storm to comfort her. Too weak to fight, he sighed and closed his eyes, succumbing to the darkness.

"I have never seen it take so long for your music to put someone to sleep, Mureln." The woman draped a blanket over Ash. "Especially two who nearly succumbed to the black water. It almost put *me* to sleep."

"They are two of the strongest souls I have ever met," the bard murmured, his eyes on his mandolin as he continued to play. He dared to flick a worried glance upwards at the impossibly slender woman. "You're sure they'll recover, Ilsa?"

Slender eyebrows rose as the woman put a delicate hand over her heart. "Mureln, I'm insulted. When have you ever known me to lie about such a thing?" The willowy woman leaned down to touch Storm's brow. "Tulis, keep changing the rags until her fever comes down." The man nodded, giving the woman a bland look that spoke volumes of her speaking to him as if he were a novice. The look was lost on Ilsa, whose attention had returned to Mureln. "I had only heard stories about Githalin Swordanzen all my life, and you bring us two. And a Forentan Illaini Magus! I can hardly wait for them to awaken so I may meet them properly!"

Mureln pressed his lips together in annoyance. "I didn't bring them here for your personal entertainment, Ilsa."

Ilsa swept behind the bard, putting her hands on his shoulders and leaning to whisper in his ear. "I have missed your entertainment, Mureln. Won't you stay for a while longer this time?"

"You know why I can't. My duty is to the music and to the Dusvet Guardian."

Tulis glanced at Mureln with an apologetic expression. "Ilsa, the woman's fever has broken, and the man is not showing signs of any. Do you wish me to have the guest hall prepared for the Dusvet Guardian and his party?"

"Yes, of course, Tulis." Ilsa went to the man to kiss his cheek lightly. After Tulis had departed, the willowy woman sighed dramatically as she moved over to a cabinet in the room, taking down two glasses. "You always did favor landwalkers over your own people, Mureln. Those two brutes—"

"Emil and Emaris are like brothers to me, Ilsa." Mureln's annoyance lent an edge to his music. The sleeping pair roused, their expressions reflecting the agitation in the music, until Mureln mastered his emotions and returned to his muted playing. The two settled back into a sound sleep. "I would appreciate if you would stop distracting me, hm?"

Ilsa brought over two glasses of dark-colored wine. "Please, Mureln. You have put me off ever since we were children. Just this once, could you at least *pretend* to be my husband?"

"I'm grateful to you for saving the lives of my friends, but I won't play your games just to amuse you." He looked up at the woman with a displeased expression, taking the glass to drain quickly then resuming before Storm and Ash roused. "Our parents arranged our pairing. We never formalized it. We are not now, and never will be, married."

"We could be if you would just stay," Ilsa pouted, resting a hand over his heart. "Please, Mureln. I'm lonely."

"You have Tulis. You're not lonely, you're bored." Mureln gently but firmly removed her hand from his shoulder. Noticing both mage and warrior struggled to awaken, he quickly resumed playing his music. Both went still again. "There is no more patient man in Vodanya than he. But right now, my friends need to rest and recover from the black water. Show your patients the compassion and consideration you have denied me all our lives."

"Tulis isn't as fascinating as you, Mureln." Ilsa sighed again. "But you're right. They need you more right now than me." She drew a gauzy veil over her hair and straightened. "I'll go speak to the Dusvet Guardian and your other companions to reassure them you had arrived in time. *We* can talk more later." Mureln closed his eyes as she left, less than eager.

THE GRAND DOORS TO the chamber where Almek and the others waited opened, and Ilsa entered with an ethereal elegance. She approached Almek, offering her hands to him as she knelt respectfully before him, eyes lowered. "Water's Resonance is honored for your visit, Dusvet Guardian Almek Two-Tones. I am Ilsa, master apothecarist of Water's Resonance."

"What of my students?" Almek's worry for the pair shortened his patience with formality, though he accepted her offered hands, squeezing them.

Ilsa smiled in understanding as she rose to her feet. "The black water is purged. Mureln is with them, bringing them ease with his music so they may recover their strength and heal faster." Her smile faded to something more serious. "It would have been otherwise if you had arrived any later. You should permit them to recover fully before you resume traveling. All of you are welcome to remain among us until then."

Almek nodded, relaxing. "Your generous offer is very much appreciated, Ilsa. Thank you."

Emil was talking with Terrence when the man laughed wryly. "Lad, I ha' been travelin' wi' Mureln fer almost as long as ye've been alive, land an' sea both, and I ain't never seen no beasts like what nearly killed yer master 'n th' Swordanzen." He glanced at Skyfire, cleared his throat, and amended, "th' other Swordanzen." Skyfire grinned at him.

Ilsa shook her head, elaborate braids dyed in pale blues, greens and violets swaying with the motion. "Kraken seldom come so near the surface. Their domain is the depths far from any shore."

"Something must have disturbed it." Tulis entered, bowing deeply to Almek and introducing himself before taking Ilsa's hand briefly, lightly kissing her cheek. "It's not unknown for one of the ocean lords to claim ships. But it is equally uncommon."

"What may have disturbed it is what concerns me," Almek mused, half to himself. "It is too much for me to think it is merely a coincidence two of my strongest students were nearly killed."

Tulis considered. "Many more attuned to the ocean's rhythms complain of dissonances in the currents. Lurkers who have become bolder each time the greater moon shines her face upon the waves."

"Darklings?" Taylin wondered.

The Vodani man shrugged one shoulder. "I suppose they would fit the Forentan definition." When the Sevmanen traded confused looks, Tulis explained patiently, "Light can only reach so far into the water's depths. You cannot have shadows where there is no light. For us, they are the unnatural things that lurk in the depths." A hint of amusement touched the Vodani man's otherwise impassive face. "Of course, most landwalkers consider what we call 'natural' to be quite unnatural."

Ilsa was studying each of the newcomers and tilted her head. "Was there not another Forentan with you? A woman?" Her eyes fixed on Skyfire for several moments, the Desanti man beginning to fidget under the intensity of her stare.

"She decided it would be best for all concerned—especially herself—if she stayed in her quarters on the ship." Taylin's voice held such uncharacteristic sharpness that her companions had to choke back their laughter.

"A pity. I am *always* fascinated when we have visitors from the mainland. It's especially rare for Forenten to come here." Ilsa's strange gaze now studied the Sevmanan woman. "Interesting," she murmured, approaching the healer, offering her hand to her. Uncertainly, Taylin gave Ilsa her hand in return, looking uncomfortable. "It has been a long time since I have met a Sevmanan healer. One with true power. Your skills are quite the talk of the ship's crew. Perhaps later we can meet to talk?"

Tulis approached and put a hand on Ilsa's shoulder, giving her a long, meaningful look. "They are our guests, Ilsa. Shouldn't we let them settle into their rooms before dinner?"

"Oh, yes, of course, dear Tulis. I'm so forgetful sometimes." Releasing Taylin's hand, Ilsa made a grandiose wave towards another set of double doors two young servants opened. "It *is* rare that we have mainland guests. There are rooms for each of you down the hall. Or you may share," she added with a twinkle in her eyes. "They are quite comfortable. A youngling will come for you when the evening meal is ready."

Almek nodded to Ilsa. "The generosity of Water's Resonance is appreciated."

"Of course, Dusvet! We would never neglect our duty to Fortress." Smiling coyly, Ilsa said, "And do tell your other Forentan companion she is welcome to join us. It would be such a pleasure to meet her. If you will excuse me, I will go see how Mureln fares with your companions." With a final bow, she swept out of the room, leaving the group in stunned silence.

"She must b'kidding," Emil finally stated, crossing his arms. "She can't be *wantin'* t' meet th' ice queen."

Almek shook his head. "Oh, stars no, I'm afraid she isn't kidding. Vodani are...ah, rather unique. To some degree, they all live to experience the world. Joy, grief, pleasure, pain...They even regard death as the last adventure." He patted Taylin's shoulder comfortingly. "If anything a Vodani asks of you makes you uncomfortable, just be firm and say no. It is rare that they will impose anything on the unwilling."

Skyfire coughed nervously, scratching his jaw. "Many women have looked at me before. Never like that." He glanced towards the door and then shook his head.

Storm gasped as she woke abruptly, looking around in disorientation as she reached for weapons that were not there. Looking around in rising panic, she relaxed when she saw them all neatly placed on the table at the foot of her couch.

"You are absolutely impossible to keep asleep." Mureln shifted to a new song. "I expect *he* will be waking soon if you've managed to wake despite my best efforts."

"Desanti rarely sleep long out of necessity," Storm stated absently. She looked at the bard and then followed his gaze to the sleeping mage. Green-gold eyes stared unblinkingly at Ash, the Swordanzen's expression unreadable, breaking her silence after several long minutes. "It was not a nightmare. It was real."

"Very much so." Mureln watched her as his fingers moved along the strings of his mandolin. "You and Ash saved the rest of our lives, however accidental your parts in it may have been."

"I am glad," Storm replied with distracted politeness. She pushed herself to her feet, wobbling a bit before she went to the window to look outside. "This strange place. It is your home."

Mureln arched an eyebrow. "I grew up here, but I have not been in Water's Resonance for many years."

Shaking her head, Storm clarified. "I meant it is the home of your birth."

The bard blinked in surprise. "You can tell?"

"The essence of home is imprinted on all who embrace their being part of the world, not separate from it." She gazed out of the window in silence. "The currents are deep here, giving a hum to this island of crystal. It echoes within you. This is not Lord Almek's. His soul echoes of crashing waves and whispering winds across the land."

"Almek is over five hundred years old! How can you—?" Storm turned, almost smiling. "Why am I surprised?" the bard asked the ceiling before looking at Storm again. "Are you alright?"

"I am whole." Storm looked over at Ash. Standing by the chair he slept in, she brushed his hair back in place gently. "Do you consider the Forentan mage a friend?" the Desanti woman asked slowly, choosing her words with care. Mureln nodded, watching Storm in silence as if not daring to risk interrupting the Swordanzen. "You must stop him."

"Stop him? From what?"

"Feeling anything other than duty towards me." Green-gold eyes met Mureln's startled sea blue-green ones. "Swordanzen are forbidden ties to anything but our duty to Desantiva. It is especially forbidden to Githalin."

"You do not have to—"

"Understand this, Bard. Duty must always come first. Always. He deserves better than the likes of me." She walked to her couch, methodically putting her weapon belts back in place. "Before that...creature attacked the ship, he told me he thought Swordanzen had greater freedom than mages." She did not look at Mureln as she spoke, the bard wide-eyed. "It is enough I fear my and Skyfire's association with Lord Almek risks danger to his students because a Swordanzen must answer all challenges and we have sworn to protect him and all his students."

"Storm," Mureln began, his playing long stopped. He started to rise, but stopped when she raised both of her hands.

"My father gave me His blessing to make new patterns. But there were reasons the patterns were made so long ago. I will not break them just because I might..." She leveled a look at the bard, the man drawing back as if physically struck. "If you truly consider yourself his friend, stop him before he has to choose between his duty and his heart. Please."

Mureln inhaled sharply as he realized, "There isn't anything going on between you and Skyfire, is there?"

"Skyfire and I are *th'yala*. We are an oasis to each other where we are now the outlanders. We are kinsmen and comrades-in-arms. Friends. Having that much between us will be dangerous enough. Skyfire understands now more than ever being Githalin Swordanzen. But." She turned towards the door. "If it makes it easier for Ash to believe there is more, let him." She paused by the door, bowing her head and said with a voice that made Mureln's heart ache with its poignancy, "It would be better if we hated each other as Desanti and Forentan should. Then it would not hurt."

Mureln could only watch as the Desanti woman left, the door closing quietly behind her. "Oh, Storm. *You* deserve better than what you allow yourself." The bard looked over as Ash began to rouse, closing his eyes in a wince when it was Storm's name on his lips.

Chapter Forty-One

Much like the Desanti, the Vodani did nearly everything together as a community. The main meals of the day were no exception. Striations of the same purple crystal that made the spires lined the walls of the massive cavern that served as the great hall, glowing with the sunlight that exposed crystal captured, casting kaleidoscope patterns across the polished stone floor. Hanging from ornately carved pillars that supported the vaulted ceiling, oil lamps added their warm light to the illumination as the crystals' glow dimmed with the setting sun.

The Vodani clustered in various groups, from the various schools of learning within the community to ship crews that were often a single clan, with the youngsters clustering together at smaller tables suited to their diminutive statures. The sounds of chatter and laughter mingled with the distant sound of ocean waves coming from the outer windows.

Ilsa invited the Dusvet Guardian and his students to sit at her table. The Vodani woman watched the group's interactions over the edge of her glass with keen interest. She spoke to the bard seated to her right with a careless nonchalance. "I see now why you stay with them. It is like watching oil and spirits mix and needing only the tiniest of sparks to ignite things." She smiled when Emil turned to scold Emaris again. "How fascinating!"

"Ilsa, just keep your curiosity to yourself." Mureln struggled to keep his voice even, not wanting to draw his companions' attention.

She chuckled softly at the bard's stern expression. "Lighten up, Mureln. You're taking things too seriously. I promise I'll be on my best behavior. Anyway," she indicated the Desanti and Forenten with a small motion, "it's only a matter of time. They don't need my help for that to occur."

At the far end of the table, Storm and Skyfire quietly spoke as they poked at the unfamiliar food. Without warning, Storm spun around on her bench and came nose to nose with a young Vodani boy about eight years old, who froze in shock, his finger outstretched, caught mid-attempt to touch one of her swords. Wide eyes stared at the gleaming blade Storm had drawn, the point hovering right in front of his nose.

Storm smiled as she put her knife back in its sheath. "You are very good. I almost didn't notice you." The boy just stared in outright terror. "My name is Storm." She offered her hand in greeting, the boy shakily responding to the gesture. "What is your name?" she prompted.

"J-J-Jakkee," the boy stammered.

"I am very pleased to meet you, Jakkee." Storm turned around in her seat to face the boy, crossing her arms as she studied him. "Do not worry. I don't bite."

"Unless ye ask," Emil piped up. "Ow!" the Sevmanan yelped as he got an elbow from each side, glaring at Emaris and Skyfire. "Ye all got no sense of humor."

Jakkee clapped his hands over his mouth to smother giggles, relaxing. Storm glanced over at a small gaggle of children hiding behind the nearest column, whispering to each other and pointing excitedly. "I see you were the only one brave enough to come meet me."

"They triple-dared me to touch your sword!" he said, as if there was no choice.

"Ah, I see." Storm nodded with complete understanding. "Surely, such a brave young warrior could not retreat from such a challenge." She stood, the boy shuffling backwards and falling on his backside. "I should like to meet your friends, Jakkee. Would you honor me by introducing me to them?"

Jakkee's eyes lit up. "Really?!" Jumping to his feet, he grabbed Storm's hand and pulled her after him.

"Your Swordanzen certainly makes an impression wherever she goes, does she not, Dusvet?" Ilsa asked Almek, smiling indulgently. "Already she has won the hearts of Home Port, the *Wave Dancer's* crew, and now the youngsters here."

"She is not that impressive," Amelana stated loftily.

"Oh?" Ilsa replied before anyone could scold the Forentan woman. "And what have *you* done to compare to the Swordanzen woman?"

"My family is—" Amelana began.

Ilsa interrupted. "Not your family. I neither know nor care about your family. This is Vodanya. We care little about your landwalker social hierarchies. They are meaningless here. The only thing that carries weight to the Vodani are only your own achievements. This is about you. Tell me what makes *you* better than the Desanti woman?"

"My great grandfa—"

"*You*," Ilsa repeated, but this time with more of an edge. "Surely *you* have done something to make your family proud to call you one of their own." She gestured towards the others at the table. "You keep company with the Dusvet Guardian, a master bard, a master healer, an Illaini Magus, and two Githalin Swordanzen." She glanced at Emil and Emaris, adding grudgingly, "And masters at other things. Surely you must excel at something to be more impressive than a Swordanzen." When the Forentan woman didn't respond, she asked, "At least equally impressive?"

Amelana flushed as others at the table began to chuckle, either hiding it behind their drinks or not bothering to hide at all. She glanced at Ash, who did not look at her as he drank his wine. Verging on tears, Amelana ran out of the hall.

Mureln looked aggrieved. "Ilsa."

Ilsa rose as most of the others in the hall did, tables and benches being moved aside, ignoring Mureln. Gliding over to Taylin, Ilsa smiled warmly. "My dear, would you honor me with your company? Sevmanan healers have always fascinated me, but they so rarely leave their temples on the mainland. I would very much like to speak with you about your arts. Apothecary shares the same goal of easing life's ailments for the suffering, you know."

Taylin smiled at Ilsa, still chuckling from Amelana's verbal smack down and nodded. "Of course, Ilsa." She fell in step with the willowy woman.

Almek put a hand on Mureln's shoulder to restrain him. "Taylin can take care of herself."

"Ilsa seems to enjoy creating waves," Ash observed as other Vodani, emboldened by seeing Storm with the group of children, eagerly approached Skyfire, Terrence, Emil, and Emaris to invite them to various entertainments of dancing, gambling, or storytelling. No one was quite brave enough to approach Almek and Ash as they spoke together with Mureln. "Another sister of yours?"

Mureln shook his head sharply before turning on his heel to stalk away. "My betrothed."

Almek nearly choked on his wine and stared after Mureln. "Betrothed? I suppose I can still be surprised, even at my age. I had no idea."

Watching Mureln leave, Tulis approached, offering the two men a respectful bow. "I see Ilsa has been seeing how many ripples she can create again. I apologize on behalf of my people, Dusvet Guardian Almek. She is not a representative in her behavior."

"She and Mureln seem to have a history," Ash commented, sipping his wine.

Tulis smiled warmly, shrugging one shoulder. "It's more the lack of history that makes him so intriguing to Ilsa. Because our people live in such small, distant groups, it's not uncommon for families to arrange marriages to keep the bloodlines strong."

"And he turned down the arrangement," Ash concluded, watching after the bard with empathy for his situation.

Tulis shrugged one shoulder. "Mureln could not abide Ilsa's manipulations and refused to make the match official. In fact, once he reached journeyman rank as a bard, he left Water's Resonance altogether by hiring on with one of the trader ships. Ilsa and I married shortly after. From his messages, he'd encountered you at the third port the ship stopped at, Dusvet. And then, once the music called, he never looked back. We were all surprised to learn he is a student to you again. But grateful, too. Many worried his decision to leave your tutelage was an insult to Fortress."

"Perhaps to some other Guardians, but never to me, I assure you." Almek finished his drink. "A divided heart would have been a detriment to everyone, and my Mistress."

The Vodani man's expression spoke of his relief and gratitude. Waving a server over to refill their glasses, Tulis added, "Mureln is the one person Ilsa has desired but has never been able to bed despite many attempts to convince him otherwise."

It was Ash's turn nearly to choke on his drink. "Excuse me? Isn't she still your wife?"

Tulis tilted his head, puzzled for a moment. "Oh, forgive me. I forget how restrictive you landwalkers are about your pairings." He waved a hand. "Marriages are for having children. The act of copulation is a sharing of pleasure and company, a celebration of life. Something Mureln has outright refused Ilsa. That has made him something of a personal challenge for her."

"So, Vodani do not stay faithful to one person?" Ash asked, fascinated despite himself.

"The way you landwalkers do? Why? Life is for living." He looked between Almek and Ash. "It's a belief that has its roots in our Desanti ancestry. Mureln says the Desanti belief is to enjoy the moment, for tomorrow you may die. Vodani are not so morbid." He smiled faintly. "But life is to be experienced to its fullest, don't you agree?"

Ash stiffened, irritated that no matter how he answered, he believed Tulis would mock him for it. "Forgive me, I thought there was some...attachment between you both."

The Vodani man's smile was so without malice, Ash could not help but relax. "Ilsa and I have been companions for many years, especially because we both study the apothecary arts. We had only one daughter, who died during her adulthood trial. Ever since then, Ilsa has been more interested in meddling in others' lives. She means no actual harm. She has always had the best interests of Water's Resonance at heart. Unfortunately, when she is not focused on her art, she enjoys instigating reactions from people."

Almek mused. "At the moment, she seems more interested in causing Mureln grief than in Water's Resonance's welfare."

"Ilsa was the only person who could get under Mureln's skin, ever since they were children. She delighted in unsettling him. It's probably why my brother rarely comes home anymore."

"Brother?" Tulis inclined his head to Ash in acknowledgment. "I see." Ash finished his wine and gave the glass to a passing serving girl, who blushed and curtsied to him. "I should check on my journeyman. If you will excuse me."

"Of course." Almek turned to Tulis. "Perhaps you could enlighten me on the news of lurkers your people have reported?"

"Of course, Dusvet. I would be honored," Tulis replied, guiding him towards one of the remaining groups of people.

CHAPTER FORTY-TWO

"YOU HAVE NO IDEA how much of a pleasure it was to see Amelana put in her place, Ilsa." Taylin followed Ilsa into a small library filled with scrolls and books alike. "She has been absolutely impossible."

Ilsa smiled indulgently. "I'm glad you were pleased. I believe everyone was amused. Except for Mureln." Tsking, she went to the table where a carafe of wine sat, topping off her drink.

"I'm surprised, honestly," Taylin admitted. "It seems like he has spent half his time putting her in her place. It never seemed to affect her nearly as much as when you did it."

"Ah, my dear, a man can never truly criticize a woman like that Forentan girl effectively. She will always dismiss anything that displeases her because of his gender." Smiling as she languidly stretched out on one of the two couches, she waved Taylin to the other. "Treat her as one who is beneath you and ignore any of her attempts to make you feel otherwise. That will bother her more than any well placed insults."

Taylin sighed as she settled. "She makes it difficult."

"Mm." Ilsa sipped her wine, studying the healer. "Using your skills to cause her pain as you had must have been satisfying, but it does little to teach her sort. They are willfully intransigent." Taylin paled, looking up sharply. The Vodani woman tilted her head to one side. "You feel guilty for using your gifts. Why?"

"It-it is not right to use my skills to cause pain," Taylin replied sharply.

The Vodani woman's eyes stared intently at the younger Sevmanan woman. "You don't feel guilty because of some arbitrary rule about when you should or should not use the full breadth of your skills, do you?" Ilsa's eyes did not waver from Taylin. "No, that's not it. You feel guilty because you felt pleasure when you caused someone else pain." Taylin turned bright red, looking away. "My dear, you shouldn't feel shame for using your skills, nor for enjoying the use of them. They are yours for a reason. If you have the ability, then it ought to be used. It's not like you abuse your gift and *over*use it."

"Killing someone is an ability, but it's not right," Taylin shot back.

"Is that what you think of the woman Swordanzen?" Ilsa asked mildly. "Her skills are at their heart about dealing death. Are they wrong because they are so often used to kill?"

"That...that's different. Storm didn't have a choice. We were attacked."

"Mm hm. And before you stepped foot in Desantiva, do you think she had not killed before?"

"I doubt Storm kills for pleasure," Taylin retorted.

Ilsa waved a dismissive hand. "As do I, but I imagine she takes some amount of pleasure because when she does, there was a reason." Ilsa's voice was soft. "As I'm sure that you had a reason when you used your gifts to cause pain." Taylin was silent, unsure what to think, frowning as she looked at her hand resting on her knee.

"Well, then, if you believe it's wrong to cause pain, what about giving pleasure?" At Taylin's shocked expression, she asked, "You *do* give pleasure with your gifts, don't you?" Ilsa rose from her seat, walking around slowly.

"Huh?" Taylin looked up sharply, then over at Ilsa. "Wh-what are you talking about? My gifts are to mend wounds. To ease pain."

"You can do that, you know. When I was much younger, I remember a Sevmanan healer I met who showed me his talents." Ilsa rested her hands on Taylin's shoulder, leaning down to whisper in the healer's ear. "And with your strength in the art, you touch would give such exquisite..."

"What? No! That-that's not—"

"Not what? Not right?" Ilsa slid her hands down Taylin's arms, pressing her cheek against Taylin's hair. "You shouldn't limit yourself, lovely one. There's so much pleasure in life you forbid yourself by rules imposed on you by others."

Taylin shivered at the closeness of the Vodani woman. "S-stop it," she whispered desperately.

Ilsa backed off, but not completely, still whispering in Taylin's ear. "My goodness, are you still that innocent? I am surprised Mureln hasn't enlightened you on some of life's most exquisite pleasures himself."

"Mureln is a good man! He would do nothing improper!"

Ilsa moved to Taylin's right to stare at her incredulously. "My Mureln? Nothing improper?! Oh, my dear girl!" The Vodani woman's laugh echoed in the chamber.

"What do you mean, 'your' Mureln?" Taylin asked guardedly.

"Didn't he tell you? He's my betrothed." Taylin gasped, going still in shock, oblivious to Ilsa sliding her hands down her arms again. "You are truly missing something then, my dear. He has such exclusive tastes. And with hands as skilled as his, he could play your body with the skill he plays his mandolin..."

Unable to bear hearing anymore, Taylin instinctively turned to face Ilsa, putting her hands on the Vodani woman's cheeks. Ilsa gasped, collapsing to her knees in pain. Taylin did not remain; instead, she fled the room, nearly blinded by tears.

Pulling herself up to rest her elbows on the couch, Ilsa sighed wistfully. "Such power! Ah, Mureln, how I envy you!" Resting her chin on the back of one hand, she grinned a little. "Do enjoy my gift to you, Mureln, dear."

TAYLIN FLED DOWN THE hall, looking back over her shoulder when she ran into a distracted Mureln in the hall where their rooms were. The man caught Taylin before she fell, looking alarmed at the tears on her cheeks. "Hey! Hold on there." Putting one arm around her, he turned her face towards his, trying to catch her eyes. "Taylin, what happened? What's wrong?"

Struggling to get away at first, Taylin abruptly buried her face against Mureln's chest, sobbing. The bard wrapped his arms around her, stroking her hair and quietly hushing her. He stiffened when she finally stammered, "I-I-Ilsa s-said—"

"Ilsa?!" Mureln scowled, glaring up the hall, then gathered Taylin against him and drew her with him to the privacy of his room. There he held her tightly, letting her cry.

"I-Ilsa said," Taylin began, stopping when Mureln touched her lips with his fingers gently, hushing her.

"I would slap the daylights out of Ilsa for upsetting you, but she would enjoy that too much," Mureln said sourly. "Ignore her. When she is not bound by duty, Ilsa lives to see how much disruption she can cause. The greater the reaction, the happier she is."

"She said...she said you are her betrothed."

Mureln sighed, closing his eyes. "Present tense for her. Past tense for me." Smiling wryly, he tenderly brushed a tendril of hair out of her eyes. "I left Water's Resonance a long time ago because Ilsa's games nearly drove me mad. I would as soon be land-bound for the rest of my life than bed that manipulative woman."

Sniffling, Taylin rubbed her eyes with the corner of her sleeve. "S-so sh-she was lying to me?"

"No, probably not," Mureln said with another heavy sigh. "Ilsa doesn't lie, but she tends to twist truths or near truths to get the most reaction out of people. In her mind, we're still betrothed. If we would both be alive a thousand years from now, the last humans in the world, she would still say we were betrothed. And I still would not bed her."

Taylin sniffled some, calming. As she reached up to tuck the escaped strand of hair behind her ear, he caught her hand in his, gently bringing it to his lips to kiss softly. She pulled away, turning bright red as she turned her back to the bard. "She said...she was surprised y-you and I...hadn't...she laughed at me when I told her you would never do any-thing improper."

"Oh, dear gods." Mureln sighed, looking upwards for patience. "Taylin, I am who and what I am. I won't lie and say I have never sought a woman's bed for a night, or won't in the future. You deserve nothing but honesty." He put his hand on her shoulder, turning her around to face him. "But I would never. Ever. Do anything that would hurt you." Caressing her cheek, he looked into her eyes. "Nothing." He smiled gently. "The first time I saw you in Ithesra...I could find no words to describe what I felt then. Just that I was drawn to you as a moth to a flame."

Taylin lowered her eyes as he pulled her into a warm embrace. "Truly?"

"Truly," he murmured, his face so close to hers, she could feel the warmth of his breath, the brush of his lips against her cheek. "You are the most beautiful woman I have ever met, Master Healer Taylin."

Tentatively, Taylin tilted her head to kiss him shyly. As he returned the affection with such unblemished intent, her kiss intensified with a sense of desperation. She looked hurt when he pulled back. "But...but I thought..."

"Not now. Not like this." Mureln smiled crookedly.

"D-don't you want me?" Taylin asked, hurt.

"Shards! Yes, I want you." Pulling her against him, he buried his face in her hair. "You deserve so much more than I can give you. So much better than the likes of a wandering bard like me." Sighing, he pulled back to look down into her eyes, rubbing his thumb against the line of her chin. "I know you are still...untried. I don't want your first time to be tainted. Not like this."

"I-I don't understand?"

"Do you trust me?" Mureln asked with a trace of hope in his voice. He relaxed when she nodded without hesitation. He pulled her against him, holding her tight. "Then please. Believe me. You will understand when it is right." Still bewildered, Taylin nodded, leaning into his embrace, the pair sighing together.

CHAPTER FORTY-THREE

THE BRILLIANT LIGHT OF the rising sun climbed up the silken bedcovers covering the sleeping man and woman, the man facing away from the woman who wrapped herself around him. As the sun crested the horizon, the sounds of the Vodani going about their lives grew louder, drifting in the open window. When the sun reached their faces, the pair roused.

"Don't these people ever sleep?" Amelana complained sourly, rolling away from Ash and pulling the covers over her head. "They're just as noisy now as they have been all night."

"We leave for the mainland today." Ash rose and got out of bed without a lingering look or touch for the woman.

Amelana sat up, the covers sliding to her waist. "Ash, don't you want to stay here with me?"

"No," Ash replied bluntly without looking at her, tugging his belt in place. He hesitated, and then picked up the delicate, slender dagger given by the Heart of Desantiva, staring at it. He ran his thumb across the desert design on the hilt, feeling the heat of the fiery land in the metal. "No," he said in a quieter, more resigned voice. "You should return to your room to make certain you have all your belongings."

Rolling her eyes, Amelana sighed. "Do not worry, Ash. We'll soon be back in Forenta, where it is much more civilized." Yawning, she lay back down and rolled over, pulling the covers over her head. "Where they wake up at a more *civilized* hour."

Ash lingered at the threshold, casting a final irritated glance at Amelana before easing the door shut behind him. The soft click of another latch echoed across the hall. He looked up to find Storm watching him; her face hardened into an expressionless mask. "Storm," he said, the word hanging incomplete between them. She pivoted sharply and strode away. "Storm, wait!" he called after her retreating form.

Hateful green-gold eyes turned on the mage when he grabbed her arm. "Do not touch me." Her voice was as cold as the desert sun was hot. With a sharp motion, she pulled her arm away.

Perplexed at the sudden change in the Desanti woman since before the kraken's attack, Ash reached for her again, stopping when her hand fell to one of her weapon hilts. "Storm, what happened? I thought we had found...an understanding between us. Between Forenta and Desantiva."

"We found nothing, treewalker. Whatever you thought you found was caused by Vodani seasickness." Storm brushed back his hand when he tried to reach for her again. "Nothing more than that, mage. Once we are on land, you will realize that."

"Storm?" Skyfire called from the main room's archway, looking quizzical.

Ash looked between the two, blinking once. "I see." With lips thinning, he turned away, shouldering his belongings and heading from the main room to the hall. "You are probably right. Good day, Swordanzen."

Skyfire's brow furrowed as he watched Ash pass him and then disappear down the hall. He joined Storm, placing a hand on her shoulder. Quietly in Swordanzen, he murmured, "He cares about you, Storm. More than I would ever have imagined one of his kind could care about one of our people. More than some of our people care about our own."

Storm brushed his hand off her shoulder, bitterness heavy in her voice. "You know why I cannot let him."

Skyfire sighed. "Yes. I know. Come. We should take time to train properly before we return to that infernally rocking ship."

Chapter Forty-Four

THE GROUP GATHERED AT the rail of the ship's bow as the mainland coast emerged from the morning mist, a verdant wall rising from the sapphire waters. Ganessi's white stone buildings gleamed like scattered pearls surrounded by darker wooden structures farther from the affluent quarters against the emerald backdrop, their red- and blue-tiled roofs catching the sunlight. The Desanti warriors stared in stunned silence at the sight of forests and fields so dense they appeared as a single undulating entity. Towering evergreens mingled with a multitude of varieties of deciduous trees, creating a tapestry of varying greens that stretched beyond sight. "It is beautiful," Skyfire breathed, his voice uncharacteristically brittle. He looked down at Storm, her knuckles white against the weathered rail, and placed his calloused hand on her trembling shoulder.

On Storm's other side, the bard glanced over and saw a tear tracing a path down her cheek. He touched her arm. "Desantiva will know this again someday."

"How much had Desantiva suffered?" Heedless of the tears that continued to fall in grief for her homeland, the woman could only stare into the distance. "I never understood until now how deep the land's wounds were. How much my Father has suffered!"

Mureln flicked a glance at Ash on his other side. As much as the mage appeared to be oblivious to the Swordanzen's reactions, the tension in his jaw belied the turmoil of emotions he locked away.

Amelana gushed as she nestled against Ash's side. "It will be wonderful to be back where we belong, won't it, Master Ash?" The woman seemed oblivious to the Illaini Magus's sullen brooding, or how the more she spoke, the worse his mood became. Without a word, the man turned to return to his cabin, Amelana firmly attached to his arm.

An unholy, baleful shriek from below startled everyone from their thoughts, and Storm immediately turned to go below deck. "The drizar smells the land. He is growing impatient. I will keep him calm." Skyfire followed her, his worry for the woman apparent. She paused by Almek, putting a hand on his arm. "Home is always home," she said simply.

"I kenna wait t' see how people react t' the desert folk." Emil grinned up at Emaris. "Bets on how long before someone does somethin' stupid when we're on land?" The big man just snorted, shaking his head.

Troubled, Terrence jumped when Almek put a hand on his shoulder. "Forgive me, Master Almek. I should be happy to be going home. But..." The young man sighed despondently. "I don't know. If feels...strange. Like it isn't...home as much as it had been before I left it. I don't know if...anywhere is home."

Smiling wanly, Almek patted the young man's shoulder. "It's often how Guardians feel, especially the wanderers. Like the Swordanzen among their own people, Guardians belong to all nations, and belong to none. Either the person or the place changes...often both. And what you remember is no longer what is."

Terrence blinked in surprised shock. "I...I am a Guardian? I-I thought only Master Ash...I was following him, not you! You didn't want me or—"

"Not just yet. There's still a lot for you all to learn before you can earn your colors. Guardians come in various calibers. My goal was to find those with the potential to become Dusvets. I thought you might have the potential to become an Unsvet at the very least," he said with a weary smile. "It is difficult to devote enough attention individually when there are many individuals. What I didn't want are those who did not *choose* to follow me. You followed me through your master. But you also have considerable talent as a mage. My mistake was underestimating how powerful the combination of these talents could be."

Terrence blushed. "I don't think anyone could've anticipated anything that has happened, Master Almek. I'm just glad I wasn't a burden to you or Master Ash."

"Yer never a burden t' us, lad," Emil said emphatically. "Never have been, never will be. Don't ye forget it, neither." The skinny mercenary wagged a finger at Terrence like a scolding uncle, making the young man laugh.

More seriously, Almek spoke with quiet emphasis, hand on the young man's shoulder. "Terrence, don't belittle what you have accomplished. If it weren't for you, I don't think the Raging One would have been as receptive to any of us. You followed your instincts and joined your master. Your choice allowed the status quo that has endured for over two thousand years to finally change." Almek smiled at the humility that brought a fierce blush to Terrence's cheeks. "Now go down below and make sure you have everything packed. We will not be staying overlong in Ganessi before we head back to Forenta."

"Yes, Master Almek." Emil and Emaris joined him, the smaller man slapping a hand to the younger Forentan's back.

Mureln studied Almek for a time. "You're troubled. I worry when you are troubled." Taylin moved closer to the two men.

"I never could hide much from you," Almek commented with a weary smile. "It's nothing, I think. I'm just worried about the Desanti. Vodani are mostly harmless in their curiosity."

Taylin blushed, looking down. "Unlike Sevmanen or Forenten, who often distrust everything different from what they have always known."

"Trust me, I'm quite aware of the differences between the natures of the four nations." Almek sighed, leaning on the rail again. "I would prefer to avoid Ganessi altogether, but it's asking too much of the drizzen to continue all the way back to Corast. Much less the Desanti. They are both getting restless with being confined to the space of this ship." He closed his eyes. "I've watched this city grow from a small town. I have intimately known Ganessi's darker side since before I became a Guardian."

Mureln glanced back over his shoulder, then at Almek. "What Storm said to you...Ganessi is your birthplace?" The Dusvet Guardian merely smiled, nodding. Mildly exasperated, the bard threw his hands into the air. "I don't understand how she can tell..."

The Guardian was amused. "Storm is an exceptional young woman. Many of the abilities of a Guardian she has, she has simply accepted and uses instinctively. The problem is she does not understand what she sees or knows much of the time. It makes teaching her much more difficult."

"Can *you* tell a person's birthplace?" Taylin asked curiously. When Almek shook his head, she was startled. "No? But you said...?"

"I suspect it's something unique to the Desanti. They are...different from the other races. They have maintained a purity that the rest of the nations have not simply because of crossbreeding at the borders." Almek smiled apologetically at the bard. "No offense, Mureln, but Vodani have changed over the centuries. It's not just the soothing rhythms of the currents. Some blending of Sevmanan and Vodani bloodlines has blunted some of the Desanti edge."

Mureln straightened, staring at Almek. "You are calling me a half-born?" The hurt in his voice was apparent.

"No." Almek gazed into the distance. "I am calling myself a halfborn."

Taylin gasped softly, covering her mouth. "Oh, Master Almek...I thought what I sensed when I healed you before was just because...because you are so-so old..." She hugged Mureln's arm. "He is both Vodani and Sevmanan." The bard drew back, staring.

Almek sighed, closing his eyes. "The mixing of nations happens more often at the border towns, and Ganessi is one of the oldest Vodani port cities that Sevmanen encroached upon. The division is still notable...the more inland you go, the more Sevmanen it becomes. In fact, the Vodani are content to let the Sevmanen believe they rule here." He smiled wanly over at the startled pair. "It wasn't always so disdained, having mixed heritage. Many Guardians are actually of mixed blood. Once they have survived their trials and bear the mark, their birthright is meaningless. Or should be, anyway." He shook his head. "Sometimes, the only way to be truly accepted is to leave all of what you were behind."

Mureln closed his eyes. "Forgive me, Almek. I should not...I guess I have some biases about purity from my upbringing." He smirked and shook his head. "Even though if someone has other parentage, if they identify as Vodani, we consider them Vodani and ignore anything else."

"There is nothing to forgive, Mureln. I am five hundred years removed from these people. No one remembers I came from here. Ganessi has both changed and not over my lifetime. Even after all these centuries, it can stir old memories. I've never forgotten what life was like as a bordertown child." He bowed his head as Taylin moved to one side to put a comforting arm around him, resting her head on his shoulder. Mureln leaned on the rail on his other side, his presence enough to give comfort.

CHAPTER FORTY-FIVE

THE LUSH COASTLINE RECEDED as Ganessi emerged—a jumble of structures where towering, pristine spires cast shadows over squat, dingy structures. Storm and Skyfire stared wide-eyed at what the others called buildings, explained as permanent 'tents'—structures that never moved from the locations they sat, pressed so close together they almost touched.

"There must be as many people in this city as there are in all of Desantiva." Skyfire looked both awed and troubled. "The bard says many live in the same place all their lives. I cannot imagine life never moving with the herds."

Storm's narrowed eyes fixed on the edge of land as the *Wave Dancer* neared the piers. "That means they will be more familiar with the area. We will need to be vigilant."

"Storm," Mureln chided patiently. "There won't be a fight everywhere you go. Relax." The bard drew back as the Desanti woman gave Mureln her full attention. He held up his hands. "Okay, okay. Never mind me."

Almek's hand settled on Storm's shoulder, his touch firm but gentle. "Vigilance I understand, Storm. But not every unfamiliar shadow hides a blade." The corners of his eyes crinkled as he gave her shoulder a light squeeze. "This world will seem alien to you both, but most of its strangeness poses no danger."

Skyfire's fingers found Storm's hand on the rail, warm against her knuckles. Storm's gaze dropped to the weathered planks beneath them, her exhale carrying the weight of concession. "I will try, Lord Almek," she said, lifting her eyes to his. "I can only promise I will not draw a weapon unless someone draws one on me first. Nothing more."

Smiling, Almek patted her shoulder. "That is all I ask, my lovely warrior." He chuckled when she made a disagreeable noise at the word 'lovely.'

Not long after the *Wave Dancer* docked, crowds started gathering as word spread about the desert folk and their beasts arriving. Skyfire and Storm sat astride their drizzen once they were on the dock, both aloof and unconcerned at the attention. At least, they projected that appearance. When something or someone spooked the drizzen, hands fell far too quickly to sword hilts.

The group rode through town slowly, too many people crowding the streets to allow them to move any faster. Mureln had just suggested a place on the edge of the town to avoid the throngs when a group of drunkards stumbled out of one of the many taverns along the street. Taylin stiffened, remembering the men from Ithesra who behaved the same. Mureln glanced at her and moved between her and the scruffy men.

"Lookit! It be one of them desert dogs. And he's got his bitch with'im." The men laughed, amused at their 'joke.' "Hey, girly, why you got all them blades on ya? Ye might hurt yerself ye know!" Admirably, Storm and Skyfire ignored the hecklers, navigating the nervous drizzen around the people who tried to cross the street too close to the nervous reptilian beasts.

Without warning, the drizar shrieked and reared back when one man came too close to him, the brilliant metal that covered his claws making sparks as he struck the cobblestones. Screams and shouts of panic filled the air as the man drew a wicked-looking axe, raising it to attack the unsettled creature. Storm suddenly stood on the moving drizar's back, crouching as she placed a foot in the man's throat.

The screaming and shouting subsided as the attacker staggered back, gurgling before he dropped to his knees, then onto his face, unmoving. Wide eyes turned to stare at Storm, who balanced half-crouched on the drizar's broad back with her paired single-edged blades drawn as she waited for someone else to be fool enough to get near enough to threaten.

Five black horses approached the group, the crimson and silver uniforms marking them as the city guard. What remained of the crowd melted back, watching attentively. Would the savage woman attack them, too? Would five guardsmen be enough for two savages? The whispers were ill-concealed, but to their credit, neither Desanti nor the guardsmen reacted to them.

The Dusvet Guardian made a gesture to Storm. She nodded slightly, lowering her weapons but unwilling to relax and sheathe her swords, eyeing the approaching men. Almek turned towards the man with more ornamentation on his uniform and nodded, smiling in recognition, both of rank and the man himself. "Captain Dylar. A surprise and a pleasure to see you." Gesturing to the rank insignia, Almek smiled faintly. "You have done well for yourself."

It became clear from the man's reaction that news concerning the Dusvet Guardian's arrival had lost the race with reports of violence. "Ah, Dusvet Guardian Almek?" He looked towards Storm and Skyfire, waving a hand towards the darkly tanned pair of warriors. "These are with you?" Storm and Skyfire awarded the guardsman captain with hostile frowns. "Could you get the woman to put her blades away, perhaps? It would help in calming the crowd immensely."

"Lord Almek, could you get the man to *ask* the woman to put her blades away, perhaps?" Storm's heavily accented trade common was icy and mocking. Locking eyes with Dylar, she stated, "I am neither animal nor stupid." Ritually sheathing the weapons, she gracefully resumed her seat, icy gaze never leaving that of the guard captain.

The captain's subordinates were at a loss, looking between the two as if trying to decide what they should be doing. The captain and Swordanzen stared at each other until the man grinned. "I like her, Dusvet. Bold as brass and tough as nails. Some of my boys could stand a bit more backbone like that."

"I'm sure if they wanted to learn some of the desert warrior arts, your men need only ask." Almek tempered his reassurance with caution. "However, do be warned. They are strictly, hands on teachers." He glanced at Storm and Skyfire, who traded looks and then offered a polite nod to the guardsmen. "It has been many years since I was here last. I wondered if you could direct us to the Blue Rose Inn, please? It has been a very long, eventful voyage."

Dylar nodded. "Allow my men and me to escort you so there are no more..." He looked at the fallen man. "Adventures." He waved to three of his men to take up escort positions, the fourth remaining to see the body attended to.

"Thank you, Captain," Almek said with a faint smile.

"Sorry I was not here sooner, Dusvet. I know some of the less desirable sorts here can get unruly." He glanced over his shoulder. "Though I doubt she'd have much problems dealing with any trouble."

"I would rather not risk my Swordanzen so soon." Almek kept his voice even. "They are both rather important, else I would not have brought them with me."

"Edgy though. Dangerous around here. It can draw unwanted attention from some of the less trustworthy in the more influential quarter of Ganessi. More money than sense, if you get my meaning."

The Guardian offered a polite nod to the worker near the Blue Rose Inn stables as they arrived at the remote inn, younger stable hands emerging and gaping at the pair of desert mounts. "Your warning is duly noted, Captain Dylar."

Dylar nodded as his men moved back behind him, waiting to depart. "I suggest you leave as soon as you're able, Dusvet. There is only so much my men can do. The reverence for Fortress isn't what it should be these days."

Almek nodded, resigned. "Of course. We will not be lingering any longer than necessary. My thanks, Captain."

The Sevmanan innkeeper came out, looking at the assorted members of the group, eyeing the Swordanzen with skepticism before going pale to see Almek. "Dusvet Guardian?!" Bowing low, the man hastened to make up for his disrespectful reaction. "W-we are honored you have ch-chosen our humble esa-esta-estaba-ba, ah...*place*. Please do come in."

Storm dismounted, holding her mount's reins. "I will be in shortly," she promised. "The drizar dislikes the scents here. He will require coaxing to behave." Turning to the monstrous-looking creature, she cooed to him like an aristocrat would to a small pet. The drizar lowered his head, nibbling her shoulder. He flinched and looked like a scolded puppy when she swatted his nose for a too hard nip.

"I ain't never seen a hangdog expression like that b'fore," Emil said, staring at the otherwise violent beast.

"See why I don't cross her when she is in a temper?" Skyfire moved to his drizzen's other side, away from Storm.

The mercenaries chuckled as the Desanti led the animals into the barn and gave Almek an offhanded salute. "We will wait for 'em, Dusvet." Emaris nodded in mute agreement. "We do not need t'have no more twits comin' around." The implied meaning was clear. It was too risky to leave the two desert folk alone.

Chapter Forty-Six

To honor the Dusvet Guardian and his companions, the Blue Rose's innkeeper provided a bountiful meal. Despite Almek's reassurances, the man continually apologized for being unable to provide as lavish a meal as was due to a Guardian, much less *the* Dusvet Guardian.

It was not long before the tension between the Forenten and Desanti became noticeable. The two Swordanzen eyed the food with keen distrust, reaching for nothing and pushing away anything set before them.

Taylin attempted to coax them with reason, her tone matter-of-fact. "You can't go without food forever, Storm."

Storm's expression resembled that of a vexed feline when she pinned an annoyed look on the Sevmanan healer. Sitting back with a child's petulance, she crossed her arms. "Watch me."

Seated across from Storm on Almek's other side, Ash looked up to pin a cold look on the Desanti woman. "You're being unreasonable." He met glare for glare when she turned her irritation away from the healer onto him. "It's nearly two week's travel just to reach the borders of Forenta, and another week to reach our destination. If we don't have to stop to rest or resupply."

"I am being unreasonable." Storm's scowl darkened. "*I* am being *unreasonable*?! I did not come to this land to be held to outlander standards!"

"It doesn't matter your intentions, Desanti. You will be held to standards here different from those your people hold so dear in your barren wastelands!" Ash snapped back. He inwardly cringed the moment he spoke, knowing he erred when Storm's eyes dilated. Skyfire grabbed one of her arms, Almek putting a hand on the other to restrain her from lashing out physically.

Almek fixed a disapproving look on the Illaini Magus. "Stop instigating. The Great War ended over two thousand years ago. I won't have the two of you start a new one!"

"Stupid savage," Amelana muttered, yelping when red wine suddenly splashed over her. She glared at Terrence. "You stupid boy! I should—!" She gasped when Emil made a show of tripping and splashing her with his own drink. Apoplectic, the Forentan woman ran up to her room, trailing a stream of invectives.

Terrence coughed, unable to hide a smile behind his hand. Schooling his features, he looked towards Ash and Almek. "Forgive me, Master Ash, Master Almek." Both men waved to the apprentice mage dismissively, more engrossed with the matter between the Illaini Magus and Githalin Swordanzen. He blushed when Mureln gave him a thumbs up, Taylin winking at him.

Almek turned his attention to Storm. "Look at me, Githalin Swordanzen." When the woman finally turned her attention away from Ash and onto him, he stated, "I will not have you starve yourself. You need to eat."

"No, I do not need to eat. I am not hungry, and I will not be hungry for days." Storm flashed a dark look at Ash. "Thanks to the defilers, what is unreasonable for them has become reasonable for our people." Standing, she hissed, "Are you not proud of what you have done?" Before anyone could speak, she turned on her heel and stalked towards the door leading outside.

Skyfire quickly got to his feet. "I will make sure she does not go far, Lord Almek." Not waiting for Almek's assent, Skyfire hurried to catch up to her.

"By Zeridis, I have never seen such a temper." Taylin clasped her pendant unconsciously for reassurance. "Even the Raging One did not seem so...uncontrolled."

Mureln shook his head. "That was controlled, Taylin. Given her youth and the demands we are making of her as well as those she makes of herself, she is doing quite well." He glanced sideways at Ash. "And with nearly everything here being unfamiliar, it's a lot to take in. I am sure she will relax once she acclimates."

Emil and Emaris gazed at the large amount of food, then traded looks. "Well, best not be lettin' all this go t' waste, eh?" Both he and Emaris reached for the platters nearest them. Mureln shook his head, rescuing a few servings to offer to Taylin graciously. He smiled faintly noticing Terrence wrapping some small meat rolls in a cloth to tuck in his pocket.

Terrence smiled sheepishly at Mureln with a small shrug. "Perhaps later they will want something?" The bard nodded, patting the young man's arm.

AFTER THE CONTENTIOUS EVENING meal, Mureln remained downstairs to play for the inn's patrons, as much to repay the innkeeper for his generosity as to gather news and gossip, Almek and the rest having retired to their rooms upstairs. As he was making his rounds of the tables, he was surprised to see Ash sitting alone at the small table in the room's corner. Noticing the mage's dour expression and notable absence of Amelana, he respected the man's obvious desire to be alone.

As the evening wore on, most of the patronage departed, save for those few more engrossed in their drinks than the bard's music. Deciding his efforts for the evening were done, Mureln joined Ash, taking a seat across from him without asking if he wished any company.

Mureln started to pour himself a drink from one of the bottles already at the table and blinked, shaking the empty container, realizing all were empty. "You don't seem the sort to drink to excess, Master Ash." His concern deepened when the mage's answer was to wave to the innkeeper's assistant to bring him another bottle. "Ash," he chided quietly.

The mage made a dismissive gesture. "Don't worry, Bard, I am perfectly capable of functioning while intoxicated." Ash spoke with precision, but slowly, focusing on each word. If he noticed Mureln's skeptical expression, he did not show it.

"It still seems unusual to me." After pouring a drink from the new bottle, Mureln frowned as Ash refilled his own glass. "Is Amelana being herself again?"

Ash snorted, bitter. "When is Amelana *not* being herself?" He sighed, putting his forehead on the back of his hand. "Why can't I get her out of my mind?" he lamented in a low voice.

Mureln squinted. "Amelana?" he asked incredulously.

"Not Amelana. That damned Desanti bitch," he growled. Draining half of his glass, he regarded the bard. "No matter how much I try, she is there. I hear her voice mocking me in the back of my mind. Being with Amelana sickens me more and more because I wish it was *her*, with her dark copper skin, her beautiful hair, her..." Shaking his head sharply with a wordless sound of self-disgust and frustration, he drained his glass and topped it off again.

Mureln reached over to put a hand on the glass, keeping the mage from lifting it. "Drinking won't help anything, Ash. You know that."

Ash shoved the hand off the glass. "I see them together all the time. Storm and Skyfire." Ash laughed bitterly. "He doesn't deserve her. How can he understand what she's had to endure? Everything she has suffered. He cannot!" Sighing, his head dropped to the palm of his hand, propped up. "I can, though. We are not so different, she and I."

"No, you aren't." Seeing behind the mage's iron-like façade made Mureln realize how similar the Illaini Magus and the Githalin Swordanzen truly were. His face was a mask of sorrow.

"Tell me how to forget her, bard?" Rubbing his cheeks, Ash looked upwards, then over to Mureln again. "The pain I felt when Dessa died...is nothing compared to the hole she left in the way she looks at me since we were in Water's Resonance."

Mureln pressed his lips together tightly. "Come on, Ash. The hour is late. You need to sleep."

The mage reluctantly got to his feet, looking surprised to discover he had trouble keeping his balance. Miserably, he grumbled to himself, "I deserve Amelana."

Mureln let Ash lean on him, leading him up the stairs. "No one deserves Amelana," the bard countered immediately. "Especially not you." They navigated the stairs carefully. "Hopefully, Taylin has a way of mending hangovers, my friend. You are going to have one hell of one in the morning."

"After everything I've done, you still consider me a friend?" Bitterness and self-loathing soaked Ash's voice as they reached the landing. "I do not know if I deserve anyone calling me a friend." He looked at his scarred palm as Mureln led him across the dimly lit common area. "It doesn't matter whether it was me or my ancestors. The blood of Desantiva is on my hands. No wonder she hates me. It's all I deserve." When the door opened, Ash looked up and frowned. "This isn't my room."

"You need to sleep, Illaini Magus, and you know your Journeyman will not permit that if she knows where to find you. You can sleep in my bed."

Mureln looked over his shoulder for a long moment before guiding the mage inside.

Ash sat on the edge of the bed, oblivious to the bard taking his boots off and undoing his belt. But when Mureln removed the Desanti knife, Ash snatched it back, glaring at the bard. "You will not take this."

"I won't take it," Mureln reassured him emphatically, holding his hands up. Ash lay down, hand tight around the sheathed desert blade, lying on his side. A moment later, he had fallen into a fitful sleep. The bard draped the blanket over him and just watched him for a moment before returning to the common area. He looked towards the figure in the shadowed corner, his voice flat and disapproving. "I hope you are satisfied. I didn't think anyone could drive him to incapacitate himself, but it seems you managed it."

"He is drunk?" Storm asked from where she stood guard over the group's rooms, her tone and expression unreadable. The bard nodded. "I do not understand. Why?" She frowned at Mureln in accusation. "Had you not talked to him as I asked?"

"I did. Repeatedly." Mureln shrugged. "He chose not to listen to me. It was your words in Water's Resonance and since that cut deep."

"It was necessary!" Storm shot back.

The bard said quietly, "He loves you."

Storm paled, taking a step back. In the space of three words, she changed from a legendary, self-assured warrior to a girl barely a woman. "Impossible! He is Forentan. I am Desanti. Our people have been mortal enemies since before the war. It is how it has always been. It cannot be changed!"

Mureln crossed his arms and repeated firmly, enunciating each word, "He loves you, Storm il'Thandar." Studying her for a moment, he moved nearer, his voice soft. "And you love him."

"No. No!" Storm raised a hand as if to slap Mureln, but the bard caught it easily. "You lie! He cannot love me. He must not! I could not ask him to risk turning his back on his duty to his people. It hurts too much watching someone you cannot save die because duty had to come first." Mureln held her wrist, keeping her from turning away. "I know..." She looked away, voice catching. "He can't suffer that. Not for me."

"Is it you do not want him to suffer it? Or are you afraid you will again, should he be the one who falls first?"

Storm glared at Mureln. "Bastard," she hissed. "Let me go!"

Turning her hand to kiss the back lightly, Mureln smiled sadly at her. "Our time on this world is often so short. *You* know this better than anyone." Releasing her, he said gently, "You are allowed some moments of pleasure, too." He turned away, heading to his room. "Good night, Githalin Swordanzen."

Chapter Forty-Seven

THE SUN BARELY PENETRATED the heavy curtains drawn over the windows, keeping the room blessedly dark. But nothing diminished the shrill, half-panicked voice of Amelana that shattered the morning peace. "Master Ash?! Master Ash, where are you? *Master Ash?!!*"

Both Mureln and Ash startled awake, the mage groaning as he lay back, holding his head. Mureln shifted stiffly where he had been sleeping in the chair, squinting sourly at the door. "What do you mean he is sleeping? He isn't in his room, you idiot Desanti!" There was a brief pause. "How dare you call me a— Are you threatening me?!"

"For the love of gods." Mureln growled, pushing himself to his feet. "Can't leave either of those two alone for a minute."

"Wait." Ash gritted his teeth as he sat up. "I'll deal with Amelana. She is my responsibility."

"You're in no shape to be dealing with anyone, Ash." Ash pushed himself up, hand to his head. The bard sighed. "Stubborn mage," Mureln muttered, lending Ash support. They opened the door to see Storm and Amelana nose to nose with each other, the others drawn out of their rooms in various states of alarmed wakefulness.

"Journeyman Amelana." Ash's own voice hammered against his skull, forcing him to squint against the pain. Both women pivoted toward him. Amelana's face transformed into a theatrical mask of concern that made his stomach churn for the obvious hypocrisy, while Storm's features hardened into something unreadable save for a flicker behind her eyes that he couldn't bear to meet. He grimaced when Amelana's fingers dug into his forearm, her touch as unwelcome as her presence.

The Forentan woman gushed effusively. "Oh, Master Ash, I was so worried about you! When I couldn't find you, I thought the worst—"

"Journeyman. Keep your voice down." The edge in his voice arrested Amelana's loud vocal fawning. "I had been up later than I realized speaking with Master Bard Mureln." He did not glance at the Vodani, though he could feel his eyes on him. "Is there something you require that necessitated waking everyone, including the dead?"

Amelana swallowed nervously as Ash's hard gaze bored into hers. "I...ah...It is such a lovely day, Master Ash. I was planning to go into the civilized districts of Ganessi—where one needed worry about pickpockets or the stench of unwashed laborers—and thought you might like to accompany me." She lifted her chin slightly. "I wished to visit an old family friend of my mother's—someone of proper breeding—who thankfully maintains a residence far from these dreadful lower quarters." The insulted expressions of the others regarding her opinion of the 'lower classes' were lost on the woman.

"No, I do not," Ash replied tersely, pushing the woman off his arm.

"But Ganessi is so dangerous! You saw what happened when we first got here!" Amelana argued. Several of the others rolled their eyes, returning to their rooms. Except for the Desanti. While they did not appear to be giving any attention to the Forenten, Storm had resumed her post of guard, leaning against the wall with arms crossed. Skyfire was speaking quietly with her in Swordanzen, making small gestures towards Ash and Amelana.

Being the focus of the Desanti pair's discussion bothered Ash more than Amelana's wheedling, making his irritation grow. "You are a *journeyman* mage, Amelana. You should be quite capable of protecting yourself if the need arises. If you wish to go into the city, by all means, go." He turned to go back into the bard's room. "Right now, I have a headache."

"I can stay if you need me..." Amelana started to follow the Illaini Magus when Mureln blocked her from entering. "Excuse me, Master Mureln," she said icily.

Mureln replied in equally icy tones. "This is *my* room. You are unwelcome, Journeyman. I suggest you depart."

"*I* suggest you listen to him," Taylin added in a low voice at Amelana's shoulder. When the Forentan woman looked at the healer, her eyes went wide in fright when Taylin simply held up one hand as if to touch her. Amelana hastily excused herself and fled down the stairs. Satisfied Amelana was gone, Taylin smiled gently at the bard. "You look tired."

"It has been a long night." Mureln moved aside, inviting Taylin into his darkened room with a grand gesture. "Have any cures for hangovers?" He nodded towards Ash in answer to Taylin's questioning look.

"Not really." The healer sat on the bed next to the mage as he slouched forward and held his head in his hands, as if trying to keep it from exploding. "Alcohol is much like black water or any other toxin. I can do nothing about them directly; I can only heal the damage they do until the body purges them." She rested her hand on Ash's shoulder, waiting until he finally looked at her. "You would still be very sensitive to noise and light, but I can banish the pain so you can sleep."

Ash nodded slightly, closing his eyes as her cool fingers touched his forehead with a light caress. He nearly collapsed with the sudden relief. "Thank you." He started to reach to gather his things to leave when Mureln put a hand on his shoulder.

"Stay. Your journeyman knows better than to come in here. Sleep yourself out." The bard forestalled Ash's argument. "Sleep, Andar." Ash finally relented with a nod. Satisfied, Mureln took Taylin's hand and left the room.

Taylin looked over where Storm had been and blinked in surprise to see Terrence. The young man smiled sheepishly and shrugged one shoulder. "Lady Storm asked me to keep watch so Master Ash can rest. She and Skyfire went outside to train." He paused for a moment. "Do the Desanti never sleep?" He could not suppress the mild exasperation with the desert folk in his voice.

Mureln chuckled a bit. "I wonder that myself sometimes. A lot of times, honestly. Is Almek awake?"

Terrence nodded. "Yes, sir. He is with the Swordanzen. He said something about assessing or determining something. It was very confusing, and he wasn't really speaking directly to me. I didn't wish to appear rude."

"Terrence, you are far from rude. In fact, you are painfully polite." Mureln shook a finger. "Sometimes it can be a detriment. Remember." Mureln tapped his temple. "There are times matters require us to cross lines of propriety for the good of those we most care about. Like accidentally spilling wine on a shrieking harpy to avert bloodshed."

Blushing at first, the young man frowned as he considered the bard's words. Smiling after a moment, he bowed deeply. "I'll remember your words, Master Mureln. Have a good day at the Ganessi market, Master Taylin, Master Mureln." He added with a twinkle of amusement in his eyes, "Make sure Master Emil behaves himself."

"*Always*, lad," Mureln said with such emphasis Taylin and Terrence both chuckled. "Always."

Leaning on a stool, arms crossed and drumming his fingers with impatience, Emil looked at Mureln as he and Taylin appeared. "About time ye both got down here." Emaris ignored his friend, finishing a rather large breakfast under the pleased observation of the innkeeper's wife. "Emaris here be happily eatin' everythin' served t' him, completely ignoring th' fact that *we* has t' pay fer it."

"Are you mad he is spending your future gambling winnings?" Mureln showed no sympathy as he tucked Taylin's arm in his.

"Money ain't growin' on trees, ye know!"

"And if it did, the forest would be nothing but denuded limbs in your wake," Mureln replied drolly, eliciting laughter from Taylin. Emaris grinned, elbowing Emil.

The wiry man waved his hands around irritably. "Th' Guardian be lucky he has us along t' get supplies fer 'im."

Taylin arched an eyebrow. "Oh? Why is that?"

Mureln said dryly, "When it comes to dickering with merchants, Emil is a master at robbing them blind. Legally." After a pause, the bard added with a teasing tone, "Most of the time."

"I ain't a thief!" Emil looked affronted as Emaris downed the last of his enormous breakfast, rose, and offered the matronly woman a deep bow in thanks, giving her several coins.

"Now there is a man with a healthy appetite," the woman said approvingly to one of the serving girls as she cleared the dishes. "Good to see not everyone is some anemic waif what could be blown away in a stiff breeze."

"Anemic?!" Emil exclaimed, looking at the woman. "I ain't knowing what anemic is, but it sounds like an insult- Hey!" He looked at Mureln and Emaris who each took an arm and dragged him outside backwards. Taylin laughed merrily, shaking her head.

The Ganessi market was considerably larger and more crowded but just as chaotic as the Desanti one. By late morning, simply hearing one another speak had become quite a challenge. They stopped at one of the Gyspari merchants, his wagon displaying a wide range of items. "Etaio!"

The Gyspari , bearing the distinctive aspects of both Sevmanen and Vodani, recognized Emil, holding his arms open wide in greeting. "Emil, ye old thief! I'd begun t' think ye got yerself locked up finally with yer antics. Ye still keepin' with yer brother and that bard?" He looked around behind Emil, grinning hugely in welcome to the other men. When he spotted Taylin, he brightened. "Oh, ho! Who be this lovely thing?" The man bowed with deep flourish, taking Taylin's hand with embellished reverence. "Ye are far too fine a lady t' be keeping company wi' this lot."

Keeping a possessive arm around Taylin, Mureln said archly, "This is Master Healer Taylin and Guardian Adept. She is one of the Dusvet Guardian's students."

Etaio looked surprised and impressed. "Truly? Then I be both surprised and honored t' meet ye, m'lady." He looked at Emil. "Hard t' imagine ye be doin' anything that actually be respectful. Guess Mureln finally rubbed off on ye." He winked at the larger mercenary. "Or Emaris finally beat enough sense into ye."

Emil feigned shock, his hands over his heart. "Etaio! Ye wound me!"

The Gyspari snorted. "Try that wi' someone who don't know ye, ye thick-headed lemur." He looked at Taylin speculatively. "So, th' Dusvet's student, eh? How can ol' Etaio serve Fortress t'day?"

"Well, we be needin' some new travel supplies..." Emil and Etaio relaxed into what was obviously a long time verbal dance as they fell into a lively discussion. Looking confused when half of the things they were talking about made no sense, Taylin opened her mouth to interrupt, falling silent when Mureln hushed her quietly, winking at her.

Emaris stood patiently, easily carrying everything they had already purchased. He glanced over towards a meat pie merchant across the way, frowning slightly.

Mureln looked up as Emaris nudged him, glancing over to where the huge man indicated. A cluster of men, looking like long-unemployed caravan guards, had their heads together by one of a merchant's standing tables. It took a moment for him to recognize them from the encounter on their way from the docks to the Blue Rose as associates of the man Storm had killed. The bard excused himself for a moment, making his way to the stall nearby to listen to the men.

Adjusting his hat to better conceal himself from the men, he used examining the various metal craft items as an excuse to hover nearby within earshot. The Gyspari merchant at this wagon was about to address him when Mureln looked up, making a hushing motion, tossing him a silver coin. The merchant caught the coin and nodded, turning his attention to another customer.

"I'm telling ya, we can't be lettin' them desert demons be wanderin' free. Ye saw what th' woman did t' Ulsen! Ye want t' wait and see what th' man will do?"

"How can ya kill a demon, though?" one of the others asked. "Demons be immortal, ain't they?"

"Not sure, but I'll be figurin' somethin' out. My boss says they are stayin' at th' Blue Rose in the northern quarter. Not too many patrols out that way." He smirked a bit. "Helped m' boss with a couple of problems out that way before."

"I guess," one said reluctantly.

"It'll be easy. And th' pay be sweet. We can get th' whole lot of them at once and then bring th' heads of those monsters them desert demons ride back t' Lord Ganessi."

"What about the Guardian? He be the Dusvet. People won't be happy if he got killed with th' rest of 'em. Guardians ain't got no patience when it be one of their own. I seen what an Unsvet Guardian did t' Joban when he were too drunk t' think straight." He shuddered. "It weren't pretty."

The man snorted derisively. "If th' Dusvet were really worried about us, he'd not have been bringing demons out of th' gods forsaken pits, now would he? C'mon. Th' boss said he was gettin' more information. I don't care how sweet th' deal be, I ain't doin' nothin' without half up front, ye know? Th' 'good lord' likes t' forget his coin pouch at home."

The men disappeared into the crowd like raindrops into a river. Mureln glanced down at the small metal flask in his hand, now warped from his unconscious grip while eavesdropping. He dropped extra coins into the vendor's palm before hurrying back to where Emil still haggled with Etaio. Leaning close to his companions, his voice barely audible above the market's din, he said, "We have problems. Almek needs to hear about this. Now."

Chapter Forty-Eight

THE GROUP GATHERED IN the privacy of the common area outside their rooms. Once Mureln finished relating everything he had heard at the market, all eyes turned to Almek. The Dusvet Guardian's visage was grim as he considered the options. "If we ration our supplies well, we should have plenty. We should leave tonight regardless of the dangers on the roads after sunset."

Both Swordanzen straightened up in surprise, Storm looking affronted. "You want to run away? *Let* them come!" She smacked the surface of the table with both palms as she stood. "I do not fear anyone who would be foolish enough to attack. We should not allow the likes of fools to dictate our behavior!"

"While I know you and Skyfire could easily handle thuggery such as these men, there's always the chance of something going wrong. You are both too important to risk losing. Nor do I wish our hosts to suffer for their willingness to house us."

"It is an act of cowardice to flee!" Storm argued, green-gold eyes flashing with emotion and looking quite willing to go hunt the men down that instant.

"Sit. Down." Everyone flinched at the tone Almek used. Reluctantly, the Swordanzen woman obeyed, crossing her arms. "There is a greater challenge ahead of you, Storm il'Thandar. A task much greater than clinging stubbornly to your tradition of meeting every challenger keen on making a name for themselves." Her cheeks colored at the rebuke, looking away with her jaw clenched to not respond.

"The road to Forenta from Ganessi is desolate." Having been awoken by Terrence only a little while before, Ash's voice was low, eyes narrowed against the returned, roaring headache. "We should not need to worry about more than a few hungry animals."

Suddenly, Storm jerked upright, eyes wide and staring at nothing. "Drizar!" Before anyone else could react, she bolted from the inn. A heartbeat after, one of the stable hands below shouted, "Fire! Fire in the stables!"

"Storm!" Almek was barely on his feet when the others headed down the stairs after Storm.

Attempting to follow, Ash nearly tripped over Amelana when she got in his path. "Ash!" Amelana desperately held onto his arm. "Don't go! It is too dangerous!"

The mage stared at her. "What is wrong with you, woman? One of Almek's students needs help!"

Amelana desperately clung to him. "Let her take care of herself. I don't want you in danger!"

"The duty of a mage is to protect others from danger by stepping into it himself. I taught you this! Now let go of me!"

"I won't let you go! Not when you are nearly mine!"

Ash growled, shoving her off his arm. She stumbled back into her chair, eyes wide. "After all we have gone through, after everything we have seen, have you not realized your entire petty world is at risk of being destroyed? Or are you so conceited you refuse to accept some things are more important than you?" Turning his back on her in disgust, he rushed to catch up with the others.

✦·—·—··—⟩C·⟨—··—·—·✦

FROM INSIDE THE FLAME-ENGULFED barn, they could hear the sounds of angry drizzen and panicked horses trapped inside. The sky, dark and heavy with an impending storm, rumbled ominously but offered no relief.

"The door be barred!" Emil shouted as he and Emaris tried to get the main doors opened. "An' I hear sword fightin' inside!"

"Storm!" Skyfire looked ready to find a way to leap into the burning structure. The young Forentan apprentice grabbed him, barely restraining him. The large Desanti man glared down at the smaller Forentan, balling a fist to punch him. "You would see her die?"

"I would not see *you* die trying to help her, Lord Skyfire," Terrence said firmly. "I can help! Have faith in me. Please." When Skyfire nodded once, Terrence stepped forward, closing his eyes as he started reciting words of magic. As he spoke, the clouds swirled darker, flickers of lightning brightening the deep gray with increasing frequency. With desperation born of necessity, the Forentan apprentice mage commanded such energy it made the hairs on the backs of everyone's necks stand up.

Emaris was throwing himself against the doors, the wood squealing at the assault, but not yielding. Abruptly, the man stopped, pressing his ear against the door. He took a step back at the same moment Terrence yelled, "Back!"

Emil managed to shove the huge man away as lightning struck the doors. The weakened, seared wood exploded open in flying splinters as diamond hard, metal shod claws finished the destruction. The sight of the drizar screaming in defiance framed by flames lent a horrifyingly surreal feel to the sight. Giant drops of icy water started pelting the ground.

The drizar bolted out, followed by the other drizzen and all the horses stabled there. The winds began to rise, and rain began falling in heavy sheets, called by the mage apprentice. The flames recoiled from the assault. Terrence shifted his posture, and the winds seemed to obey his gestures, the heavy rain blowing inside the doors and dousing the inferno inside.

"Stop!" Mureln shouted, and Terrence dropped his hands. The winds abruptly calmed and the rain waning to a drizzle. The bard got to the apprentice's side as the younger man grabbed his head, making a sound of pain. "I've got you, Terrence," he reassured.

From the darkness of the bowels of the stables, Storm staggered out, supporting two stable hands. Once beyond the barn's creaking structure, the three collapsed to their knees, coughing.

The innkeeper's wife ran over to one boy, pulling him tightly against her. "Tomi! Tomi, my baby!" She looked at Storm, who stared at her dazedly. "Thank you, Swordanzen. Thank you for saving my baby's life!" Storm only nodded, trying to catch her breath.

Emil looked over at Ash as the mage finally caught up to them and said sarcastically, "Nice of ye t' join us, mage. Good thing yer apprentice got skills." Emaris looked at Ash in disappointment as took over supporting Terrence as Mureln joined Almek entering the still smoldering stables. The young mage grimaced, his hand held against his head, pain contorting his features. Ash scowled and then looked for Storm.

Storm waved Taylin away, coughing violently. When the healer would not stop trying to help her, the Desanti woman grabbed her hands and put them on Tomi, giving the healer a meaningful look. Taylin nodded in understanding, healing the two stable hands first. Only then did Storm allow the healer to touch her.

Skyfire knelt on one knee by Storm, a hand on her shoulder while Taylin healed her. "I know there is a bond between a Swordanzen and their drizzen. But I have never known or heard of anything as strong as between you and the drizar, Storm." He looked up as the drizar dipped his head over Skyfire's shoulder, nibbling his shoulder lightly. The Desanti man smiled, patting the beast's nose. "Forgive me for doubting you would protect her." Bumping Skyfire's cheek lightly, the drizar walked over to the horses, the animals hovering around the full male obediently, despite him being nothing near equine.

Storm pulled Taylin's hands away, shaking her head. "That is...enough. The rest...I can heal...on my own." She coughed lightly.

"Storm, there is no need to deny healing," Taylin scolded, stopping at Storm's sad expression.

"No need...to heal fully...right now." She coughed again. "Not sure...all enemies...dead. Might need...to heal others. Conserve...strength."

Taylin opened her mouth, and then shut it again, lowering her eyes. "Very well. Though more healing would be better," she added tartly, earning a smile from the Swordanzen woman.

Mureln emerged from the barn with Almek, the pair grim as they rejoined the others. "It was the same men from the market. What's left of them. They are...*missing* a few chunks." Mureln glanced over at the drizar. The animal met the bard's eyes, then raised his head to shriek to the skies, long teeth bared. The bard shuddered a bit.

"Do not know...who they were...or why...they were here." Storm tiredly leaned against Skyfire as he put an arm around her to keep her on her feet. "Nor do I...care." Coughing lightly, she closed her eyes, focusing on trying to catch her breath.

"Dusvet Almek," the innkeeper said gruffly. "Your Swordanzen saved my only child's life. Anything we can do for you, just name it."

"We do not want to endanger you any more than necessary," Almek began, when others from the nearby houses and businesses spoke up.

"We'll keep watch for others," a man said, others behind him nodding grimly, murmuring in agreeing solidarity.

The others gathered started talking all at once. "Was our neighbor-hood you all saved. Won't let no one burn us out again." "My father died when someone set fire to the tailor shop next door to mine." "Don't want to see anyone die like that again." "Specially don't want to bring the wrath of the Guardians on us for allowing the Dusvet to get hurt...or die!"

Almek looked at the gathered city folk and finally nodded. "Thank you. All of you." He looked at Storm with concern when a fit of coughing caught her.

"She will be recovered by morning, Master Almek," Taylin assured. Looking annoyed, she added, "She permitted me to heal her *almost* completely." Storm looked unrepentant.

"Please, Dusvet, stay as long as you need," the innkeeper begged. "It's the least I can do to repay you and your students for my son's life."

Almek considered, then nodded. "Very well." He gave Storm a stern look. "We will speak later about how you continue to put yourself at risk, Githalin Swordanzen."

"Yes, Lord Almek." Pausing to cough, Storm spoke quietly to Skyfire, who reluctantly left her and followed the others into the inn. Pausing only a moment, Storm approached Ash, pausing behind him. "Mage," she rasped quietly.

Ash flinched at her rasping voice. "Swordanzen." He looked down when he felt her take his hand, pressing something into it. "What is this?"

"One of the men who...set the fire...had this in his...hand." Her words were quiet, slow, as if focusing her entire will on speaking. "I barred the doors...to prevent his escape. Before I knew...how fast fires spread here." She scowled, glaring at the stables. "Should have...killed him...quick."

Ash opened his palm and scowled at the soot-tarnished pendant. He looked up at Storm. "You know this belongs to my journeyman," he stated rather than asked. She nodded once. He pressed his lips together, closing his hand into a fist around it. "Thank you for not letting the others know of this."

"It is a matter...between you and your...student...alone." She looked away when he opened his eyes to study her in surprise at her consider-ation. "I would not be...a hypocrite."

Remembering her words wishing his and his people's deaths in the desert when he'd succumbed to dehydration, the Forentan mage could not help but be impressed. "I would have thought you would have demanded to avenge the attack on you or the drizar."

Storm shrugged, not meeting his eyes. "Things are...more complicated here. Lord Almek told me...they would be. I am beginning to understand what he...meant." Looking towards the street where some people still loitered, Storm sighed. "I cannot be certain...she had any...part in this. It would...be dishonorable to seek justice...blindly."

"Do you think she had a part in it?" the mage asked her quietly.

Storm was silent for a long time. "My heart...wants her to be. To have...just reason to wring...her neck with my...bare hands and..." She cut her words off, her hands clenched in fists. Forcing herself to calm, she exhaled. "But I do...not know...she had any part in...this. She might have dropped the pendant. Somewhere."

Ash sighed. "Yes. She might have." His voice did not reflect his belief in his own words. "Thank you," he said, eyes downcast. He looked startled when she pressed a small pouch into his other hand. "What is this?"

"They are herbs that...will help with...too much...alcohol." He looked up at her sharply as she said softly, "I will not allow...you to suffer more...because of...me." She turned her face away, but he caught a glimpse of the flush of emotions she tried to hide from him. "I have been the cause...of enough suffering and death."

"Storm?" He reached for her as she turned away and walked back inside. He stared at the two objects in his hands, lost in thought before he returned inside as well.

✦—•—•——♦⟨♕⟩♦——•—•—✦

ASH CLENCHED HIS TEETH as Amelana approached him, putting her arms around his, nattering obsequiously, going on about how relieved she was that he was all right. He headed up the steps and into her room.

She threw her arms around him, pressing herself into him. "Oh, Ash, I am so relieved—"

"Where is your pendant, Journeyman?" Ash's voice was devoid of emotion.

Amelana's eyes went very wide, her hand going to her throat instinctively. "My pendant?"

"Your family crest pendant, yes," Ash pressed. "The one that no one of your breeding would be without." Raising his hand, he let the soot-covered object fall, dangling from his hand.

Amelana stared, going deathly pale. "Wh-where did you find...?"

"Where do you think it was found?" He spat, dropping the thing onto the table. Grabbing her upper arms, he pulled her close, glaring into her eyes. "Do you take me for that much of a fool?"

"I-I don't know what you are talking about! I-I had lost it during that commotion on the street when the Desanti woman killed that man in cold blood."

Ash glared at her before releasing her with a shove. "I tire of you, Journeyman. I tire of your clinging to the honor of my master's family name to cleave to me." His cold eyes were unwavering as he snatched the pendant off the table. "When we return, I will be formally dismissing you as my student." He turned to go towards the door.

"Master Ash!" the woman said, running to catch him, almost taking his arm to hold him back, but freezing at the dark look he gave her. "Master Ash, please! You-you need me!"

"*I* need *you*?" He stared incredulously. "Do not make me laugh, Amelana. A courtesan would serve me better than you have. They are better tempered, much more discreet, and have more promise to be a master mage than you ever will."

Amelana gaped in shock, and then scowled. "How dare you compare me to a-a courtesan!"

"You're right," Ash replied sharply. "Courtesans reflect their breeding better than you. You have brought shame to the Avarian family name. The family of my master! And shame to our people, and I will be certain the Edai Tredecima knows it."

Outright terror filled Amelana's eyes. "You...you wouldn't!"

"What choice have you given me? You have dishonored the Magi Laws, and you have dishonored the ancient traditions. You will be lucky if the Avarians even acknowledge you when I am done with you." He paused halfway through the door, turning back to fix an icy glare on her. "You will be less than lowborn, because I doubt even the lowest of the low would accept the likes of you." He slammed the door with finality.

Chapter Forty-Nine

Seated at one of the stained-glass windows of the Dove and Lily Inn, the Dusvet waited patiently, offering a polite smile to the young girl who brought him wine in a glass etched with the emblem of the establishment.

Cleaned up and dressed in new clothes, Emil reached up to tug at his collar, muttering under his breath. "Don't know why I had t' get all gussied up fer ye. All I'm doin' is playin' bodyguard. Emaris'd done better." Standing near Almek's shoulder, the man swore colorfully. "This feckin' itches like all hells."

"It was too short notice to get proper clothes that fit Emaris and I do not want to be too blatant." Sipping his wine idly, he glanced over his shoulder at the Gyspari . "This is one of the best restaurants in the city, Emil. It would be insulting for you to look like you just rolled off a wagon."

Emil grumbled. "Rather be rolled over by a wagon."

Almek tsked. "I *am* paying you to play the part."

"Barely enough t' put up with these snotty horses' arses." Emil glanced towards the door and put his hands behind his back. "I think yer company be here. Arrogant lookin' bastard, too."

Almek did not look, simply nodding slightly. "Behave yourself, Emil." He did not bother reprimanding the Sevmanan man for the colorful swearing under his breath. The mercenary fell silent before the elegantly dressed man came within earshot.

Almek looked up as the man offered the Guardian a deep bow. "You wished to speak with me, Dusvet Almek Two-Tones of Fortress?" he asked formally.

"Yes, Lord Anton Ganessi, thank you." Almek waved a hand to the seat across from himself.

Both silent while the serving girl poured the nobleman a drink, Anton looked over Emil with a critical eye. "A Gyspari-born bodyguard, Dusvet Almek? Surely Fortress can afford better than the likes of that to serve you."

Almek regarded Anton steadily for a long moment. "I appreciate the concern that prompted you to question my choices," he stated tonelessly, the nobleman lowering his eyes at the pointed rebuke. "I find it easier to travel with those more accustomed to a less fixed lifestyle."

"Of course, Dusvet Almek Two-Tones. I meant no disrespect." Settling back in his chair, the nobleman returned his gaze to the older man. "How may I be of service to you?"

"I am concerned, Anton," Almek stated in a low voice, setting his glass on the table.

"Oh?" The blond man arched an eyebrow. "Nothing too dire, I hope?"

"That would depend on what part you had in the fire at the Blue Rose's stables." Almek studied the other man for his reaction.

Anton paused a moment, his glass almost touching his lips before taking a sip. "I heard it was some hooligans who set the fire. Truly, it is the gods' own blessings that a Forentan mage extinguished the blaze with such alacrity. Captain Dylar tells me there will be no need for any trials because of the desert demon..." He paused, cleared his throat, and said, "woman." Anton reflected the noble breeding of his family, the toned, slender build of an outdoorsman blunted by a life filled with servants doing most of the menial tasks. "Surely, you do not believe I would have ordered such a thing?"

Almek's expression remained mild. "Of course not. It would be beneath your station to use such crude methods." He tilted his head to one side. "It has been a few years since I last visited Ganessi. I believe you were just a boy then. Does your family still have aspirations of building stronger ties to Forenta?"

Anton was silent for several minutes, his expression guarded. "Perhaps we do, Dusvet, but that does not mean I would have ordered anyone to do anything as foolish as attack a Guardian." The nobleman looked more annoyed than concerned. "Having the wrath of Fortress brought down upon my city would have destroyed anything we accomplished."

Almek nodded, sipping his drink, eyes not moving from Anton's. "It is good you remember the consequences should any harm come to a Guardian within your auspices." He narrowed his eyes. "But you *were* aware something was amiss?" His words were more statement than a question.

"I might have heard rumors," Anton stated airily, waving a dismissive hand. "But you know rumor is often the fabrication of jealous fishwives. If I paid attention to every little snippet of worrisome drivel, I would get nothing accomplished."

"It would behoove you to pay attention to such rumors, Lord Ganessi. Fortress is not so forgiving of 'accidental' slips of duty." He paused, the two men's eyes fixed on each other as the serving girl returned to refill their glasses.

"Of course," Anton replied when the girl left. "I am quite aware of the consequences of angering Fortress. No one in my family has forgotten what happened to my uncle."

"I am glad," Almek replied, tones conversational, pleasant. "The Vodani would be quite cross about disruption in one of their oldest ports because the Sevmanen could not police themselves adequately. I am sure they would be quite eager to help if you need aid."

Anton's smooth features hardened a little. "I can assure you, Dusvet. Vodani *help* will be quite unnecessary."

"That's good to hear. I would suggest, however, it might lend you some credence if you would make it well known that to attack my students is to attack me. Any harm to them is an attack on Fortress." Almek's voice hardened a little. "This includes the two Desanti and their beasts."

"You are well aware of how large Ganessi is, Dusvet. I cannot control everyone," Anton replied in a low, sneering voice. "Accidents happen all the time. People get ideas in their heads thinking they know what is best to protect their families. I am sure you knew the risks when you removed two of Forenta's ancient enemies out of the confines of the desert wastelands to these much more civilized lands. It would have been safer for everyone if they had remained locked in their prison away from the rest of us."

"Do not fool yourself, Anton," Almek stated as he put his empty glass down. "The desert folk *choose* to remain within their borders. Nothing binds them to their land. If anything were to happen to either Desanti with me, believe me when I say word *would* get back to their people, and it would draw more of them out of their desert and for less amicable reasons than trying to heal the wounds caused by the Great War."

Almek sat forward, his gray eyes hard as flint. "The war between mages and warriors ended two thousand years ago. Do not be foolish enough to start one anew between the four nations. Be the man your people rely on and protect them from foolish games of posturing and glory-seeking."

Anton grimaced and nodded. "I will consider your words with the utmost urgency." The man rose, back stiff. "If you will excuse me, Dusvet Guardian."

Almek's eyes remained fixed on the nobleman. "I certainly hope you consider my words. Good day, Lord Ganessi." Waiting until Anton Ganessi had departed, Almek rose and walked out as well, offering polite nods to those who greeted him with varying levels of respect as he passed.

Emil fell in step with Almek, the two leaving the Dove and Lily Inn at a confident, leisurely pace. Once they were outside, Emil muttered, "What a pretentious pri—"

"Very much so," Almek interrupted. "I'm certain Lord Anton Ganessi played some part in the fire, but I do not think he instigated it. He's far too lazy."

"Yeah?" Emil raised an eyebrow. "Ye think another be pullin' th' strings? One of them darklings?"

"Perhaps. Now that I'm looking closer, I can see some ripples, but their sources still elude me. More than time and complacency from lack of conflict erodes the respect owed to Fortress and to my goddess." Putting a hand on Emil's shoulder, he grinned. "So how much did you manage to get off of Lord Ganessi when he passed by you?"

Emil turned his head sharply to stare at Almek. "What makes ye think...?" The Sevmanan man sighed. "Man, can't pull nothin' past you Guardian types." Emil whispered, quirking a faint smile, "His money pouch an' his pretty silver dagger with th' amethyst. Th' dagger alone'll pay for th' supplies. I'd've given it back if he weren't such an arse." He snorted indignantly. "Insulting th' Gyspari folk! Th' nerve!"

"You've not been trying to snitch from any of my students?"

"Are ye kiddin'?" Emil's expression filled with honest shock at the idea. "I have no wantin' t' see what Storm'd do t' me if I even *thought* th' idea too loud. I like livin' and if I has to die, I want it t' be quick, and I know full well she'd make it last a long time." Almek chuckled, patting Emil comfortingly. Pausing a moment, Emil looked at the Dusvet Guardian's profile. "Ye be certain Ganessi had somethin' t' do wi' the fire?"

Almek's expression darkened as he nodded once. "I have no doubts, believe me. I'm all too familiar with the Ganessi family temperament. Save for a few anomalies, it has not changed at all since I was a boy."

Emil blinked. "What? Ye were one of their servants 'r somethin'?"

"No. One of their bastards," Almek said bitterly. The Gyspari blinked, then looked over his shoulder before putting a hand on Almek's shoulder.

Chapter Fifty

THE INN DOOR SWUNG shut behind Ash as he squinted into the midday glare. He flinched backward when a pack of shrieking children darted past him toward the Blue Rose's corral. His momentary irritation softened as he watched them race ahead.

Across the dusty yard, Storm and Skyfire worked over their mounts with coarse-bristled brushes. Under their ministrations, layers of grit fell away to reveal scales that shimmered between sapphire and emerald in the harsh light. Storm, her feet bare against the creature's hide, balanced effortlessly as she scaled her drizar's flank. The beast lifted his massive horned head, metal caps gleaming dully, allowing her access to polish them.

Children's voices rose in a chorus of excitement. The two Swordanzen exchanged knowing glances, lips quirking upward. Storm clicked her tongue once, and the drizar responded instantly, carrying her in a smooth trot toward the fence. She crouched low on his back, addressing the wide-eyed audience. "You wish to know about my companion, yes?"

When Storm addressed the children, it unleashed a flood of questions and comments. "What is that?" "It looks like it'd eat a whole horse!" "I bet it eats anyone that annoys him." "Would you let it eat my annoying little sister?"

Storm chuckled, hopping down to the soft dirt. "They are called drizzen." She put a hand on her companion's shoulder. "He is a drizar. He is to drizzen what your people call a stallion for horses." As if knowing they were discussing him, the drizar bobbed his head, picking up his feet to show off.

"He's kinda ugly," one girl said, the others looking at her in panic, shushing her.

Storm laughed, a quiet, gentle sound. "His beauty is not out here." She put her hand beneath his jaw, unconditional love for the animal in her eyes. "It is in his heart. We have been together since we were both young." She looked at the children. "Would you like to ride him? He will allow you if I ask him."

As several of the children begged for permission to ride the drizar, Storm picked them in pairs, a small child, and a larger one. Instructing the older child to hold the smaller one, she whispered something to the drizar. The animal calmly trotted around the corral to the delight of the riders and those waiting to ride.

"You have a way with children," Ash observed, watching the drizar as he circled.

A small smile soften Storm's expression. "Theirs is a purity of heart and joy of life that I swore to protect for as long as it can endure." The drizar lowered himself to the ground to let the children dismount without help, two more children climbing astride, screaming in delight as the animal rose again to trot in a circle.

Ash looked at Storm's profile, studying her for a long time. His lips curved into a faint smile, leaning on the fence next to her, content to watch the children ride the drizar with her. "You enjoy sharing it with them."

Once the children had all had their turns, the drizar trotted over to Skyfire's drizzen, the Desanti man having drawn his sword out. "Through them, I know what I lost." Drawing her own dual-edged blade, she looked to Ash with a matter-of-fact expression. "And I know intimately why protecting it is so important."

As the clash of blades brought awed silence to the children, Ash watched the two Githalin Swordanzen train. "You didn't lose it entirely," he murmured to himself. He looked over his shoulder as Almek joined him. "Was your discussion with Lord Ganessi fruitful, Master Almek?"

"Rather, but I'm uncertain if it will be for good or ill yet." Almek leaned on the fence next to Ash. As the wind gusted, Almek half closed his eyes, then glanced at the mage, observing the slight shift in his posture. "Can you feel the change in the wind, Ash?"

The mage closed his eyes, going quiet. "Yes, Master Almek, I do. Something...has shifted. But it's just beyond my grasp."

"Hold on to what you sense, and open your eyes," Almek instructed quietly. As the mage obeyed, Almek nodded as Ash's expression hardened. "What do you see?"

The mage's fingernails dug into the wood as he replied in a low voice. "I see shadows around the Swordanzen. Especially Storm. Though the shadows cannot quite reach either of them. I can almost see...something. But it's like seeing faces in the curl of candle smoke." He looked at Almek, expression bleak. "Do you see these shadows all the time?"

"Not only such dire things," Almek assured him. "It's unfortunately easiest to teach you to recognize and interpret seeing time traces when danger looms. That you can glimpse images at this stage of your training as well reflects your natural strength." He pressed his lips together. "Look at the Swordanzen's eyes. You can tell they can sense it, too."

Ash studied the pair, their swords clashing, and bodies moving with instinctive, deadly grace. "It seems...different for them. They see without seeing. Know without knowing." He propped his chin on his fist, feeling a twinge of envy. "They had embraced the gifts of the Guardians and made them their own long ago."

"Not exactly." Almek's words drew a surprised look from the mage. "For the Desanti, survival requires anticipating their opponents. They have honed the art of future sight by seeing the minute futures of their opponents' intentions. I believe they have bred the Guardian gifts into their people, made it a part of their culture.

"In Desantiva, only the strongest survive. To be strong, they must constantly test themselves, prove themselves. Swordanzen are the best of their people. What they have embraced of the Guardian gifts has become so ingrained, I don't know how to help them grow beyond their patterns, however willing they may be to learn them."

"I don't understand." Ash frowned, troubled. "The same training you give the rest of us should work for them."

"It's different for you and the others. You, Taylin, and Mureln each mastered unique arts with unique aspects of temporal energy used for each. But the training for your arts is quite similar to the training used by Guardians to manipulate temporal energy." Almek paused as he and Ash looked at the Desanti when the children squealed in delight. Storm swept her blade low, Skyfire diving over top of her to roll back to his feet. She spun, the two once more facing one another. "For you, it's expanding your first instruction to the greater breadth of Guardian skills. The instruction method is familiar; only the medium has changed."

"But if Desanti can use Guardian magic," Ash asked slowly, "they're not completely bereft of magic as my people assume."

Almek sighed, shaking his head. "You know that what you define as magic is life energy. The Desanti and their kinsmen, the Vodani, are...different. In their souls, they lack a connection to what you and Sevmanen possess—the capacity to gather and wield life energy external to yourselves. The size of your capacity shows whether you have the strength to be a mage, or a healer, or the others who trained in its use. Temporal energy is not the same.

"To be a Guardian isn't about capacity. A songbird or a rock has as much capacity for temporal energy as I do. What's different is my awareness of time and its flow. The Guardians' purpose is to ensure that no stone thrown into the River of Time, whether or not unconsciously, upsets the great balance. It takes only a strong desire or even happenstance for something to set events into motion to bring about enormous changes. We try to ensure that the results are not disastrous."

Ash considered Almek's words, eyes following the Desanti. "So, it's akin to someone gifted in numbers versus someone gifted in horsemanship. Both require education in their specific facets, but there is no difference in the fact that they require some education."

"Correct." Almek sighed softly. "The Desanti use of temporal energy and perception is more primal. Instinctive. Unless it is damaged, we are born with the ability to see, hear, taste. The stronger the sense, the easier it is to use well without training. If you do not realize that what you see is not what others see, or those around you see similarly, you simply accept it as fact. Desanti learn simply because temporal sight has given them the edge to survive. They learn...by using it, by *needing* it to survive."

Ash considered the Desanti. Having watched others train in the physical arts, he realized what seemed peculiar to him about their training. "She's teaching him. Helping him hone his skills."

The Dusvet Guardian nodded, expression grim. "I fear the day when Skyfire is Storm's equal." Ash focused on Almek, the ring of blade on blade a mere background sound. "It's difficult to scry the future of those poised to change the course of the river of time. It's been especially difficult to scry anything about Storm. But I have seen..."

Almek exhaled, eyes closing, shoulders sagging. "I've clearly seen what will happen when they are truly equals. That day, if they have not found their true paths as Guardians, if I have failed to expand their world, they will fight. But it will be no training fight. It will be to the death."

Ash inhaled sharply, looking back at the desert folk. "Can you see...which one wins the contest?" he asked, an icy knot settling in the pit of his stomach as he followed Storm's movements.

The Desanti's training came to a halt, the two straightening from their fighting stances. "There will be no winner. We will lose them both."

The Swordanzen bowed to each other, teacher to student, sheathing their swords. Skyfire went over to the gate that joined the two halves of the corral, letting the crowded horses into the half they had taken over for their training. Storm approached the two men, bowing to Almek.

A pebble struck the back of her head just as her lips parted to speak. Storm whirled, her incredulous stare meeting Skyfire's mischievous wink before he darted away. Without hesitation, she vaulted the fence in pursuit, her fluid movements betraying her deadly training even in play. The children erupted in delighted cheers, abandoning their posts to follow the two warriors, who had momentarily shed their deadly grace for childlike abandon in their impromptu chase.

"Can you tell them what you have seen? Warn them away from the danger? Order them not to...No." Ash shook his head, answering his own question. "They cling too stubbornly to their traditions. They would not listen to you, even with Storm having sworn an oath to you. She holds her people's ways more important than her own life."

The Guardian sighed softly. "And though I believe their temporal perception exceeds that of most Unsvet Guardians...I'm not sure how to teach them because I can't determine what they really sense."

Chapter Fifty-One

Since their departure from Ganessi, the group quickly fell into a routine of travel and stops that would normally swiftly become boring, particularly since they encountered little more than solitary farms or small inns solely existing for travelers on the road. But the camaraderie that had developed made for many discussions that explored different points of view of the world, sometimes lively. For a change, Amelana was silent, eyes downcast. Many noted the condition not only for how unusual it was for her, but for how welcome her silence was.

The travel would have passed faster but for the pair of Swordanzen. The Desanti slowed their travel with a constant childlike curiosity and incessant explorations. Every strange rock, every plant, every creature they saw demanded investigation. Even the dew in the early morning was cause for wonder. It reached a point, Almek had to reign them in.

"Storm, Skyfire. I know there is much you wish to explore." Almek's paternal smile was as gentle as his words. "But you have a task that needs completing. We should try to get to it as quickly as possible."

The others had to repress laughter at the uncharacteristic sheepishness of the Desanti's expressions. "Of course, Lord Almek. Forgive us." Storm's bow from the drizar's back was almost regal. Until the drizar bowed as well, mimicking his rider's intent and earning scolding for nearly throwing his rider as she jumped off instead, inciting amused laughter.

"Hey! Mage!" Ash arched an eyebrow at Emil. "When we get t' Ithesra, ye think ye could give me an' Emaris directions t' a pleasure house, maybe?" The Gyspari man affected a child's pleading expression. "We ain't stopped long enough anywhere, and it's been years! Oof!" He glared at Emaris then corrected himself. "Months!"

Ash smirked. "Perhaps. We'll see when we get there." He rolled his eyes at the whoop and rather detailed plans Emil gave voice to. Terrence blushed, chuckling at the smaller mercenary.

Ignoring Emil, Taylin watched Storm as the woman urged the drizar some distance away, standing on his back to extend a hand. The healer smiled when a songbird alighted on Storm's offered finger and trilled. When Mureln joined Taylin, he followed her gaze. "I never realized how much I had taken for granted before we went to Desantiva. I don't know if I could ever return to the desert." She looked at Mureln, troubled. "What will it be like for them to return to the wastelands after being here?"

Mureln shrugged with a wan expression. "I don't know." Smiling gently, he leaned over to capture her hand and place a chaste kiss on her knuckles, smiling when she blushed. "Don't let such thoughts occupy your mind, my lovely healer." He watched as the songbird took wing, Storm watching it until it vanished. "I find it remarkable, honestly. They aren't as bitter at the bounty here as I would have expected."

Ash rode over to Terrence, the young apprentice sitting hunch-shouldered with his cowl drawn forward. "Apprentice." The young man jumped, startled. "Relax, Terrence," the mage said calmly. He studied the young man. "Something is bothering you." The master mage realized that moment how much he had neglected his apprentice because of the demands for attention caused by Amelana's ineptness.

Surprised and gratified to be Ash's focus, Terrence blushed and looked away, the cowl hiding his features. "It is...difficult to watch the Desanti, Master. I...I still remember the things Dzee showed me...of Desantiva before the Great War, and it is just...just..." The anguish in his voice spoke the feelings he could find no words for.

"Everything serves a purpose, Apprentice." Ash's gaze drifted toward the desert folk, his voice dropping to a murmur. "Even the darkest moments contain seeds of growth. Look at the Desanti—forged in fire, yet flourishing where others would wither. Our people wait for calamity to transform them, when transformation could be a choice."

The master didn't notice his apprentice smiling at him. "Yes, Master Ash."

The wind gusted, and both Swordanzen straightened, looking in the same direction with alert expressions, hands fallen to sword hilts. The others stopped to scan the area, wondering what had brought about the sudden change.

Almek studied the two, tilting his head. He rode over, putting himself in front of the drizzen. "What do you see?"

Neither Swordanzen reacted as if the question were something unusual to ask. Skyfire frowned before focusing on the Guardian. "I am not sure what I see. I have no words to describe it. But I feel something is not right." He regarded Storm, the woman still unmoving.

"Storm?" Almek frowned. "Storm!"

Storm's gaze fixed on some distant point beyond the visible world, her statue-like stillness so complete that Almek's words seemed to go unheard. The beast shifted nervously beside her, nostrils flaring until she absently placed a steadying hand on his neck. Her touch calmed him, though his muscles remained taut and his claws dug gouges into the soil. "I see flickers of ghosts dancing in the trees," she murmured. "Betrayal. Regret. Forgiveness. Mourning." She shook her head sharply, as if clearing cobwebs from her vision, then swung herself fully into the saddle. "We should go." Without waiting for a response, she urged her mount forward, leaving Skyfire to exchange a confused glance with the others before hastening after her.

Mureln looked at Almek's blank look of surprise. "Dusvet?"

"I may have underestimated Storm." Almek's thoughtful words brought no comfort to any of them.

Ash studied Almek. "She may know more of the Guardian gifts than you estimated?"

Almek looked at Ash soberly. "She doesn't just see. She feels across time. Farther and more deeply than I expected. Only a handful of Guardians ever achieve that level of ability."

The mage backed away from the intense look the Guardian fixed on him. "What?"

"I wonder what unexpected facets *your* gifts will bring the Guardians, Illaini Magus." Almek's expression softened as he smiled at the startled mage before he turned his horse to catch up to the Desanti.

✦————·—··—-≻ͼ·2≺--—··—————✦

As it had been for the days since their departure from Ganessi, the ride continued without event...up until both drizzen abruptly balked, hissing malevolently. The others swiftly drew back as the Desanti focused on getting them calmed again.

Emil looked as bewildered as the rest. "What be that about?"

Ash pressed his lips together before he finally answered the Gyspari mercenary. "We are on the border of Forenta." He pulled his mare around, turning away from the pair of Desanti. "I did not realize they would be able to perceive—"

"Of course we can sense the magic that stands against us." Storm's words were clipped. Flashing an irritated look towards the Forentan, she clearly struggled to reign her own temper in while endeavoring to calm the drizar. "Why would you defilers not block everything Desanti access to your lands when you failed to destroy us? We can feel it! It is a part of us." She leaned forward, vigorously rubbing the drizar's neck, murmuring in Desanti to calm him.

Ash grimaced, staring at the back of his right hand. Decisively, he spurred his mare across the invisible border, then turned back. "From this day forward, Forenta extends welcome to Desantiva's children."

The others stared in bewilderment when the pair of drizzen abruptly calmed at the Illaini Magus' simple words. Flattened ears swiveled forward, tension draining from their haunches. Even the two Githalin Swordanzen relaxed. With only a moment more hesitation, the four desert dwellers crossed into Forenta as though nothing had happened.

Almek came up beside Ash, considering him. "The Knowing One welcomed them?" he asked in a low voice.

Ash's expression hardened. "Not precisely. My master used to tell me about the days shortly after the Great War. How we shut out all things foreign, especially the warriors." Ash closed his eyes, looking away. "After we recovered enough from the last battle of the Great War, we welcomed our Sevmanan cousins and accepted the seafaring Vodani. Of course, no Desanti had ever come.

"To break a warding, one of those warded against must stand at the threshold and be formally received. I doubt anyone remembers a warding existed." He looked up, watching the Desanti as they examined the fruit of the nearest tree along the road. "Bennu always emphasized the importance of that history never being forgotten. He would say it was so it could be made right one day. I don't know if this was what he meant, but..." The ghost of lingering guilt for performing an act that could be considered treasonous by his people haunted the Illaini Magus's eyes. "I can tell you She is...not pleased with me."

"Bennu was always a wise man, even in his youth. He would be proud of you." Almek smiled gently at Ash's surprised, grateful expression. "Come on, if we do not distract them, we'll be here all day while they explore."

"Let them explore. Travelers frequently use the clearing up ahead for camping. It's only several more days ride to reach Naveene's Rest in Ithesra." Ash's expression softened when Storm laughed, hanging onto the back of the drizar as he balanced on his rear legs to reach the fruits almost out of reach. "They wish to learn about the world beyond their borders. I don't wish to discourage them."

Almek looked surprised before an understanding smile curved his lips. "The Knowing One emphasizes gaining knowledge." He called out, "We will be making camp!"

"Finally!" Emil made a show of holding his stomach. "I be starvin'!" His horse danced sideways before Emaris's shoulder punch landed. "Hah! Missed me! Let's get t' work. The sooner we be settled in, th' sooner we eat!" That was all the encouragement the mute Sevmanan mercenary needed, the two guiding the pack horses on to the clearing ahead.

By evening, the group had settled in for the night, the single tent nestled between two old trees that, while larger than in Sevmana, were still considerably smaller than those farther into the interior. Storm and Skyfire were crouched by the stream on the side opposite the road, watching the shadows of tiny fish darting back and forth.

Taylin smiled indulgently when she looked towards the pair. "Supper is almost ready!" She chuckled when they both waved hands dismissively, not looking away from the water. "I cannot understand how they can eat so little, but they do not seem to show any weakness from starvation." She smiled at Mureln as he bumped her shoulder 'accidentally' while he helped with the evening meal, reaching for the teapot.

"We're making good time, even without my encouraging the horses to go faster." Mureln poured some tea and offered it to Almek before grabbing another cup to serve the others. "We should be in Ithesra by high sun the day after tomorrow, even with Storm and Skyfire's constant explorations delaying us." He frowned when the pair jumped to their feet, hands on their sword hilts. "What's bothering them all of a sudden?"

Just as the Desanti reacted, Ash looked up from his meditation, and frowned as he squinted into the branches of the trees. He leaped to his feet, snapping out the words of a spell that created a barrier over the camp. Eerie sounds of arrows bouncing off the invisible shield echoed hauntingly. "Terrence!" he barked. "The branches!"

Terrence held his hands out, directing powerful gusts of wind into the upper branches, knocking several men to the ground. The young man's eyes went wide as several others emerged from behind the trees, swords and axes drawn as they advanced on the travelers.

Storm and Skyfire charged one group, Emil and Emaris taking on those from the other side. The battle cries filled the glade as chaos ensued. Ash fixed his gaze on another archer in the branches, sending a bolt of lightning that landed square in the man's chest.

Mureln stood over Taylin and Almek protectively, deftly fending off two smaller men. A large man shoved him aside, easily knocking Taylin away with a backhanded fist. With bared yellow teeth showing, the grinning man reached out to wrap his hands around Almek's throat. "First you, then the rest," the man promised. "Ganessi's payin' extra to kill you for interfering, Guardian."

Dazed, Taylin and Mureln looked up in panic, then stopped, gaping as Almek put his hands on his attacker's wrists. The man's flesh seemed to ripple and wither as he aged decades in mere seconds before their eyes. His scream of horror died to a whisper as he crumbled into a pile of dust and dry bones. Drained by both effort and attack, Almek sucked in air, covering his throat protectively.

Storm turned sharply when Ash cried out and collapsed with an arrow sprouting from his back. Heedless of the danger the archer still posed, she ran over to the fallen Illaini Magus. "Mage!" She grabbed his shoulder. "Ash!"

Ash gasped in pain, half clinging to her as she tried to help him up. "Take my hand. Now!" Storm did not hesitate, holding his hand tightly in hers. She gasped as a surge of power blinded her for a heartbeat.

The burst of energy exploded from the huddled pair of Forentan and Desanti, flowing out like the ripples from a stone dropped into a pool. While the energy flowed harmlessly around their companions, it exploded into the attackers no matter where they hid themselves, killing or incapacitating them.

Storm blinked rapidly, her sight slowly clearing as she attempted to stumble back from the mage. "What did you—?"

Keeping a tight hold on her hand as he sank to his knees, Ash grinned. "I used your instinct of identifying ally from enemy to protect our own."

Her surprised expression drew more of a smile from him. "Forenta and Desantiva can make a powerful team, hm?"

"No." Dazed, Amelana emerged from the shelter she'd hidden in during the attack. "No! It wasn't supposed to be like *this*!" The Forentan woman shrieked in maddened fury, her hair in disarray as she fixed a hateful glare on Storm. "*She* was supposed to *die*! You *all* were supposed to die!" Stabbing a finger towards Storm, she shrieked, "It's your fault! You poisoned Ash against me! You ruined *everything*!"

"Amelana." The pain in Ash's voice took the edge off the angry warning in his tone.

"Shh." Storm put her fingers to his lips. "This is my challenge to answer. And I must answer it alone. Let Taylin heal you." When he tried to argue, she said, "Trust me, Mage." Leaving Ash in Terrence's care, she stood.

With hands curled like twisted claws in her fury, Amelana hissed. "Desanti bitch! You'll suffer for what you did to me!"

"Shut up and attack me," Storm ordered, holding her arms out to her sides. "But know your first attack will be your last." Eyes narrowed as she took a step closer, then another. "Make it count, you harpy vulture."

Amelana screamed epithets at Storm before she spat a spell. Flames erupted from her hands to crash against the Desanti woman, enveloping her in the angry conflagration. Everyone cried out in horrified dismay as the wash of flames concealed the Desanti woman. Amelana looked on when she stopped casting the spell, eager to see Storm laid low. Her glee faltered when the flames sputtered out and only thick, dark smoke remained.

When the smoke cleared, Storm remained standing, her tattooed arm raised over her face, only her clothing showing signs of damage, herself unharmed. As she lowered her arm, she met Amelana's terrified eyes with stony cold ones, jaw clenched. Drawing the smaller knife, Storm crossed the distance between her and the journeyman mage. She grabbed the front of the journeyman's robes, jerking her forward and snarling at her.

Amelana's eyes went wide in shock as the blade sank deep into her. Storm hissed between gritted teeth, "Now you can know Desantiva's pain, daughter of defilers." Shoving Amelana away, Storm stood over her a moment before turning to stagger a few steps, collapsing against Skyfire.

Skyfire looked at Storm in horrified realization as her eyes rolled back and she went limp. "Healer! Come quickly! She is burning within!"

Terrence looked at Ash, eyes wide. "Master, Amelana used forbidden magic! I-I do not know how to counter such spells!"

Ash grimaced, putting the pain of the arrow shaft still protruding from his back out of his mind. "Get me on my feet, Terrence." The mage staggered over to Storm and Skyfire, dropping to his knees. Without hesitation, he put his hands on the exposed flesh that roiled grotesquely, closing his eyes.

So focused on unwinding the wild magic coiling within the Swordanzen woman, Ash did not notice Taylin easing the arrow from his back and closing his wound. Nor did he notice the others gathering around the pair. Their voices were only an annoying buzz to his ears. He felt a tingling under his hands as he swept away the last of the perverted magic and opened his eyes to see Taylin's hands on either side of his, sensing the damaged flesh beneath mending. He sat back on his heels, focusing on getting his emotions—fury at Amelana's further betrayal, fear he was too late—under control.

"Master Ash," Terrence whispered, his eyes wide in fear as he knelt by the man. "How? How could she have...known forbidden arts? When she couldn't even manage basic spells?"

"I don't know, Terrence. I know only that she has squandered her honor and stained the Avarian family name." When Taylin sagged wearily, he met the healer's eyes and relaxed at her imperceptible nod. "But at least we've undone the evil of it." He turned his hand up to look at the star-shaped scar and relaxed with a knowing smile. "Thank you, Mother," he murmured.

The sound of others entering the encampment roused the weary travelers to prepare for another attack. Ash called out, "Hold!"

The guardsman captain Nolyn Lirai swung down from the branches, with an incredulous look on his face. "Illaini Magus Ash Andar? Someone attacked you?" He stared in horrified shock the moment he spotted Almek being helped by Mureln and Taylin. "Foreigners attacked Dusvet Guardian Almek Two-Tones? On Forentan soil?!" The other guardsmen's faces turned sickly pale, realizing the potential retribution looming over their nation.

Almek shook his head, leaning on Mureln for support. "You bear no fault. You couldn't have known. I still live, so Fortress remains unaware."

The reassurance helped assuage some of the fear, though the worry lingered.

Terrence helped Ash to his feet. With effort, the Illaini Magus moved away from his apprentice and stood on his own. "Master Nolyn Lirai," he greeted with traditional Forentan formality. "Forgive us for being unable to give you a proper welcome. We were unavoidably distracted."

The guardsman master mage rolled his eyes, but that was the extent of his response to the man. He clasped Ash's star-scarred hand with his own bearing the twin to that scar. "We happened to be nearby when we felt the ripple of forbidden magicks." Nolyn's eyes widened as his scanning eyes fell upon the Desanti. "Forgive us for arriving...late." After a few seconds, he asked, "Are those Desanti?!"

Ash managed a wan smile. "Indeed they are, Master Nolyn. We welcome your arrival, however belated the circumstances have rendered it." He looked down at the fallen Forentan woman, his face twisted in rage and grief. "My former apprentice employed forbidden magicks against the Swordanzen. The Dusvet Guardian and his students bear witness to the journeyman's unprovoked aggression." Pausing, he withdrew a small pouch from his robes, extending it formally to Nolyn. "Furthermore, she conspired to orchestrate the demise of the Dusvet Guardian. The Desanti warriors stood in his defense. And she," he indicated Storm with a respectful gesture, "administered justice when Journeyman Amelana persisted in her malevolence."

Dragging his stare away from the Desanti, Nolan's gaze fell on Amelana who twitched, moaning. Nolyn looked surprised. "She didn't kill her? I'm impressed. I always thought the warrior folk were ruthless murderers." Skyfire gritted his teeth, but held his tongue, cradling the unconscious Storm.

Nolyn snapped his fingers. Two more guards dropped out of the trees to gather up Amelana. "She will stand before the Edai Tredecima for the crime of using forbidden arts. Until then, she will remain bound and in custody." Nolyn put a hand on Ash's shoulder. "Her actions will not reflect on her family, my friend. I promise you. Master Bennu's memory will not be tarnished."

"I'm grateful for that, Master Nolyn." Nolyn caught Ash's elbow as the Illaini Magus's knees buckled. "My pardon," Ash began.

Nolyn shook his head, straightening as he assumed a more formal air. "You need not apologize, Illaini Magus Ash Andar. You had to guard against foreigners foolish enough to attack you on our soil. We should have arrived sooner to prevent this atrocity against Fortress within Forenta's borders. Permit my people to stand guard and escort you to Naveene's Rest." He flicked a glance as Amelana was carried away. "The High Council will require your presence for the woman's trial."

Ash nodded once. "Of course. Thank you, Nolyn. But if you would excuse me now." Terrence hurried over to lend his shoulder to his master as the Illaini Magus's knees threatened to buckle again. "I think I need to rest now."

"That goes without saying, Ash." Nolyn turned to bark orders to several men and women in the trees.

Taylin and Mureln could not help but stare at Almek after things calmed. The old man quirked a sad smile. "Not everything a Guardian can do is benevolent, children. The world is not always a benevolent place." He accepted the cup of tea from Taylin, ignoring how it trembled in her hands. He met her eyes. "Only intent determines whether a skill is good or evil. Not the skill itself. Remember that."

"Yes, Dusvet." Taylin kept her gaze fixed on her trembling hands. When Mureln's fingers brushed her shoulder, she startled. His arm encircled her, drawing her close, and she buried her face against the rough fabric of his tunic. The reality of what they had experienced crashed over her like a wave, and her body shook with an upwelling of emotions that she could no longer hold back.

Skyfire carried Storm to the shelter, followed by Terrence and Ash. The two Forentan watched Skyfire lay Storm down and drape a blanket over her. He glanced at Ash, then turned and left without a word. Ash studied Storm for several heartbeats and then closed his eyes in utter exhaustion.

At a loss, Terrence said, "Master...I do not understand everything that happened. But—"

"Go," Ash ordered simply. "Watch over Master Almek. I'll be fine." The young man hesitated, then nodded and left the shelter.

Ash stared at the ceiling for many long minutes. Eventually, he dragged himself to his feet, stumbled the few steps to Storm, and dropped to the ground by her side. He touched her cheek, his hand shaking. "Storm," he murmured, the fear of what could have happened and relief she survived soaking the single word.

Green-gold eyes opened, and Storm reached up to cover the hand on her cheek with her own, her whisper barely audible. "Ash. Forgive me. I—"

"No," he interrupted her gently. "Don't apologize. Nothing you did caused any of this. You did what you had to do. Amelana brought this on herself. I don't know how you withstood her spell, but I am...very grateful you did." His thumb traced the edge of her lower lip. "My beautiful Storm."

Agonized, Storm tried to pull his hand away. "Ash, please. Don't. We can't...our peoples..."

"Shhh. I know. I don't care about them."

"But—"

Ash smiled tiredly. "Shhh. Storm, stop. Listen to me." He paused, looking into her eyes. "All my life, I have been alone. You were right when you said I chose solitude. But I chose it because I was afraid." He closed his eyes for a moment, taking a deep breath. "No one could truly understand the wounds on my soul. There was no one I trusted to know my heart because I feared they would use it against me, or those I trusted would become targets to reach me. And so I suffered alone, thinking myself superior to everyone else because I endured what would have crushed them and excelled beyond their paltry attempts at power."

"Ash—"

He pressed a finger gently to her lips. "Then I met you, and suddenly all the walls and barriers meant nothing. You saw through them all." His voice caught. "And when you saw what lay beneath, you never used it against me." The corner of his mouth lifted in a half-smile. "Instead, you drew your blade for me instead. To protect me. No one has ever stood between me and danger before." He paused, searching her eyes. "Our peoples may forbid more, but perhaps..." His voice lowered to barely a whisper. "Could we stand as allies?"

Storm held his gaze, the silence stretching between them. Finally, her lips curved upwards. "Allies," she agreed softly. Ash's shoulders dropped, tension flowing from him like water. She reached for him, pulling him down beside her and drawing the blanket over them both. In the quiet darkness, they found an unexpected peace in each other's presence as sleep claimed them.

Chapter Fifty-Two

Ash jolted awake, blinking rapidly as the shadows resolved into the shelter's interior. Outside, familiar forest sounds washed over him—wind-stirred leaves, the cacophony of birds calling raucously to each other, distant lupine howling to one another—a symphony that comforted him in its familiarity. His hand found only empty space where Storm had lain beside him, stirring anxiety over her absence. He scanned the other sleeping forms, then slipped quietly from the shelter. Relief flooded through him as he spotted Storm by the campfire, absently stirring the embers with a branch.

"You should be sleeping." He brushed the log beside her with his hand before settling onto it smoothly. "Even with Taylin's healing gifts, injuries requires time to recover from."

She almost smiled, eyes fixed on the hot coals. "If I slept this much back home, I would likely wake up with a flock of harpy vultures taking pieces out of me because they would have thought me dead for not moving for so long."

Ash frowned, reminded of her harsher homeland, but said nothing. They both looked up at the howl of a lupine much closer than the others. He noticed her hand had fallen onto one of the twin single-edged sword hilts. "It's just a lupine. A giant wolf. They won't bother us. Especially not with them standing guard." He gestured towards the men in forest green and black garb, who nodded to Ash in acknowledgment. The mage's attention returned to studying the silent young woman when she silently returned to staring at the fire. "Storm?"

"There is so much life here." Storm continued to stare at the flames, her voice low. "At home, I could tell you where each plant, where each animal was. Even if it were hidden from my eyes." Sighing, she reached over for a piece of dead wood, picked it up, but hesitated to put it in the fire, stroking it like one might a beloved pet that died. "I feel very overwhelmed." She finally leaned forward to set the wood into the fire with something akin to religious reverence, murmuring a few words as if in prayer.

Ash tilted his head as he studied her. "You pray over the wood?"

"We pray for all whose souls we set free, to thank them for providing their bodies to sustain or protect ours. Plants are no less alive than we are." Storm scrutinized him. "You do not?"

Ash stared into the dancing flames, his expression thoughtful. "Perhaps I should," he said finally. "In Forenta, we offer gratitude to the Knowing One for Her gifts, but..." He traced a finger along the grain of the log beneath him. "Many just say the words without embracing the meaning of them." When he looked up at Storm again, his eyes lingered on the hilts at her waist. "I've noticed how you handle your blades—they hold similar significance for your people, don't they?"

"They are symbols of what we live for, what we die for." Storm looked at his waist, where his desert knife rested. "Like those given to you and the rest of Lord Almek's true students, the purest blades are gifts from the Totani themselves, given when they grant us our adult names. They are a lesson and a reminder that, above all else, the sacred balance of life and death must be kept. They always have two edges."

Drawing her own long knife, she held it up, studying it. "This is the first Naming Blade. All who reach adulthood receive one, gifts from the Totani signifying the Heart's acceptance of them." Sheathing it, she touched the two-edged sword's hilt. "This is a Swordanzen Naming Blade, given only to those who survive their final trial and are deemed worthy to be Swordanzen by the Totani." She smiled when Ash glanced back towards the shelter. "Kailee has always been a temperamental Totani. She makes nothing easy for anyone, especially those she holds dearest to her. True, Totani-blessed blades always have two edges."

"Except for your Githalin blades." Ash pointed to the two single-edged blades resting across her lap.

Looking down at them, her expression gentled as she smiled. "These are given by the Heart Himself, when He blesses the joining of Totani and human into Githalin. If you lifted a sword to fight, you would fight with a sword. When I lift a sword to fight, I am the sword, and the sword is me." She held up her hands. "I have two hands. Two halves."

"Two swords," Ash finished, his intrigue showing through his aloofness. "With two edges."

"It is the mark of the Githalin. God-chosen."

Falling silent, Ash looked into the fire as the wood popped, sending out sparks.

"Who was she?" Storm asked simply. "The one you grieve for still."

Ash closed his eyes, grief constricting his heart at the memories that resurfaced with her words. "Someone I couldn't protect." He expected her to ask about Dessa, unsure he could speak more of the loss, of his failure. Her words startled him.

"The deepest wounds we bear," Storm murmured, drawing Ash's gaze to her, "are for those we could not save."

With an earnestness he could not contain, Ash put a hand on her wrist. "I will let nothing happen to you or Skyfire. Amelana isn't representative of all of my people."

"She represented some," Storm stated tonelessly. "And it would only take one to kill me. I knew the taste of your magic in the desert. And now I know the taste of magics no one should. I will not hold you to promises you cannot keep. Even the gods cannot control the actions of individuals with free will." Getting to her feet, she drew her swords. "Do not fear for me, Mage. I can take care of myself."

As Storm began moving through her sword training routines, Ash could sense the eyes of the Forentan guardsmen turning towards her, sense their uneasiness. "She is no murderer," he stated flatly in Forentan. "She is Master Almek's student." He turned his vivid azure gaze towards the branches. "If you fail to protect any of them, Fortress will be the least of your worries. My anger will know no limits."

"Yes, Master Andar," various voices murmured, some contrite, some bemused. Ash snorted and went back to watching the Swordanzen train by herself until the others roused to begin the last leg of the journey to Ithesra.

THE DEEPER INTO FORENTA's territory the group traveled, the more withdrawn and wary the pair of Swordanzen became. When they reached the first bridges that led into the towering trees above, only the soft glow of hundreds of lanterns illuminated the darkness beneath the nighttime canopy of leaves and night sky.

The drizzen balked at the foot of the bridge, reflecting the unease the Swordanzen could not conceal. "No," Storm stated adamantly as the others dismounted to walk their horses up the bridge. Skyfire was equally resolute.

"The bridges are perfectly safe, Desanti," the senior guardsman stated with a hint of impatience. The man's hard expression faltered when the Swordanzen turned dark looks on him.

Ash approached the pair, waving the guardsman off. "I will escort the Swordanzen. See to Master Almek and the others' comfort." The guardsman looked torn between relief and his sense of propriety. He opted to let Ash handle the Desanti, turning to follow the rest of the party up the bridge.

"I am not going up there." Skyfire crossed his arms across his chest, his eyes challenging Ash to say otherwise.

Ash studied them. "It is better than the rigging on the Vodani ship," he assured, keeping his voice carefully neutral. "There's more surface area than the ship's ropes or railings, and it doesn't move so much."

"I could see the ship below me," Storm snapped at Ash. She waved a hand upwards. "How high does it go? I cannot see the sky from here!" The drizar made a barking noise, grabbing a mouthful of moss, dirt, and stones, munching all of it.

Skyfire grumbled, stroking the neck of his drizzen. "It is unnatural."

Ash opened his mouth then shut it again, deciding against a retort about what was and was not natural. Closing his eyes, he took a deep breath to calm himself and reclaim his patience. "It's natural here." Skyfire growled and turned away.

"We will wait here," Storm stated. "On the ground."

The Forentan mage considered the pair, and then the branches above. "After everything I have seen, I never would have imagined this." A carefully condescending tone colored his voice.

The two Desanti fixed hostile glares on the mage. "Imagined what?"

"That Githalin Swordanzen would be afraid of trees." He remained outwardly unmoved as both drew swords, his hands remaining tucked into his sleeves. He held tight to his forearms to conceal the instinctive fear the pair and their weapons inspired. The underlying challenge in his words had the desired effect.

"We fear nothing!" Skyfire snarled at the mage.

"You don't? Then come stay with the rest of us at Naveene's Rest." Ash met Storm's eyes and held her gaze as he let a hint of challenge seep into his voice. Then, feigning dismissal, he turned his back on them and started up the ramp at a regal pace.

Storm fumed and finally shoved her sword back in its sheath. Jerking the drizar's halter, she started towards the bridge. Hesitating a moment, she finally took a resolute step onto the wooden planking and forced herself to go forward. Skyfire hesitated a little longer before he followed her. Both drizzen did as their companions, though their claws left deep gouges in the wood.

Ash released a long-held breath when he heard their footsteps behind him on the wooden planks. His eyes lifted briefly skyward in silent gratitude to the Knowing One that his challenge hadn't earned him a blade between his ribs. He kept his gaze fixed ahead, careful not to glance back—acknowledging their unease would only transform their fear into rage.

Chapter Fifty-Three

In the elegant main room, Almek and the others sat around the large table towards the back of the main room. They watched with pleased surprise as servants placed many enormous platters and tureens containing an abundance of food fit for royalty on the table. Several young men and women poured wine, fawning over the travelers with youthful innocence and curiosity. When Ash and the two Swordanzen finally arrived, they flocked to attend to them. Most, however, shied away from the Desanti, avoiding meeting the hostile glares of Storm and Skyfire.

Almek smiled as Ash sat beside him, the two Desanti on the mage's other side. "It seems the Edai Tredecima has reconsidered its position on the issues you had reported prior to your departure."

Watching the Desanti from the corner of his eye, Ash said distractedly, "Oh? Do tell."

The Dusvet Guardian chuckled at Ash's droll tone. "Indeed. Without you to handle matters, they have been unable to wave off the seriousness of what you repeatedly reported to them. They wish to speak with me about some occurrences since your departure...after they attend to the less pleasant business of your former student."

An older woman approached Ash, bowing to him as she took his travel cloak. "Tonight we celebrate Forenta's Son's return and honor Dusvet Almek and his students! I am Headwoman Kelafy. Please enjoy Naveene's hospitality. You will find no better in all Forenta."

"Lookit all this food!" Emil called to the warrior pair. He smiled up at a pretty girl who leaned down by him. "Now *this* is how Almek's students should be treated!"

Mureln arched an incredulous eyebrow at Emil, Taylin giggling behind her hand. "'Almek's students'? You are including yourselves now?"

"Hey now! We been pullin' our weight!" Emil countered, the serving girl tittering in amusement. "Ah, ye lovely thing, thank ye fer th' wine, but I am wondering if ye do have something a little stronger, mayhaps?"

"Of course, Master Emil!"

"Ye see? *Master* Emil!" Emaris rolled his eyes, shaking his head at his brother, who puffed his chest proudly. Emil glanced over at the Desanti who sat with backs stiff, expressions grim. "Skyfire, lad, c'mon! Cheer up!" The Desanti man gave the Gyspari a side-eye glare, unmoved.

A young woman barely out of her girlhood put her hands on Skyfire's shoulder, leaning over. "Master Warrior, would you like some food or wine?"

Startled at such open friendliness from a Forentan towards him, Skyfire looked at her, and shook his head once sharply. "I am not hungry." As an afterthought, he added in an effort at politeness, "Thank you."

"As you wish, Master Warrior," the girl said brightly. "But if you change your mind, please ask for Lyra." She glanced down and back up. "I have never seen a Desanti before."

"You would not have. Desanti do not leave Desantiva. Except for us." He glanced at the Forentan girl, drawn out of his bad temper by bewilderment. "I am Skyfire," he responded automatically to her oblique introduction.

Lyra smiled with a sweet, guileless innocence. "Are all the men in Desantiva as handsome as you, Master Skyfire?"

Skyfire glanced over at Storm with a helpless expression. The Desanti woman simply shrugged, arms crossed and sitting stiffly in her chair.

"Mistress Warrior," a young man chided teasingly. "Would it kill you to relax and enjoy yourself?" Without any warning, Storm's hand shot up, grabbing him by the front of his shirt. He made an inarticulate noise as Storm jerked him down. She glared at him, nose to nose with the terrified man.

"My name," she stated in annoyance, "is Githalin Swordanzen Storm il'Thandar, and I am here because I must be here. I will not relax, I do not intend to enjoy myself while I must be here, and I will leave the soonest I can. Do you understand?" The terrified young man could only nod furtively.

Ash put a hand on her other arm. "Swordanzen, please don't manhandle the servants. It's their assigned duty to see to your needs."

The young man stumbled back a few steps as Storm released him with a disagreeable sound and crossed her arms again. "I need nothing from anyone here."

Making a gesture of dismissal to the perplexed man, Ash reached over for the water pitcher to pour a glass for Storm and sat it in front of her, then poured his own from the same pitcher. The Forentan servants stared, chattering among themselves at seeing the Illaini Magus serving the Desanti woman.

Storm noticed the servants' reaction, her eyes narrowing as she studied the glass, then Ash. "What? Are you going to try to throttle me now?" he asked, one eyebrow raised. When her gaze flicked to the whispering servants, Ash made a sound of understanding. "In Forenta, those of lower station serve their betters, and equals serve themselves. I feared that in your foul temper, you might bite someone. I considered it my duty to spare them and accepted the risk as my own, propriety be damned." The corner of his mouth twitched as she snatched the glass with a low growl. Though she only took a single sip, Ash counted this minor concession as a victory in their unspoken contest of wills, though he kept his satisfaction carefully hidden.

As the evening wore on, Ash remained as silent as Storm, watching how his people behaved with the foreign members of the group. He was pleased to note that the normal Forentan hostility was nearly nonexistent, undoubtedly because of the older woman in charge of who chose whom she allowed to attend them. Eventually, the overwhelming desire to escape the cacophony of the main room surpassed his intention to remain near Almek.

Almek put a hand on Ash's shoulder, leaning close to murmur in his ear. "Why don't you take Storm up to our rooms? Perhaps she will relax away from so much unfamiliar chaos." Grateful for the excuse, Ash nodded and stood. He didn't even need to say a word to Storm about his intentions. The mere touch on her shoulder served as well, the warrior woman standing with fluid grace. If either took notice of the many eyes watching them depart, no one could tell.

THE PAIR ASCENDED THE wide, curving staircase to the uppermost floor, far enough from prying eyes that no one could claim "accidental intrusions" to be coincidentally "just passing by." The landing opened to four curtained archways, with an exterior balcony visible between heavy drapes. Ash paused at the top of the stairs, watching Storm prowl the perimeter like a caged desert cat examining unfamiliar territory. "Skyfire and Master Almek have the other sleeping areas on this level," he said. "Though I imagine we won't be seeing either of them anytime soon."

Storm tugged back the curtain of one of the sleeping areas, then let it fall back again, walking to the balcony to look outside, an unexpected melancholy in her eyes. "Even up here, I cannot see the sky. Tell me, treewalker, before you came to my land, had you ever seen the stars?" Before Ash could answer her quiet question, Storm spun around suddenly, drawing her twin swords. Hearing footsteps on the stairs, the mage raised his own hands instinctively to attack the unknown intruder.

"Wait!" an old man's voice called. "Do not attack! I mean no ill to either of you!"

The mage froze in shock at the sound of the voice. He held his hands up to forestall Storm, stepping in front of her protectively. "Hold!" Sensing Storm lowering her swords slightly, Ash called, "Come."

Storm looked warily at the stooped figure of an old man as he continued climbing the stairs slowly with the self-possessed air of an aristocrat. Lowering the swords further, the woman inquisitively studied the old man. "You know him?"

"I do." Ash offered a stiff, respectful half-bow to the elder Forentan. "Master Ellis Avarian, this is Githalin Swordanzen Storm il'Thandar, Daughter of Desantiva." Storm turned her attention from the old man to Ash at the abrupt shift in his posture and demeanor to a formality she had never witnessed. "Swordanzen Storm, this is Edai Magus Ellis Avarian, head of house for the Avarian family, Amelana's great grand uncle, and my master's twin brother." Storm frowned at the bitterness in Ash's voice, puzzled, but remained silent as she turned her attention back to the elder man.

Ellis's expression did not falter, turning azure blue eyes towards Storm to appraise her as openly as she appraised him. "Blessings to you, Githalin Swordanzen Storm il'Thandar, Daughter of Desantiva," he greeted formally with a polite nod.

Sheathing her swords once assured there would be no attack, Storm outright stared at the old man. She moved forward with light steps, circling him like a great cat would an entrapped prey. With wide eyes, Storm reached up to touch his pure white hair. Her hand moved to touch the deep wrinkles on his face. She drew back sharply, deeply worried. "The cracks in your face...they do not hurt?"

Ellis endured the examination patiently. Although he was not smiling outwardly, his eyes sparkled in amusement. "No, child. They are just wrinkles. They are the price for the one hundred and twenty-some odd years I have survived."

Storm finally looked down, her cheeks coloring. "Forgive me, Ancient. I meant no disrespect." Her reverence for his age verged on a religious level.

"'Ancient?'" Ellis blinked and then smiled reassuringly. "No apologies are necessary, Githalin Swordanzen." He looked towards Ash. "I was hoping to speak with you prior to my great grand niece's trial before the Edai Tredecima."

Storm backed away a step. "I will leave." Before she could leave, Ellis put a hand on her arm to forestall her; she froze in place, not a twitch towards a weapon.

"No, young Storm, I meant I wished to speak to both of you. Please remain." Storm nodded and moved away from the stairs, her attention fixed raptly on the older Forentan.

Ellis took a deep breath, folding his hands into the sleeves of his robes. "On behalf of House Avarian, I wish to beg forgiveness for the shameful behavior and reprehensible actions of my great grand niece Amelana Avarian."

Ash's expression hardened before he turned his back on both Storm and Ellis, walking the several steps to the balcony archway to stare outside in silence.

Storm squinted in puzzlement over Ash's behavior. She looked between the young man and the old man in silent thought. With realization in her eyes, she looked back at Ellis. "You were the one who wanted to bind Amelana to him to mate with her."

Ellis stared at Storm. After a moment, he smiled, almost wistfully. "Plain spoken. You remind me of Ash when he was a boy." Ash shot a glare over his shoulder before looking away again. "In answer to your question, 'mating' was not my primary intention."

"Oh, really? It certainly seemed to be Amelana's," Ash snapped, turning to glare at Ellis.

Ellis raised his eyes to look into the young man's fury-filled gaze. "I had only your best interests at heart. And it would have helped restore some of the family's prestige to have an Illaini Magus among us. You would have had the respect of being a member of one of the ancient Houses instead of the abysmal treatment you receive because of being seen as lowborn."

Storm considered her words before speaking. "Ash deserves a better mate. I had seen better breeding in the sickly stray dogs in Ganessi."

The Desanti woman's forthrightness caught the older Forentan off guard. Recovering from his surprise at the crude yet somehow elegant observation, Ellis chuckled ruefully. "I would take insult if I could disagree." Ellis sighed, closing his eyes. "I had hoped that..." His words drifted off, and he shook his head. "Well, I'm sure you don't want to hear a tired old man prattling on about nonsense—"

"It would be the greatest of honors to listen to an elder of elders prattle on about whatever he wished for as long as he willed," Storm interrupted with such heartfelt sincerity, both Forentan men looked at her in surprise. "*You* do not need to apologize. Amelana made her own choices; she will suffer the repercussions for them. If she had been Desanti, she would never have survived her adulthood trials to begin with, or lasted long if she had. It is fortunate she has not bred any more like her."

Looking at Ash for several moments, Storm changed the topic. "I must go check on the drizar. He will be useless to me if he eats too much." Offering a respectful bow to the old man, Storm walked down the stairs.

"Well spoken, if about as blunt as a fallen branch on the head. Not what I would have expected of a Desanti," Ellis mused in Forentan as he watched Storm vanish from view.

"What could you have expected? All we knew of the warrior people were the stories that had been passed down for generation after generation after generation." Ash pointed out coldly, "Inaccurate stories."

"Very true," Ellis mused. "She shows me more respect than most of what remains of the Avarian family."

Turning away to stare into the murky darkness of the upper branches, Ash spoke without inflection. "You are already more than three times older than the oldest among them. Anyone who lives to get old is accorded great respect among the Desanti. Storm is barely more than a child herself."

"Three times?" Ellis looked back down the stairs. "I could see the girl is young, but I find it hard to believe someone considered a master of her arts is as young as I am inclined to guess she is."

Impatient, Ash interrupted the old man, arms crossed. "What is it you really want, Ellis?"

Ellis regarded Ash in silence for a time. "I want what I said earlier. Your forgiveness for what Amelana had done. You know I was the one who arranged for her to be assigned to you."

"Of course I knew it was you," Ash replied bitterly. "I could have turned her out within a year. But you knew I would keep her despite her complete worthlessness as a mage. All because she was part of Master Bennu's House, and I would do anything to honor my master."

"Yes, I knew." Ellis stood proudly, shoulders squared, unrepentant.

The pair stared at each other for many minutes. Finally, Ash broke the silence. "Just tell me one thing. Why her? Was she a punishment because I could not save my master's life?"

"What? Don't be ridiculous, Ash," Ellis said, his voice sharp with irritation. "I promised Bennu I'd look out for you if anything happened to him, and I intend to honor that promise. No matter how difficult you make it! The Avarian name would have shielded you from those who seek to diminish you." Ellis's jaw tightened as Ash turned away, muttering something indecipherable. He added, each word clipped. "The moment Bennu's funeral was over, you vanished, only to reappear demanding your mastery trials. You knew precisely what you were doing—once you were declared a master, you'd be beyond anyone's authority."

"I was not about to allow the Edai Tredecima to destroy me by assigning me to some hateful fool hell-bent on making certain I knew my place as a lowborn." Ash faced Ellis, fists clenched at his sides. "Master Bennu was the only one who believed in me. I would not let him down."

Glaring back at Ash, Ellis nearly shouted, "If you had told me you were so dead set against marriage, I would have adopted you myself, to hells with traditions and the Se'edai Magus!" He gestured sharply with his hands. "But you discussed nothing with me before forging ahead—"

Ash's anger faltered a moment before the wall around his emotions slammed back up. "You can say that now. When I was a boy, I heard you both talking. *Master Bennu* wanted to adopt me. *You* wanted to be rid of me before I shamed the Avarians."

"I wanted nothing of the sort!" Ellis spat, clenching his fists so tightly his knuckles turned white beneath the fabric of his sleeves. His voice cut through the air like a blade, icy and unforgiving. "Despite all you've achieved, Ash, you remain unchanged—stubborn and filled with defiance. You're still that furious young man, desperate to prove your independence. Master or not, you are still consumed by rage, rejecting any connection to your former master's family, refusing any help, determined to stand alone."

"So you forced Amelana on me to prove I would have to deal with the Avarians whether or not I wanted to," Ash accused.

"You know Amelana was the only girl in the family of marital age who had an inkling of talent," Ellis responded, unable to reclaim his calm façade. "So much of the true talent of the Avarians and other powerful families has died protecting Forenta. I had hoped that under your tutelage she would make something respectable of herself."

Ash waved a dismissive hand. "You knew she would fixate on becoming my wife rather than becoming a proper mage. She has only ever hungered for position and prestige—and what quicker path to both than to ensnare the Illaini Magus?" Behind his heated accusations, shame roiled in the pit of his stomach at memories of years of empty sex with the shameless woman, taking advantage of what she offered without remorse while having no intention of giving her more.

"I had hoped she would see the truth about the kind of man you are and transform into a woman worthy of you!" Ellis retorted, his face flushed with fiery indignation. "Instead, she almost got you killed and brought shame upon the entire House!" Ellis's shoulders sagged under the weight of his disappointment, his voice heavy with exhaustion. "Bennu and I had such hopes...but what does it even matter now?"

"It doesn't." The bitter words made Ellis visibly flinch.

"If you can find it in your heart, forgive your master's brother for his foolishness." Ash turned his back on the man, silent. Ellis sighed, closing his eyes. "I understand, Master Andar. If you will excuse me." He turned to make his way slowly down the stairs when Ash's voice stopped him.

"I cannot forgive you, Ellis. Not now. Maybe not ever."

The old man remained motionless for a time, searching for words that could change the status quo, and coming up empty. Resigned, he continued down the stairs.

On one of the lower landings, Storm stood with her back against the wall, a sentry to ensure no one would interrupt the private matter above, never having gone far. Ellis paused to regard the Desanti woman until she raised her eyes to meet his steady, sad gaze. "Watch over him, Githalin Swordanzen Storm il'Thandar. Please."

Storm blinked once. She simply nodded, uncertain what to say. As Ellis left, she stared upwards for several moments before returning to the topmost landing.

Facing away from the stairs, Ash stood at the balcony arch, fingers digging into the wood as he leaned, his shoulders shaking with the effort to suppress his emotions. He flinched when Storm put a hand on his shoulder, starting to turn away until she spoke a single word.

"Allies."

The single word hung between them, carried on a breath so soft it might have been mistaken for the rustling leaves outside. Her fingertips rested lightly against his shoulder—a steadfast warmth that somehow anchored him to the world even as his composure crumbled. She offered no platitudes, no questions, just the silent solidarity of her body angled slightly toward his, a living shield against whatever might come.

Chapter Fifty-Four

As the forest thinned, the ancient mountain revealed itself, rising above the tallest trees like a guardian watching over its domain, dwarfing even those silent wooden sentinels. Within its stone heart lay the Magus Academy, home of Forenta's magical legacy. Generations of mage-artisans had carved and shaped the mountain interior over centuries, imbuing the stone with residual power that hummed beneath one's feet or tingled under fingertips brushing walls and columns.

The Majestic Hall opened before them, a cathedral-like cavern where stone balconies circled the walls, each marking a passage deeper into the mountain's heart. Mages crowded these upper levels, their ceremonial robes creating ripples of motion against the static gray rock. Their whispers echoed through the chamber, all focused on the coming trial of Amelana Avarian—a scandal they clearly savored.

Ash stood alone near the floor's central mosaic—an ancient tree inlaid in stone—positioned across from where the thirteen council members would sit. He caught fragments of sneering comments about the "desert savages" from the upper galleries and shot a venomous glance upward, relieved his Desanti companions couldn't understand the Forentan tongue.

Awed and perplexed, Storm and Skyfire stood near each other, looking at the hundreds of people, speaking to one another in Desanti. "I understand their contemptuous regard of us, but of one of their own? They remind me of harpy vultures; they seem so happy to see this woman's fall." Skyfire crossed his arms, shaking his head with disgust. "They should feel shame one of their own has fallen so low, betraying their goddess and Her ideals."

Dubious, Storm frowned thoughtfully. "Things *are* different here than in Desantiva. Perhaps it is something we do not understand because they are civilized." Skyfire merely grunted his opinion.

Overhearing their conversation, Mureln glanced at the two warriors. He looked at Taylin when the woman put a concerned hand on his arm at his heavy sigh. "How can they be so naïve about how petty people can be? It pains me to see it."

"They will learn," Taylin assured him, resting her head on his shoulder.

The bard sighed, putting his arm around her waist and pulling her close. "Aye. I know. I wish it could be otherwise."

The council, composed of twelve male and female Edai Magi and the Se'edai Magus, filed out to the half circle of thirteen seats that loomed over the ancient tree inscribed within a half circle sun symbol, alternating bands of color framed each ray of sun that connected each council member's seat to the image of the tree. Almek's eyes narrowed as he centered his attention on the central figure of the Se'edai Magus, but remained silent.

Six Edai Magi flanked the Se'edai Magus of the High Council on each side. The tall, elderly woman remained standing as the others sat, regarding the Guardian with unveiled hostility and the Desanti with outright hatred. The dark bronze bell by her hand chimed once as she struck it, the resonating tone bringing abrupt silence to the entire chamber. "Bring forth the accused!"

Barefoot and dressed in a simple brown dress with gold shackles on her ankles and wrists that inhibited the flow of magic, Amelana walked with her head held in proud defiance of the boos and catcalls that stopped when the bell rang again. Her defiance faltered when she met Storm's unwavering glare, and she quickly averted her eyes.

Ellis Avarian rose from his seat to the right of the Se'edai Magus, his formal robes rustling against the stone chair. He fixed his gaze on the woman standing before the council and spoke with the practiced cadence of one who had presided over many ceremonial proceedings. "Journeyman Amelana Avarian, the council brings three charges against you: dereliction of your sworn responsibilities to Illaini Magus Ash Andar, conspiracy with foreign agents to harm Dusvet Guardian Almek Two-Tones of Fortress, and the employment of forbidden magicks against a student under the Guardian's protection. What say you to these accusations?"

Amelana smiled serenely. "Honored Edai Magi, I plead innocence." Cacophony filled the chamber as both jeers and cheers erupted from the audience. Ysai rang the bell again.

"Illaini Magus Ash Andar, step forward," Ysai called imperiously. Ysai leveled a cool gaze at the younger man. "You accepted the rights and responsibilities of a *teaching* master when you took Amelana Avarian as your student, did you not?"

Ash's eyes narrowed at the insult insinuated in Ysai's question. "I accepted the rights and responsibilities of a teaching master when I *chose* Terrence as an apprentice and was *assigned* Amelana as a journeyman, Se'edai Magus Ysai."

"And did you properly perform your duties as a teacher, Illaini Magus Ash Andar?"

"I did properly perform my duties as teacher and mentor, Se'edai Magus Ysai Oberlain."

A sneer twisted the woman's features. "Amelana has not successfully tested to become a master, though. Is not the progress of the student the responsibility of the master, Illaini Magus Ash Andar?" Ysai's tones grew increasingly mocking. A murmuring whisper rustled through the audience above, echoing in the massive chamber.

Ash gritted his teeth, ignoring the smirk Amelana gave him. "Yes. The master bears responsibility for the pupil, including his or her progress."

Well aware of the building emotion beside him, Almek hissed at Mureln. Each man grabbed one of Storm's arms to keep her from interrupting the proceedings, able to restrain her only because of who they were. "She mocks him," Storm hissed. "Can you not see—?!"

"Patience, Storm," Almek ordered under his breath. Storm shot him a dark look. "I do see. I *know*. Patience!" She growled, jerking her arms away from them and crossing them tight across her chest, obeying with keen reluctance.

Ysai's sneer deepened as she relentlessly drilled Ash with her accusatory questions. "So tell us, why have Amelana's abilities failed to blossom under your so-called renowned skills? Could it be that you are inadequate as a mage?" Her words dripped with venom.

"No, Se'edai Magus Oberlain," Ash retorted sharply, his patience fraying like a brittle rope. "The truth is, Amelana Avarian's skills as a student are sorely lacking." The crowd erupted into a cacophony of hoots and shouts, Amelana's eyes blazing with fury as she glared daggers at Ash.

Ysai's gaze pierced through him, cold and unyielding, as she waited for the bell's echo to subside. "Is it not improper for a master and student to engage in relations beyond that of teacher and pupil?" Her question sent a shockwave of surprise through the chamber, causing several Edai Magi to squirm uncomfortably.

Ash clenched his fists, his eyes dropping with the weight of the accusation. "Yes. Traditionally, it is improper, Se'edai Magus." His voice was firm but edged with tension.

"And yet you, a *lowborn* man, dared to bed Amelana Avarian, a scion of the Ancient Houses, did you not?" The silence was thick enough to choke on, the chamber so still that Ash's heartbeat seemed to echo in its depths. "Were you attempting to assert your dominance over your betters, Illaini Magus Ash Andar?" Ysai spat the title as if it were a curse.

The Edai stared at Ysai, their surprise palpable at her blatant disrespect. The crowd buzzed with a mix of confusion and shock. Ellis, standing to Ysai's right, regarded her with a look of offended reproach. "He is Illaini Magus, regardless of his birth, Ysai. The goddess's choice is beyond question." His voice was low, intended only for those of higher rank. "Disrespecting rank so openly will sow discord in our society. You're being reckless!" Ysai flicked a dismissive glance at Ellis, a smirk playing on her lips.

Almek caught Storm's arm again, restraining her firmly. He grabbed her chin. "Look at me," he ordered in a sibilant voice. When he caught her eye, he spoke with hushed intensity. "You are my student. Listen to me. Gods damn it all, girl. By your oath, listen to me!" Her rage did not abate, but she lowered her eyes, listening as he whispered in her ear. "Allow me, my lord," she whispered. He paused, then nodded once.

Ysai continued on, ignoring the growing disapproval of the twelve Edai. "And how is it you were unaware of Amelana's knowledge of the forbidden arts? Or was it not forbidden arts but the failing of inferior instruction by an inferior, lowborn teacher." She waved a hand, standing. "It is clear it is not Amelana Avarian who should be punished, but her master Illaini Magus Ash Andar."

"No." The single word, spoken with such strident clarity it cut through the confusion of the distraught Forenten, shocked at the sacrilegious idea of punishing an Illaini Magus. Without the prompting of Ysai's bronze bell, a profound silence consumed the massive hall, all eyes on the Se'edai Magus and Illaini Magus.

The shrew-faced woman scanned the sea of faces along the many balconies, her voice imperious. "Who dares interrupt the Se'edai Magus? Step forward, or your punishment will be far more dire for your disrespect when you are identified."

Storm took two resolute steps forward from the group facing the high council, her hard green-gold eyes fixed on Ysai. Her companions watched with concern but remained silent at a gesture from Almek, not interfering. "Githalin Swordanzen Storm il'Thandar, student of Dusvet Guardian Almek Two-Tones, *Daughter of Desantiva*, dares to interrupt you." The ring of challenge in her voice carried to the highest point of the vaulted ceiling, setting the watching Forenten to whispering.

Ysai waved a dismissive hand, turning her nose up haughtily. "Feh. You have no voice here, savage. Go sit down and be quiet like a good little Dusvet lapdog."

"I thought 'civilized' meant being wiser. Everyone here but *you* seems to remember their place with the Fortress of Time." Storm spoke to the woman with a feral, hateful snarl, each step that of a stalking lioness, green-gold eyes glittering dangerously. "What is the matter? Do you fear the words of a mere warrior? Or do you fear all of *them* knowing the truth about you?" She spread both arms wide, raised towards the audience above.

Ash hastened to Storm's side, grabbing her arm with more concern than disapproval in his touch, keeping his voice pitched for her ears alone. "Storm, this is a Forentan matter. Don't get involved."

The Desanti woman looked at Ash, but spoke so all could hear. "I *am* involved in this 'Forentan matter.' I was involved the moment Amelana attacked me with your forbidden Forentan arts." Her gaze fixed on Amelana as she stepped towards the shackled woman. Amelana's eyes went wide as she backed away. She fell on her backside as her feet got tangled in her ankle shackles in her careless haste to get away from Storm. The Desanti stopped her advance at the heart of the tree image, fixing Ysai with a hard look. "I will not stand by and watch this farce of a trial any longer. The truth will be known."

The Se'edai Magus looked around as the whispers of the audience grew. Her expression reflected her growing anger as her absolute control was slipping away. "Where is this 'truth,' Desanti?" she asked mockingly.

The hiss of the two-edged sword clearing its sheath and the flash of metal brought a collective gasp when Storm drew the weapon. Storm's eyes locked with Ysai's as she wrapped her hand around the blade, pulling it through, red staining the metal. "The truth...is in my blood." She opened her bloody palm, blood dripping steadily. "I am Storm il'Thandar. Githalin of the Heart of Desantiva. Let all see Amelana's truth!" Reversing the bloodied blade, she shouted as she drove it into the center of the stone of the tree image she stood on, the blade sinking into the stone as easily as if it were merely butter.

Cries of pain erupted from all those watching as a wave of power centered on the blade exploded outwards, including Almek's students who were unprepared for the sudden sharing of the moment of Amelana's attack on Storm, the scene blazing behind eyes, the searing pain, the hatred behind it. That it was forbidden magic was undeniable. And behind it, the pact made by Amelana with Ysai to learn the dark art for the promise of winning Ash after he returned as Illaini Magus.

As people recovered, they looked to see Ysai, her hands contorted into gnarled, almost clawlike appendages, covering her face, caught in the throes of something else in that explosion of power. Almek took a step forward. "Come, Ysai, let them see the whole truth. Let Forenta see what you truly are!"

"You have no power here!" Ysai shrieked. "*I* am the Se'edai Magus! *I* rule here!" Lowering her hands, the woman's face contorted into something dark and monstrous that most believed were merely myths to scare children until that moment.

"Darkling!" The room erupted into a chaotic panic as every Forentan recognized Ysai for what she was, frightening tales brought to life as terrifying fact.

Raising his hands, Almek concentrated on Ysai, his power ensnaring the shrieking creature and pulling it free of its human host. The old woman's body collapsed like a rag doll. Writhing, the darkling's screams echoed in the halls even after Almek crushed it out of the physical plane. A dazed stillness overtook the gathered.

"What...what happened to Ysai?" one of the other Edai Magi asked slowly. He knelt by Ysai's body, reaching to close her dead eyes, then covering her face with her hair veil. "She-she could not have always been..."

With only a shadow of pity, Almek's grim words carried as easily as Storm's had. "I suspect the darkling had consumed her soul long ago." He scanned the upper levels where the Forenten stared, stunned. "Had I met her before today, I would have recognized her for what she truly was."

Dazed, the Swordanzen remained on one knee, head bowed. Booted feet in her periphery drew her attention, and she raised her gaze to meet Ash's eyes. Without a word, he offered her his hand. She put her hand in his, shaking her head to clear it as she let him help her to her feet. As she stood, she withdrew the blade from the stone with her still bleeding hand, turning a malevolent look on Amelana, baring her teeth. The shamed woman stared at her with terror. "Do not worry, Forentan bitch," Storm assured. "It was never *me* you needed to worry about."

Amelana's eyes darted from Storm to the Illaini Magus who moved past the Desanti with purpose. "No!" Amelana whispered as Ash deliberately advanced on her. "Master Ash...no, please!" Paralyzed in fright, Amelana fell to her knees, begging for mercy. She screamed as Ash put his hands on her head. After several minutes, she collapsed in silence. Whispers of "Morelmi!" floated from the mass of observers, a tangled mess of shock, amazement, awe, and horror that fell silent when Ash moved.

Emil tiptoed nearer, squinting. "Ye didn't kill her?" he asked in amazement.

"I did worse," the mage intoned, his whole body taut with physical pain, looking down at the fallen woman. "I stripped her connection to magic." He turned and walked towards the hall's exit amid the awed silence.

Without a word, Storm walked with him, ignoring the eyes that followed them. He faltered a step as they reached the archway, beginning to succumb to the extraordinary effort to strip Amelana's magic from her. Storm caught him, putting her arm around him as they left.

Chapter Fifty-Five

ASH ROUSED FROM A deep sleep, his eyelids heavy as river stones as he rubbed away the grit of exhaustion, his whole body aching. The distant metallic song of steel kissing steel pierced his consciousness like lightning through fog. Wearing only his trousers, the cool morning air raising gooseflesh across his bare chest, he rushed to the intricately carved balcony rail in alarm, his knuckles whitening as he gripped the polished wood and scanned the verdant expanse below.

On one of the swaying rope-and-plank bridges that spanned the gap between massive tree trunks, Storm and Skyfire faced each other like predatory cats. Their two-edged swords caught the dappled sunlight filtering through the canopy, sending prismatic flashes with each parry and thrust. They moved in perfect counterpoint, her lithe form a blur of copper skin and leather against his taller, broader silhouette, both of them dancing across the gently undulating structure with the fluid grace of water over stone. Dozens of Forenten, with wide eyes, lined every available vantage point—hanging gardens, spiraling staircases, moss-covered platforms—their collective breath held in rapt fascination at the deadly ballet unfolding below.

"Oh, thank the gods, you're finally awake." Almek joined Ash, offering him a cup of water. Following the mage's worried gaze, he smiled in understanding. "I had to send Storm out to burn off some energy. She would not leave until I assured her I would remain and watch over you." The Guardian, aged more than before the trial, appeared amused. "I can assure you, there is nothing more nerve-wracking than a worried Desanti pacing an enclosed area and jumping at shadows, more often than not with a weapon in hand."

"Storm was that concerned about me?" Not entirely awake, Ash drained the cup of water to clear the rasp from his voice. "How long was I asleep?"

"Three, nearly four days." Almek patted Ash's shoulder. "I have noticed that sleeping longer than four hours makes our Desanti fret about people." He looked down at the training warriors. "She was frantic. At least, what passes for frantic for Storm."

"Four days?" Ash considered and nodded to himself in satisfaction. "That's not bad at all. It usually takes no less than three mages chaining to strip the magic from the condemned without risk to the mages, and then no less than five days for them to recov—Storm!" Ash's heart nearly stopped when Storm missed the edge of the bridge and fell. She deftly caught one of the ropes looped underneath and used the momentum to swing back onto the bridge and land lightly on her feet behind Skyfire. Her eyes turned unerringly up towards Ash and Almek.

Almek put a hand on Ash's shoulder to reassure him. "She has done well in becoming accustomed to life in the trees."

Skyfire followed Storm's unwavering stare, relaxing from his fighting posture and sheathing his blade. He caught Storm's hand, the rope seemingly having reopened the wound from the trial. He pulled out a strip of cloth, deftly wrapping her hand as he spoke to her.

The woman eventually uncoiled, returning her blade to its sheath, her eyes still never wavering from the balcony the two men stood at until she turned to run back towards Naveene's Rest. Skyfire followed at a considerably more sedate pace.

The sky seemed to echo the Desanti woman's mood, rumbling with the promise of an impending thunderstorm. Ash gazed at the sky in bemusement. "She *is* aptly named, isn't she?" he said more to himself than to Almek. He turned to the Guardian. "Perhaps you should go check on the others before she gets here?"

Almek nodded, putting a hand on Ash's shoulder in concern. "I have nearly lost you both at least once already. Just don't kill each other, please?" Ash shrugged one shoulder noncommittally. Alone, he returned to his sleeping area to await Storm's arrival.

Hearing footsteps, Ash rose just as Storm nearly pulled the heavy privacy curtain off its fixture. She closed the space between them, raising her uninjured hand and slapping him with a sound crack. He did not block the strike, touching the corner of his mouth and examining his blood as she seethed.

"I thought you were dead! You risked your life for *nothing*!" Green-gold eyes glittered with emotion. She raised her hand again, but this time he caught her wrist, holding her. "Let me go!" she demanded, trying to pull away.

Calmly, Ash shook his head. "What I did to Amelana had to be done. I didn't trust the Edai Tredecima would follow through with the morelmi, despite the laws dictating it had to be done."

"I do not care what it was. It nearly killed you!"

The mage's nod was grave. "It would have, but for you." His lips twitched into a rueful smile. "As I saved you from your Final Dance, you saved me from mine."

Storm stopped struggling, studying him with wary suspicion. "I did nothing. I have no magic as your people have. What little I have of Guardian power is novice at best."

Ash could not help but smile openly. "If what you displayed in the Majestic Hall was novice, you will be fearsome once you master it." He allowed her to tug her arm away, watching as she turned her back on him to hide her emotions.

"Father taught me that a Desanti's true power is in their heart. A matter of focus, of will. We have nothing as your people. You—" She stopped and corrected herself. "Your ancestors stole it from us in the Great War." Bitterly, she whispered, "Yours are the more powerful of our peoples."

Ash shook his head, his words echoing the gesture. "I disagree. I reached this place only with your help before I had to give in to sleep. If the burden of casting the spell to break the connection to magic is not shared, it is lethal to the caster...usually." His voice was hushed as he took a step nearer to her. "Alone, it is akin to your Final Dance."

Storm finally whirled around, her eyes blazing, her fists clenched so tightly her knuckles blanched. "What I did in Desantiva and what you did here are *nothing* alike!" Her voice rose to a ragged shout. "Those raiders would have hunted you down like *animals*! They would have torn you apart limb by limb while you still breathed! I had to slaughter every last raider. Every. Single. One." She advanced on him, trembling with fury. "But Amelana?" She spat the name like poison. "That treacherous snake was just one pathetic woman. She was not worth anything. You nearly died for *nothing*!"

"Amelana knew the dark arts. The corruption had to be removed; else her poison would have spread. The danger to my people and to you was just as much of a threat as the raiders had been. But..." Ash looked away. "Our reasons for self-sacrifice were not dissimilar."

Snarling, Storm turned to stalk out. "Liar!"

Ash grabbed her and forcibly turned her around to face him, holding her by both arms. "You felt shame for things you believed were failures to your people. It was how I felt about...Dessa. Bennu. All those I could not save."

"Let go of me," she demanded, trying to pull away.

"We both sought death to atone for those failures," Ash stated intently, gripping her arms. "It's as your father said. Your power is in your heart. When I hovered on the edge between life and death, I heard you." She stopped struggling, her expression dubious. "How could I abandon you? I could feel your wounds. I knew your pain. I could hear your tears."

"What are you talking about? I have not shed tears since the Vodani ship. And that was for my homeland. I do not shed tears for myself. That is weak!"

Ash smiled, touching her cheek with the back of one finger as if catching a tear. "No. You do not shed tears for yourself. Not where anyone else can see, you don't." He held her tight as she tried to pull away again, pulling her against him, and wrapping his arms around her. "I'm sorry I frightened you," he said with soft sincerity, resting his cheek on her hair.

Briefly, Storm struggled to pull away before returning the embrace. She held on with the fierce intensity of a frightened child, trembling. He looked down at her as her embrace loosened. The mage staggered a few steps to lean on the wall when she slapped him hard again.

"If you ever almost die like that again, I will kill you myself," Storm stated heatedly before turning on her heel to stalk out.

Ash looked down at the floor, blinked at several small shining pools of dark red. Realizing why he could physically overpower the woman so effortlessly, the mage pushed off the wall to run after her. "Storm!"

He caught her at the top of the stairs before she fell, grabbing her wounded hand at the wrist to slow the flow of blood. "Taylin!" the mage bellowed down the stairs as he sat with Storm on the top step. "Foolish girl, haven't you eaten anything since we got here?! Or let the healer tend to you? Your obstinacy is going to kill you yet!"

Before the running feet below reached them, he whispered in her ear harshly, "Don't think I won't do the same to you if *you* almost die again." Seeing Storm smile faintly, Ash just shook his head, tightening his arm around her as Taylin arrived, immediately taking her wounded hand to heal. "Stubborn Swordanzen."

"Stubborn mage." Taylin flicked a glance up at the pair and rolled her eyes.

Chapter Fifty-Six

Unperturbed by the biting, icy rain that drummed relentlessly upon his shoulders, Ash stood resolute before the imposing door for what seemed like an eternity. Finally, he extended a hand to the intricately designed knocker, letting it resound with three deliberate taps against the metal plate embedded in the wooden surface. As the door creaked open, he was greeted by the wide-eyed gaze of an elderly woman, who seemed momentarily taken aback. "By the goddess!" she exclaimed, her cheeks flushing a deep crimson as she quickly averted her eyes. "Illaini Magus! It's been such a long time since you last visited. I beg your forgiveness for my disrespect—"

"You need not lower your eyes to me, Clarissa," Ash reassured her gently, his voice carrying the weight of familiarity. "You've known me since Bennu first brought me home."

Clarissa looked up, her eyes softening as she studied his face with a penetrating gaze. Her demeanor shifted to one of gentle admonishment, her voice tinged with maternal warmth. "Come in before you catch your death of a cold, young man."

A small smile tugged at Ash's lips. "I would never have imagined I would have missed hearing you chiding me, Clarissa." His expression grew somber as he glanced down the dimly lit hall. "Is he home?"

"Of course. He has been in his study since the trial." With practiced ease, Clarissa lifted the sodden cloak from Ash's shoulders, her touch both firm and comforting, before resting a hand on his arm. "Do be kind to him, would you? That girl's antics broke his heart." Ash offered a silent nod, gently patting her hand in acknowledgment before making his way down the shadowed corridor.

He opened the door to the study, memories of his childhood flooding his mind's eye briefly. He closed his eyes, letting the scent of the cherrinut wood carry him to a happier time when he sat on the floor in front of the fire with Bennu, learning how to read from one of the ancient tomes lining the walls.

Opening his eyes to the present, he noticed how much things had changed. Before, the twin mages were all but inseparable, always together in this room. Now, Ellis sat alone, staring into the fire, looking even older than before. "Master Ellis?"

Ellis's eyes snapped open, and he straightened in surprise. "Ash! I did not expect—"

Ash lowered his eyes and said simply, "I know. May I come in?" he asked, remaining at the threshold.

The old man smiled tiredly. "Of course, dear boy. You have always been welcome here." He gestured for Ash to come in and sit. "How is your Desanti girl doing? I heard a rumor that she had fallen ill after the trial. That was quite an impressive display. And only a student of the Dusvet Guardian? Ithesra is still buzzing about it."

Ash entered slowly and bowed respectfully to Ellis before pausing by Bennu's empty chair, caressing the carvings lightly before sitting. "Storm is doing well. Master Almek and the others are making sure she allows herself to recover completely." He shook his head in wry bemusement. "The woman refused to rest until I woke up. She is incomprehensibly stubborn."

The old man chuckled. "Reminds me of a boy who used to sit with his master by this very fire not so many years ago."

The Illaini Magus smiled briefly. He sighed, lowering his eyes as he spoke. "Master Ellis, I wanted to apologize about how I handled Amelana—"

Ellis shook his head, scowling. "Do not mention that creature's name. The remaining members of the Edai Tredecima gave me a boon and stripped her of the Avarian name so her blight no longer taints my House." He flicked a nutshell into the fire, the ashes bursting in a small cloud of sparks before settling. "She was as much my fault as yours. If I had not been so determined to hold on to you, so desperate to restore the Avarian House, I'd never have let that slut's spawn near you."

Ash blinked several times. "I beg your pardon, Master?"

Ellis did not look at Ash, grumpily shifting in his chair. "Neither that creature nor her mother possessed a drop of Avarian blood in their veins. Her mother had married into the family. I was quite aware Amelana was not her father's child, but an Oberlain bastard."

The fire crackled in the silence before Ash spoke again. "Then why...?"

"Because she was the only means I knew to give you your name back within our people's traditions and still protect you." Ellis's frustration was obvious. "I was foolish enough to let myself believe there was some hope she would change for the better in your company."

Ash just stared at Ellis uncomprehendingly. "Give me my name back? What do you mean?"

Ellis exhaled loudly, closing his eyes. "I suppose it's time to stop trying to protect you and explain. Especially now that Ysai is gone." The old man turned melancholy eyes towards Ash. "Long before you were born, Bennu and I could see that the Great Houses of Forenta were growing weaker. Poor matches produced weaker instead of stronger children. Strong mages fell to an ever-growing number of mishaps or illnesses. Even promising children were dying before they could even begin to seek their destinies. All those from the old families appeared to be targeted.

"Bennu and I...we watched so many of our sons and daughters, then our grandchildren...die. Others in the House and even many in other Houses. None were excluded. Not all of them, but...more than misfortune alone could account for. About twenty years ago, there was a darkling attack on the main city of Andar in the Gallilae region, the Avarian's ancestral home, where Bennu's youngest son had settled with his new family while most of us served elsewhere. He sent us a message about something stalking the city, begging for help. By the time we got there, everyone was...gone. Except for Bennu's grandson...you."

"...what?" Ash stared at Ellis.

"You were so weak. Near death for so long...we feared your becoming a target. The only way we knew to protect you was to let people believe we brought back a lowborn foundling." Ellis looked at Ash, tears shimmering in his eyes. "It broke our hearts watching you grow up being treated so horribly. Feeling so alone and isolated. Bennu wanted to adopt you, to give you a true family. But you showed promise so early, and I feared if you had the Avarian name at all, that whomever or whatever had targeted the gifted would discover the ruse." He rested his head against the back of the chair. "We used Forentan bigotry against them."

Ash sat back in his chair, staring in shock. "Bennu...was my..."

"Grandfather," Ellis confirmed. "After Bennu died, you were furious at everyone. Most of all, you were livid with yourself because you couldn't save him. When you returned Chosen by the goddess, I wanted to tell you the truth then. Goddess, how I wanted to tell you. But you avoided me, and Ysai..." He spat in disgust. "She eroded the respect for the goddess and the Illaini all because she believed you were merely lowborn. And so many never argued, or reveled in the implied permission to treat lowborn as less than human. But it kept her from seeing you as more of a threat. Perversely.

"Our people put so much weight on birthright, I feared...what would have happened if you were not only an acknowledged master, but highborn." Ellis said bitterly, "I would rather have had the Avarian name die than be the cause of my brother's grandson's death." Ellis closed his eyes. "If you never forgive me, I couldn't blame you."

Ash looked up at Ellis. "You were still family in spirit to me, even if I did not know we were family by blood. There is no excuse for my behavior, even if I felt justified then. I shouldn't have turned my back on you." He managed a sad smile. "I do not know if...I would have been as receptive to all this before now." He looked down at the star-shaped scar in the palm of his hand. "So many things have changed."

"Many things have, yes," Ellis agreed. "Dessa...she was a bastard child of one of the other Ancient Houses. A strong family. We had hoped to match you with her to strengthen the Avarian bloodline. No one should have cared about two lowborn youths. But then you both were attacked, and you blamed yourself for not being strong enough to keep her safe, even though you were only a student, not even a full apprentice. You were fiercely protective of her, but you never let her get close." Ellis sighed softly. "You never let anyone close. Then, when Bennu died..."

Ash closed his eyes tightly, Storm's words echoing in his mind. "I chose to be alone," he murmured dismally.

"Unfortunately, perhaps the wisest course. Gods know what that creature might have done had she been able to get close to you. Or worse." The old man's face was grim. "What you would have done in your grief if you had lost yet another person you cared for."

Ash sighed, leaning forward, putting his face in his hands, struggling to come to terms with the old beliefs of his life and the new realities. "I...have a family?"

"If you choose, Ash. Establish a new House as Andar. Take the mantle of the Avarian name and the history and responsibility that entails.

Names mean nothing at the end of the day. You are Illaini Magus, and I know...your parents would have been proud of you." Feeling Ellis's hand on his shoulder, he looked up at the old man. "Let someone into your heart someday, Ash. No one should spend their life alone."

"I will...Uncle." Ellis smiled, a tear rolling down his cheek. Ash stood and embraced the old man tightly.

Chapter Fifty-Seven

The evening meal at Naveene's Rest transformed into a jubilant celebration, as the Illaini Magus's miraculous recovery lifted the spirits of everyone inside, despite the cold, dismal rain that continued to pour relentlessly outside. Inside the warm, candle- and oil-lamp-lit tavern, Naveene spared no expense, treating Almek and his students to a sumptuous feast, with tables overflowing with an abundance of savory dishes and brimming mugs of ale and wine.

Ash sat quietly next to Storm, their presence a stark contrast to the animated chatter and laughter that filled the room. The mage and the warrior remained silent, an island of calm amidst the lively celebration. Despite the enticing aroma of roasted meats and spiced vegetables wafting through the air, and regardless of the gentle coaxing of their companions, Storm steadfastly refused to partake in the feast. Ash, though tempted to chide her for her stubbornness, found himself unable to muster even a flicker of impatience. How could he, when so often her actions stemmed from such pure, selfless concern for his well-being that she entirely neglected her own needs? In stark contrast, Amelana...

Shaking his head, Ash firmly pushed the distasteful memories of the years with Amelana and her poisonous motivations out of his mind. Unlike that hated woman, Storm had proven herself time and again to have only the most honest motivations behind her often bewildering behavior. Knowing it was no attempt to garner pity or attention, Ash tried to understand why Storm would continue to risk her health.

Mureln and Skyfire drew the mage's attention. The bard was praising a particular vintage of wine given to him, and took a sip from his glass before offering it to the Swordanzen man for him to taste himself. He thought about the ritualistic gesture when the Desanti would drink from their waterskins before offering it to another.

Memories of when the Desanti brought them food in First Home came to mind. At first, they all assumed the picking bits of the food was a childish behavior, or one born of living in wastelands that snitching bites of food was a habit born of necessity. Knowing the Desanti culture was not as childishly naïve as he had once assumed, he realized the actions may have been rooted in another reason. To test his theory, Ash pushed his plate between himself and Storm. He continued eating calmly, watching her. It was not long before she wrinkled her nose before daintily eating the offered food.

Ash could not help but be surprised he guessed correctly. "Is that why you won't eat? You don't trust it?"

"Eating what you do not recognize is asking to be poisoned," she replied simply. "I was lucky to survive poisoning once. It is not an experience I want to repeat." She glanced at Skyfire and shook her head. "Some are more trusting than others."

"Most people would not starve themselves to death," he pointed out with a half-smile. She just looked at him sidelong and he held up his hands. "Forgive me. You are not most people." Her brief, faint smile faded and she became troubled again. His own smile faded in concern. He touched the back of her hand to get her lost attention again. "What's wrong?"

"I miss my home." Silent for a time, she glanced up briefly as Mureln began playing his mandolin at the others' urging. "I do not belong here."

Ash frowned and looked around the room. "Have you been harassed by my people?"

"Not openly. I know they fear me. They fear you, too. But they love you. You are one of them. The best of them. I am..." She sighed. "An enemy." She spoke slowly, choosing her words carefully. "No matter the outcome, once I have done what I came here to do...I must return to where I belong. I must return to Desantiva."

Ash snorted dismissively as he reached over to replenish the food on their shared plate. "You belong with Master Almek. You have sworn yourself to him just as I had. You can't leave him."

"Do not make this harder for me than it already is, mage." Storm fixed him with a hard look, her voice as sharp as the edge of one of her blades. "I do not belong here. No Desanti belongs outside of Desantiva."

Ignoring the silence that had fallen over the others at the table, Ash met glare for glare with the Swordanzen. "Stop acting stupid, Swordanzen. You belong anywhere you want to belong, and you belong with Master Almek."

"I have already spoken to Lord Almek! He understands why I must return to my people." Storm shoved the plate away and stalked out of the Rest. Servants nearly fell over themselves to get out of her way, whispering amongst each other as they stared at the retreating Swordanzen woman's back and flicked glances at the Illaini Magus. Ash rose with a scowl on his face, intent on following her.

Almek waved a discrete hand towards Mureln as he rose. "Master Andar!" The mage froze for a moment when the Guardian spoke sharply. "A word with you, please." Ignoring Almek, Ash took another step after Storm. "Now!" The mage grimaced but obeyed, stiffly following Almek out of the main room.

Away from the others, Ash spun on Almek. "How can you let Storm leave?! She has so much unrealized potential; it will be wasted in that desert. You saw what she is capable of already! Talent like that can't be left untrained. It is too dangerous! And I...*we* need her!"

Almek remained silent, letting Ash vent. When he finally fell silent, the Guardian's voice was calm, but uncompromising. "I won't force anyone to be my student, no matter what sort of oath was sworn to me. If you wished to leave, I wouldn't stand in your way. Each of you has the power to make your own decisions. I won't take that from any of you."

"For all her skill and knowledge, Storm is little more than a naïve child," Ash seethed. "All she's ever experienced in her life is that godsforsaken wasteland she calls home. Children need someone to guide them because they don't know any better. She has to be made to understand there is more to the world than that." He started to stalk out to find Storm, freezing at the Guardian's words.

Almek tilted his head, studying the mage. "Storm knows very well there is a greater danger, and that leaving likely will condemn her to death. She also believes she is a liability to us. She has chosen to leave for that reason."

Ash spun around, staring incredulously. "*What?* You didn't tell her she was wrong? Why not?!"

"Think about it, Ash. You've seen much more of the world than she has. Even if your people's attitudes towards Sevmana and Vodanya were...wanting, you had been exposed to different peoples, different ways of life. Storm had never left Desantiva. Ever since the disaster of the Great War, no Desanti had." Almek's eyes held Ash's, keeping him from leaving.

Ash crossed his arms stubbornly. "It doesn't make her a liability. She is quick witted and intelligent. She can learn to become accustomed to it."

Almek sighed, putting a paternal hand on Ash's shoulder. "Ash, you said so yourself. She's still a child. She's a child who is homesick with the weight of the world on her shoulders. It's distracting her, and for a warrior, distraction can be deadly.

"We are already demanding a great deal from her, and she is trying very hard to answer all those demands without fail. But perhaps what we are demanding, what she is demanding of herself, is more than she is able to give. It's cruel to ask more."

Ash clenched his teeth in silence. "I don't want her to leave. We need her. I..." He looked away, eyes shut as he confessed, "*I* need her."

Almek sighed. "None of us wants to lose her, Ash. But for now, she is still with us, and she will not leave until she has done what she promised her Father she would do. Don't taint the time we still have her with us with anger. Respect her decision." He smiled sadly. "We'll all need to let her go."

Shoulders slumping slightly, Ash said barely loud enough for the Guardian to hear, "I don't know if I can."

THE SOFT RUSHING SOUND of falling rain became more muted as Mureln entered the tree-bound stables several measures below Naveene's Rest. The sounds of animals shifting in their stalls replaced the rain as he lowered his hood, shaking off the water that clung to his cloak. He squinted into the darkness for several moments, uncertain. "Storm? Are you here?" he called in Desanti.

Storm's embittered voice floated from the furthest stalls, where the drizzen had been stabled. "What do you want?" Eyes finally adjusting to the dim light, he saw her, sitting on the drizar's bare back, lying against his neck.

"I wanted to make certain you were alright." Approaching slowly, Mureln held up a hand to allow the drizar to sniff it. The beast, half asleep, only chuffed softly, head drooping. The bard blinked several times in disbelief at the uncharacteristically docile behavior. "He really is useless when he eats too much, isn't he?"

Storm could not help but smile, though the expression was fleeting. "Drizzen eat constantly in Desantiva because they have to. And they eat literally everything. Meat. Plants. Rocks. Meat and plants are more nourishing but..." She sighed and rubbed the somnolent beast's neck fondly. "He has never been in a place where good food was so plentiful." She exhaled softly. "I suppose letting him eat himself into a stupor is useful to keep him from goring people randomly."

Taking a prudent step to one side of the beast, Mureln nodded. "It's very useful, yes." He studied her again. "You are avoiding my question. Are *you* all right?"

Hiding her face on the opposite side of the drizar's neck, Storm gave vent to her feelings. "No, I am not all right. I hate it here. I wish I never met any of you. Never came to this gods forsaken place. I want it to be the way it used to be. The way it has always been." She tightened her embrace around the reptilian beast's neck. "I want to go home where I belong!"

Ignoring her words as emotional turmoil and not what she honestly felt, Mureln considered Storm for a long time. Seeing what lay below the turmoil on the surface, his expression saddened in sympathy. "The mage doesn't hate you. There are few he trusts enough to consider a friend, and when he does, he holds onto them tightly. He just doesn't let go of those he cares about easily."

"He never should have started caring about me to begin with," Storm said bitterly. "Forenten live forever. Desanti are mere sparks in the night. At least I would not have known his heartache with my death. This...it is so much worse this way."

Raising his hand hesitantly, Mureln put a hand on Storm's shoulder, feeling the unnatural heat from the Totani mark. "Give him time, okay? The news came as a shock to him."

Pushing herself upright, Storm looked at Mureln, her expression pleading for understanding. "I never wanted to hurt him, Mureln. But it is just too much for me. Too much to learn. Too much to watch. I cannot sleep. I cannot eat. It takes every shred of will not to attack everything that moves—or doesn't—that I do not understand. It will not end well if I remain. I will become the monster the treewalkers always believed my people to be."

"I have faith you can tolerate this land in time. But I understand, Storm. Truly, I do. The others will too. Eventually." He took her hand, squeezing it when she looked away with a pained expression. "However, we are all Almek's students. Even Emil and Emaris, in their own ways, the louts." Storm couldn't help but smile at the fondness in the bard's voice talking about his brothers-in-arms. "That makes us a kind of family. A tribe."

Storm closed her eyes, looking away. "Tribes take care of their own. I am Swordanzen. We have no tribe. It is tradition."

Mureln squeezed lightly. "You do not need to stand alone, Storm. I'm always here to talk to if you need. Or any of the others. Okay?"

Storm took a deep breath and nodded. "Okay. I will try, but I cannot promise anything."

"Just promise to try." Mureln smiled encouragingly. "That is enough."

Storm considered. "I promise to try."

"Good." Turning to leave, he said over his shoulder, "Come back upstairs when you're ready. I bet we can get Emil to make a fool of himself dancing before he's too drunk to see straight." The bard smiled when he heard her laugh.

Chapter Fifty-Eight

Seven days of unrelenting rain had transformed the world outside Naveene's Rest into a sodden blur, bringing with it a bone-deep chill that permeated the warmest of clothing. Storm glared through the archway, shoulders hunched beneath her heavy travel robes as she clutched the fabric tighter against the biting cold. Her knuckles whitened as she gripped the carved threshold. "The skies mock me," she hissed through clenched teeth. "It is as if they plot against me!"

"The rains here are very different from home," Skyfire said, huddled under his own travel robes as he stood on the other side of the archway. "Instead of swift and violent, they are quiet and unending." He peered up at the sky and sighed. "And it is so cold, the trees are dying!" He patted the edge of the archway mournfully. "Poor, ancient tree."

Lyra approached, carrying a tray with two mugs filled with steaming cider, giggling. "The trees are not dying, Master Skyfire. It is just autumn." The Desanti traded quizzical looks. Lyra pursed her lips, never having had to explain seasons to anyone before. "Some call it fall, too. It's the time of year that the trees prepare to sleep in the winter cold. The leaves will turn very pretty colors before they turn brown and fall off." At the Desanti's alarmed looks, she hurriedly added, "Oh, not forever! New leaves will grow in spring when the weather warms again. It's the natural progression of the seasons through the year."

Skyfire considered Lyra's explanation for a moment. "We have only two...seasons...in Desantiva. The wet season and the dry season. The wet season is much shorter. " He accepted one of the mugs, sipping it. His warm smile of gratitude brought a faint blush to the fair girl's cheeks. "Thank you, Lyra. This is very good." The Desanti man looked at the sullen Storm. "You should have some of this. It is very warming."

Storm took the other mug, but only nestled it against herself, hugging it for warmth.

Lyra's smile faded to one of concern. "Mistress Storm, the cider is very good."

"I am sure it is," Storm replied, not looking at the girl.

"Would you like something different? I would be happy to bring you something you would like better," she offered hopefully.

"No."

Lyra sighed. "Mistress, please. Everyone is so worried about you. Is there nothing you would like?" Storm remained silent, ignoring Lyra instead of lashing out as she had with the servant their first day in Naveene's Rest.

Skyfire looked between the concerned Forentan girl and the ill-humored Desanti. Stepping away from the arch, he reached over to exchange mugs with Storm. Looking up at Skyfire in vague annoyance, she turned her attention back outside, sipping the drink.

"I...do not understand. They are the same." Lyra looked at Skyfire, perplexed.

"Traditionally, my people will only eat or drink what they have themselves made or only if they see another taste it first," Skyfire explained to the girl with a shrug.

"You don't, Master Skyfire," Lyra pointed out.

"I should," the man admitted. Then he grinned at the slight girl. "But I figure people would be more afraid of *her* wrath if someone poisoned me, so I do not worry so much." Storm snorted softly, rolling her eyes, not deigning to make any comment.

Lyra was silent for a time, thoughtful, before she finally spoke. "Your ways are very strange. But I will remember, Master Skyfire."

"You are very kind," Skyfire said to the girl, who curtsied with a blush before leaving.

Storm said in Swordanzen, "You are smitten with her."

Skyfire bristled defensively. "She is very sweet. Very innocent." He sighed softly, putting his arm around Storm comfortingly. "Things are different here. You do not need to hold so tightly to the desert traditions. Not all of them are necessary here."

"I devoted my life to protecting and honoring our traditions." Storm allowed herself to lean against him, half closing her eyes. "If I lose them, what will I have left to me? A lifetime focused on perfecting how to kill?" She looked away from him. "How to murder?"

"You are not a killer or a murderer," Skyfire said firmly. "You are a survivor and protector." He tightened his arm around her. "There is no shame in that." He rested his cheek against the top of her head when she closed her eyes with a sigh, laying her head on his chest.

At one of the small tables, Mureln sat with Ash, watching the two Desanti. "You cannot keep putting her off. The rain will eventually have to stop. And even if it doesn't, you know Storm will eventually try to find Her on her own. Might even succeed, given her stubbornness and the fact she was raised by a god and his divine servants." Mureln could see by the slight twitch in his expression that Ash was not ignoring him. "Making it rain like this is only delaying the inevitable."

"I'm not making it rain," Ash said sourly, glowering at Mureln before looking back at the two Desanti staring outside. "I'm strong in wielding Forentan magic, but even I can't make it rain for a week." At Mureln's dubious expression, Ash scowled. "Don't look at me like that. I know my limitations."

"Then convince me I'm the only one who can tell this rain is unnatural." Mureln squeezed Ash's shoulder. "Some way, somehow, the weather is responding to *you*. Before Ithesra washes away into the ocean—and believe me, my people do not want *your* trees in *our* waters—we need to go see Her. *She* needs to see Her."

Ash pushed himself to his feet. "Fine. The sooner we get this done, the sooner we can be rid of the Desanti bitch and life can get back to normal." As Ash stalked to the stairs, he nearly ran into Taylin, who pressed herself against the wall to get out of his way.

"I am not sure which is gloomier. Him or the weather," Taylin said as she slipped into the chair next to Mureln. She laced her fingers with his, leaning close to kiss his cheek.

"He's trying to convince himself he wants her gone now," the Bard said sadly. "And failing hopelessly." Wearily, he rested his forehead in his palm, closing his eyes. Nearby, Terrence turned his attention from Taylin and Mureln to where his master had disappeared.

⁕ ⁕ ⁕

TERRENCE CLIMBED THE STAIRS, smoothing the new robes that marked his promotion, his hands trembling with the same anxious energy he'd felt when the Illaini Magus first took him on as an apprentice. On the uppermost landing, silence reigned, broken only by the low rumble of thunder outside, barely lit by the muted daylight filtering through the balcony arch. He murmured a quick incantation, summoning a tiny sphere of magelight that hovered in midair. "Master Ash?" he called, voice tight.

From beyond the curtained alcove where Ash slept, a sharp voice replied. "What is it, Senior Journeyman Terrence?"

Terrence closed his eyes and inhaled slowly, bracing himself. "I must speak with you, Master." When no answer came, he drew back the curtain and peered into the dim chamber before stepping inside.

Ash sat cross-legged on the bed, his eyes shut in an attempt to meditate. He made no move when Terrence let the curtain drop behind him. The younger man stood in silence until at last Ash's deep azure blue eyes flicked open and fixed on him with frosty displeasure. "So speak. Then leave. I want to be alone."

Terrence pressed his lips into a thin line. "Master, I...I know you're angry that Mistress Storm has chosen to return to Desantiva." He dared not meet Ash's glare. "But isn't it better if she is somewhere she can be happy? It's obvious she's been miserable since we arrived at Naveene's Rest."

"She won't find happiness there," Ash retorted. "She gave what we call a Soul Oath to Master Almek—just as I did. Even if he allows her departure, the decision will destroy her. And there'll be no one to restrain her from self-destruction. Not even Skyfire."

Terrence frowned and sank onto the chest at the foot of the bed. "You think she'll die if she leaves." He tilted his head. "But she's the finest warrior I've ever known. How can you be certain?"

Ash seethed, his lips twisting into a bitter smile. "Because I know her, Terrence. She'll be consumed by guilt for failing in her vow to Master Almek. She'll throw herself into her duty without rest or caution until something—some merciful accident, some lucky challenger—ends her suffering. I know because..." The smile vanished as Ash's fists clenched. "Because I'd do exactly the same in her shoes."

Terrence's eyes widened, and he sprang up. "We must tell Master Almek! He'd never stand by and let her perish—"

"He already knows," Ash interrupted, voice low and hard. "He sees every possible outcome. But he believes people must choose their own paths—even if it costs them their lives." He paused, bitterness seeping into each word. "Even if it means damning the world."

Terrence frowned in thought. "Mistress Storm wouldn't be so selfish as that. I'm certain of it, Master."

Ash growled as he stood. "That's the problem, Terrence. She is *not* being selfish." Rubbing his face, then pinching the bridge of his nose, he composed himself. "She believes herself a danger to the rest of us."

"A danger?" The young man stared at Ash without comprehension. He opened his mouth to argue that, then closed it again as he remembered the many times Ash had endured Storm's violent explosions of temper, and the wounds he suffered without complaint. "I can see why she would believe so," he murmured. After several moments, he sighed. "I feel so sorry for her."

The Illaini Magus looked sharply at the young journeyman's odd tone of voice. "Sorry for her?"

"Yes, Master." Terrence met his master's intense gaze. "Everyone here sees her as a master of weaponcraft. Which she is," he said hurriedly before Ash scolded him for even hinting Storm was anything less. Looking down, the young man touched his temple. "I...While I sheltered Dzee, she told me about Desantiva...of the past, at least. She said being Swordanzen—especially Githalin—is much more than just knowing how to fight well."

Ash's bitter expression melted into one of blank surprise at the interactions he had been unaware of. "Of course," he responded automatically. "She knows how to survive in the harsh environment of Desantiva's wastelands, how to protect the life there to sustain her people. She is the keeper of her people's history and traditions."

Terrence lowered his hand from his temple, looking at Ash. "She is to Desantiva as an Illaini Magus is to Forenta." Terrence smiled sadly. "But it meant little to be the Illaini Magus in Desantiva. You knew nothing of their language or their culture. Nothing at all about how to survive. You just happened to be a powerful wielder of magic."

"Get to the point, Terrence," Ash said impatiently, crossing his arms.

"Master, when we went to Desantiva, we knew we would not be there long, and none of us plan on ever returning. We had little reason to learn more about the Desanti, though I am sure Mistress Storm would have taught us if we had asked her." He leaned forward, looking up at his master. "But none of us asked because...well. Desantiva is of very little value to us. To us, it's just a lost, forgotten land we are eager to forget again. It reminds us of our ancestors' mistakes and makes us uncomfortable."

"Terrence—"

"Master, allow me to finish," Terrence stated so firmly, Ash blinked in surprise and fell silent as his student requested. "If the Desanti would remain with Master Almek, they know they are likely never to see their home again. Everyone treats both Storm and Skyfire as masters. But they aren't. Not here. Here, they are two people who are very good at using weapons. You taught me yourself; a master is both teacher and student. Part of the Swordanzen patterns must include those aspects. Especially Githalin."

With a hint of urgency, Terrence asked, "Master. Who is teaching the Desanti? Who is *learning* from them? No one. Why should Mistress Storm consider herself necessary when all of us, even Master Almek, dismiss almost everything about her but her warrior skills as unnecessary?"

Ash opened his mouth to answer, then shut it again, frowning.

✦·—··—·—·⟩⟨ ·⟩⟨·—·—··—·✦

THE MOOD IN NAVEENE'S Rest was quiet, with only a few Ithesrans leaving their homes amidst the ongoing rain. The constant low rumble of thunder and the patter of rain created a gloomy backdrop for the evening meal. All of Almek's students, except for Ash, gathered at the table reserved for them. The Sevmanen and Forentan were laughing at a story Mureln was narrating with lively enthusiasm. The Desanti, as was their custom, sat apart, sharing a plate of food and conversing softly with each other.

All eyes were drawn to Ash as the self-possessed mage joined them, his hands tucked within his sleeves. Even though the others offered him greetings of varying degrees of warmth, his attention was only for Storm. "Githalin Swordanzen Storm il'Thandar, would you honor me with a moment of your time in private?"

Storm and Skyfire traded quizzical looks, Skyfire shrugging before Storm rose without a word. The two left the main room for a private one. A small table with a crystal lantern glowed with a warm, soft light on several platters of food. He moved to one chair, pulling it out and waiting patiently when she balked. "Please," he requested simply.

Hesitating a moment more, Storm finally agreed to the implied invitation, sitting stiffly. Moving to the seat across from her, Ash took bites from each of the platters before serving them both.

Storm watched him with silent intensity. When he finished, she stared at him a little longer. "There was food with the others. And Mureln was telling a story you probably would have enjoyed."

"You did not seem to be enjoying it," he pointed out neutrally. Cheeks coloring, she looked away, falling silent. Ash reached towards her, resting his outstretched hand on the table. The gesture drew her eyes back to him. "I wanted to apologize to you. I reacted poorly when you told me of your plans to leave, and I have been behaving even worse since."

After a moment, Storm shook her head. "I do not fault you. There is no need—"

"Yes, there is a need for an apology, if only for myself." Ash looked chagrined. "I'm the Illaini Magus. You're a guest in my land, and I've been negligent in my duties to you. And...I should have been more understanding." He took a deep breath. "When it's time for you to leave, I won't stop you." He added softly, "No matter how much it will pain me to lose you."

Looking sad, Storm started to speak then stopped, letting him take her hand. Finally..."I accept your apology, Illaini Magus." Tilting her head to one side, she gestured towards the meal in puzzlement. "But why all of this?"

Ash smiled sadly. "Because I wish for you to teach me. About your people. Your culture. Your beliefs. Everything you can in the time we still have together." Feeling grateful for her surprised reaction, he could not help but feel some guilt for his own blindness. "When you leave, Desantiva leaves with you. I don't want to lose it...or you...forever." He extended his other hand to her beseechingly. "Githalin Swordanzen Storm il'Thandar. Please honor me and teach me about Desantiva." He squeezed her fingers lightly at her nod of acceptance.

CHAPTER FIFTY-NINE

WITHIN DAYS OF STORM and Ash's reconciliation, the relentless downpour that had soaked Forenta for weeks finally surrendered to sporadic drizzles, leaving behind a forest that exhaled mist with each breeze. The air carried the sharp tang of decaying leaves and fresh sap, crisp with autumn's unmistakable bite. Overhead, the once-uniform emerald canopy had transformed into a tapestry of flame—crimson blazing beside gold and burnished copper. Sunlight, so long absent, now pierced through gaps in the foliage, casting dappled medallions across the forest floor where mushrooms sprouted in fairy rings around moss-covered stones.

Almek smiled indulgently, the others laughing, as the good humor of the Swordanzen returned with the change in the weather. "I was beginning to believe we would never see the sun again!" Skyfire stretched his arms expansively, turning his face into the sunlight. "Kailee's tail, I will never again take it for granted."

Astride her drizar, Storm squinted upwards, shading her eyes. "I have never known the sun to be so bright yet the day so cold." She blew on her cupped hands to warm them.

"Githalin Swordanzen." Ash stepped off the ramp to the forest floor, followed by Lyra. Each carried a large bundle. Both Desanti looked over with curious expressions, Skyfire's eyes lighting up seeing the young Forentan woman. "The days are only going to grow colder. I would be remiss in not assuring our Desanti guests were better protected against it."

Taking the bundle from Lyra, Skyfire unfolded the heavy, fur-lined oilskin cloak dyed a rich rust color, putting it over his shoulders. Lyra beamed up at him as he fastened it securely. "It fits you well, Master Skyfire. And there are gloves to match!" She cast her gaze down shyly. "Allow me to help you with them?" She looked up when he offered her his hands, smiling brightly.

Ash offered a similar set of cloak and gloves to Storm with a small smile. "For you, my Swordanzen." She slid off the drizar's back, looking both curious and appreciative.

Storm arched an eyebrow as he moved behind her to drape the deep crimson cloak around her shoulders. "'Your' Swordanzen?"

She closed her eyes as he leaned close to whisper in her ear. "Yes. *My* Swordanzen." Moving around her to fasten the clasp, he stated, "In Desantiva, I met your Father. Today, you will meet my Mother." He smiled at her expression before reaching for her hands to help her with the gloves.

WITH THE HELP OF Mureln's music, the ride went by swiftly. But the easy camaraderie that had grown between Almek's students shattered when they reached the hidden glade. The moment the drizzen entered, clouds of forest sprites swarmed the two Desanti, cutting and stabbing the desert warriors with thorns and other tiny weapons. Despite desperately trying to protect their faces, arms, and legs, neither Swordanzen drew any weapons against the tiny guardians.

"Stop this!" Ash bellowed, but was unheard over the shrill voices of the sprites. "Stop!" Finally, given no choice, he raised his hands, a burst of wind sweeping the tiny creatures away from the Swordanzen. He ran to stand between the Desanti and the swarm. "I said stop!"

One familiar sprite flew to Ash, hovering in front of him with angered agitation. "All Mother must be protected! They will kill All Mother! Why bring murderers?"

"They are not murderers, Li!" Ash glanced back over his shoulder, frowning. Both Desanti slumped in their saddles. The others hurried to help the pair dismount their agitated beasts. "Do you think I would have brought them here if I believed they meant harm to Her?"

"Confuse you they must have." Li crossed her arms, adamant in her belief. "Li not allow All Mother harm."

"Skyfire, lad, what be wrong?" Emil asked worriedly. Emaris frowned as the Desanti man's knees buckled. "It just be little bee stings. Ye be tougher than that!" But no amount of cajoling seemed to help; the Desanti man's eyes rolled back. Emil felt his throat for a pulse desperately. Stricken, Emil looked up at Almek. "I-I kenna find a heartbeat, Guardian!"

Taylin and Mureln were having similar issues with Storm, the woman limp despite their support. "I-I can't heal her faster than whatever is hurting her." Her expression fell moments later, and she closed her eyes. "No," she whispered in disbelief. Almek frowned as he tried to rouse the Desanti woman, calling to her. But there was no response.

Ash's eyes went wide in horror before he spun on the tiny creature that drew back in shock. "Li, what have you done?!" He ran to Storm, taking her from Mureln and Taylin as he fell to his knees. "Storm, no." He cupped her cheek in one hand, trying to find even the tiniest spark of life and finding only emptiness. "Please, Mother, no! Storm!"

The sprite flew closer to Ash, looking perplexed. "Li do what must. No more evil ones. No more danger to All Mother. Eep!" She squeaked as Ash grabbed the tiny creature. She stared at him. "You cry for evil one?"

"She. Was. Not. Evil," Ash grated out. With a wordless growl, he flung Li away from him to embrace Storm, burying his face in her hair as the drizar shrieked, slashing his horns at the cloud of sprites. "Storm, forgive me."

Without warning, Storm and Skyfire both jerked, gasping like drowning victims breaking the surface of the depths. Shaking uncontrollably, Storm tried to smile at Ash, one hand grabbing the front of his robes. She tried to speak several times, closing her eyes to focus. "N-no...need..." Swallowing tightly, she held tighter to him. "Forgive..."

Almek was as dumbfounded as the others at the unexpected resurrection. "You're both alive?! How is this possible?"

Clinging to Ash, Storm struggled to speak through the spasms that wracked her and Skyfire mercilessly. "P-plant...poi-poison...d-doesn't..." The woman whimpered as she tried to regain control of herself. "I-it..."

"Shhh. It doesn't matter. I didn't know this would happen. We'll protect you both, Storm. For however long you need to recover. I promise you." He scowled as Li alighted on his shoulder to stare at Storm, starting to slap the sprite away again, but Storm caught his wrist in a tight grip. She held out her other hand to the sprite in invitation.

Li fluttered to the shaking palm extended to her, crouching down. Storm managed to smile. "F-fearless...one...We-we ask...s-safe...pa-pass-passage..."

"Hush," Ash ordered softly, brushing Li away to take Storm's hand, holding it tightly. "Shhh. Rest." He brushed his fingertips over her eyes as he murmured the words of magic softly. Her body relaxed, the spasms easing to deep shudders. Terrence followed his master's lead, doing the same for Skyfire. Emaris hefted the man across his shoulders with a grunt, waiting patiently.

Li hovered near the mage and Swordanzen for a long time and then flew to the vines that continued to flower despite the cooling season. The other sprites joined Li without a sound and solemnly drew back the vines, exposing the passage.

Mureln put a hand on Ash's shoulder in wordless question. "I will carry her. I would carry her to the ends of the world if that was where she wished to go," Ash stated as he got to his feet determinedly, cradling the unconscious woman.

THE COLORS OF THE coming twilight painted the sky in brilliant pastel ribbons as the group emerged on the other side of the passage. Naiya hopped down from the upper branches to the lowermost reaches of the great tree, her expression a twist of horror and fear. "Ash, what is this?"

"You are the Voice for my all-knowing Mother," Ash said coldly as he laid Storm's trembling form on the still sun-warmed stone before the goddess. "I am surprised you do not know."

Naiya stiffened at Ash's tone, the tree rustling in the still air. "I never claimed to know all things. Neither has She. You know what *they* are to Us. Why have you brought Her Brother's people into Her presence?"

The others kept back from Ash, even Almek knowing better than to intrude between the Illaini Magus and the Forenten god. Mureln's gaze shifted away from the confrontation with a frown. Silently, he put a hand on Almek's arm to get his attention, touching his ear with the other hand. Almek listened for a moment, then also frowned.

Defiant anger all but radiated from Ash's posture as he stood before the majestic tree. "She is Githalin Swordanzen Storm il'Thandar, Daughter of the Raging One, the Heart of Desantiva. She wished to speak to you on behalf of her father because He cannot speak for Himself." With one more worried look at Storm's shuddering body, he returned his attention to the tree. "She came in peace and good faith. I gave my word that I would protect her. She was attacked unprovoked—"

"Her presence is provocation!" Naiya's voice and posture reflected the goddess speaking through her. "The warriors bear no love for My mortal children. They must be punished."

Ash's face contorted with rage. "*Punished?*" The word exploded from him like a curse. His fists clenched so tight his knuckles blanched white. "The warrior folk who should *hate* us honored *our* request for safe passage while You—" He jabbed a finger towards Storm's trembling form. "Look at her, Mother! *Look*! What's her crime? Being born Desanti? Having different beliefs? Seeing the world through a different light? Sharing the blood of ancestors dead two millennia?" His voice cracked as he slammed his palm against his chest. "I *swore* they would be safe! I *failed* because You're too blind to see anything has changed!" Ash's eyes blazed with furious tears as he positioned himself between the tree and Storm. "She can't speak now, so I will on her behalf."

Naiya frowned delicately, the branches above rustling in agitation. "Very well. We will listen."

Ash took a deep breath and straightened. "Neither the Raging One nor those beholden to him will bring any harm to You or Your children." Ash regarded Naiya with a hard look. "He has been imprisoned for far too long. He and his children suffer."

The dryad was still for a long time. "You want Me to believe He does not wish to harm Us?" Naiya shook her head once. "I will never believe that. He is the Raging One! Violence and destruction are all He knows."

"You can't condemn the Desanti to keep suffering!" Ash's hands curled into fists in frustration. He took a deep breath to reclaim his composure before speaking again. "I have been to Desantiva, Mother." His stony gaze fixed on the branches above. "I witnessed the devastation that was wrought on their land. I have seen, despite the deep scars that disfigure their land, a fierce determination to survive. I have seen the prices they pay for that survival."

Naiya shrugged one shoulder. "You know We did what We had to. They were dangerous. Uncontrolled. They would have attacked us without a second thought to destroy Forenta."

"Lies!" Ash shouted, making Naiya flinch back. "The entire heart of their beliefs is about balance and self-control! If they had attacked, it would have been to test themselves against the best of Forenta. You allowed an outsider to play on Your fears and manipulate You to attempt to destroy an entire race. To destroy Your own Brother!" He took a step forward. "You charged me to keep the Great Balance, yet You allowed my ancestors to use the most heinous of spells and nearly ripped all the life from Desantiva. How is that protecting the great balance?"

Naiya lowered her eyes. After a moment, she raised them again, squaring her shoulders. "We realized Our mistake nearly too late. But We will not regret our actions. We acted on what We knew to be truth. We ended the attack before all was destroyed."

"You *left* them to suffer! You left the land twisted and grotesque. You knew it was a lie, yet you willingly cursed them to watch their children die, their families suffer, and left their god to suffer their pain but unable to do anything to help them! Generation after generation, left only to look forward to their deaths because their lives are too short to truly live. No one," he said intently. "*No one* should have had to suffer as they had." He took a step forward imploringly. "Why, Mother? Why did you damn them to that hell?!"

Naiya crossed her arms, her expression chill. "If you met Our Brother, then you know why. He would not hear Our words, Our reasons. He was unrepentant of the threat His children posed to Ours. Unapologetic."

Ash was incredulous. "You wanted Him to *apologize*? But the Desanti had not attacked first! *We* did! Their blood is on our hands."

"Irrelevant," Naiya stated with deceptive mildness.

"The Heart of Desantiva suffers the pain of each of His children's deaths. Deaths that come far more frequently for Desanti than for any other race because of what *we* did to their land. And His children suffer with Him. He is trapped, chained to rock that gave Him no respite from His own pain, or that of His land, unable to free Himself from the bindings You put on Him."

"If anything had changed, He would have been freed long before now. You know why the bindings hold," Naiya replied with maddening serenity. "He thinks as We believe. We fear He means Us harm. He wants to harm Us."

"How can you blame Him?!" Ash demanded hotly. "But wanting to do something doesn't mean he would actually follow through with it! He loves His children as much as You love Yours. But He cannot spare them the suffering they have been condemned to because of Forentan arrogance and ignorance."

"We have done what He allows. We have kept Our children away from His," Naiya stated, an edge to her otherwise mild tones. "It would have been simple to kill all that were left. It would be simple to finish it now. But We did not allow it then, nor will We allow it now." Naiya closed her eyes, speaking for herself. "She offered to help mend things, but He shut Her out. He shut everyone out."

"You want Him to accept blame for the chosen path of the Desanti." Ash shook his head. "You cannot ask that of them. They are no more at fault than we are for *our* beliefs. Their strengths and ours complement each other." Plaintively, he said, "They and we both believe that family is the most important thing. Do you still honestly believe the Raging One would harm His own Sister? That He would not come to You if You were in need?"

"Almek!" Mureln said sharply, interrupting Ash and Naiya, his eyes unfocused, listening to something. "Do you hear it?" As the others looked around, trying to find the source of the sound slowly increasing in volume, the bard ran to the cliff edge, looked down towards the ocean far below and swore colorfully as he swiftly backed away.

The Guardian did not waste time, barking orders. "Emaris! Emil! Get the Desanti to safety!" Almek looked directly at Naiya. "If you've others who protect You, call them."

"There are no others! The Trisari are still missing!" Naiya looked to the branches and nodded, then lightly ran towards the root that curled towards the cliff wall. "Over here, Gyspari sons!"

A horrible screech tortured the air, vibrating through bone and tooth as a massive abomination cleared the cliff edge. Twice the height of a man, its malevolent eyes fixed unblinkingly on the sacred tree. Its mottled hide—black as pitch in places, translucent as fog in others—writhed ceaselessly. The creature seemed composed of countless distorted smaller versions of itself, each with its own gaping maw and twisted limbs, moving independently within the greater whole. They pushed against their shared skin from within, creating rippling bulges and hollows like a nest of venomous snakes given a single grotesque corporeal form, their collective hunger radiating outward in waves of palpable malice.

Taylin recoiled in horror. "What is that thing? It-it looks like-like those things from the Rumblelands crushed together."

Almek grimaced. "That is exactly what it is. They could not harm the Raging One as many separately." He pressed his lips together. "I don't know if I have the strength to banish so many at once. Together they possess nearly the power of a god." His eyes went wide as he realized its goal. "They seek to kill the Knowing One!"

With bellowing battle cries, Emil and Emaris charged the monster with weapons drawn, the mages pairing with them. The fighters' distractions gave the mages the time they needed to prepare their own strikes. The combined physical and magical attacks, while powerful and accurate, dislodging and banishing significant chunks of the whole, met with only limited effect on the massive beast that kept inexorably moving closer towards the immobile goddess.

Mureln closed his eyes, holding his hands apart as he focused. Beside him, Almek murmured instructions, working with the younger man to defend the Tree. Waves of raw sound coupled with temporal energy crashed into the monster, which shrieked in pain, blindly trying to stop the bard and the Guardian. The fighters and mages harried it, distracting it away from the two as they moved out of its striking distance.

Naiya crouched behind the roots where the Desanti had been hidden. The relentless march of the dark creature slowed, but did not stop. Tied to the Knowing One, she cried out in agony as hideous claws dug into the main trunk. The dryad looked down when Storm grabbed her wrist.

Storm looked into Naiya's eyes. "C-call...Him," she said intently. "C-call m-my Father!"

"We cannot! He will kill Us!"

"She...is His...S-Sister..." Pulling out her knife, Storm pointed it at the dryad and demanded, "Call Him!"

Moments later, a thunderous crack split the air, followed by a challenging roar. Almek and the others looked up in shock to see the dark, scarred figure of the Raging One diving for the beast. They bolted away barely in time to avoid the impact of the massive dragon with the darkling monster.

The monster backed away a pace, hissing malevolently. "Two gods for price of one," it said with ominous glee. "Master will be pleased."

The Raging One did not bother to speak, lunging for the monster's throat with jaws that could crush boulders. The two titanic bodies crashed into one another with a thunderous impact that shook the very earth beneath them, grappling and clawing viciously, scales scraping against the writhing darkness. The effects of having been so long imprisoned became apparent as the struggle lengthened—the dragon's once-mighty muscles trembled with fatigue, his obsidian scales dull. The Raging One's moves grew less quick, less certain, his breathing ragged and labored. Crimson blood welled from deep slashes in the dragon's flanks, while viscous black ichor oozed from the dark monster's wounds, hissing where it touched the ground.

Without warning, the conglomerate beast shook the dragon off with a violent twist of its malformed body, flinging Him into the cliff face with such force that rock shattered and cascaded down in a shower of debris and choking dust. The darkling monster's countless mouths twisted into grotesque grins as it prepared to finish the stunned god, when thick, gnarled roots burst through the soil like wooden serpents, coiling around the beast's limbs and torso, ensnaring the monster where it could not reach the dragon. It shrieked its fury at being denied its victory.

Dragging himself up on trembling legs, the Raging One gathered His remaining strength, His eyes blazing with ancient fury as He lunged forward, massive jaws clamping down to rip the monster's throat out in a spray of black corruption. The beast broke apart into dozens of individual bodies that squirmed and writhed like maggots, then vanished with tortured shrieks that clawed at the mind, echoing across the valley before leaving behind a silence so complete it pressed against the ears like a physical weight.

The soft patter of the dragon's blood dripping onto stone and His labored breathing broke the oppressive silence as He stood, swaying unsteadily. He staggered over to the tree, standing in front of it, staring.

Naiya emerged from her hiding place, walking forward to touch the dragon's foreleg. He lowered His head to the dryad, sniffing at her. "You are wounded, Lord Desantiva."

"So is My Sister Forenta," the Raging One replied wearily. He staggered a few steps, collapsing and resting His head on a root. "I am glad You are safe, Sister."

Taylin ran over to the dragon, ignoring the burn of His blood on her hands as she focused on closing the worst of the open wounds. The dragon raised his head, eyes dull. He snaked His tail around her, pulling her away. "You are in pain," she rasped, trying to finish her work.

"I will not have you die for Me," the dragon intoned. "Your help is appreciated. But I will heal." He dropped his head back to the root, closing His eyes. "Pain is nothing new to me. Your mortal family needs your touch more."

Naiya had gone to where the evil beast's claws had dug into the wood, gently and carefully aligning the pieces as best she could. "Oh, Mistress,"

Naiya lamented, tears in her own eyes as she tried to mend the wounded tree. She jumped when Almek joined her.

Looking nearly as ancient as he actually was, Almek reached into an inner pocket to pull out the small wire-wrapped bottle given to him so long ago. He opened it and poured the gift of temporal water over the damage. The pieces melted together, healing completely, but evidence of the wounds remained, marring the formerly perfect trunk. "A gift from the Timeless One," he explained simply, wearily.

Naiya wrapped her arms around Almek in gratitude, and then straightened as the branches above rustled. "The Mistress requests you honor Her by remaining here to recover." Looking to the Raging One, she added, "All of you. It should be safe enough. It is the least She can offer."

Almek cast a wan smile towards the Vodani bard and Sevmanan mercenaries, who were leaning on each other to stay upright. "I do not know if we have much choice about whether or not we stay, but thank You for welcoming us."

Ash staggered over to the Desanti, dropping to his knees in exhaustion. "Storm," he murmured worriedly, pulling her deeply shuddering body into his lap and cradling her as he leaned against the tree's root. He saw her ungloved, bloody hand and her knife half embedded in the dirt. He frowned. "Storm, what did you do?"

Skyfire, in relatively better shape than Storm, dragged himself to sit upright, leaning against the root near the pair. "Sh-she made s-sure *He* h-heard *Her*." Ash squinted at Skyfire. The Desanti man guessed the question behind the expression. "D-Desanti...are immune to...p-plant t-toxins. Th-they a-are n-not l-l-lethal...to us." He made a face. "B-but takes t-time t-to re-re..." He swallowed, shudders wracking him uncontrollably as they overwhelmed him. His determination to regain control was obvious, the shudders subsiding again. "Recover. C-cannot pr-protect se-self l-like th-this un-until b-body purges it."

Putting his hand on the other man's shoulder, Ash said firmly, "Skyfire. I will watch over you both. Rest." The Desanti man nodded, closing his eyes as he stopped trying to fight the tremors that crippled him. Ash did his best to bind Storm's bleeding hand. "Stubborn Desanti," he muttered crossly. A small, unnoticed smile touched Storm's lips.

Chapter Sixty

THE RAGING ONE SAT along the edge of the ledge that opened out over the water, watching the sun glitter off the waves. He looked down at the sound of slow, uneven footsteps approaching and fanned a protective wing over Storm. She walked alone with sheer determination, fighting the poisoned induced tremors that still shook her, despite a week having passed since the attack.

"Daughter," the dragon intoned, lowering His head towards her.

Raising her hand to touch the tip of His snout, Storm managed a shaky smile. "F-father. I am glad Y-You are f-finally f-free." She looked towards the others seated together near the foot of the great tree. "Th-the mage h-helped very m-much."

The dragon rumbled deep in His chest in amusement. "He is tolerable for one of Hers." Exhaling warm air over her to banish the chill air, He murmured, "My children will always surpass the children of magic. But none will ever compare to you, My beloved Daughter."

"I d-do not f-feel v-very im-impressive right n-now. C-can b-barely w-walk." Storm closed her eyes. "W-will be f-forever b-before I c-can...be u-useful."

Bumping her with His nose, the dragon chided, "You know your usefulness extends beyond your skills with the physical disciplines. What troubles you? It is unlike you to feel sorry for yourself."

Storm closed her eyes, leaning against the massive shoulder, soaking in his warmth. "F-father...I want t-to c-come home. Wh-where I b-belong."

The dragon brought His wing forward more, creating a small area of warmth, concealing them both from the others' eyes. He considered her for a long time. "Is that what you truly want, Daughter?" Storm nodded, huddling in the crevice of the dragon's shoulder muscles. Blowing warm air on her, He said simply, "No."

Stung, the young woman looked up at the dragon god. "N-No? H-have I f-failed You, F-father? H-h-have I n-not done all Y-you asked of m-me and m-more?" Stricken, she asked, "I-I am c-cast out?"

The dragon sighed heavily, touching her with His nose gently. "No, Daughter. In fact, you have done the opposite. You have done more for Me, for Desantiva, than any of My children since the earliest of days, both mortal and immortal. Desantiva needs you...here. You need to bring an understanding of our world to the outlanders. To begin the healing so the tribes can trust again." Grumbling, he added, "And the outlands need your skills to protect them from the shadows."

"Father, please," she implored, burying her face against Him. "I m-miss Desantiva. I m-miss my home."

"Daughter, Desantiva will always be with you because it is a part of you. You only need to seek it within yourself." He bumped her back gently. "You already know this. There is no need to return to Desantiva when it is already here."

"No! I w-want to go home! I w-want to leave th-this h-horrible place wh-where th-they hate us."

The dragon rumbled. "Storm, Mine is the domain of the heart. You do not want to leave." With the utmost gentility, he shifted position so she was between His forelegs, keeping her close to Him. "You are afraid to stay."

"I am afraid of nothing." Her whispered voice carried a note of desperation.

The dragon said nothing, simply letting her lean against Him as the sun touched the horizon. Finally, he carefully rose, stretching His wings, drawing the attention of the others. "It is time. I must return."

"Father," Storm begged, kneeling on the ground, holding her hand out to Him.

"Be strong, My Daughter." He reared on His back legs, wings beating the air. "Yours and Skyfire's patterns will be the patterns of Desantiva's future."

"Father, please! Don't leave me!" Storm cried, stumbling to her feet, reaching as if to catch Him as He leapt skyward. She would have stumbled over the edge except for Ash, who pulled her back firmly to safety.

The dragon's mind touched Storm's as He spiraled higher. *<I am always with you. As is he.>*

The others ran to join the Swordanzen woman at the ledge, all watching the dragon fly until He vanished with a soft rumble of thunder. All but Ash, who frowned in worry at Storm. He put a hand on her shoulder, wanting only to offer some comfort. She looked back at him, eyes wet with tears that were for herself. Pulling her close, Ash held her as she hid her face against his chest and wept.

GLOSSARY

a'alisna — (ah-ah-LIS-nah) Vodani term for the nomadic urge to move from place to place

Almek Two-Tones — (AL-mek) The last living Guardian of Time bearing two colors on his divine mark. Oldest wandering Guardian at over 500 years old; Sevmanen-Vodani halfborn

Amelana Avarian — (ah-MEH-lah-nah) Great grandniece of Ellis Avarian; Ash Andar's journeyman student

Ancestral agony — Vodani term for the Psia Re

Ancient Trinity — The first gods, Creator, Destroyer and Time

Anton Ganessi — Head of the noble house that rules the Sevmanen region of the port city of Ganessi

Arrowhawk — A black falcon with blue markings used by the Vodani people to carry messages

Ash Andar — Forentan man, youngest master mage and only living Illaini Magus

A'tyrna Ulan — (ah-TIR-nah OO-lahn) Stone pillars that are the remains of ancient Desanti-Forentan halfborn

Avarian family — (ah-VAH-ree-ahn) One of the oldest of the Ancient Houses in Forenta

Bard — A wandering minstrel and neutral arbiter, usually Vodani-born

Before Time — Desanti term for the time before the Great War

Bek — A crude Sevmanen caravan worker

Bella — A Vodani Unsvet Guardian

Bennu Avarian — (BEH-noo) Deceased Forentan mage, Ash's former master, twin to Ellis

Black water — The ink produced by squids

Blood Oath — A mystical bond created between a Forentan and another

Blue Rose Inn — A tavern the travelers stay at in Ganessi

Chlayxin — (CHLAY-zin) the buildup of pressure caused by using Forentan life magic, also called magic backlash

Chok — A crude Sevmanen caravan worker

Clarissa — Headwoman of the Avarian household

Corast — (KOR-ahst) A Forentan-Vodani border port city

Council of Elders — The ruling council of Desantiva comprised of the oldest members of the Desanti people

Creator, the — One of the Ancient Triad; The Unchanging One

Cursed child — A surviving child of a dead Desanti tribe

Darkborn — A human born with the soul of a darkling

Darkling — An entity that crosses into the physical plane from the River of Time that preys on the souls of the living

Defiler — A derogatory Desanti term for a Forentan

Dinnais — (dih-NAY-ss) A Desanti term for a darkling

Desanti — (deh-SAN-tee) Singular or plural term referring to a human from Desantiva; adjective describing anything from Desantiva

Desantiva — (deh-san-TEE-vah) The barren wasteland southern territory claimed by the Desanti people; The name of the Desanti's dragon god

Dessa — (DEH-sah) Ash's only servant, companion since childhood; Killed by a darkling

Destroyer, the — One of the Ancient Triad; The Changing One

Dove and Lily Inn — Upper class establishment in Ganessi

Dremmen — (DREH-men) A Forentan Unsvet Guardian

Drizar — (DRI-zahr) The term for a full male drizzen, synonymous to stallion

Drizzen — (DRI-zen) Vicious, reptilian omnivores that replace horses in Desantiva

Dulain — (doo-LANE) Senior Unsvet in charge of the Guardian city in Fortress

Dusvet Guardian — (DOO-sveht) A Guardian of Time marked with a metallic mark of two colors on the right cheek

Dylar — (D'EYE-lar) Guardsman captain of Ganessi

Dzee — Rainbow wyvern Totani

Edai Magus — (eh-DAH-ee) One of the mages on the Forentan mage high council

Edai Tredecima — (eh-DAH-ee treh-DES-ee-mah) The thirteen member mage high council

Elder — A Desanti who is 35 years or older

Elder bear — A giant bear native to Forenta

Ellis Avarian — (EL-lis) Forentan mage, twin brother of Bennu Avarian, second highest ranking mage on the Edai Tredecima

Emaris — (EM-ahr-ihss) Mute Sevmanan gypsy mercenary, brother of Emil

Emil — (EH-mill) Sevmanan mercenary-thief, brother of Emaris

Etaio — (eh-TIE-oh) Gypsy merchant in Ganessi

Final Dance — A Swordanzen attack that leaves the attacker impervious to injury, but kills the attacker once completed

First Home — The only permanent Desanti city in Desantiva

First Sundering — An ancient cataclysm that created the Forentan and Desanti nations

Forbidden arts — Forentan magic that has no limitations that end a spells effects

Forenta — (for-EHN-tah) The heavily forested northern territory claimed by the Forentan people; name of the Forentan god

Forentan — (for-EHN-tan) Singular term for a human from Forenta; adjective describing anything from Forenta

Forenten — (for-EHN-ten) Plural term for a human from Forenta

Forge, the — Desanti term for the hottest part of the day

Fortress of Time — Solitary mountain near the World Spine, home to the Guardians of Time

Ganessi — (gah-NESS-ee) A Sevmanan-Vodani border port city

Githalin Blades — (gith-AH-lin) The divine created single-edged paired blades given to Githalin

Githalin Swordanzen — A god-touched Swordanzen

Great Barrier — The dividing line between the physical plane and the River of Time

Great War — The war between Forenta and Desantiva that ended in the Second Sundering

Guardian Adept — A person formally identified to be training to be tested to become a Guardian of Time

Guardians — Short form for Guardians of Time

Guardians of Time — Nearly immortal servants of the Timeless One

Gyspari — Sevmanan nomads

Halfborn — Anyone with parents from two nations (example: Sevmanan and Vodani)

Hall of Remembrance — Chamber in the butte of First Home with mosaics depicting moments of Desanti history

Heart of Desantiva — Name for the Desanti God

Home Port — The first Vodani city, only non-Desanti city in Desantiva

Hollow — A Forentan term for an inn, usually lower class

Illaini Magus — (ill-AEE-nee) A god-touched mage

Ilsa — (ILL-sah) Master Vodani apothecarist of Water's Resonance

Immortal servant — a minor divine entity that serves one of the gods
Ithesra — (ih-THEHZ-rah) Capital city of Forenta
Jaison — (JAY-sun) A Vodani Unsvet Guardian from Desantiva
Jakkee — (JAH-kee) A Vodani boy of Water's Resonance
Joban — (JO-bahn) A Sevmanan man punished by a Guardian
Kailee — (KAY-lee) A silver desert cat Totani
Knowing One, the — The Forentan tree god
Kraken — Giant, deep-ocean squid
Landwalker — Vodani nickname for anyone from the landbound nations
Li — (LEE) Forest Sprite guardian of the entrance to the Forentan god's home
Lowborn — Forentan term for someone of the lower classes
Lupine — Giant wolf native to Forenta
Lurkers — Vodani term for temporal shifters
Lyra — Forentan servant at Naveene's Rest
Magelight — Light generated by Forentan magic, often imbued into lanterns to allow minor talents to use them.
Magus — Archaic term for a mage, used as part of titles for the senior most mages
Magus Academy — Forentan school of magic that occupies an entire mountain
Majestic Hall — Largest room within the Magus Academy
Maternasi — (MAH-ter-NAH-see) Largest of the Vodani ships, home to an entire Vodani clan
Mia — (MEE-yah) Mureln's sister, owner of the Silver Seagull Inn
Morelmi — (mo-REL-mee) a spell used to remove the magic from a living being, generally considered fatal to the caster
Morlaiz Clan — (more-LAYZ) The gypsy clan Emil and Emaris are from
Mureln Nadeesi — (mur-ELN nah-DEE-see) A Vodani master bard; Almek's student
Naiya — (nah-EE-yah) The dryad divine servant of the Forentan god
Naming Blade — A two-edged knife given to a Desanti child by a Totani to acknowledge their transition into adulthood
Navar — (nah-VAR) A Forentan village
Naveene's Rest — (nah-VEEN) a Forentan upper class inn
Nolyn Lirai — (NO-lyn lih-RAI) Forentan master mage and guards-man captain in Ithesra

Oberlain Family — (OH-ber-layn) One of the oldest of the Ancient Houses in Forenta, rival of the Avarian family

Perisi — (peh-RIH-see) The last Illaini Magus 300 years before Ash

Psia Re — (SEE-ya RAY) The tie between the Desanti born and the Desanti god only recognized by mortals as sharing the pain of the trapped god

Radisen na'Citali — (RAH-dih-sen nah-cih-TAH-lee) A Desanti warrior

Rage wind — Sand storm attributed to the expression of the Desanti god's fury

Raging One, the — The Desanti dragon god

Rest — A Forentan term for an inn, usually upper class

River of Time — The area outside of the physical plane

Rumblelands — The volcanic plain home/prison of the Desanti god

Rusty Pelican — derogatory nickname for the Silver Seagull

Second Sundering — An ancient cataclysm that created the Sevmanan nation out of the Forentan nation, and the Vodani nation out of the Desanti nation

Se'edai Magus — (SEH EH-dah-ee) The senior member of the Edai Tredecima

Seeing One, the — The Sevmanan god

Selina — The mermaid divine servant of the Timeless One

Sendarli — (sen-DAHR-lee) a Desanti monster that resembles vine covered rock that cannot be killed with normal weapons

Sevenday — a unit of time equal to a week

Sevmana — (sehv-MAH-nah) The grassy lowlands south of Forenta claimed by the Sevmanan people; name of the Sevmanan god

Sevmanan — (sehv-MAH-nahn) Singular term for a human from Sevmana; adjective describing anything from Sevmana

Sevmanen — (sehv-MAH-nehnPlural term for a human from Sevmanen

Shadowlord — mysterious entity that causes chaos

Silver Seagull Inn — The most popular in of Corast owned by Mureln's sister Mia

Singing One, the — The Vodani God

Skyfire il'Kailee — The Githalin name of Radisen

Soul Oath — A mystical bond created between a Desanti and another

Storm il'Thandar — Desanti Githalin Swordanzen; Almek's student

Sumalen — (SOO-mah-lehn) Desanti warrior

Sundered Lands — The term describing the nations of Forenta, Sevmana, Vodanya and Desantiva

Swordanzen — (sohr-DAN-zen) mortal servants of the Desanti god, charged with protecting the people and the land

Swordanzen Naming Blade — A two-edged sword given to a Desanti by a Totani to acknowledge their passage of the Swordanzen tests

Taylin — Sevmanan master healer of the Zeridis temple

Temporal shifter — a non-corporeal entity from outside the physical plane

Terrence — Forentan mage, Ash's apprentice student

Thandar the Golden — Desert golden eagle Totani, Storm's guide

Th'yala — (th-YAH-lah) Desanti term for a long term companion that shares all things but children

Time of Gathering — Traditional time when all Desanti tribes gather in peace at First Home

Tomi — (TOE-mee) only son of the Blue Rose Inn's innkeeper

Toss stone — A dice game

Totani — (toe-TAH-nee) immortal divine servant of the Desanti god, singular and plural form

Traveler's Hollow — An inn in Ithesra frequented by lower class citizens or most non-Forentan visitors

Tree of Knowledge — Name for the Forentan god

Treewalker — A Desanti term for a Forentan, only derogatory by vocal inflection

Trifold stone — A stone found in deep waters of the ocean with unique properties of being able to draw or locate pieces of the same stone; used primarily with arrowhawks

Tri-tailed deer — a giant deer native to Forenta with three tails

Tulis — (TOO-lis) Mureln's brother, Ilsa's long term companion

Tyrsan — (TIR-sahn) Sevmanan Unsvet Guardian, Dulain of Guardian settlement

Ulsen — (UHL-sehn) Sevmanan drunkard in Ganessi, killed by Storm

Unsvet Guardian — (UHN -sveht) A Guardian of Time marked with a metallic mark of two colors on the right cheek

Verris na'Zhekali — Senior Elder of the Desanti, Storm's grandfather

Vi'disa tribe — (vih-DIH-sah) Desanti tribe wiped out by a dinnais attack

Vodani — (voh-DAH-nee) Singular or plural term referring to a human from Vodanya; adjective describing anything from Vodanya

Vodanya — (voh-DAH-nyah) The ocean and islands where the Vodani people call home; name of the Vodani god

Warriors of heaven — Desanti term for shooting stars, believed to be
   the freed souls of a Desanti who recently died
Water's Resonance — Vodani island marked for having natural purple
   crystal spires
Wave Dancer — Vodani ship that Almek's students travel on
World Spine — Impassable north-south running mountains on the
   western side of the main continents
Ysai Oberlain — (yih-SIGH) The Se'edai Magus of the Edai Tredecima
Zeridis — (ZEHR-ih-dihs) A divine servant of the Sevmanan god, patron
   of healers
Zoey — A Forentan girl, Magus Academy student

ABOUT THE AUTHOR

Lexy Wolfe began by crafting vibrant genre-blurring adventures where Saturday morning cartoons collided with interstellar stakes and fantastical mysteries, imagining what encounters with a multitude of characters and universes would be like. Her worlds, forged through decades of shaping stories that honor both childhood wonder and adult resilience, are a testament to an obsessive love of world building. A lifelong devotee of science fiction and fantasy, she had scribbled cross-universe escapades in notebooks long before fan culture embraced such mashups, their teenage self painstakingly drafting tales by hand ("the trees still haven't forgiven me"). Early respect for creative ownership led her to pioneer original characters—quirky, flawed, and disarmingly human—who navigate worlds where, one day, laser swords might duel enchanted dragons, and spaceship crews trade banter over alien campfires.

A U.S. Army veteran, mother of two, and grandmother of one, Lexy Wolfe balances high-stakes plots with wry humor and emotional authenticity, drawing inspiration from her late husband—a steadfast champion who believed in her stories long before they reached print. After navigating the early trenches of self-publishing, they found success collaborating with a close-knit creative team, releasing two beloved series and the start of a third that blended nostalgic charm with nuanced explorations of loyalty, reinvention, and found family. Following a decade-long hiatus after the passing of her spouse of twenty-five years, and the demands of work—as a techie/non-techie translator and application designer and tester—that feeds the insatiable appetite of bills, mortgage, and (according to them) starving cats, she is revitalizing her catalog with revised editions, weaving fresh depth into cherished narratives while honoring the muse who first urged her to share her voice.

When not resurrecting half-finished manuscripts or appeasing their clowder of feline editors and home office managers, Lexy Wolfe counsels aspiring young authors, advocating for persistence as much as craft. Her work invites readers to reclaim forgotten playgrounds of imagination—one wisecracking cyborg or misfit wizard at a time.

9 780984 000388